Praise

'This is heartache for grown-ups. *The Weight of Love* pulls you in and does not let go.'

Anne Enright

'Beautiful and painful, exquisitely written, shot through with nostalgia for our earlier selves.'

Marian Keyes

'Fannin writes with acute insight on loss, grief, and the ways in which time folds in our lives. We are not long into 2020, but Fannin's novel is already likely to be a serious contender for one of the books of the year.'

Sunday Times

'Incredibly beautiful, aching; it feels like it's being whispered to me. The story unfolds so naturally in prose at once delicate and powerful, hypnotic. Gorgeous.'

Donal Ryan

'A masterful dissection of romantic love . . . This novel is still revealing new unexpected depths until the final page.'

Sunday Independent

'An absorbing, cleverly structured, yet very human novel. It is hard to accept that it is Hilary Fannin's first.'
Roddy Doyle

'An exquisitely written, deeply moving novel about the agonies of love, intimacy, and the harm we inflict upon one another in the name of romance.'
Louise O'Neill

'A tender, beautiful novel that sparkles with humour.'
Danielle McLaughlin

'It's a gorgeous read; delicate, well crafted, full of clever insights into relationships, loss and the human condition of the calibre you might expect from Anne Enright.'
Irish Times

'Wise and beautifully bittersweet, *The Weight of Love* explores how we can be haunted by our own ghosts and the ghosts of others, by versions of our younger selves and the lives we failed to lead.'
Irish Independent

'Intimate and moving . . . It is all in there: family love, friendship and romantic love. Hilary looks at these universal themes with microscopic precision.'
Irish Examiner

'Fannin proves the efficacy of fiction as a medium for truth – and in doing so, exceeds all expectations.'
The Irish Times Ticket

'This beautifully written and intimate story is profoundly moving.'
Irish Sunday People

'A startling debut.'
Must Read, Image Magazine

'An utterly beautiful book.'
Michael Harding

'A beautifully written account of a love triangle that feels so real I could have lived it myself.'
Kathleen MacMahon

'Gorgeous, romantic, sad, melancholy, wise, amazing. I really recommend it . . . One of the best books of the year.'
Seán Hewitt

'*The Weight of Love* left me with a feeling I so rarely get with fiction – a sort of drunkenness, an ease. I sank into it and when I got to the end, I wanted to turn it over and start again.'
Sunday Business Post

'Wonderful . . . A novel about lots of different forms of love . . . Everyone should buy it.'

Miriam O'Callaghan, *RTÉ Radio 1*

'Stunning . . . perceptive, pitch-perfect.'

Saga Magazine

'Beautifully written . . . profoundly moving.'

Sunday Mirror

the weight of love

HILARY FANNIN

TRANSWORLD PUBLISHERS
Penguin Random House, One Embassy Gardens,
8 Viaduct Gardens, London SW11 7BW
www.penguin.co.uk

Transworld is part of the Penguin Random House group of companies
whose addresses can be found at global.penguinrandomhouse.com

First published in the UK and Ireland in 2020
by Doubleday Ireland
an imprint of Transworld Publishers
Paperback edition published 2021

A CIP catalogue record for this book
is available from the British Library.

ISBN
9781784163365

Typeset in 9.8/16pt Haarlemmer MT Pro
by Integra Software Services Pvt. Ltd, Pondicherry.

Printed and bound in Great Britain by Clays Ltd, Elcograf S.p.A.

The authorized representative in the EEA is Penguin Random House Ireland,
Morrison Chambers, 32 Nassau Street, Dublin D02 YH68.

Penguin Random House is committed to a sustainable future
for our business, our readers and our planet. This book is made
from Forest Stewardship Council® certified paper.

For Giles

PROLOGUE

London, October 1995

Robin looked across the yard. At first, he didn't quite believe what he was seeing: Joseph, whom he had forgotten might turn up, standing talking to Ruth. Around them, freed by the ringing bell, children fled the school like uncaged birds. Halted, Robin stood at the staffroom window and watched Ruth's head incline and the toecap of her boot lift and graze the ground while Joseph unravelled his persona: artist and occasional invalid, and not necessarily in that order. As drizzle scribbled on the windowpane, Robin stood and watched his hopes of spending the evening alone with Ruth evaporate.

'There you are,' Joseph said, as Robin walked towards them. 'Apparently you two are going to see something at the Renoir. Am I interrupting?'

'Yes, you are. Ruth, this is Joe. Joe,' Robin said flatly, 'is an old friend.'

'So I hear.'

'Cup of tea on the way?' Joseph asked. 'I promise I won't detain you.'

At Joseph's suggestion, the three of them left the schoolyard and walked down Judd Street to a cafe where they could get out of the rain and continue their introductions. Winding their way through the wet streets, their conversation curtailed by the traffic and the sharpening rain, allegiances were brewing and rivalries being stoked, and it would be tempting to say that by the time the three of them had turned down Woburn Walk, a narrow Dickensian passageway where the window of the Sorrento Cafe glowed pale and yellow in the dusk, what would happen had somehow already happened, the loving and mourning had already begun and already ended. Even though, in real time, as the rain fell over London on that autumn evening, Ruth had only known Joseph for an instant.

Reaching the Sorrento (which Ruth and Joseph would later rename the Kurdistani cafe), Robin pushed open the door for Ruth, and Joseph followed her inside. The cafe was warm, sour with the smell of the weather, and they took a table by the bay window, looking out through the thick glass at wet flagstones and a neat little man with an umbrella nipping through a wrought-iron gate opposite and down to the tailor's in the basement. And there was something raw and unsettled in the air between the three of them that was more than just the dubious freedom of a Friday afternoon.

Two solemn, baggy-eyed old men sitting at the next table paused their conversation to look at the newcomers when they came in. Robin, deep in the cave of his new coat and wondering if he should have bowed to the inevitable and simply gone home, watched the old men watching them and saw what the old men saw: two young men, one dark, shabby and assured, one fair and reticent, and a young woman in her mid-twenties, small and watchful underneath her green scarf.

Joseph, unaware of being observed himself, slouched down at the table opposite Ruth, looking at her in that unabashed way he had of looking at people, as if he was trying to figure out the puzzle of her construction, weighing up skin and bone, categorizing shape and shadow, measuring, proportioning. Soaked to the skin in his ratty jacket, he was looking at Ruth's face over the previous occupants' dirty crockery as if he was trying to memorize her, and Ruth, braving his scrutiny, was staring right back. Robin, wearily disappointed and unsurprised by the turn of events, briefly considered putting his fist through Joseph's delicate face and blurring his painterly vision before he himself sat down. Instead, tethered to kindness (even when he felt unkind and rebellious) and knowing that Ruth was poor and Joseph poorer, he picked up the dirty cups and went to the counter to place their order. And the old men, absorbing the presence of these ordinary strangers in the damp cafe, resumed their conversation.

While Robin waited at the counter, Ruth, defeated by Joseph's stare, looked away and began listening to the old men's talk. They were speaking of disasters. Small, personal disasters – the kind that would never make headlines. Cherished disasters, Ruth thought, aware of Joseph's gaze shifting away from her. The old men's stories were, she considered, smooth as pebbles from the number of times they'd been pulled from memory and fondled with words and sighs. One of the men was remembering how, decades before, his wife had left their infant son parked in his pram outside a hardware shop on Pentonville Road and walked all the way home with a brand-new whistling kettle before she noticed the child's absence. And although parents and infant had shortly been reunited, the boy had grown up so entirely devoid of talent or luck that his father strongly suspected the child had been switched.

Ruth turned to look at Joseph and saw that he had taken something from his pocket: a notebook and pencil. The second old man, commiserating with the first, agreed that his companion's son was indeed a fool and, as Joseph picked up his pencil and began to draw, recited his own story about falling from a stepladder while unscrewing a spent light bulb and almost lobotomizing himself on the contents of his wife's much-loved ornamental umbrella stand.

'It could be worse,' the first old man soothed. 'We could be halfway up a Kurdistani mountain.'

'We could indeed,' agreed his companion, sipping his tea. 'We could indeed be halfway up a Kurdistani mountain.'

Ruth reached across the table for the notebook, and Joseph handed it to her, and she saw that he had made a line drawing of the old men, a free-flowing yet perfect miniature. Joseph smiled at her and she held his gaze, and Robin, returning with a tray of tea and three stale pastries, already felt like an outsider.

Joseph took tea with his sugar, pouring sachet after sachet into his cup while he and Robin talked about teaching and art. Joseph, arrogant and combative, leaning back in his chair and rolling a cigarette, said that he could never work in a classroom, no matter how skint he was (and fuck it, he was skint now). He refused to waste his time, he said, perched on a radiator, talking about light and the absence of light, while forty students stuffed putty rubbers up their adolescent noses and fantasized about shagging each other blind. And Robin said that, as he had no particular objection to people thinking about shagging each other, blind or otherwise, while he attempted to engage the remainder of their imaginations, teaching suited him just fine.

'You're a good teacher,' Ruth said, breaking her silence because she knew, from the way he spoke to the students in the school where they both worked, that Robin was a patient man.

'Thank you,' Robin replied, and for the first time that afternoon he looked directly at her. Ruth looked away and out of the window at the passageway outside, so arcane, so quaint, that she half expected to see women in crinolines wandering through the drizzle and was surprised when, instead, two emaciated young girls, grey-faced and frantic, rushed down the wet road, cropped hair sticking to their bony faces.

'So what's on at the Renoir?' Joseph was asking.

'An Irish film,' Robin replied.

'A film about small-town Irish friendship,' Ruth interrupted, and the words sounded so much more dismissive than she'd intended.

'It's probably too late anyway,' Robin conceded, and Ruth felt angry with him for sounding so resigned.

'I never promised you anything,' she wanted to say, but the words stayed inside her.

The coffee drunk, Ruth's pastry uneaten, Robin stood and put on his gaberdine. Ruth saw that the rain that had earlier tattooed his shoulders had dried into the fabric, and briefly she wondered if the rain had been trying to leave a message they had failed to decipher. She stood, picked up her father's old satchel, which she carried everywhere and which had nothing much inside except a paperback, bookmarked by his tattered photograph, and her purse, and put her hand on Robin's arm.

'I'm sorry about the film,' she said, and she meant it.

'Some other time maybe.'

'I should probably go too,' Joseph said, buttoning up his skimpy jacket. Ruth looked down at the table and thought she recognized her own profile etched out in the spilt sugar.

The Kurdistani mountain men had begun talking about disasters again. Ruth slowly rewound her scarf, delaying her departure, so that she and her companions could listen. The old man who had fallen from the stepladder and almost lobotomized himself on his wife's umbrella stand was telling his friend how, after his tumble, he had got to his feet and stormed upstairs to berate his wife, only to find her in her bath, the water cold, her body grey.

'Dead as a doornail,' he said, as if the memory still confounded him, and before he reached into the water for her, he said, before he even called out her name, he had wondered if, at the moment of her departure, she had pushed him off his pedestal.

Leaving the cafe together, they walked towards Russell Square, unwilling, despite the silence that had settled over the three of them, to part. Reaching the square, Joseph, searching his pockets for skins to roll another cigarette, found a forgotten ten-pound note and offered them a celebratory drink in The Lamb. It would, Ruth persuaded herself, have been churlish to say no.

Later, much later, that evening they ended up in the pub in Camden Town. It was there that Joseph asked Ruth if she thought the dead ever truly left, ever really relinquished their hold, and she said the dead were as empty as her glass. And Robin took Ruth's empty glass and Joseph's empty glass up to the bar to buy another round, and Joseph said that he thought death was a spectrum and that the recent dead were almost present, were swathes of colour, warm as a breeze, listening and lingering and waiting to grow cold.

When Robin came back with the drinks, they moved outside and sat on a picnic table under hanging baskets withered by the onset of winter. Crowded together, sitting on the tabletop in a line like expectant children, their feet on the bench, they drank a toast to the dead wife of the old man in the cafe and to her malevolent spirit in the bath. Ruth, drunk and cold, shivered, and Robin took off his coat and spread it over her shoulders. And then they drank a toast to Robin's 100 per cent wool gaberdine coat, which had been an anniversary present from his girlfriend, whom he didn't have the courage to leave.

'It's a very fine coat,' Joseph said, inhaling his cigarette. 'Maybe love grows.'

'Maybe it doesn't,' Robin replied.

And then, because they were talking about love and death, or because Ruth thought they were talking about love and death, she told them a story about a delivery boy called Len whom she had quietly fucked in her aunt's utility room in New Jersey some months beforehand, on a night when she had been so washed out with sadness she could barely speak. Surefooted now, picking her words with ease across the running stream of her drunkenness, she told them that although she had only known the boy for an hour, maybe less, her memory of him was crystal clear. She told them how, on that first night of a sad Long Island holiday, just weeks after her father's death and with her grief-stunned, jet-lagged mother upstairs in the bed she would later share with her, she had made love alongside the softly rumbling washer-dryer to the gentle boy, who had small hands and curly hair and a weekend job delivering delicatessen meats to the suburbs, conveying late-night cold cuts to households weighted down by friends and relations.

The boy, she told them, had introduced himself as she stood looking at the stars in her aunt's clipped garden. He'd told her he was an astronomy student and had pointed out Mars, pinkish over the horizon, and a blur of light below that he said was a rarely seen constellation. Ruth suspected it was just the reflection of the lights on the highway, just traffic trailing towards the toll plazas, creeping towards Manhattan, which, had she had the courage to smash through the awful torpor of the night, would have been her choice of destination too.

'What is it you're looking for?' the boy had asked her, and she'd told him she was looking for signs of life, and she'd laughed, and he'd kissed her, and she'd been grateful for his touch, grateful that she was alive enough to notice that his tongue tasted like his cinnamon-flavoured gum. Afterwards, she told Robin and Joseph, the boy had driven away in his refrigerated truck and she had spent the weekend looming around the turkey roll and the pastrami, wondering if she'd ever see him again.

'Did you want to see him again?' Joseph asked.

'No. No, I didn't.'

Joseph bent down and blew fallen ash from his cigarette off her thigh, and when the ash was gone she saw that there was a tiny hole in her tights, her skin just visible through the aperture, like a distant star in the night sky.

'I'm sorry,' she said then, although she had no idea why she was apologizing or to whom.

'Sorry for what?' Joseph asked, as Robin, who had listened to her story in silence, stood and went into the bar for a slash. And Joseph picked up her satchel and slung it across his back and turned his collar up against the rain, and Ruth slipped out from under Robin's warm coat. And when Robin returned to the table, they were gone. There were just the withered baskets and Ruth's glass, half full or half empty, and his coat, a carapace that still held her warmth. Robin picked up the coat and walked back into the bar while, all over the rain-washed city, people were losing and finding each other, and beginning and ending and ending and beginning, ordinary strangers spooling and unspooling into the night.

ONE

Ireland, May 2018

Robin left his class as soon as he got the call, and picked up his jacket from the staffroom, which was empty bar Harry Coleman sleeping deeply on a swivel chair.

'Rough night?' Robin asked, waking him.

'Outrageous.'

'Go in and intimidate 3E for a bit, will you? I've left them unsupervised.'

'Skiving?'

'I need to get on the road. My mother's taken a turn for the worse.'

Dublin to Bantry in just over four hours. A lone bullock stood stock-still on the motorway outside Fermoy. Transfixed. Stunned. Elemental. Traffic ground to a gobsmacked crawl.

Robin spent the night in a chair by her bed, woke to the yell of peacocks on the hospital lawn; three peacocks, strutting around in broken circles as if they'd lost their wedding party. He wondered if he might be hallucinating. The door opened. A woman introduced herself, offered him tea from the breakfast trolley in the corridor.

'I'm Joy,' she said, coming in and handing him a cup and saucer. 'Biscuit?' she asked. He declined. Joy stroked his mother's hand. He watched from the window. 'Poor lamb,' Joy said. 'Poor little lamb.'

'Peacocks?' Robin asked, to steady himself.

'Full of themselves,' Joy replied, returning to the urn and closing the door behind her.

Soon after, two nurses came in to change his mother and make her comfortable and told him to go into the ward kitchen, where he could make himself another cup of tea. He complied. The consultant will be in to see you at eleven, they told him when he returned, leaving him to stand watch over his mother, wax-still on crisp sheets, her oxygen tube secured by surgical tape.

The consultant arrived at quarter to one.

'There will be no recovery,' he said.

'Her hands,' Robin said. 'She was a potter. I've never seen her hands so still.'

'Would I know her work?'

'I doubt it,' Robin replied.

'I suggest you go home and telephone whoever needs to be telephoned.'

Robin got back into the car and drove south, stopping at the garage just outside town for diesel, bread and milk. He arrived at Popes Cove late afternoon.

Two low cottages stood side by side, their gable end shoulder to the wind. His mother's neighbour, Suzi, was standing beside the ornamental wishing well in her front garden, alongside her gnomes, waiting for Robin to turn off the engine. He could have wept. Gnomes? Dwarfs? He counted six of them as he followed her inside.

'I telephoned the hospital,' she said. 'They told me you were here.'

She told him to sit down, said she was going to make tea. 'You must be desperate for a cup.'

'Really,' he said, 'I'm fine.'

He wanted to go next door, let himself in, shower, sleep. Sit and look out at the water.

Suzi went into her kitchen to boil the kettle. He turned on his phone. Nothing.

A cloth dachshund with a tartan bolero was sitting on the chair Suzi had indicated – a draught excluder. There was no draught; Robin would have killed for a draught. Waves of heat rolled off the radiators. Early May, milder than most. He sat down. From the opposite chair a rag doll with a rosebud mouth looked at him like he was a serial killer. He stood up, put the dachshund on the floor. Sat down again. China shepherdesses multiplied on the mantelpiece, net curtains iced the glass. Coasters on the occasional table – English country garden. This was an occasion, he supposed, for an occasional table.

'Do you remember the goat?' Suzi said, returning with a tray, tears falling, making firebreaks on her powdery face.

'Of course I remember the goat.'

How could he forget? He was thirteen. The sight of the goat nibbling on Suzi's washing line of alarming underwear, like a teasing lover, had haunted his dreams.

Robin and his mother had watched, from their door, the goat being delivered to Suzi's cottage by a boy in a Morris Traveller. Suzi had had her hair done. Cash changed hands. The boy licked his fingers to count it, undid the chain holding the van doors shut and dragged out the reluctant goat, handing the rope to Suzi before reversing at speed down the stunted boreen. There was dried shit around the goat's arse. The bemused animal had taken a moment to steady itself, to get the lie of the land. Robin had seen it glance over Suzi's garden wall to where they stood, his mother in her overalls, he in his Scooby Doo T-shirt which, by the end of that summer, the animal would have soundly masticated. Suzi had bought the goat a bell, had hung gingham curtains in the lean-to where it was to sleep in a crate in the corner, plumped up with her former husband's showband flares. Robin hung over the garden wall separating their two houses while Suzi hosed down the goat's hindquarters. Eyeball to eyeball with the goat, he blinked first.

It didn't take the new arrival long to realize his power. By that evening, he'd trampled Suzi's hollyhocks, eaten a pair of tights from her washing line and made a good start on the gingham curtains. That night, sprightly and quivering with certainty, he'd pushed open Suzi's kitchen door and trotted around the house looking for her. She woke up in a nest of her own shredded valance, the goat lying next to her. It was the way he had looked at her, she told his mother the following morning, while Robin listened from under the kitchen window. It was a look that reminded her of her husband, the goat's pale eyes wide open when she woke, coldly appraising her crumpled breasts, her slack mouth. It frightened her, she said. She'd had it with goat husbandry, she decided, with husbandry of any kind for that matter. She'd been a fool. The knicker-eater was to move in with them.

'Of course I remember the goat,' Robin said. 'Gilbert.'

'Gilbert,' Suzi repeated.

His mother had loved Gilbert. A long, hot summer, remarkable for its rarity, and his mother, broad and strong, on her knees, dragging lacy straps and metal sinews out of the goat's gurgling throat, and Suzi, in varying states of fury, hurdling back and forth over the wall that separated their dominions.

'This is exactly what he wants, two women fighting over him!' Suzi had roared one August afternoon, mid-flight, a black brassiere unravelling in her grip. And Robin's mother had sat back on her haunches, a mangled underwire in her hand, and laughed. Lay back on the rough seagrass and laughed and laughed, and Robin had never heard her laugh like that before. Both of them, Suzi and his mother, laughing. He remembered them so clearly, two raw women, younger than he was now, much younger, their backs to the dry-stone wall, their legs, bare and white and heavy, stretched out under the unaccustomed sun, drinking gin and barley water out of his mother's misshapen mugs. The gin that had been under the sink for years. Years.

'Sometimes he was glorious,' Suzi had whispered to his mother.

'Who was glorious?' Robin had asked from his apron of shade, and his mother asked him to take the now tethered goat for a walk.

Goat on a rope, and the sky too blue, an unfamiliar, compressing blue, and the sharp, dry gorse around the inlet, and the wading birds tracing the jigsaw of cracked mud with their beaks. And the goat dragging his feet until he could slip the rope and chew on a D-cup. And Robin wanted it to be just him and his mother again, under an ordinary gnarled-up sky, the way it always had been. He wanted the smirking old goat and Suzi, with her mascara-stained tears and her memories of glory, back in her own house where she belonged.

And it occurred to him now, sitting in Suzi's hot little sitting room, the china tea cup snap-light in his hand, that when Joe had turned up at his mother's cottage a couple of summers later, wary and arrogant and wild and unhappy, Robin had felt the same way, misplaced and exiled and abandoned, excluded from his mother's steady gaze. Joseph, he should have said. Joseph. Ruth would never call him Joe. As if his name held water that she didn't want to spill.

Exhaustion threatened to beach him on the dachshund's velveteen chair, to leave him adrift in an eternity of antimacassars.

'Where will I be without her?' Suzi asked.

Robin stood, picked up a sparkling china milkmaid, turned her over in his hands.

'I must sleep,' he said.

He left Suzi and her plaster army, pitting their painted faces against the gathering rain.

He walked to his mother's front door, let himself in and went into her small blue bedroom that smelt like fish and jam. He cleared the medication off the bedside table, picked up her open book, marked the page before he closed it, and lay down on her single bed. Robin slept and dreamt that his mother was at the cottage door, rattling the handle to get in. And in his dream he sprang up from the bed and opened the door with such force that it dissolved in his hand, and then there was nothing, no door, no house, no mother, no landscape.

He woke, hollowed out, heart pounding. He looked around the room, breathed in its presence. Next to the bed was a photograph of them both, his mother in one of her heavy dresses with diamonds of glass sewn on to the embroidered front, her blonde hair plaited around her head, haversack on her back, square feet in solid sandals. In the photograph Robin was leaning back against a magnolia tree, long and thin and white and blond, scowling into the camera, his adolescent rage shadowing the sunlit road.

He got up, went into the kitchen, leant on the table, facing the window. The tide was low, the lobster man puttering out to his nets. Mustard-coloured weed shouldered the rock. The cloud had evaporated while he'd slept; the evening, not quite done with rain, washed the sky yellow.

Less than a week ago Ruth had sat at their own kitchen table and asked: 'Why now? Why now, Robin, after all these years, are you behaving like someone who has been betrayed?'

He had turned his back to her, horsed around with a saucepan, pretended not to understand.

'What is this?' she'd asked. 'Revenge?'

He had left the house then, saying nothing, had cycled the narrow city streets of their neighbourhood. He had pedalled the length of Oxmantown Road, a long, unbroken terrace of two-up-two-downs, originally the homes of abattoir workers on a street that ran with blood, now the properties of galvanic couples in information technology or arts policy or new media, who dressed in ethical cotton and painted their front doors duck-egg blue. He had turned left, had cycled along a wide road of high red-bricks, many clad in scaffolding, the uniform of gentrification, where bedsits were being obliterated and partitioned homes brought back to singular glory. Soon, Robin thought, the avenue would be a sea of SUVs and sugar-free children in tutus tottering up the power-washed paths.

He had turned the bike into the park, wide and flat and empty, a sheen of recent rain over the stretched grass, had cycled as far as the obelisk, which loomed in front of him like a big grey dullard, a long thin fool. He'd stopped the bike, sat on the plinth, watched a jogger trying to outrun some fucking fate or other. Watched until the man evaporated into the distance.

'Who are you?' he'd asked himself. 'Who are you, with your ordinary little secrets and your basil plants on your windowsill?'

He'd cycled home, pushed the bike through the kitchen and out into the yard. He'd found Ruth upstairs in Sid's room, lying on the empty bed.

'I'm sorry,' he'd said. 'I don't know how to explain it.'

She'd looked at him for a long moment.

'I need to compose myself,' she'd said, and the words had sounded too big for her mouth, as if she was a child playing at talking.

'I'm sorry,' he'd said again. 'It's over. Whatever it was, it's over.'

She'd turned away from him, drawn her knees up to her chest, and he'd gone to the hot press on the landing, taken out Sid's uncovered quilt, laid it over her and left the room.

'I'm sorry,' he said out loud now in his mother's empty kitchen. 'I'm sorry,' he said to the lobster man, to the bleached rocks, to the dresser full of his mother's crude pottery, to the sooty range where she had cooked their soups and stews.

'What?' he asked his mother's wooden armchair. 'What do you want me to do?' he asked the patchwork cushion, each hand-sewn square a remnant of their life together. If the range had been lit he would've burnt it, would've stuffed the cushion into the flames, would've incinerated the sweetness, the careful repair, the patient, loving alteration. He sat down and closed his eyes.

He'd often envied Ruth's ability to cry, something she did solemnly, with her eyes wide open, a mute, solid grief, and when she was finished she'd wipe her eyes on her cuffs and smile or shake her head, or make tea or pour wine. And Robin, left in the shallows of her grief or rage or disappointment or regret, would think, fuck it, I wish I could do that. I wish I could weep and then stand up and walk away to sew on a button, or cycle to the fishmonger, or wash my hair or change a bloodied sheet.

He sat now in his mother's kitchen and thought about crying, and couldn't. He needed to focus, get his thoughts in order. Ruth. He should have gone home when he got the call, and left Ruth a note in case she came back: 'Gone to Popes Cove, Mother dying.'

Or maybe 'Mother dying, gone to Popes Cove' might have been a more appropriate construction.

Friday, last class before lunch break, Robin had been doing the anniversary of the Somme with his third years when the call came about his mother. (The war poets, poor bastards, lying in mud and rats, squeezing beauty from a dewy cobweb.) He'd asked his class of bored, largely over-privileged fourteen-year-old boys – who, had they been born in a marginally different time and place, might have been obliged to add their limbs to the slaughter – what in that trench was destined to survive? Sonnet or spider? What, he asked, endures?

'The spider, sir, definitely the spider,' said Heap, sitting up straight in his seat, electrified by the arachnid prod.

'Thank you, Heap.'

'Cockroaches would definitely endure, sir, as first-tier decomposers.'

'Great, Heap, thanks.'

'Sir, they can break down dead matter, like the dead soldiers, into more manageable particles for bacteria to work on.'

The blue veins that meandered over Heap's long, pale head pulsed.

'Great, Heap. Anyone else?'

'And, sir, cockroaches are impervious to radiation.'

Heap's pale hands fluttered, boys sniggered into their V-necks. Robin's phone had pulsed in his trouser pocket.

'The spider is just as fucked as the soldier. But at least it's not following orders. At least it didn't volunteer to be slaughtered.'

This from Fogarty.

'Language,' Robin said automatically.

Heap trembling, Fogarty smirking, the question lost, the back row stretched out indifferently on their chairs. The veins on Heap's head stopped pulsing and resumed their watery journey until Buchan had farted and, in a familiar ritual of mock-disgust, hit Heap hard on the back of the head while the class pissed themselves.

Fogarty didn't laugh. He'd looked straight at Robin, and some slow percolation of arrogance and fear had reminded Robin of Joe. Joseph.

'Buchan!' Robin had shouted, surprising even himself with his fury.

'Sir?'

'What would you say, Buchan, if your next breath was your last? What glorious imprint of yourself might you possibly leave if that spider in its glistening web was the last thing you would see?'

'Sir?'

'I'd stand up and walk away,' said Fogarty. 'My choice to die, rather than wait.'

'All right, good. Buchan? Care to illuminate the class?'

'What about you, sir?' Fogarty continued. 'What would you do? Wait for someone to come along and save you?'

'Take out your books,' Robin had instructed, ignoring Fogarty and taking his phone out of his pocket to check the message while the boys rummaged in their bags. It took a moment for the words on the screen to convey their meaning.

'Sir?' Heap was speaking. 'Please, sir, may I be excused?' He looked spent.

'What? Yes, yes. Go. The rest of you memorize the Sassoon. There'll be a test on Monday. Buchan, you've earnt yourself a detention point.'

'For what?'

'Take your pick.'

Robin had followed Heap out of the class. Closing the door on Fogarty and the dying fragrance of Buchan's generous emission, he had hurried towards the staffroom.

Robin stood and opened the kitchen door for his mother's hungry cats, who, woken from a long sleep in their woodshed berth, were arching along the windowsill. Hunkered down on the floor, filling their dishes, he smelt their metallic breath, the crusted stench of their unwashed bowls, and felt, with each slow action of feeding them, the notes and beats of himself, so carefully arranged, fall off the stave.

'Why now,' Ruth had asked him, 'are you behaving like someone who has been betrayed?'

'It was a fair enough question,' he admitted to the cats. 'But, in truth, we both already knew the answer.'

On Sunday morning, five days before Robin received the call about his mother, Robin and Ruth had been lying in their bed, Ruth flicking through digested news on her telephone, Robin pretending to sleep. Outside their bedroom window, rain had shrugged down on their terraced Dublin street of two-up-two-downs, on Sunday-morning shoppers walking home from the refurbished corner shop with soya milk and organic granola.

Robin, wide awake under a mask of sleep, was thirsty and dismayed and needed a slash. He'd opened his eyes, looked at the ceiling, at raindrops reflected on the bloated paper shade. He had dreamt about Fogarty. It was coming back to him in fragments: a border crossing, Fogarty on the other side pointing Robin towards a trough. 'Drink,' Fogarty had commanded.

'You awake?'

'Kind of.'

'Heavy night. I'm sure Helen is counting the empties.'

'Yeah, it was a bit.'

'There's coffee made downstairs.'

'Thanks.'

'You were grinding your teeth.'

'Sorry.'

Fogarty had been in uniform, something military. He wore gloves, white.

'They're saying here that no one will be able to afford to live in Dublin soon, that the city is becoming beyond the reach of ordinary people. Apparently we're going to end up like London, full of oligarchs and roof gardens and celebrity chefs.'

'My jaw hurts.'

'I'm not surprised.'

It had occurred to Robin, standing over the bowl, that Ruth had slipped up. She so rarely mentioned London, so rarely allowed an opening to the past, and he had failed to take her cue, to trace the line back.

He watched the water circle the pan, washed his hands, looked at his face in the mirror: pale, crumpled, defeated.

Downstairs a box of Sid's football boots sat by the front door, the last of his possessions to have been packed up before he went to Berlin, yet to be ethically redistributed by Ruth, who was entirely scrupulous in such matters.

In Robin and Ruth's articulate kitchen, iron pots hung above the hob, bleached wooden shelving bowed under the weight of cookbooks and patio-garden manuals. Robin had poured his coffee, opened the fridge for milk. Magnetized poetry, faded now and worn, clung to the fridge door. Robin could clearly remember Ruth lifting Sid up on to a kitchen chair to make a poem, watching his small hands fish in the box. Robin had waited for the child to pull out 'love' or 'song' or 'frog' or 'ball', but he had pulled out 'torrent' and 'blade'.

Robin took his coffee to the table. Three black-and-white photographs hung on the wall opposite. The session with the photographer had been a wedding present from Helen and Colm that neither Ruth nor Robin wanted. Helen had driven them to the photographer's studio, all the way across Dublin city and through its northern reaches to a harbour-side block, Sid sprawling across Ruth's knees on the back seat. They had walked to the studio from the car park, heads down against the wind, gulls reeling, masts clanking, Sid swinging from Ruth's arm. Smile, click, wave-crash, smile, click, wave-crash.

Helen had flitted around in the background, wiping non-existent spittle from Sid's sweet mouth. Ruth and Robin were silently angry with her extravagance, her boom-time propriety. Afterwards, the squall almost blown out, they had gone for a walk. Helen and Ruth had sheltered by the big granite steps at the end of the pier, and Robin had held Sid's hand while they looked into empty fish boxes, until they'd found one with a dead fish in it and Sid had looked up at Robin in awe and astonishment, his mouth as round as the mackerel's cloudy eye.

And there they were, all these years later, framed on the kitchen wall, the three of them, Ruth small and fair, Robin pale and translucent, Sid determined and curious and beautiful.

Robin had stood and carried his coffee back up to the bedroom. He'd sat down on the small blue couch, their clothes strewn around him, her shirt lying across his jeans. He'd picked up one of her socks, absurdly small, polka dotted. On the chest of drawers at the foot of their bed: beads and pens, loose coins and scribbled envelopes, lotions, a crooked vase that Sid had once made so diligently.

The grey light beyond their bedroom window had deepened; it was beautiful, almost operatic. Ruth had closed her eyes, her glasses pushed to the top of her head, her phone on the bedside table. Robin had watched her sleep, her mouth slightly open, her jaw soft, he looked at the cloudy skin underneath her eyelids, at her lovely neck, her freckled shoulders, the crumpled straps of her T-shirt, her hands, dark against the white duvet cover, nicked and cut, small and dry and strong.

'Ruth? Ruth? Ruth, wake up. I need to talk to you.'

Robin waited, crouched down on the floor of his mother's kitchen, while the cats demolished the dish of food, nudging each other away, pausing occasionally to look up at him as if he might pounce. He stood and began looking for a water bowl, and, for a moment, Robin forgot the present. He was not this man, this teacher, this husband, this father, this fool; he was a boy, here in his mother's kitchen, feeding the cats. Just boy and mother and goat, and tide, filling and receding, and the soup on the hob as thick as fleece, and the scrubbed table, and the sated cats padding away to sleep on his mother's narrow bed.

He was unable to find a bowl for the cats' water – the right bowl, that is – among all the stout rejects that filled his mother's cupboards, dish after dish that wouldn't be quite right to put on the kitchen floor or leave outside on the stoop, bowls that his mother had thrown and glazed and painted and fired, an endless parade of fucking bowls. How many bowls could one woman possibly need, he said to himself, his hands full with another piece of lumpen pottery. How many rejects can one woman save, Robin asked, coming back to the squalid, fucked-up present. How much shit can one life accumulate, he wondered, smashing his fist against the cupboard door and scattering the cats under the table.

TWO

London, October 1995

The first time Ruth slept with Joseph was in his broken bed in his basement flat. The cracked slats underneath his mattress created a dip in the centre that rolled the sleepers together, or would've rolled the sleepers together had she been asleep, which she wasn't. She lay on the edge while he absorbed the hollow, arms thrown wide, head tilting towards his shoulder. He slept crucified. She put her hand on his stomach, bird-light; he held his breath, she held hers. In those halted seconds, the room felt very still. Ruth took her hand away; he exhaled.

She lay that first night on the rim of his bed, half submerged under city streets that nobody wanted to walk on after dark, the flat metallic taste of knife and cheese in her unwashed mouth, and wondered if she should get up, find her boots and skirt, her cardigan and tights, her coat and bag, and leave. She thought about retracing her steps along the ribboned streets he had led her through, back to Euston Road, where she could cross over to the station and wait on a bench until it was light. Wait, upright, her satchel on her knee, until morning commuters with clean teeth and clean underwear began to fill the concourse, and she too could begin her journey home.

Home: a strange concept in this city.

Ruth considered her not inconsiderable fear – an empty station save for the mad, the dangerous and the bereft – and, weighing it against the embarrassment she would feel in the morning if she stayed until he woke to find her still there, decided to go. But in the margins of the deciding to depart and the departing, she drifted off to sleep, and when she woke again to find herself still on the lip of his bed, morning was breaking through his basement window, ice-light in the boxed glass, wintering in the rotting frames. She lay, still as still, watching him, despairing now that if she moved he might wake and not recognize her. She lay looking at this man she had known since ten minutes past four the previous afternoon, and words like 'alabaster' sprang to mind and, mortifyingly, the phrase 'carved saint' floated up from somewhere, floated up from under his basement floor, wriggled up the leg of his broken bed and crawled into Ruth's ear.

Carved saint, she thought. Fuck's sake.

The dust spores of a national affliction – the habit of sublimating desire, of wishing every gash a stigmata – must have settled on her.

Careful as she'd been to shake her off, the knee-socked little girl framed on her mother's sideboard in Communion dress and veil, knitting her pink rosary beads through her white-gloved fingers, must have climbed into her haversack last summer and crossed the Irish Sea to London with her.

Joseph's flat was on a side street off St Pancras Station, in a red-brick housing-association block, sooty, Victorian, ornate. The dwellings – that is how they were identified, on a carved brick scroll on the outside wall – had been built to house the city's poor, Joseph had told her the night before.

'Who built them?' she had asked, anchored to his kitchen table, his thigh between her knees, the toe of her boot grazing the concrete floor, her mouth opening for the cube of cheese he offered, pierced by the one clean knife.

'Who built them?' she had asked, even though she couldn't have cared less.

'They were built by a man making provision for the repose of his soul,' he had replied. 'A man who believed in salvation and the curative power of vinegar and brown paper.'

The fluorescent cheese, like the withdrawn knife, had tasted flat and metallic in her mouth. The telephone rang for the first time. He'd ignored it.

'Say that again,' she had said.

'Say what again?'

'Vinegar and brown paper.'

'Vinegar and brown paper.'

She liked the smudge of his voice, liked the sound of his consonants falling off his vowels, as if the letters had lost interest in making words. She had put her fingers on his mouth; he'd lifted the hem of her skirt with the blade.

'Stay,' he'd said.

'Cave' was another word Ruth thought as she lay in his bed, looking at him.

Cave was a safer word than saint. Cave, not induced by anything Neanderthal (as in caveman) or even masculine (in truth, he looked more like a boyish girl); cave because of the grey-blue sockets of his eyes and the hollow places around his neck and shoulders. He was beautiful; it was plain as day. Far too beautiful for her, that went without saying. (But she heard it said anyway.)

He was long and hollow and graceful and cautious. And beauty, real beauty, is unwelcoming. That kind of beauty pours itself a drink and drifts off into the garden while you're still lingering by its door.

In that moment when he'd lifted her skirt with the blade, she'd felt fearless. She had stood to walk behind him to his bedroom, and when his telephone rang, for the second time, and he had returned to the narrow hall to answer it, she had stepped out of her skirt and tights and stood, in her green shirt, on the blue rug, her legs bare and white, and waited, breathing in the damp and cigarette smoke and something that smelt like paint thinner, while he took the call.

There was his bed, empty as a hungry mouth, and on the floor an ashtray full of butts, a torn envelope scribbled over with numbers, a cigar box filled with dirty chalks, and two glasses, both of them cloudy and used. On a card table next to the bed were three paperbacks, another ashtray – less full – and a photograph, a pinkish Polaroid, unframed, propped against the stem of an Anglepoise lamp. Ruth had stepped forward to look: the photograph was of a young woman, brittle, bone-thin, blunt blonde, her mouth leaning in to kiss the lens.

'She's here,' Joseph was saying to the caller. 'She's with me.'

She'd stepped back on to the rug as he entered the room.

'Was that Robin?'

'Yes,' he'd answered, and sat on the bed, where he began to undress.

She'd watched him take off his jacket, his shoes and socks, his shirt and his jeans. She waited.

'Aren't you cold, Ruth?' he had asked.

'Yes,' she'd replied from her small blue oval of frozen tundra.

He had looked at her then as if seeing her for the first time, as if the ringing telephone had broken the spell of her, had sharpened the light around her, had revealed her for what she was: an ordinary girl, small and pale, undressed on his rug.

'To amputate or resuscitate?' she had asked herself. But in the spill of the night, she didn't really know where those words had come from.

He'd held out his hand to her, and when she had negotiated her way across the ice and lain down next to him, he brought her hand to his mouth and kissed it.

'Of course it was Robin on the phone,' he'd said. 'Robin loves you.'

'We're just friends. Robin and I are just friends.'

'Go to sleep,' he'd whispered, closing his eyes.

And she had felt foolish and disappointed and failed, and the city seemed to have turned its back and quietly closed its door against the best she had to offer.

Cold and sleepless under his grimy sheets, Ruth, in her loneliness, felt almost brave. This sleeping Englishman was not, after all, someone she had known her whole life. She was not sharing this stale bed with some lad whose cousin once worked for her father, or whose uncle had sold her mother a second-hand car. She had never inked this sleeping man's name on to her pencil case, or stood shivering on the sidelines while he hurled himself around a bog-wet pitch. He wasn't some boy, familiar to her as rain, thighs shaking on a candlewick bedspread, school tie pulled from a raw neck, who had looked at her afterwards with awe and hate.

This man was a stray. He was not of her tribe.

And there was, Ruth considered while she watched him sleep, so much to tell him, were he ever to wake up, yet so little to reveal.

'Who are you?' he might ask, could well ask, would be quite entitled to ask. And what would she say?

She was Ruth. She was Irish. She was twenty-four years old. A daughter. That much was true, was indisputable.

That she had failed was also true: failed to finish her education; failed to remain where she was needed; failed, even after her father's death, to offer anything much to anyone.

She could tell him about growing up (school kilts and knee-socks and listening on the stairs to quiet rage), but that would bore him. She could tell him about her home town and all those games of love and nothing that went on for years. Years of girls crying and brushing their hair in bathroom mirrors. Years around the back of the Spar on drizzly Saturday nights, boys and girls in tattered gangs, the lads leaning and smoking, framed against a wire pen of empty packaging, waiting, everyone waiting, for something to happen. She could tell him about sex – but then the sex she'd had amounted to little more than barter. She could tell him that when, briefly, she'd been a student in Dublin, she'd been so lonely she thought the trees were whispering about her. She could tell him how she went home every weekend on the bus to witness her father's slow departure. She could tell him about death when it finally came, and about the days before her father's funeral when she lay stunned on the bathroom floor.

'For the love of God, Ruth, will you get up off the floor?' her mother had whispered through the keyhole. But love, or the lack of it, couldn't shift her.

This morning, lying as still as she could in Joseph's bed, the icy light from his basement window creeping along the bed, she thought about the night before, when, just hours after meeting Joseph for the first time, the two of them and Robin had sat outside the bar in Camden Town. They were, all three of them, drunk and sitting on the wooden picnic table under the empty flower baskets, sitting up on the table like children, their feet on the bench, and she'd told Joseph and Robin about fucking the American boy in her aunt's utility room in Long Island. She had told them that it had felt true, even though everything that came out of the American boy's mouth was a lie.

Joseph had bent down and blown the fallen ash from his cigarette off her thigh, and Robin had looked at her, and his look was hard to decipher. Anger? Disappointment? Resignation? He had stood up then and gone inside to the bar.

'Come home with me, Ruth,' Joseph had said to her then, when the story about the boy was still suspended in the smoky night air and the small hole in her tights threatened a dam burst. 'Come home. I'll make you cheese on toast.'

It was the most plausible, plainly decipherable thing that Joseph had said all night. She'd stood up and he had locked his fingers around her wrist and they had begun walking, fast, towards King's Cross. And Ruth knew, following Joseph along Camden High Street, that she had told them the story about the American delivery boy not just because she was drunk but because she had wanted Joseph to know that she was not afraid.

They had crossed Euston Road on the way to his flat, his fingers around her wrist, the traffic belting, regardless of the moonlight. Euston Road, he'd told her when they were running for the other side, was where he once saw a naked man wade into the traffic with a sword in his hand.

'What happened?' she'd asked, but he hadn't replied.

His slip-knot fingers around her wrist were an indication of his interest in her, a fragile interest, Ruth suspected, but then, in her brief experience of him, there was little about him that wasn't fragile.

She had hoped 'cheese on toast' wasn't a euphemism, and also hoped that it was. She'd been hungry. She'd eaten nothing since Robin had bought them all apple strudel that afternoon in the Kurdistani cafe which wasn't really a Kurdistani cafe and where, aware of Joseph watching her, she couldn't eat anyway.

'Are we really having cheese on toast?' she'd asked.

'Of course,' Joseph had replied.

She had thought, following behind his inky jacket, that he might have kissed her somewhere along the route. On the empty streets of Somers Town maybe, where he might, if only out of curiosity, have pushed her against a night-blind wall, his tongue in her mouth, the heel of his hand against her crotch. But he hadn't kissed her, in Somers Town or anywhere else. She could have pushed him against a wall, her tongue in his mouth, her hand on his crotch, but somehow she knew not to puncture the caul of him uninvited. He was shivering; maybe she should have offered him her coat.

With each step away from the pub in Camden Town, Ruth had felt less and less familiar to herself, losing her outline somewhere between Mornington Crescent and Somers Town, dissolving almost entirely at St Pancras Station into the leaking gutters, into the stain and spall of the masonry.

Locked at the intersection of his fingers and her wrist, she had become, as they walked, rain and brick, ironwork and shadow, the headlights splashed along Euston Road. By the time they reached King's Cross, she'd blazed with the neon strips of the kebab houses that washed the pavements yellow. Shapeless and afloat, drenched and polluted, she had looked up at the too-bright-for-night London sky above her head and opened her mouth to the rain.

She'd been drunk, naturally. They'd all been drunk. Ruth, though, had been airborne drunk, an elusive drunkenness that you can try to find again and never will. A kind of drunkenness where the centre of yourself unfurls and a big, raw wound, grateful for the light, arches up inside you, revealing you clearly as you are. And some alchemy then, of the drink and the night and the ordinary truth of the matter (that nothing actually matters except this moment), sets you free.

Outside King's Cross Station, closed for the night, there had been a man and a dog and a shouting drunk, and a child, statue-still, huddled between two women who were holding on to one another, crying or laughing – Ruth had been moving too swiftly to tell.

It was only when they'd left the road and burrowed through narrow unknown streets between blocks of flats that Ruth had become frightened that Joseph might splinter into the dark and disappear.

'And then where will you be?' she had asked herself.

He had swerved into a corner shop, open still, although it must by then already have been tomorrow. He'd bought a block of cheese and a packet of fags from the Indian man, in turban and knitted cardigan, behind the counter.

'Ruth, this is Nish,' he'd said. 'Nish works nights.'

'Yes, we keep the same hours,' Nish had concurred, holding out his hand to shake hers.

Next to Nish's counter was a magazine rack – a sad princess and girls with breasts so big you'd want a compass to navigate them. Joseph had asked Nish for bread, but all the bread was sold.

He'd pocketed the fags and cheese, taken her hand again and crossed a narrow street, passed through an iron gate that didn't properly close, and on into a courtyard studded with cramped trees, to the door of his basement flat.

Inside, she had noted the cement floor, the board covering the bathroom window, the dirty kitchen. He'd dredged the sink for a knife while she sat on the edge of the table next to a jam jar of bluish water and a black banana. He'd taken the cheese from his pocket, wiped the knife on the leg of his jeans and slit the parchment. Behind him, on the draining board, among the unwashed mugs and plates, was a single crystal glass, dignified and absurd, an unexpected addition that must have come from somewhere else, that mustn't ever have really belonged to him.

Ruth needed to move. She needed the bathroom. She was thirsty. She still had her knickers on. She needed to get out of the bed. She had no toothbrush. She needed to find her bag, see whether she had any money or not. She remembered ordering a round the night before, remembered searching in her purse, remembered Robin leaning across her to pay the barman. She would pay Robin back when she could. She remembered her tights parachuting to the floor.

'Aren't you cold, Ruth?' he had asked. 'Aren't you cold?' As if the words exhausted him, as if, by standing on the rug, she had already worn him out.

When, in the night, she had touched him, pooled still in sleep, he'd caught his breath and held it, and Ruth had understood that his stillness was not anticipation of pleasure but pure, animal caution.

Light seeped around the edges of the board covering the bathroom window. The towel was damp, his sink matt-grey; the floor, though, was painted crimson. His bath was deep and almost clean, a bar of soap on its lip. She picked it up: lavender. She washed quickly at his sink, rubbed his toothpaste over her teeth and gums. She looked at herself in the mottled mirror. It wasn't necessarily to her credit that this room made her happy.

Since she had arrived in London the summer before, Ruth had been living in a house-share in Streatham with three Irish girls who were all doing nursing, where there were scented candles in the living room and potpourri on the bathroom windowsill and cleaning schedules stuck up on a noticeboard in the kitchen. She lived in a house where there was a kitty for home improvements and where rolls of peach-coloured toilet paper bred in a wicker basket next to a pristine toilet bowl. She lived in a house where there had been excited talk about buying a tumble dryer.

In Joseph's kitchen there was a cooker that would have made the nurses retch, and on his wooden table a beautiful turquoise bowl that she hadn't noticed the night before, Moroccan maybe, filled with papers and bills. She picked out an envelope. His address: Midhope House. His name: Kazargazof. Joseph Kazargazof.

There was no kettle. There was a saucepan she filled with water and set on a sticky gas ring. Matches everywhere; she lit one, lowered the flame.

There were drawings pinned up, and others chalked directly on to the walls; they lined the narrow corridor between the bathroom and his bedroom. Many more drawings scored the walls in a small bare studio where the basement windows revealed the pavement outside, legs and feet hurrying along the wet street towards St Pancras Station. There was a drawing of Robin taped to the wall, Robin standing waist-deep in water, his body raw-boned and translucent. There were sketches of other people she didn't recognize, but most were delicate but disturbing drawings of the woman in the photograph next to his bed, that looked to Ruth's untrained eye as if the artist was deliberately trying to make the viewer feel uneasy. In one, she was lying down, reading; in another, she was sleeping; in another, she sat upright, a burning cigarette in her hand, a look of amusement, or maybe contempt, on her face.

Ruth returned to the bedroom with two mugs of tea, stood in the doorway and watched Joseph sleep, still and intact, watched the rise and fall of his chest.

The boys from her home town would have been floored by the pure insolence of it, by the casual, girlish beauty of him. Look at him, sleeping when he could be riding, when he could be pumping away like a dog.

His shoes were blue. She'd noticed them yesterday when he'd stood in front of her, blocking her light. In the shipwrecked bedroom his clothes washed around the floor, but the shoes were moored side by side at the foot of the bed.

She needed to find out the time. There was no sign of an alarm clock, no clock at all as far as she could see, nothing to suggest hurry, no cupboard sheltering a suit or tie or overcoat. The boys in her home town had plans, they had matches to win and accountancy degrees to pin down and pillowy girls to plunder and bungalows of their own to build. They had mothers who picked their damp socks off the bedroom floor and plucked sticky hankies from under sour mattresses, closing their eyes against the very thought of it.

'Who are you, Mr Kazargazof?' Ruth wondered, looking at the chalky parade on his bedroom walls. And then, just as rapidly as the confidence to use his soap, and boil the water, and peruse the artwork, and wake him with a mug of tea and thank him for providing a bed for the night, had struck her, it deserted her entirely.

She placed the mugs next to the ashtray as quietly as she could and picked her tights and skirt from the floor. She was desperate now to leave before he woke, to walk out of his front door and pretend she knew where she was going. Straightening up, crumpled skirt in her hand, she saw him open his eyes and look at her, and the word 'ice' slipped into her empty mouth. 'Ice' because in the bleached stillness of this wintery morning his eyes were the colour of frozen things, of trapped things, of subterranean things, of things that are lost. He sat up, pushed back the bedclothes, held her gaze, and she felt a bolt, a charge, that made her want to sink to the floor. Here it is, she thought, here is love, and fear.

She let her skirt drop, crawled to him across the wasteland of his broken bed.

THREE

Cork, May 2018

Robin ran water into a saucepan and herded the startled cats from under the kitchen table and back outside, leaving the pan on the step. He was starving. He found a tin of sardines among his mother's stash of dried pulses. Sardines on toast and a drink. His search unearthed a bottle of cava – it was the same one he'd bought her on a visit late last winter.

'Goodness, are we celebrating?' his mother had asked. Relieved when he'd told her the bottle was on special offer in the garage before the roundabout, and that he'd picked it up on impulse, she'd thanked him and put it away.

He'd spent the better part of that weekend helping her clear up her studio, a corrugated-roofed lean-to at the side of the house. It was a pleasantly haphazard space where her most recent work (which was scant) dried out on wooden planks supported by a low scaffold, and where her rejected pots, those whose lips sagged or whose bottoms blistered, sat together in amiable groups like war veterans at a picnic. That Sunday morning, when the narrow room was in order, her kiln swept and her potter's wheel cleaner than he'd ever seen it, they'd moved outside to the woodshed. While his mother had fretted around him, clapping her gloved hands together to shake out the cold, Robin dragged out bloated canvas deckchairs, an old pug machine for mixing clay and a bicycle of hers that she would once have insisted on trying to repair. Piling up the contents in readiness for a skip, he'd tried to talk to her about her reluctance to get back to work. But she'd resisted his efforts and found him another task.

'If you empty the top shelf in the kitchen, you'll find a soup tureen that Ruth might like. It's a very fine dish. I didn't make it myself, make sure to tell Ruth that. It came with the cottage; it's probably antique.'

Robin had been bored, tired, beginning to get irritated.

'We don't need a soup tureen, thanks. We had to let the butler go, he kept dribbling into the potted shrimp.'

'I don't understand you, Robin.'

'Thank you, but Ruth won't want a soup tureen.'

'Sell it, then.'

'Why would I sell your soup tureen?'

'Sell my car. Give the money to Sid.'

'You need a car. You can't live out here without a car.'

'I haven't been driving.'

'You need to drive. I'll check the tyres before I go back.'

'So how are you feeling?' he'd finally managed to ask later that afternoon, having taken her car into town and adjusted the tyre pressure. He had lifted a cardboard box of papers from the top of her wardrobe and put it on the kitchen table – his final task, he'd hoped, before he could reasonably depart.

'Unafraid,' she'd replied.

'What do you mean?'

'Oh, you know,' she'd said, fishing old photographs and damp Christmas cards out of the box. 'I just need to shake this thing off.'

Robin, who'd been leaning against the rail of the Aga watching her, went over and pulled a wilted wedding invitation from the box. It had been a big country wedding; the groom, whom Robin knew from surfing, had inherited his father's drapery business in the town and was marrying Maria, who worked alongside him. The couple had met in primary school. 'A whirlwind romance, then?' he remembered Joseph remarking, having gatecrashed the wedding party. They mustn't have been more than seventeen or eighteen, Robin thought, drinking vodka from the free bar. Joseph had been visiting from London, steadily sleeping his way through Robin's friends' girlfriends, while Robin spent the summer nights lying awake scowling at Joseph's empty sleeping bag and wondering when his life was going to begin.

'Oh my goodness, look at this!' his mother had said, handing him a newspaper cutting from a craft show she'd entered a decade before.

'Top of the Pots!' read the headline, above a photograph of his mother holding up a bulbous vase. The photograph had caught Robin short. In it, she looked as he expected her to look.

'Promise me you'll go back to the doctor. Yeah?'

'I'll be fine, Robin.' She'd turned to him and raised her hand to touch his cheek. 'You look a little tired yourself.'

'I'm good. All good.' He'd moved away from her, replaced the cutting in the box.

'And Ruth? How is she?'

'Good. Busy.'

'Maybe next time she'll come down with you?'

'Maybe. I should probably think about getting back actually.'

'And are you happy, Robin?' She had moved towards him again, her hand reaching for his.

'Happy?'

His desire to get out of the kitchen had felt overwhelming, the ceiling beams seemed to be descending on him, the walls swelling, the scent of cats and cumin thickening with each breath.

'I would very much like to know that you are happy.'

'Why wouldn't I be?'

'I don't know. You don't tell me.'

'Go to the doctor. That'll make me happy.'

The ginger tom was yipping outside the window; Robin had lifted the sash, grateful to breathe in the wet scent of winter.

'Can I do anything else before I go?'

'You don't want to eat?'

'No. I'll get on the road.'

He'd been impatient to get going, to avoid Sunday-evening traffic on the outskirts of Dublin. If he got back early enough, he'd call Celestine, maybe meet her in the bar on the canal. Maybe she'd be alone in the flat. Ruth wouldn't be expecting him till late.

'You need to get back behind the wheel,' Robin had said to his mother. 'Both wheels.'

'Suzi offered to pick up anything I need from town. I've asked her to buy me yarn. I need to do something with my hands.'

She'd followed him to the bedroom and was sitting on the edge of the bed while he threw his clothes into a bag.

'Do you have to go?'

'I'm teaching tomorrow.'

'It's early.'

'I'll come down again soon, I promise. Meanwhile, please don't knit me a jumper.'

'No?'

'I'm not standing in front of thirty adolescent boys bleating on about Orwell in another purple tank top.'

'Who says this one will be purple?'

She had walked him to the gate. The Christmas roses were dying, the flat white flowers wilting against the black foliage. He'd kissed her cheek.

'It's cold,' he'd said. 'Go back inside.'

Through the rear-view mirror, he had watched her walk to the house, watched her turn to wave from the low red door. He'd saluted and left.

Somewhere outside Naas, the car radio warning of the catastrophic environmental consequences of being alive, he had heard the words she had spoken. 'I am unafraid.' It was a thing she did, he'd reassured himself. Still, after all these years, she sometimes used language in a peculiarly arcane way.

'My spectacles behave as schoolchildren,' she'd sighed during his visit. 'Hiding whenever I'm looking for them.'

She'd be fine, he'd reassured himself, she was always fine.

With one hand on the steering wheel, he had freed his phone from the pocket of his jeans. The Bluetooth thing was broken, as usual. Sid knew how to get it working, but Sid was in Berlin. As the city-bound traffic thickened, he'd glanced down at the phone and pressed the call button, followed by the loudspeaker. Propping the phone on the dash, he'd listened to it ring.

'Hi,' Celestine answered.

'Hi,' he'd replied, leaning back into his seat while, outside, the bruised evening turned to black.

In his mother's kitchen now, Robin folded a piece of toast around the oily sardines, stood by the window, looked out over the hushed water, and ate. He'd made two phone calls after he woke: one to Helen and Colm to see if they'd heard anything from Ruth (they hadn't), the other to Bantry Hospital.

'There is no change,' the ward sister informed him. 'She's comfortable.'

'She's sleeping?'

'Yes.'

'I'm coming in,' he'd said. 'What time are visiting hours?'

'Don't worry about visiting hours, Mr Wolfe, you're welcome to come in and out as you need.'

Robin washed, then realized that in his haste to get out of Dublin he'd packed nothing. His shirt stank. In his old bedroom the handful of clothes, hanging in the wardrobe for decades, taunted him. A lean man, he couldn't ever remember being that thin. There were a couple of shirts in his mother's wardrobe that she wore in the studio. He pulled one on. Collarless and flannel, clay-stained at the cuff, he was grateful for its familiarity. In the kitchen he put the unopened cava in the fridge, found his car keys and, before he left, just on the off-chance, phoned Ruth.

'Ruth's phone. Leave a message.'

He was going to speak, going to repeat what he'd already said in earlier calls, that he was in Popes Cove, that his mother was in a hospital where peacocks strutted on the lawn. He was going to say that he missed her. He was going to ask her where she was, ask her when – if – she was coming back. He was going to repeat his litany of regret. But he didn't. Pocketing his phone, fearful of alerting Suzi and her gnomes, he quietly closed the cottage door, slipped the car into gear and left.

Driving to the county hospital along narrow country roads, past sloping fields dotted with black-and-white cows, stock-still, gazing seaward at a silver ocean, Robin, immune to this quotidian beauty, thought about Celestine. It was, he attempted to console himself, as if those months he'd spent with her had happened to someone else, as if he'd been some other self, a portrait, a man who'd stepped out of the frame and lived as Robin wouldn't have dared. That he'd seen her waiting at the bus stop that autumn night after the parent–teacher meeting, alone in the rain, made him feel, right from the beginning, as if he had conjured her, had already fictionalized her. Or maybe, he now considered as he approached the roundabout and turned the car towards Bantry, it was at that point that he began to fictionalize himself.

The sense, the notion, that both he and Celestine were not quite real, not quite actual, had stayed with him for the months of their . . . what? Their affair? (Robin associated affairs with hotel bedrooms and underwear slung over lampshades and anonymous phone calls at 2 a.m. to sleeping houses. And none of those things applied, had applied, to them.)

He hadn't really expected to find her that late-October evening, yet when he was driving towards the bus stop and had seen her pale coat and dark hair, when he'd pulled in and stopped the car, he'd known that somehow he would find her, and whatever rage he'd been carrying had dissolved and she had looked, he thought, terribly alone. And it had occurred to him, leaning across the passenger seat and opening the car door for her, that their previous conversation in the classroom was one she had been looking forward to, that her words had not been intended to mock him but to engage him. It occurred to him in that small, inconsequential moment that this was a beginning.

'Can I drop you somewhere?'

She'd hesitated.

'All right. Thanks. Anywhere near the canal.'

'My name is Celestine,' she'd said, buckling the seatbelt. 'I don't know if you knew that.'

'I didn't. You don't drive?'

'No, I don't drive.'

Her proximity was absurd. He could smell rain and cigarettes and musk. He'd driven towards the canal that partly encircled Dublin city.

'I should apologize,' Robin had said, changing lanes. 'Back in the classroom, I didn't mean to cut you short.'

Breaking the silence that followed, she'd asked him if she could smoke. 'You'd probably hate it, right?'

'No, not at all,' he'd lied.

She had lit a cigarette, cracked open the window and seemed to relax. Robin had asked her to talk to him about her son, who was one of his pupils. And Celestine, almost jaunty now, told Robin that Dylan was her only child and that it mattered to her to do her absolute best by him, to work to give him a good education, a head start, something she felt she hadn't had. Dylan could play guitar, she said, and make a chicken curry, and she was proud of the books he bought. Just sixteen years old, and he went unbidden into the bookshop in the city that sold cut-price classics.

'I don't know if he actually reads them,' Celestine had said, 'but I'm glad that he thinks he might.'

They'd gone, quite naturally, for a drink in a bar she knew on the canal, the kind of bar that used to be the haunt of phlegmy old men nursing harsh whiskies. Reborn now in the republic of hip, it was a place that served craft beers to sleek young Dubliners who paid cruel rents to live so close to the city. Midweek the place was almost empty, just a couple of girls with very red lips grouped around their half-drunk pints and, at another table, a middle-aged man picking at a cheeseboard which, according to the blackboard menu behind the bar, came replete with pickled kumquat. The barman, who was older than he looked, had tiny silver rings threaded through his beard. His name was Luca, Celestine said, which felt like another fiction.

'I'll get these,' she'd told him, and Robin had chosen a table underneath a string of prayer flags. He'd sat down, and wondered what the hell he thought he was doing. One of the red-lipped girls, he noticed, was crying. She looked up at him, challenging his curiosity; embarrassed, he had looked away. Celestine had joined him then, with two bottles of beer. Sitting opposite him, she stretched out her legs.

'Why did you stop the car? Were you looking for me?'

'Of course not.'

He'd picked up his bottle, brought it to his mouth.

'Cheers,' she said.

'Yes. Sorry. Cheers.'

When he'd first met Celestine earlier, at the third-year parent–teacher meeting, it would, he had hoped, be his last encounter of a long and tedious evening. She'd come into the classroom alone and sat down at his desk. She had been wearing white gloves, maybe leather, which she removed while they spoke, pulling the fingers free with her teeth. He'd watched her, before shuffling through his papers, looking for her son's report. Glancing up again, he'd noticed that she had spread her fingers out, fan-like, on his desk and Robin, somewhat alarmingly, pictured himself lifting her hand from the desk to warm her fingers in his mouth. Instead, however, he had delivered an efficient, if curt, precis of her son's prospects in his Junior Certificate English exam (must use more quotations, good textual understanding, can expect a reasonable result if he puts the work in). When he'd finished speaking, she'd looked down at her starfish fingers.

'It's so cold,' she'd said, smiling. 'My fingers look like Dylan's mice.'

Bewildered, Robin had said nothing for a moment. 'Mice?'

'Frozen mice. I buy them online for his reptile collection. They're delivered in batches. Has he told you about his reptiles?'

'I'm your son's English teacher,' Robin explained, thinking she might somehow have mistaken him for Harry Coleman, who was rumoured to teach biology.

'He wants to be a writer, you know.'

'I didn't.'

Robin had shifted in his seat, unfurled his back. He'd been sitting for hours. This was all he needed, another delusional parent who thought a four-line ditty about a sunset was proof of their child's poetic genius. Robin had already seen dozens of parents that evening, had witnessed a parade of middle-aged, middle-class couples, stubbornly clinging to their belief in their sons' sparkling prospects. The idealized offspring of these conscientious parents rarely, if ever, resembled the sprawling masses of anxiety and arrogance he met in his classroom.

Had he seen Dylan Fogarty's mother earlier, when he still had some hope of surviving the evening without feeling like a fraud, he might have felt more tolerant. He might have told her that Fogarty interested him, unsettled him, that the boy had an unnerving calm, a self-belief that Robin felt tempted both to crush and to nurture.

'He has a brilliant imagination,' she'd continued. 'He invents lives for people; our neighbours in the flats, people on the bus. He's even written about the mice, about them coming alive, becoming monstrous, annihilating us.'

'Good stuff.'

She was looking straight at him, smiling. She was young, Robin thought, although lately he had begun to feel as if everyone was young, younger than he was anyway – newsreaders, politicians, doctors. This woman was in her late thirties maybe. Her hair was scraped back, her mouth thin and red, her teeth small and white and even, as if she might start at the edge of you and nibble all the way in. What the fuck was he thinking? He was tired, he needed to get home.

She'd reached down into her bag. He could see her scalp through her parting; the line of grey roots through her black hair surprised him.

'I told him to tell you. I said, "You should tell Mr Wolfe, you should show him, he's your English teacher, show him your stories." But he won't. So I brought you one myself.'

That she was on her own was unusual. Unlike any school Robin had taught in before, the majority of his pupils seemed to come replete with a full set of progenitors: pert mother and balding father. There had been just a handful of single parents at his desk all evening, a couple of mothers and one father, a widower, whose phone had rung twice during the course of their discussion.

'Thank you,' Robin had said, taking the torn copybook sheets from Dylan's mother. 'I'll certainly take a look at that.'

'He thinks you're unhappy.'

'Me?' Distracted, Robin thought he'd misheard.

'Dylan says you look as if you're thinking about something else, as if the walls of the classroom crumble and you're looking at something that no one else can see.'

Robin had felt doused in fury. How dare the little shit observe him. What fucking business was it of a sixteen-year-old to decipher his fucking expressions?

Fogarty's mother was still smiling, her eyes bright.

'And is this a phenomenon he's noticed with other teachers?'

'Phenomenon,' she had repeated slowly, her smile fading. 'No, Mr Wolfe, it is not a phenomenon he's noticed with other teachers.'

'I can teach your son. I can't, however, modulate my expressions to please him.'

She'd stood, put her hand out for the papers she had just offered him and picked up her bag and gloves.

'Thank you for your time.' She smiled tightly. 'I'll pass on your advice, tell him to keep his eyes on his book and use more quotations. Gold dust, I'm sure.'

Robin had watched her walk away. His knuckles were white; he'd wanted to hit her. He'd never wanted to hit a parent before.

He'd taken a breath, stood, walked to the classroom door, looked along the line of plastic chairs outside his room. She was gone; the line was empty. He'd turned, pulled the scrawled paper sign off his door – 'R. Wolfe, English' – balled it up and slung it in the bin. He'd put on his jacket, gathered up his notes and the roll book that he'd have to take back over to the staffroom before he could get out of the fucking place. He'd kill for a pint; maybe he'd stop on the way home. Or maybe he'd go to the off-licence and buy a bottle of wine.

He'd picked up his copies of *Animal Farm* and *Hamlet*, put them in his bag. Fuck them, every last pig and prince. He was tired. Tired tired tired. 'He thinks you're unhappy!' Really? Well, who gave him permission to think?

'Excuse me?'

Heap's parents were standing by the open classroom door; he recognized them immediately. Wearily pleasant, they were panting a little, their four round eyes already brimful of apology and understanding. They reminded him of middle-aged Labradors.

'We were waiting over in the science block for Mr Coleman, the biology teacher, but I think he may have already left.'

'That's pretty likely.'

'We were awfully worried we'd missed you. Are we too late?'

Robin's desire to see Dylan's mother again felt inexplicable, primitive.

'Sit,' Robin had commanded. 'I mean, sit down. Please.'

He'd give them five minutes of what they wanted to hear. He might still be able to find her.

And find her he did, in the rain, and it was almost, he let himself believe, as if she had been waiting for him.

Robin went to the bar to get another beer for Celestine. Declining Luca's inducement to buy himself a non-alcoholic beverage made from kefir grains and blueberries, he'd chosen an overpriced bottle of water instead.

'Nice place,' he'd said, while the barman poured. Luca hadn't deigned to agree or disagree.

'Do you like teaching?' Celestine had asked him when he returned to the table.

Robin sipped his water.

'How could I not?'

'I think it's the most important job in the world.'

Are you fucking kidding me, he'd wanted to say. No, I don't like teaching. I'm barely making it through the term. I no longer believe in what I'm doing. I feel obsolete. I am dressing them up for a wedding and leading them to a wake. I am redundant and failed. I wake up in the morning exhausted at the prospect of another day standing in front of a classroom of adolescent boys. I wake, he was tempted to add, wondering how it all came to this, to a twenty-year-old marriage, to a job I no longer want, to a lightly boiled speckled egg and the very occasional fuck when my wife feels like she once did, warm and present.

'Teaching, it's . . . it's challenging,' he'd heard himself say. 'Certainly challenging. What about you? Do you work?'

And she had told him about her job with a market research company, finding people for focus groups, people to fill in questionnaires, to offer their opinions on anything from cryptocurrencies to sugar-free cereals.

'I find people, and then I find out what they like and what they don't like. That's my job. And I'm very good at it.'

'And there's just Dylan? Just you and Dylan?'

'And my father,' she'd told him. 'He lives with us in the flat, but he spends most of his time with his girlfriend in Tenerife. They go dancing.'

'Ballroom dancing?' Robin had enquired, though he couldn't have said what put that idea into his head.

'It's all in the stance, or so he says.' Celestine had looked dispassionately at the weepy girl at the other table. 'My father's probably not that much older than you. Do you go ballroom dancing?'

'No.'

'How old are you?'

'Fifty-one.'

'He's fifty-nine. You're married, obviously.'

And he'd told her he was married to Ruth and that they lived, alone now, near Phoenix Park in a small house that they'd often talked about moving on from but somehow never had. He told her that they had one son, Sid, who'd been in art college but who had deferred and recently moved to Berlin to try to be a DJ.

'What kind of DJ?' Celestine had asked, and Robin said he wasn't entirely sure but there had been a lot of talk about his intention to strip out post-industrial something or other and do something else that sounded painful and involved neural networks and shattering things into fractal pieces.

'You were listening, then?'

'That's all I could do.'

'What does your wife do?'

'She's a framer. A fine-art framer.'

'For a minute, I thought you said she was a farmer. A fine-art farmer.'

'No, there's no livestock involved in her work, just quite a lot of still lifes with withered peaches. And children, she volunteers with refugee children. Making things. Making art.'

'She sounds kind.'

'She is kind. "Kind" is a good word to describe her actually.'

'I have to go,' Celestine had said then. 'I don't like leaving Dylan alone too long.'

He'd been grateful that she wanted to leave; the spontaneity was killing him. The unexpected nature of their encounter, of the night itself, begun with verve, with anger, was threatening to paralyse him. It had been so long since he had acted on impulse that he no longer knew what impulse was. He was working too hard to sound casual, he was fraying around the edges.

'Are you sure?' Celestine had asked when they went outside into the rain. 'I could walk the rest.'

In the car, she'd said she was hungry. Robin's heart sank.

The chipper was called Luigi's.

'It's Italian,' she'd told him in the queue, as if she was speaking to a child, or maybe an invalid.

'I gathered,' he'd replied.

'It's OK, you know, Mr Wolfe,' she had said, looking up at him. 'We're just getting chips. We're just two people going to get chips. We're just ordinary strangers, so ordinary we're almost invisible.'

'Will you tell your wife about tonight?'

They were sitting in the car outside Celestine's block of flats. To their right was a circular dome housing the stairwell. She'd taken her shoes off. Her legs curled under her, she was rolling a very thin joint. Outside, the rain was beginning to bore itself. She'd lit the joint, took a long drag, and passed it to Robin. He felt the smoke make a playground of his lungs, felt a forgotten needle-thin tingling around his jaw. Silently they passed the joint, watching the rain. After a little while, she had uncurled her legs and begun to put on her shoes.

'It's been good, Celestine.'

'Has it?'

She was bending down to pick up her bag. He ran his finger along the line of her scalp. Under the cold arc of the courtyard light, the grey roots shone silver. He recalled a tide mark, a salt mark, crisp and iridescent, a white moon; a night, some night that he couldn't grip, the memory of it rising and sinking, washing away.

She'd straightened up.

'When the classroom walls crumble, I see the past,' he told her. 'I try to fit it together. I try to know it.'

She had brushed a thread of tobacco from his lower lip. 'Thanks for the lift. And the chips.'

'Tell Dylan not to give up. Tell him giving up is the only failure.'

'OK.'

'Celestine?'

She'd opened the car door. 'I need to go.'

'We could go for a cycle.'

'On a bicycle?'

'It tends to work that way.'

'I don't have a bicycle.'

'It doesn't matter. Sorry. Goodnight.'

She had smiled and got out of the car.

Robin had closed his eyes, opened them, reached for the ignition. His brain felt numb. She was leaning back into the car, holding the door open.

'I have a pair of runners somewhere. We could go for a walk?'

Some of her hair had slipped its noose; it fell loose and black around her neck. He'd been about to answer her when easily, gracefully, she had kissed him. Softly, fleetingly, she had kissed him. And he had touched her neck, his fingers grazing the collar of her thin coat, and then she was gone. He'd waited, the engine running, watching until she disappeared into the tower of the stairs.

When he got home, Ruth was on the phone to Sid. 'Have you thought about what you want to do next?' she was asking.

'Where were you?' she'd mouthed to Robin.

'Pub. Harry Coleman. Sorry,' he'd whispered back, before bounding upstairs to brush his teeth. Then, realizing he was parched, he'd gone back downstairs again.

'Do you want me to talk to him, Sid?'

'I'm going to bed,' he'd mouthed.

Ruth had nodded. Knowing she was watching him through the open living-room door, he'd taken the stairs at a more sedate pace.

Robin had undressed, throwing his clothes on the small blue couch in their bedroom. He was about to get into bed and feign sleep (and, in that manufactured state, find privacy) when he caught sight of himself in the wardrobe mirror. Long and gaunt, blue veins ribboning his arms and legs, he had looked at himself and seen a route map. 'But where are you going?' he asked himself.

'Who are you talking to?'

Ruth was at the bedroom door, her reading glasses on her head. She looked drawn.

'Have you seen my charger anywhere?' she asked.

'Phone charger?'

'Laptop.'

'Did you look on the desk?'

'Yes, of course.' She leant against the frame. 'So who are you talking to?'

'Myself. I was wondering if I'd always had so many veins.'

She'd considered him for a moment. 'Not so many on the backs of your legs.'

He turned, looked at himself over his shoulder. 'Shit.'

'I wouldn't worry,' Ruth had said, leaving the room. 'I'm too shagging blind to notice.'

Unable now to sleep, Robin had gone back to the bathroom and stood under the shower. He thought of Celestine. He thought of Ruth watching him watch himself, and then he thought of Celestine again, Celestine tending trays of frozen mice, her hair falling over her shoulders. In the bar, watching the weeping girl, she'd told him the mice reminded her of embryos, that she imagined a frosted population of foetuses every time she opened the freezer. He closed his eyes, let the water obliterate him, thought of her pulling at the leathery fingers of her gloves with her teeth, of her lips around the bottle top. He imagined lifting her cold hand from the desk and warming her fingers in his mouth.

By the time he re-emerged Ruth was already in bed, glasses on, her laptop wired up and open on her knees.

'So is Harry in trouble again? What is it this time?'

Momentarily, he had no idea what she was talking about.

'Oh, you know Harry – school politics, the usual.'

'Your clothes smell of vinegar.'

'Do they? Harry bought me chips.'

'Harry bought you chips? Chips are the last thing Harry needs. God, I'd hate to be his arteries.'

He'd watched her for the slightest flicker of suspicion. There was none. Why should there be? He had never in the twenty years of their marriage been seriously interested in another woman. Ruth was wearing an old T-shirt, her hair pushed back behind her ears, a gauzy sheen of something that smelt like roses on her face. You're beautiful, he thought, and that is of no consequence to you; it is meaningless to you, your loveliness.

'How is Sid?'

'He's OK.'

'Right. When you were talking to him it sounded like something was up.'

'Did it?'

'He's all right, is he?'

'Ali moved her girlfriend in to the flat and now the landlord is hassling them. I told Sid to email me a copy of his lease agreement.'

'The lease will be in German. You don't speak German.'

'You do.'

'I can say "Good morning!", "Where's the train station?" and "I'll have mine without tomato".'

'You know that's not true.'

'They'll sort it out themselves. They're adults.'

'Are you drunk, Robin? Your eyes look cloudy.'

'I thought you were too blind to notice what I looked like.'

There was a silence. Robin could have bitten his own tongue out. Why start a row? Why, tonight of all nights?

'You think I don't see you? Don't notice things?'

'I didn't say that.'

'I'm tired, Robin. Sid asked me for help. Please don't be like this.'

'Like what?'

'Resentful.'

He lay down, turned off his light, closed his eyes, listened to Ruth tap out her endless solutions. Drifting into sleep, he saw Celestine on a bicycle, gliding along a silvery beach, saying something to him that he couldn't quite hear. Her pale limbs and dark hair reminded him of someone he had loved.

Later, he'd been aware of Ruth getting up and going downstairs. She'd lie on the couch with a camomile tea, waiting for Sid's email, which would probably never come. She'd wait, resisting for a long time the urge to turn on the late-night rolling news, to mute the presenters' prattle and scan the ribbon of carnage and despair unravelling across the bottom of the screen. Just in case there'd been an incident in Berlin and a beautiful boy with his father's eyes had been blown apart by someone else's war.

FOUR

London, September 1995

One of Robin's problems, or traits – the one he liked least about himself, yet held on to most dearly – was caution. A cautious man, he had to brace himself to crack an egg. So when Ruth had first washed up, however briefly, in the staffroom in Clerkenwell, on the first day of the new school year, when she had angrily rewrapped her scarf around her neck, bit down on her hand, picked up her clumsy bag and left again, banging the door behind her, Robin had stood stock-still next to the photocopier, a mug in his hand, and done nothing. She had slipped into the staffroom largely unnoticed that morning. (He had since observed her ability to appear and disappear easily.) Veronica, assistant to the principal – a title she never tired of repeating – had sniffed her out immediately, however, and asked for her rank and file. Ruth, unravelling a pale green scarf, had replied: 'I'm Ruth Lennon. I'm the new special needs assistant.'

Robin, recognizing her accent, had hidden behind his coffee.

Veronica, a woman with all the warmth of roadkill, had told Ruth Lennon that, brand-new special needs assistant or not, the staffroom was reserved for qualified teachers only, with the exception of herself, naturally, being assistant to the principal, and that SNAs (let's reduce her to an acronym while we're at it) took their tea breaks in the small kitchen off the domestic science room, where they also hung their coats. Being denied access to the staffroom, where a variety of men and women in dull jumpers congregated over teabags and throat lozenges, was in fact no great loss to Ms Lennon, though it was the principle of the thing that stung. And so Ruth reddened, and rewound her scarf, and bit down on her small hand, and picked up her big bag, and slammed the door behind her. And what did Robin do? Robin sipped his granulated Nescafé.

He saw her occasionally over the ensuing days, navigating her way around the corridors, and on Tuesday morning of the following week, when she had once again appeared out of thin air and asked him if he might know where her year-ten class had disappeared to, he had smiled and momentarily touched her elbow to turn her towards the computer room, which, as it happened, she was standing right outside.

It was only a couple of weeks later, after the accident in the sports hall, when Ardu, one of her younger pupils, smashed his nose on the exit door, that Robin found Ruth smoking at the back of the boiler room and introduced himself. (Though to say 'found her smoking at the back of the boiler room' might be misleading. Robin, having overheard Veronica discuss 'the matter' with two teachers who were both called Hazel and who both looked perpetually exhausted, went looking for her.)

'Irish?' Ruth asked when he spoke. 'You're Irish?'

She looked like she might bite.

'Yes. Yes, I am.'

'And your name is Robin?'

'It is, yes,' he replied, fairly bowling himself over with the chat.

'I didn't think Irish mothers called their sons Robin.'

An amateur smoker, Robin asked her for a cigarette paper and some tobacco and began to roll – a task he performed with diligence rather than panache – and told Ruth that his mother, although living in Ireland for thirty years, was German and that his surname was Wolfe.

'Robin Wolfe?' she repeated coolly. 'School must have been fun.'

She looked at him then and he noticed that her eyes were grey and so much wilder and so much sadder than she intended.

What Robin didn't tell Ruth during that first encounter – he wasn't a fool – was that he'd come to London to get away from his mother's ferocious protection. Nor did he tell her that when, in his late twenties, he'd gone for a job teaching English in this shabby Clerkenwell comprehensive, his application was optimistically predicated on his belief that he was bound to have more sex in a world capital than in a small Irish town on the edge of the Atlantic – a belief that had spectacularly failed to hold water. He didn't tell her that all he'd managed so far, almost two years into his great experiment, was to buy a small car, rent a smaller flat, fall in and out of a relationship with a lachrymose Bristolian who had a fondness for novelty pyjamas, and become thinner and paler still – if it is possible, that is, to grow paler than snow. He didn't tell her that he was lonely. He didn't have to.

Finding his voice between ragged inhalations, he did, however, tell Ruth that his German mother was a potter – not a very good potter, but an enthusiastic one – who had thought her son might follow her vocation. But the thought of being Robin Wolfe, stoneware potter, eating organic carrots on a wind-blown peninsula, and quite possibly taking up the mandolin to while away the long, black winter nights, made him feel like someone he'd never met before. He had inhabited his pale, lanky self for twenty-nine years, he told her, and no matter how hard he tried he couldn't see himself in a pair of Birkenstocks, which seemed to be the footwear of choice for just about every potter he'd ever met. And then, despairing at the sound of his own voice, he stopped speaking and waited.

'I quite like the mandolin,' she said after a moment, a thin trail of smoke whispering into the autumn air.

'Are you hungry?' he asked, and she nodded. It was lunchtime; he had a cheese and chutney roll in his backpack if she could just be persuaded to stay still. 'I have a sandwich in the staffroom. I could bring it back?'

She nodded again and her eyes filled up, and for a moment he thought his offer of half a bread roll had moved her to tears.

'I tried to stop Ardu. I ran. I heard the break. I'd asked the PE teacher to stop the game. He laughed.'

'It's not your fault. Everyone knows that.'

When Robin got back to the staffroom the entire cabal were doubting Ruth's competence, Veronica even speculating that Ruth might be let go. Keith, the PE teacher, thighs splayed so that Veronica could appreciate the hillock of Lycra between his legs, was agreeing with her.

'She asked you to stop the game, didn't she?' Robin asked, opening his backpack.

'What's that?'

'She asked you to call off the game. You ignored her.'

'She might have said something. I didn't hear her. She's one of yours, isn't she?'

'One of mine?'

'Oirish, begorra! Sorry, mate, can't understand half of what you lot are saying.'

Robin and Ruth shared the cheese roll, sitting on the boiler-room step, leaning back against the grey steel door, Ruth's head haloed by red and black graffiti: 'Dev loves Ash', 'Lai is a queer', 'Ash loves Lai', 'Dev is a queer'.

Ruth had a Time Out bar in her pocket. They'd been giving them out free that morning on the concourse of King's Cross Station.

'You get the Tube in?' Robin enquired.

'Bus from Streatham to Brixton, Tube from there, then walk.'

'What time do you get out of bed? Dawn?'

'Something like that.'

She rolled another cigarette, ran her tongue along the paper.

'Do you always bring in your lunch?' she asked, handing the cigarette to him.

'Habit.'

He lit up, letting his head rest against the door. And in the shared quiet of that shadowy place he told her how, when he was a child, his mother had sent him to school every day with sand-wiches of home-made bread, heavy and moist as a turf sod. And a banana; she always packed a banana. And sometimes, he sighed, his mother would write him a message on the banana skin, or maybe a joke, a ritual that Robin had come to despise but didn't know how to break without hurting his mother's feelings. (Why Robin was talking so much, wreathing Ruth in words, making a bouquet of his life for her, he didn't know. It was the nearness of her that mattered, her mouth blowing smoke into the stillness.) He would tentatively unpack his lunch in his small country school, hoping that today's banana wouldn't hold a message. The other children – curious, freckled, dispassionate, with jam sandwiches made on glorious shop-bought bread by mothers who were far too busy with quick-tempered husbands and moon-eyed cows and rib-thin dogs to be writing messages on banana skins, for god's sake – would crowd around his desk hoping that the banana would have some news. Then, one day, Con, the biggest boy in the class, who had a covetable if faint moustache and a father who owned a drapery in Clonakilty town, had straddled the small classroom chair next to Robin's, taken a long swig out of his bottle of red lemonade, belched, and declared Robin a spy, a suspicion confirmed when Robin took out the banana and found his mother had written to him in German.

'What does it mean?' the children had asked, crowding around his desk, their jammy mouths agape.

'I'm sorry, I'm not allowed to tell you,' Robin had replied gravely, replacing the banana in its Tupperware bed and snapping shut the lid. 'It's in code.'

And the children had fallen silent, staring at him, slowly, methodically, masticating their lunch, each chew on the cud of their processed bread raising him up on a pedestal of mystery and danger.

'What did the banana say?' Ruth asked, stubbing out her cigarette. 'What did she write that only you could understand?'

He looked at her while he debated the truth, or at least the telling of it.

'Sorry, maybe I shouldn't ask.'

'Ich liebe dich, mein blasses kleinen Sohn.'

'What does that mean?'

'I love you, my pale little son. That was it,' Robin added briskly. 'Last message.'

His words stalled then, as if the wave of their conversation had peaked but could not break. And Robin felt overwhelmed by the loss of something he couldn't define. Himself maybe, a pale boy in a wind-torn, cow-scattered world, with a mother made of sea and clay and dark, wet bread, whom he loved and hated for loving. And the realization that he knew nothing more about Ruth Lennon than he had when he had come to find her, coupled with the knowledge that she knew more about him in fifteen minutes than he would divulge to another in a lifetime, left him feeling exposed and oddly ashamed. As the bell signalling the end of lunch break sounded, he gathered the remains of their lunch and stood up.

'Why was that her last message?' Ruth asked, reaching out her hand to him. 'What did you do?'

'I started making my own packed lunch,' Robin replied, taking Ruth's hand and pulling her to standing.

They were friends then in that immediate way you can make a friend when you're young and alone. She liked him; he loved her. It was charted in an instant, engraved by the rain, as they threw their stubbed-out cigarettes into the broken dish by the boiler-room door and began walking together back to the school, stamping out their territory on the autumn mulch, a no man's land between them. They reached the door of the school; around them children flocked to their classrooms.

'I suppose I'd better go before you eat me, Mr Wolfe.'

'I'll see you later,' he called, watching her dissolve into the crowd.

Robin didn't see Ruth again that day. He looked for her that afternoon after the last period, when the school was emptying out. He saw her, briefly, out of the staffroom window, speaking with a woman he assumed to be Ardu's mother. He flung his marking into his bag and left by the side door, but when he got out to the yard she had gone. He decided to walk back to his flat in Chalk Farm. He'd walk, get a grip on himself, slow down, consider his position. Reaching his flat, hungry and already impatient to see her again, he cooked himself two poached eggs and was eating them when his phone rang. It was Joseph, yawning, having just got out of bed at 5 p.m. and ready, apparently, to accept Robin's offer – which had not been easy to swing – that he should paint a mural on the schoolyard wall.

'Cash, yeah?' Joseph asked.

'Petty cash. Veronica is holding the purse strings.'

'Veronica?'

'Assistant to the principal. Paint something pleasant.'

'Pleasant?'

'Not a woman.'

'Women are pleasant.'

'Paint flowers or something.'

'I'll paint trees.'

'Brilliant. Veronica'll be thrilled.'

Robin was going to tell him about Ruth Lennon, but decided against it. There was only so much of his life, Robin thought, pushing his fork through the molten egg, that he was prepared to divulge to Joseph. Joseph was careless with secrets, and anyway, as he frequently reminded Robin, Robin's life bored him.

'Maybe it *is* dull,' Robin had said to him the last time he'd called over to Joseph's to bail him out with fish and chips and forty quid, 'but I can afford to eat.'

'And to feed me too, mate. Employment certainly has its compensations.'

'Why don't you try to sell some of these?' Robin had asked, looking around the room in the flat where Joseph worked, the walls and floor covered in drawings and portraits. Most seemed to be of a single subject. Some were finished, others abandoned.

'I'm not ready yet. Not quite cured,' he'd replied, returning from the kitchen and spearing a piece of battered cod with a fork he'd resuscitated from the bottom of the sink.

Before Robin put the phone down, Joseph arranged to meet him at the school in a week or so to look at the space for the mural; he'd get there as soon as he'd finished the portrait he was working on.

'Who is it of this time?' Robin asked unnecessarily, maybe even cruelly.

The following morning was Friday, and Robin woke up to rain. Rain! He flung himself out of bed, showered, found a grey sweater that didn't quite make him look like a negative of himself, ate a bowl of Weetabix, packed an extra sandwich into his backpack, and before he left, his timing just about perfect, he telephoned Bristolian Vicky's Holborn office, knowing that she would be on her way to work but would not have yet arrived. Apologizing to her voicemail, he said he wouldn't, after all, be able to meet her outside the Renoir on Bloomsbury Square that evening to see that Irish film that had just opened there (a tale of enduring female friendship in a two-horse town that she was sure he'd find tremendously moving). Something had come up, he said. Work. He'd call her tomorrow and explain. He wasn't lying, he reasoned with himself, putting the phone down, he just wasn't entirely telling the truth. He picked up his car keys and drove to Clerkenwell, a thing he never did.

He found Ruth at breaktime, just before she was swallowed by the door of the domestic science kitchen.

'You can't drive me home. I live miles away!'

'I need to go to Brixton anyway.'

'For what?'

'A chicken?'

'A chicken? There are no chickens in Chalk Farm, no?'

'Nope. Not a single one.'

'Sit down,' Ruth said, her head in the fridge looking for milk.

Robin hovered in the preternaturally clean kitchen that Ruth shared with three Irish nurses in Streatham, wondering whether to remove a pair of white tights that hung over the chair back. The room smelt like a swimming pool, the plastic tablecloth shone like an ice rink. Robin was dismayed. Somehow he had assumed that Ruth would need to be rescued, though from what he hadn't really considered. However, if her home seemed alarmingly shipshape, he contented himself that her career certainly wasn't. Robin, seeing in Ruth somebody who could do better (a favourite phrase of teachers everywhere), thought she might consider going back to college, earn the degree she had abandoned and get back on track.

'I'm not off track,' Ruth replied lightly, emerging from the fridge with a carton of milk.

The job suited her, she said. She liked spending her days head down over smudged copybooks, helping children shadowed by difficulty, some who wouldn't speak, others who couldn't silence their scattered thoughts. It wasn't exactly teaching, but, as Robin had already pointed out, she wasn't exactly qualified to teach. The most important thing, however, something that Robin had failed to consider, she told him, handing him his coffee, was that if and when she felt like it, she could leave. She was, in her estimation, entirely replaceable.

'Why would you leave?' he asked, attempting and failing to sound like he was making a casual enquiry. 'You've just arrived!'

'This is Helen's milk, by the way,' Ruth said, pouring it into his sparkling mug.

'Helen?'

'Helen, whose tights you're about to sit on.'

He placed the tights on the table and sat down. The delicacy of the fabric seemed to mock him.

'I have three housemates,' Ruth was saying, spreading peanut butter on seeded flatbread and successfully turning the conversation away from herself. 'Pauline is our Mother Superior; Pauline hates tights drying in the kitchen. Then there's Helen, who washes her tights in the kitchen sink and dries them on the chair back. And Mairead, whose relationship with her tights is a mystery.

'And there are the milk wars,' she continued, licking the peanut butter off her knife. 'I'm a milk pilferer. Helen is a milk sharer. Pauline is a milk fascist, measuring it before she goes to work. And Mairead, well . . . stealing Mairead's milk could send her over the edge.'

'What's wrong with Mairead?'

'Who knows? She's from Trim. She's a dental nurse in Clapham. Very beautiful, very clean teeth, quite a lot of downward dogs and weeping in the bath. I think she's harbouring feelings for the dentist.'

'Poor Mairead.'

'At least she's got her gum health. Do you have a girlfriend?'

The question threw him. He'd been watching her talk, only half listening to what she'd been saying. She was private, he thought, using words as decoys. She hadn't looked at him while she spoke, addressing her conversation to the tabletop, the knife, the window. She turned to him now and smiled.

'Do you?'

'Yes. No. No and yes.'

'Right.'

'I mean, there is someone. Vicky. I just don't know if she's . . . I don't always know what it means.'

'What what means?'

'She. I. Her and I.'

Ruth was leaning towards him, offering honey for his tea, a tiny black seed from the flatbread caught between her front teeth.

'Are you looking for love, Mr Wolfe?'

He ran a hand through his hair, leant back in the chair, looked at her framed against the darkening evening; behind her, suburban rooftops and nearly naked trees. She had a strange authority over him, as if she could order a door within him to open, causing memories from his past to break away, shale-like, rattled by her gaze, crowding each other for her attention.

He found himself telling her about his father, whom he had met only once before he died yet in recent years had seemed to haunt him. Robin had seen the old man's face reflected on passing Tube trains, in cafe windows; he had glimpsed him at the mouth of an escalator, his image dissolving just as Robin reached the bottom.

'I can never quite grasp him,' Robin said as the evening folded into night. 'I think I have him, then I lose him in the crowds.'

It was something to do with London, he tried to explain, the sheer force of numbers, that sense of being invisible, that somehow let his thoughts freefall. It was as if, he struggled to articulate, the city's practised indifference gave him permission to think whatever he wanted to think, to see whatever he wanted to see, on the grey edges of its disregard.

Their coffees cold, Ruth stood and took the cups to the sink.

'You asked me if I'm looking for love,' he said to her back as she leant over the sink and rinsed out the cups. 'Yes, I suppose I am. Are you?'

She didn't reply, just bent her head further to her task. Why had he asked her that? Why had he intruded and scared her away?

'My father died last summer,' she said, straightening up and coming back to the table.

'I'm sorry.'

She was silent for a while, sitting, looking at her reflection in the black window, hunched over, her knees under her chin, her arms wrapped around herself.

'My father was the manager of the co-operative stores – machinery and hardware, washing lines, lawnmowers.'

On Saturday mornings, when she was a little girl, Ruth told Robin, she would stand up behind the counter beside him, trying on the gardening gloves and choosing packets of dahlia seeds for withered old ladies. She told him how, as she got older, her father taught her about the stock and suppliers, had shown her how to change a till roll and measure a yard and how to slowly, slowly, count out the change into the hands of the paunchy old farmers who came in on a Saturday morning and might just think you were leaving them short.

They went upstairs to Ruth's bedroom, which was narrow and musty and which she shared with everyone else's suitcases and a box of Christmas decorations. Pauline having banned cigarettes in the house, they leant out of the window, blowing smoke into the yellow-black night, rain glancing off the kitchen roof underneath them. Ruth told Robin how her father – a small man, a dapper man of endless cheer, a man who'd been known to recite entire Shakespearian soliloquies while he was measuring a length of nylon rope (although, to her memory, he never actually did) – was loved by his customers.

He was loved, but nobody besides herself and her mother knew about the nights he sat in their bungalow, hunched over the dying grate as if his legs couldn't move under the weight of his own despair. And it wasn't even the drink that paralysed him, Ruth said, he could handle his drink. He just couldn't handle his sadness. There was a line her father used to say to her, she told Robin, a line he would recite when she stood by the wing of his chair in her nightdress and asked him would he not go up to bed. It was a line from Shakespeare, she knew, though she didn't know from what: 'And such a want-wit sadness makes of me, that I have much ado to know myself.'

'How did he die?' Robin asked.

'Cancer. Bone cancer,' she replied, pulling the sash window closed. 'I should get rid of the evidence before Pauline comes home.'

She stood and picked up the empty matchbox that held their crushed butts. Downstairs in the bathroom, Robin stood over the cistern, breathed in a lungful of potpourri and told himself to get a grip. Slow down, he told himself. Slow down. There was a knock on the bathroom door. He opened it and was greeted by a young woman jigging up and down in the hallway, a woman in a nurse's uniform who looked like a seaside picture postcard.

'I'm Helen,' she said, 'I'm bursting.'

Robin went back into the kitchen and found Ruth leaning with her back to the sink. Abandoning his resolve, he walked over to her, put his arms around her and held her, and she didn't resist, didn't demur.

'*Merchant of Venice*,' he said, kissing her hair.

'What?'

'The quote. "And such a want-wit sadness makes of me, that I have much ado to know myself." *Merchant of Venice*, Antonio, I think.'

'And you know this because . . . ?'

'Leaving Certificate. English.'

'Top of the class?'

'Near enough.'

'Who's your friend?' Helen asked Ruth, coming into the kitchen and slumping on a chair.

'This is Robin.' Ruth moved away, took the chair opposite Helen. 'We work together. Well, kind of. Robin is a real teacher; he's allowed in the staffroom. Robin, this is Helen, my housemate, whose tights you were sitting on.'

'I like you, Robin.'

'Do you, Helen?'

'You put the toilet seat down after you. You grow up with sisters?'

'A mother.'

'She taught you well. Drink, anyone? It's been a fucking long week.'

Later, beer cans and empty cartons of Indian takeaway littering the table, Helen told them about her day on the psychiatric ward. She told them about the blind man who thought he was a crow and about the bone-thin woman who'd been rescued from the river with stones in her pocket. She told them about a young man in a tinfoil hat who'd been brought in by the paramedics earlier that evening after they'd been called to his home.

Scraping up the last of the korma sauce with her torn bread, she told them that the ambulance crew had found the young man sitting on a kitchen chair underneath a chainsaw suspended from the ceiling by its flex.

'Was it plugged in?' Ruth asked dispassionately, picking at the orange- and emerald-flecked rice on her plate.

'It was gnashing away over his little hat, apparently,' Helen said.

Ruth had tied her hair up. Sitting next to her, Robin could see dark strands gathered at the nape of her neck.

'I did the paperwork when they brought him in, and the odd thing is Chainsaw Boy and I have exactly the same birthday.'

Ruth, sensing Robin's gaze, looked up and smiled.

'I went in to see him before I finished my shift. He still had the tinfoil hat on,' Helen said. '"Trying to do away with yourself before the big three-O?" I asked. "I was protecting myself," he says. "From what?" "Aliens," he says. Fucking aliens, eh? He started to cry. It's easier if they lash out. It's the despair, the weight of it, like furniture. Like he's got a fucking three-piece suite of sadness inside him.'

Ruth stood, began to clear the plates. Robin brushed the grains of spilt rice into his open palm. In the silence, Helen looked from one to the other.

'I think we should get drunk,' she said.

Helen produced a litre of duty-free vodka from her bedside table. In the communal living room they drank and listened to music. Ruth perched on the arm of Robin's chair, curating the soundtrack from Pauline's idiosyncratic CD collection. Having deftly amputated Metallica, they watched Helen, her painted toenails breaking through the tips of her silvery tights, dance to Dolly Parton. While Dolly stood by her man, Ruth leant back against Robin's chest and closed her eyes. He let his hand stroke her hair.

'Do you want to dance with me, Robin?'

'No, Helen, I don't.'

She was craning in towards them, her fingers gripping the arms of the chair he had resolutely adhered himself to all night.

'You've kind eyes. And you're generous – the food, the beer. There are so many fucked-up people in this world, and you're not one of them.'

'You think?'

Helen looked at Ruth resting on Robin's lap.

'You like her, don't you?'

Robin didn't answer. His eagerness to shut Helen up was matched only by his desire to strangle Dolly Parton's vigorous whine.

'The boy in the tinfoil hat told me he loved me. I got him a tissue, sat down and held his hand, and he told me he loved me. Took two minutes to net myself unconditional love from a bloke who believes in little green men – not bad, eh?'

Helen was unsteady. She swayed, adjusted her grip on the armrests.

'Do you think it's possible?'

'Do I think what's possible?' Robin asked.

'To love someone after two minutes?'

Robin remained silent.

'Ruth! Wake up!'

'Don't, Helen.'

'Ruth!'

'What?' Ruth opened her eyes.

'He's the one.'

'What?' Ruth raised herself up.

'Robin is the one. Marry him.'

'Why would I marry Robin? I don't want to marry anyone.'

'I'd marry him tomorrow.'

'Yeah? Maybe someone should tell his girlfriend first.'

When Robin woke up the next morning in Ruth's single bed, he was alone. His arm, which he'd lain on all night, was still asleep. He tried to move it. Vaguely alarmed at the slow refill of blood to his limb, he lay still, remembering the night before when Ruth had pulled back the duvet cover and he had slipped underneath. She'd turned her back to him, settled into the shallow curve of his body. She'd been wearing a shirt; it was soft. He'd put his hands underneath the fabric, touched her breasts and caressed her stomach, concave and warm. He'd felt the band of her underwear, the bite of her hip. Gently, she'd stopped him slipping his hand under the waistband.

'Sleep,' she'd whispered. 'Just sleep.'

He'd woken around dawn, uncomfortable, thirsty, desperate for a slash. He'd crept down to the dishevelled kitchen to get some water, fearful of meeting Pauline coming in from her night shift. Instead he'd walked straight into a man he'd never seen before, an almost naked man in a pair of yellow Y-fronts filling a glass from the tap.

'Colm,' the stranger said by way of introduction. 'You must be Robert.'

'Robin.'

'That's it. I hear Helen led you astray with the Absolut. She's a whore for the Absolut is my Helen.'

'Is she?'

'I'm not long in off the night train. Good job I replenished the stock.'

'The night train?'

'From Holyhead. Ferry from Dublin. I was home for a couple of days, looking for a site for the business. We're heading back there as soon as we can.'

'Right.'

Despite the convivial nature of his exchange with this earnest man in the canary underwear, a man around the same age as himself, balding and all smiles, Robin had been painfully aware of his own near-nakedness and his pressing need to use the jacks.

'Have you any plans to go home yourself?' Colm was asking.

'Home? Ireland? No, no, not really. Hadn't thought about it.'

'London's grand, but it's no place for kids.'

'No? Colm, I need to use the . . .'

'Nice to meet you.' Colm was holding out his hand. 'Helen was only thrilled with her korma. She said she'd have you in a flash! I better watch myself, Robbie, eh?'

Robin stretched out his fingers, felt the blood course through them. He looked around Ruth's functional, impersonal room. No photographs, no mementos, no clues. Her ambition, she said, was to be replaceable, to leave no trace. Already she moved through the school, in her flimsy skirts and heavy boots, with a kind of ghostliness. Floating along the teeming corridors with Ardu, the child staring up at her with something resembling adoration, Ruth moved through Robin's world as if she was already elsewhere.

Crossing the Thames on the way to Streatham the previous afternoon, when she'd finally agreed to a lift home in his pale blue car ('Robin's egg,' she said when she saw it), she'd told him about a cousin of hers who was living outside Boston. The cousin, Ambrose, lived in a dry town called Belmont, where he worked in an ice-cream parlour.

'Belmont,' she'd mused, looking out of the window at the London traffic. 'Could be somewhere to go.'

'Why?' Robin had asked, not wanting to hear the answer.

'London is hard,' she'd replied. 'Everything is so big and far away and sure of itself. I could live in Belmont, eat blueberry ice cream and get some sleep.'

Robin, taking his eyes off the road, had glanced at her, at the small pink veins on her eyelids, at the dark circles under her closed eyes, at the bow of her mouth, so precise in outline and scale it looked manufactured, a mouth cut by a mouth-maker.

She'd opened her eyes, looked up at the glistening apartments along the river, their pewter-coloured windows reflecting the skyline. Robin had tried to concentrate on the traffic.

'I can't ever imagine being rich, can you?' she'd asked. 'Rich enough to have an apartment with a view of the river. I wonder if they bartered their firstborn for a balcony.'

She unnerved him. Her restlessness confused him.

'Do you want to be rich?' he'd asked.

'It might compensate for other failures.'

'What failures?'

She didn't answer.

'How have you failed? You left college. You could go back.'

But even as he'd spoken, he'd known he was way wide of the mark. Whatever failure she was referring to had nothing to do with an abandoned teacher-training course.

She'd rolled down the window, let her hand receive the needling rain. Robin, unable to manage the silence, had started speaking again.

'I certainly couldn't imagine leaving London for a dry town in New England. I couldn't imagine a blueberry ice cream hitting the spot.' (Hitting the spot? He heard his words echo back as soon as they'd escaped his mouth. Hitting the spot! Who under ninety said 'hitting the spot'? For fuck's sake.)

'No,' she'd replied, orchestrating the rain out of the open window. 'No, I don't suppose it would hit the spot.'

He'd winced.

Robin found her downstairs, cleaning the kitchen. She declined his offer of help; she declined his invitation to leave with him now and come back to his flat. He stood in the kitchen while she soaked their glasses in a sink full of water, waiting for her to change her mind. That she wouldn't come back to the quiet and privacy of his flat felt unbearable to him. He could see his generous bed under the window, the low afternoon sun, her body in the shadowy geometry of the slatted blind. But she steadfastly declined, and while he drank the coffee she'd handed him, she also declined his invitations to a cafe, or a film, or a market, or a park, or a bar.

'The zoo?' he asked at the front door.

'I'll see you on Monday,' she said, reaching up to lightly kiss his cheek.

'Robin!' she called from the door, and he turned.

'Helen was down looking for the Solpadeine earlier – she told me to tell you that she's going to bake you a cake.'

'Can't wait.'

'Reticence,' his mother was saying, 'is undervalued. The world is too quick to make itself heard. Say nothing. When she says nothing, you say nothing.'

They were on the telephone, Robin lying on the floor of his kitchenette, which just about encompassed his length. He'd been on the floor, retrieving a pair of rolled-up socks that he'd kicked under the sink during a particularly manic game of solo indoor football, when the phone rang. He stood up to answer, knowing that it wasn't Ruth, knowing the call would be from Vicky or, more probably, from his mother. Now, lying on his kitchen floor, the telephone wire stretched to breaking point, he wished he'd let it ring out.

'I rang you last night as we arranged, but you were out.'

'Yep.'

'Anything interesting?'

'A friend. Ruth. Someone I work with. I drove her home.'

'That's nice.'

'Yes.'

'What's she like, your new friend?' his mother asked, and he had told his mother that his new friend was prone to silences which he felt compelled to fill with mouthfuls of shit.

'All the yabbering people do.'

'What about it?'

He could imagine her, blowing her long grey hair away from her face, lighting her single minty evening cigarette, pleased that they had found something to talk about, pouring wine into a stoneware mug, one of her rejects with a crooked handle. (His mother's cupboards were heavy with stoneware rejects.)

'People talk too much when they are fearful. What are you afraid of?'

'I'm not afraid of anything.'

'You like her?'

'She's interesting. She's restless. She's sad. I don't know. Yes, I like her. We're friends. People like their friends.'

He listened for his mother's inhalation, the clunk of the mug against the wooden tabletop.

'Indeed they do. Speaking of which, have you seen Joseph?'

'I got him some work, painting a mural in the schoolyard. He'll turn up when he's destitute.'

'Try to take care of him.'

'I always do.'

'Did you hear that we're getting a cocktail bar in town. Can you imagine? Who's going to drink the cocktails? Sheep?'

He imagined her settling down for this delayed weekly ritual of cigarette smoke and conversation. He could see her, in her cottage in Popes Cove, stroking the cat with her rough hands, something lentil-heavy simmering on the hob. He could see the glass buoys hanging on the chalky white walls next to the water-colour of a child on a white beach that she loved, that she had wanted so much she'd persuaded the painter to barter it for a surprisingly level dish. He saw her settling against her patch-work cushion, putting her feet up on an empty chair in the warmth and solid comfort of her home, which smelt of cats and jam, and he felt his heart hammer in his chest. He felt the crush-ing, atrophying weight of her innocence, of her contentment, of her uncritical, unconditional, boundless love. He felt, lying there on his cold London linoleum, every banana skin he had ever deciphered crawl out of those pungent schoolyard bins to strangle him.

'Why would I be fearful?' he heard himself ask, interrupting her reverie about the neighbouring cattle tottering downtown for pink gins and pina coladas. 'Why would I be afraid of Ruth? I have nothing to be afraid of. She's a friend. She's just a friend of mine.'

'What did you say?'

'I have to go,' he replied, standing up so suddenly in the tiny kitchen that he staggered against the sink. 'I'm sorry, I have to go.'

Later, he sat with Bristolian Vicky on her very soft couch while she wept into a dressing gown decorated with picnicking teddy bears, watching Princess Diana, coltish and fawn-like, tell the nation that her husband was sleeping with his old girlfriend. 'There were three of us in this marriage,' the princess said, 'so it was a bit crowded.'

'Did you hear that?' Vicky asked, in excited shock. 'How could he do that to her? How could anyone be so cruel?'

'I just can't imagine,' Robin heard himself say, 'how anyone could be such a duplicitous bastard.'

And Vicky, moved by his chivalry, by the urgency of the moment, lunged across the couch and pulled his head to her acrylic breast. They had, Robin had to admit, surprisingly vigorous sex, and afterwards in her bed, while Vicky slept (she hadn't gotten back into her nightdress with the bumblebee printed on the front, which might have been a first), he resolved that he would tell Ruth how he felt about her. It was time to abandon caution. He closed his eyes, felt Vicky's beneficent bottom abutting his cold, still body.

Ruth and Robin had a gentle week. Each day Robin packed an extra sandwich, and each day Ruth brought a surprise – usually chocolate, once a packet of beef jerky. Robin talked about music, about the clubs he'd been to and the bands he'd seen. He talked about films he'd seen or planned to see in the arthouse cinemas he liked in Angel and Bloomsbury.

Finally hearing her silence, he asked her what she did with her London nights. She hadn't very much money, she told him, and since arriving in London she hadn't really gone out much.

Let me take you to the Renoir, he said, and when she hesitated he told her that the coffee came in tiny paper cups and the seats were wide and soft, and if she didn't like the film she could sleep, or listen to the audience whispering about the cinematography, and afterwards they could go to Chinatown for dim sum.

'I can't afford it,' Ruth said simply.

'I got some tax back,' Robin lied. 'Please, let me take you?'

They arranged to go the following Friday.

As the last of the school population dispersed on Friday afternoon, Robin, wearing the new beige coat Vicky had surprised him with, looked out of the staffroom window and saw Joe introduce himself to Ruth.

Tea and pastries in the Sorrento Cafe ended up becoming pints and wine in the Man in the Moon in Camden Town, until Robin, who had paid for the last round, and the one before that, and indeed the one before that, returned from taking a slash to find the empty chrysalis of his coat abandoned on a picnic table underneath a couple of withered hanging baskets. She had gone. She and Joe were gone – as Robin, who had observed them all night from under his sandy eyelashes, had known they would be.

Robin put on his coat and went back inside, stood at the bar, drunk and sober, haughty and crushed, unsurprised and confounded by this entirely predictable turn of events, and bought himself one last pint of bitter. Sinking into the new coat that smelt like chlorine, he thought about knocking on Vicky's door. He drank slowly, hunched inside the unwanted gaberdine, weighing up whether the inevitability of Vicky gently guiding him towards the mouthwash before he entered the warmth of her bed was worth the bilious self-hatred that would follow.

He finished his pint. The telephone was by the door. Joseph's number rang out. He leant his head against the wall. He needed to eat something; he felt sick, empty. He wanted to walk away, was going to walk away, when he watched his hand lift the receiver again.

'She's here,' Joe said. 'She's with me.'

There should have been some satisfaction in hearing the shadow of regret in his tone. But there was none. Robin, closing his coat against the night, felt like a cat spraying against a hard, closed door; all that howling, all that posturing, for nothing but the scent of its own futility.

FIVE

Ireland, May 2018

On Monday morning Ruth had phoned work to tell them she was sick, and had then spent the day lying curled up somewhere or other in the house, unmoving but not sleeping. And now, a day later, as she was being driven along at precisely the speed limit in the heat of her mother's belligerently fragrant car, her desire to drift off was intense. Ruth wondered how much it would matter if she closed her eyes. Not to sleep exactly, just to rest and let her mother's monologue wash over her.

Her mother was outlining, in painstaking detail, the tribulations she had endured while waiting to pick Ruth up outside the train station. Her mother had (temporarily, it should be noted) parked her car in the one remaining disabled space, directly outside the main door, attracting the attention of an attendant, who had, so she said, employed his limited prowess in the English language to persuade her to park elsewhere. Poor man, Ruth thought, he should've borrowed the strategy Ruth had employed with her mother for the best part of five decades and kept his mouth shut.

Granted, the Dublin train wasn't due in for another twenty minutes, her mother continued, but she liked to allow herself plenty of time to deal with catastrophic events, which, when Ruth was involved, invariably seemed to begin at train stations.

Ruth considered arguing the toss over whether her husband of twenty years sleeping with the mother of one of his pupils could reasonably be described as a catastrophic event, given the state of the planet, but decided to let that one go.

She had had no choice about parking in the disabled spot, Ruth's mother continued, as the small crescent around the station, which had been adequate to the needs of the town for decades, was chock-a-block when she arrived. (Chock-a-block, Ruth thought, closing her eyes. Nobody said chock-a-block any more. *I am chock-a-block with rage.* Nope, it didn't quite cut it.)

Since the advent of the new housing estates, explained Ruth's mother, parking at the train station had become such an issue that one of the nuns' fields next to the railway line had been purchased by the county council, tarmacadamed and fitted with an electronic gate that required a payment of two euro to open.

'Two euro, Ruth!'

'Brutal.'

'Well, I wouldn't call it brutal, but it's certainly inconvenient. Ruth? Are you awake?'

'Sorry. Inconvenient. Yes.'

Ruth's sleep patterns were completely wrecked, she reflected, as her mother settled into a soliloquy about living in a market town that had become part of a commuter belt. In truth, Ruth thought, her sleep patterns had been wrecked for years. After a day lugging stiff landscapes and gloomy portraiture around, and cycling home along the quays, and shopping and cooking and talking to Sid about his plans, or talking to Robin about his endless disenchantment, she would fall into bed, instantly unconscious, only to wake up two hours later wired to an electric moon and unable to slip into sleep's orbit again until five or six in the morning. She'd lie awake, waiting to hear Sid's key in the door, trying to slow down the showreel in her head: Sid falling victim to some random act of violence, Sid on life support, and then, guiltily, when she heard him come in and take his Doc Martens off at the foot of the stairs, her thoughts turned to other people's children; to oceans full of corpses and families wandering the earth in search of shelter. She'd lie there listening to Robin breathe, wondering if any of it mattered: her work with the refugee children, her signature on petitions, her paltry contributions to one relief appeal after the other, her useless despair in front of the television news.

'Ruth! Are you asleep?'

'No. Sorry.'

'I explained to the parking attendant that while I may not technically be disabled, I am, however, old enough to merit the comfort of a designated space.'

Ruth turned up the air conditioning in her mother's car and was assaulted by a lungful of Alpine fern.

'How old?'

'What are you talking about?'

'How old are you?'

'You know how old I am, Ruth.'

'I've forgotten.'

'Well, how old are *you*?'

'I'm almost forty-seven.'

'Then I'm almost eighty.'

'You were late having me, no? For the times?'

'No, I was not late for the times, Ruth. I was perfectly normal.'

Of course you were, Ruth thought.

Downstairs, in the middle of the night, nursing bitter tea, she would worry about Sid again, worry what it meant for him to have a father he'd never known, worry how that absence had made the boy restless, always anticipating the next moment and the next. And what was going to happen when, as would inevitably happen, he'd have to stop following his dreams and make some plan for his future? She should have been firmer, insisted that he stay in college, not sit around their backyard late into the night talking about his music, sometimes sharing his delicate heartbreak.

'Ruth!'

'Sorry.'

'I was saying that driving in town has become impossible. It's bad enough during the week, but at weekends this place is like the Black Hole of Calcutta.'

'Have you ever been to Calcutta?'

'Of course I haven't, Ruth. What on earth would I be doing in Calcutta? All I'm saying is, on a spring day, when you might assume that people with young families would enjoy a walk, or a paddle in the sea, when you'd be forgiven for thinking that they might like to leave their cars parked in their driveways rather than clogging up every square inch of the place with their people carriers and their double-buggies, what do they do, Ruth?'

'I don't know. What do they do?'

'Shop, Ruth! They shop. The amount of shopping these people load into their cars! In the name of God, where do they put it all?'

Ruth had gone to a reunion of sorts with a bunch of mothers from Sid's old school recently, women she had come to know and like over the years. She had sat underneath a string of prayer flags in a trendily refurbished Dublin bar while one of the women, Sinead, talked about her 'second life' now that her children were growing up and moving on. She was making plans for herself, she'd said, for her emancipation from a husband she no longer felt like appeasing, now that there wasn't a domestic peace to be brokered.

'It's his smirk,' Sinead had said. 'I hate the way he knows bloody everything.'

'Leave him,' Ruth had suggested, too enthusiastically.

'I wouldn't give him the satisfaction,' Sinead replied.

Sinead's husband was a rich man, an attractive man, who had once, during a birthday party for the couple's twin sons, asked Ruth to come upstairs and look at a painting he'd won in a charity auction. Ruth had followed him up while Sinead cooked cocktail sausages in the kitchen and Robin took penalties with the children in the long back garden. Sinead and her husband's bedroom was opulent, and Ruth had been surprised to find herself inside it. The painting hung over the bed, a watercolour of a harbour view, bland and unoriginal.

'It's a piece of shit, isn't it?'

'If you like it, it has value,' Ruth had said. 'If you don't, then give it to someone who'd appreciate it.'

He'd laughed.

'Are you really so fucking sweet?' he'd asked, moving towards her and brushing a stray hair behind her ear.

Ruth had looked out of the window at the children throwing themselves around on the frosted grass. She'd watched Robin line up to take a shot, loose and fluid, elegant and pale, and remembered a drawing Joseph had made of him, swimming in a dark lake, that hung on the studio wall.

'Piss off,' she'd said quietly to Sinead's husband, and left the room.

'What about you, Ruth?' Sinead had asked in the bar, pulling a strip of cucumber out of her gin and trailing it down her throat. 'What do you want?'

'Want?'

'You and Robin have no ties now, do you? Now that Sid has gone? You're free as birds.'

'Ruth, I need to talk to you.'

Sunday morning. She'd opened her eyes. Robin had been sitting on the bedroom couch holding one of her socks. He looked as if he'd been cored, he looked like a cooking apple, greenish and white with a hollow running right through his centre.

'I'm sorry,' he'd said, but Ruth, still wreathed in sleep, hadn't understood what he was apologizing for. She could hear his words but couldn't grasp their meaning. Mother. Pupil. Car. Rain. Fear. Boy. The words remained unstrung, floating around the bedroom, drifting over the worn duvet, arching under the paper shade. Finally, Ruth had interrupted him.

'An affair?'

'I wouldn't call it that.'

'What would you call it?'

'A friendship?'

'You're saying you had a friendship with the mother of one of your pupils?'

Robin had leant back into the couch and looked out of their bedroom window.

'More than that.'

Later, lying in the bath, Ruth had looked at her thighs, at the water rippling over her dimpling skin. I'm old, she thought.

'What does she look like?' Ruth had asked Robin sometime on Sunday night, or Monday morning. Getting up from where she'd been lying in Sid's room, she'd found him in their bedroom, lying on their bed. 'What does she look like?'

He hadn't answered.

'What does she look like? What does she look like? What does she look like?' The question asked itself, over and over again, while she swept their possessions from the top of the chest of drawers, coins and beads and papers and lotions and Sid's lop-sided vase, airborne and falling until Robin was standing, holding her arms.

'Stop it! Ruth! Stop it!'

She had sat on the floor between their bed and the window, holding Sid's smashed vase.

Robin had gone downstairs. She could hear him in the kitchen. She could smell her own breath, she could taste blood in her mouth. The thing was, she didn't care what the woman looked like. What did it matter what she looked like? She had smashed Sid's vase, that was what mattered. All that mattered.

Robin had come back into the bedroom. Standing over her, he'd handed her a drink. Brandy. For the hysteric.

'Fuck off,' she'd said, and gone back to Sid's room to curl up on his empty bed, the broken pieces of pottery in her hands.

'Mediterranean Cafe! In the name of God, Ruth! In the drizzle, Ruth? I ask you.'

Ruth's mother watched the young mothers in the town, she told her daughter, shivering outside the silly new Mediterranean Cafe Bar, which wasn't fooling anyone with its rubber plants and cheap yellow crockery. She watched them laughing and hissing and wearing themselves out with all their gaiety. She felt sorry for their squirming toddlers, kicking their chairs underneath the cafe tables, their mothers quietening them with chocolate-chip muffins and teaspoons of froth. When Ruth's mother was a young woman, long before skinny lattes were invented, children played outside in the garden while their mothers drank tea at the kitchen table, and if the day was warm enough they were taken to the beach.

'I'd like to go to the beach now.'

'No you wouldn't, Ruth. You'd freeze to death.'

Driving along Main Street past the familiar shops and bars – Eddie Quinn Family Butcher, Desirée Ladies' Outfitters, the Patriot – Ruth remembered childhood days on the beach. She remembered emerging from a greenish tide, her legs dyed blue with cold. She remembered picnics of bananas and sugar-sprinkled sliced pan, and a bottle of diluted orange squash that would travel from mouth to shivering mouth, from child to frozen child. She remembered a swarm of children, wrapped up in cardigans, crowding a dry rug, nudging at rock-warm mothers for a bit of heat, until Nancy Fitzmaurice would snap and shoo the lot of them away.

'How is Nancy Fitzmaurice, by the way? Do you ever see her boys?'

'God almighty, Ruth, Nancy Fitzmaurice has been dead for years! What made you think of Nancy Fitzmaurice?'

Her mother had reached the outskirts of town where the co-op used to be. They drove in momentary silence past the site of their old bungalow, which had gone, like everything else after Ruth's father's death. The German supermarket stood there now, sharing the concourse with a warehouse-sized hardware store selling cut-price garden furniture to decorate the town's rain-soaked patios.

'I liked Nancy.'

'I can't see why, Ruth. Two of her boys are in Silicon Valley. The other one had a tracheotomy. No oil paintings, any of them. Mind you, neither was Nancy.'

Nancy would scoot the children off the rug to bury each other in the wet sand, but Ruth would lie stock-still behind her mother (stillness being so close to invisibility) and listen to her talk. Lighting up a fag, Nancy would regale the other mothers with stories of her youth, how she'd fallen in love with a priest in her home parish, a young man, beautiful and strong and plagued with doubt. How she'd wait for him after confession, until he'd absolved his flock, and then the pair of them would whip back up to the parochial house, where she kept a baby-doll nightie in his sock drawer to please him.

'God forgive you, Nancy,' the mothers would laugh.

'I'd do it all again, even though they made him a bishop.'

Nancy would exhale, stabbing her cigarette into the sand, then roar at her boys not to suffocate each other.

They turned in behind the secondary school and parked in front of the maisonettes where, courtesy of the same county council that was so determined to relieve her of two euro to park her car, Ruth's mother had qualified for a ground-floor flat.

'Hello, Caleb,' she called to one of a group of children kicking a ball against the gable wall. 'I have a dish to send back up to your mammy. Pick it up before you go upstairs, pet.

'Sweet potato,' Ruth's mother added, turning in her seat and, finally, looking at her daughter. 'Caleb's mother made me sweet potato soup.'

'That's nice.'

'The African women don't waste their lives in coffee shops.'

'No.'

'You're trying to make yourself invisible, I take it?'

'I'm sorry?'

'I nearly didn't recognize you when you got off the train, Ruth. You used to be such a pretty child. Still, I always said it, prettiness ages faster than something more solid.'

'Yes, you did always say that.'

'Would you like to tell me what happened?'

Ruth closed her eyes.

'Ruth?'

'Robin has been seeing the mother of one of his pupils.'

'Seeing?'

'Yes. Seeing.'

'Doing things?'

'Yes. Doing things.'

'What kind of things?'

'I didn't ask.'

'Well, in that case you could probably do with an omelette.'

Opening the car door, Ruth could hear her mother's dog yapping inside the flat. She felt weary. Coming here had been a mistake.

'I'm really not hungry,' she said to her mother's departing back, picking up her bag and following her inside.

When Ruth had come home from London, more than twenty years before, her mother had gone to pick her up from the station and it was her daughter's coat that she'd recognized, not the wearer. Practical and unshowy, the green duffel coat that she'd insisted Ruth take to London had always been on the big side, but when Ruth stood on the platform, her eyes dead as spent cartridges, she was barely visible beneath it, the coat having finally subsumed the shrunken child.

Ruth had been mute in her mother's car, asking only that they pull over so that she could get out and spit bile into the hedgerow.

Ruth's mother had driven her straight to Dr McAnally. The doctor, however, had been hosting a Christmas fundraiser for the Red Cross so they'd been packed into the sunroom at the back of the surgery with half a dozen neighbours. Ruth perched on the edge of a wicker couch, staring at a handful of miserable succulents garlanded with fairy lights, a paper plate of mince pies on the table in front of her. Her mother was politely engaging in a chat about the fate of the recently arrived refugees to the county with the compassionate elderly doctor when Ruth had excused herself from the sunroom and gone out into the garden to throw up behind a display of limp tobacco plants.

'When are you due, Ruth?' Dr McAnally had asked, vaguely but audibly, on her return. The mince pies grew stone cold while the room waited for an answer.

Escaping the surgery, Ruth and her mother had gone back to the flat and, while Ruth slept, her mother had hung the green duffel coat out in the yard to air and unpacked her daughter's canvas bag. She'd been tempted to bin the T-shirts, the leggings, the unmatched socks. There was a nice green shirt that she'd decided to hand wash, and two cotton skirts that swished around when they were released from the drum of the bag. There was nothing in there that offered clues.

Ruth's mother had sat on a kitchen chair, the skirts in her hand, and taken in the situation. Ruth was pregnant. Papery and slight, the protuberance of her belly was an alien thing. Her mother would have to take care of her, make sure she didn't blow away over the roof of the co-operative store, up the hill, past the county hospital, where she had begun and her father had ended, and down again to the silver beach where the sea and the salt could claim her.

Zsa-Zsa, the punctilious new Pomeranian, which Ruth had never met before, tottered down the hall and, standing on its two hind legs, sniffed at Ruth while she searched through her pockets for her cigarettes. The imperious little animal reminded Ruth of someone, the way it was ferreting out something to disapprove of.

'Go away,' Ruth said quietly to the dog, remembering that she didn't have any cigarettes left.

'Are you planning on staying long?' Ruth's mother was already fiddling around in the kitchen with a whisk.

'A night or two. If that's all right? Could we go to the Patriot, do you think? I want to buy cigarettes.'

'You don't smoke any more.'

'I *didn't* smoke any more.'

'They've cigarettes in the garage at the top of the road.'

'I'm sure they do. Let's go to the Patriot. Just this once. I'll buy you a drink.'

Ruth took in the unfamiliar surroundings. The televisions and bar stools she remembered from her days hanging around this place were gone, and so too was the tincture of urine that used to snap at the mongrel air. Rows of optics hung, jewel-like, behind the bar. The room was furnished with low couches and smoked-glass tables. Synthetic music emanated from somewhere.

'Isn't this marvellous!' her mother said. 'I haven't been in here since the night your father died.'

Her mother, who had become alarmingly perky since the decision to go back downtown had been made, took a seat while Ruth went to the bar, where she was served by a startlingly beautiful man. He gave her a token for the cigarette machine and said he'd bring the drinks to their table. Such lavish beauty for a drizzling Tuesday, Ruth thought, going out to the beer garden for a fag. Outside, there were fairy lights and overhead heaters and a trellis of plastic ivy where there used to be crates and barrels and a floor mop in a filthy bucket, so stiff with dirt it could have pirouetted the length of the town and back.

'Artem is getting married,' Ruth's mother told her when she returned.

'Artem?'

'Artem, the barman; he's from Latvia. A summer wedding. He's marrying his boyfriend. Well, I said, your boyfriend is one lucky man. Cheers, Ruth.'

'Cheers.'

'I would have liked to marry a woman.'

'Would you?' Ruth thought she was hearing things.

'Not for the sex, although I suppose you never know until you try it, but for the companionship. My God, but your father could be very bleak sometimes. This is marvellous; it tastes like bitter lemon.'

'I thought I ordered wine.'

'You did. I told Artem I hadn't set foot inside this bar since the night your father died, and he said he had something special for us and that it was on the house.'

With the second negroni, Ruth's mother was kicking down the doors to the past, and the past, the unreliable sod, was crumbling.

'Your father put his foot down. "No more babies," he said. "I'm not having you in that state again."'

'I thought you were the one who didn't want any more children.'

'I never said that!'

Ruth had a headache; whatever distraction she'd felt by revisiting the Patriot had subsided.

'You were an angry baby, Ruth. Furious. I'd go as far as to say off-putting. The nurse handed you to me and she said: "Well done, pet, it's a girl." I'll never forget it. I looked at you, at the wet little vole in my arms, and I wanted to correct the woman. She should have said: "Well done, girl, it's a pet."'

Ruth's mother took a long drink.

'You were terribly furry, Ruth.'

'So I believe.'

'Furry and furious. "Take it back," I said to the nurse. "Back where?" says she. They took you anyway, dressed you up in a little yellow cardigan. "Are you absolutely sure it's a baby?" I asked the midwife. "It looks awfully like an otter."'

'I thought I looked like a vole?'

'They put me to bed with a Valium and a pair of plastic pants, and telephoned your father. I'm surprised they didn't put me in a straitjacket. Of course, when your father arrived you were as good as gold, asleep in his arms, flaky and puffy and human, your little skull pulsing, and I was the one who was behaving like an animal.'

Ruth sipped her drink. When Sid had been born she had looked into his eyes, spilt ink, neither human nor inhuman, and there was a moment when everything that there was to be known about him was known, his fate glimpsed. And then the shutter had closed.

'One for the road, Ruth?'

When Ruth looked up, Artem, smiling, was already coming to the table with another round.

'Thank you, Artem!' her mother sang. 'My goodness, what service.'

'You're welcome, Anne.'

'Artem, this is my daughter, Ruth. Ruth's husband's not behaving himself terribly well. He's at that age.'

'Jesus, Mother!'

'I'm sorry to hear that,' Artem said, smiling his beautiful smile.

'Don't worry, please,' Ruth muttered, standing up to make a bolt for the beer garden.

'Shit happened!'

'Happens,' Ruth corrected him. 'Shit happens.'

'I should have been waiting for you on the platform,' her mother said when Ruth returned.

'You had to defend your illegal parking.'

'I don't mean today, Ruth. I mean the other time.'

Ruth's mother reached across the table to touch her daughter's face, a gesture that surprised them both. Ruth breathed slowly, tried not to flinch, as her mother touched the blue skin under her eyes, the grey skin around her mouth. When her mother took her hand away, they picked up their drinks and normal relations resumed.

'Did I tell you I have Bluetooth, Ruth?'

'No.'

'Oh yes, it's marvellous. Sometimes I drive up to the woods and telephone Sid in Berlin.'

'Really?'

'His voice fills up the whole car. It's like magic.'

'Has he . . . ? Has Sid said anything to you recently?'

'What about?'

'The past.'

'Of course not, Ruth, he's far too busy with his present.'

'Can I pay?' Ruth asked Artem while her mother set sail for the ladies' room like a boat that had taken on water.

'They're from Dan. He sends you his love. He says he's sorry he couldn't be here, but maybe tomorrow?'

'Dan? How does he know I'm here?'

'Cameras. He's watching the bar from home. He telephoned me as soon as you came in.'

'Can I wave?'

'There's a camera behind the optics.'

Even though she was over the limit, Ruth drove her mother home. Helping her out of the car, she gripped the old woman's elbow, wing-thin under her bulky sleeve.

'I never liked your name. It was your father who wanted to call you Ruth. I wanted something special. Amanda, I wanted to call you Amanda. But your father was right – people would've thought I was looking for attention. Don't you see, Ruth?'

'Come inside. I'll make you something to eat.'

'Life is sad, Ruth. You can't go back, not even to change the smallest of things.'

Ravenous for attention, the little dog danced around the room while Ruth's mother dozed in her chair. Ruth remembered now exactly who the yappy, furious little dog reminded her of: Veronica, assistant to the principal. All those long years ago.

Ruth lay awake on her mother's sofa. She disliked this flat, had done from the first time she saw it, when, stunned and sick, she lay every morning on the cold bathroom tiles waiting to throw up.

Sleepless now, as usual, Ruth got up and wandered around the small living room. Her mother had wanted to bring nothing from the bungalow next to the co-op, where everything, she said, had belonged to the company.

Surrounded now by her mother's cheap furnishings, leatherette chairs and framed prints of unknown bridges, Ruth picked up one of the few remnants from their old life, a photograph of her father on their honeymoon, a young man shyly smiling, behind him a black fjord, ahead of him his whole life.

The night her father died, Ruth had been sitting up at the bar of the Patriot while Dan worked behind it. The place was loud with a crowd of JBFAs (Just Back From Americas), straddling the bar stools in baggy sweatpants, slopping pints on their nicely ironed Nirvana T-shirts. They were home from a summer of pot-scrubbing in Brooklyn, labouring in New Jersey, home with their red tans, looking to chase their pints with whiskey sours or a Long Slow Screw Up Against The Wall, neither of which were available in the harsh, sparsely supplied bar owned by Dan's aunt.

Dan was Ruth's best friend – her only friend, if she really thought about it. Dan had worked the bar alone every Tuesday while his publican aunt knocked spots off the Limerick Road in her soft-top car in her haste to visit her married boyfriend in Thurles. The married boyfriend was called Clive, Dan said, or maybe, he'd added, his aunt wanted him to be called Clive. 'Maybe she likes to whisper "Clive" in the dark, maybe his real name is Pat.'

On the night her father died, Ruth had stood in with Dan to give him a hand, washing pearly lipstick stains off the glass rims, listening to the boys boast of boardwalk nights in Atlantic City and nearly being knifed on steaming subways out to Flatbush.

Functional, on the cold side, laced with low notes of cigarettes and phlegm, the walls of the Patriot back then had been hung with laminated sunsets and two television sets. That night though, the coconut scent of the girls and the brash, burnt American smell of the boys had knocked the coldness out of the place, and it was possible, Ruth felt, to believe that you were somewhere else entirely.

Ruth had watched the girls shake out their sweet-smelling hair and lift their double Bacardis to their pink mouths, creamy little pouches of fat drifting over the tops of their glittery boob tubes. She'd watched the lads lean their freckled arms over the girls' naked shoulders, watched their hard fingers dimpling soft flesh. It all felt almost languid, and nothing in that town ever felt languid. The lads had no rush about them, no urgency; they knew full well, Dan had said, that after their talk of great adventures and their bountiful spend, they'd get plenty of recompense back out on the road in the bucket seats of their souped-up Fiestas. They'd be leaning back against the headrests, presenting their big pink transatlantic cocks like trophies, as soon as they were safely parked at the end of a wet lane. Even so, that night in the Patriot, those boys were as close to debonair as they ever would be, and fuck it, Ruth thought, if one of them had asked, she might have considered it.

'How is your father anyway?' Dan had asked when the drinking slowed and they were leaning back against the dirty sinks.

'He's shrivelled up, like those ancient people they found in the bog. There are needles in his groin to hydrate him. His lips are like leather.'

'Jesus, sorry I asked.'

'It can't just be this, after he's gone. I can't just be here.'

The day before, Dan's aunt had stopped to give Ruth a lift up the hill to the county hospital. It was hot, as late Irish summers often are, when the sun waits until you've given up on it entirely before it flashes its brilliance and then disappears altogether. The aunt drove barefoot, her calves dimpling over the pedals.

'Your father – is he dying?'

'Yes.'

'He won't be long, I'd say. There's very little cuttin' on him.'

A tiny fall of sweat had run down the aunt's temple. She'd driven the car like she was riding a horse, rocking forward, urging it up the hill. Ruth wished she'd walked.

Her father was small, light-footed, neat. The disease, Ruth considered, might have chosen a sturdier opponent.

'What class of cancer is it?' the aunt had asked.

'Bone cancer.' Ruth had dared herself to sound casual. She'd looked out of the window at a field of cows turning their heads to witness the aunt's rusted Scirocco scorch the hill, before nuzzling again at the grass. 'Cows really don't give a shit, do they?'

'Dan won't be any use to you in the long run,' the aunt was saying, slowing down on the silky road as the hospital came into view. 'He has his own class of fish to fry. You know that, don't you?'

'I know that,' Ruth had answered.

'You can tell your mammy she has my sympathy. If it's of any use to her.'

'Thanks for the lift.'

Dan had been three months back from a six-month stint in London.

'Why did you come home?' Ruth had asked him while the JBFAs finished their drinks, their conversation turning to the clack and smack of the weekend match.

'I lost my nerve,' Dan had said.

Ruth had been glad when Dan came home. She'd been lonely in Dublin, lonely in her digs, lonely in teacher-training college, lonely on the Friday-night bus back to her town, lonelier still when she reached the familiar street, the pompous church, the leery bars. She would walk from the bus stop to her parents' bungalow determined that the next week, regardless of her father's deterioration, she would invent something she had to do in Dublin, and stay there.

She would walk her rosary of recognition from the bus stop to the bungalow: betting shop, post office, the Spar that sold briquettes, the pharmacy behind the yellow glass; Desirée Ladies' Outfitters, with a window full of truncated plaster torsos, each wrapped in a flesh-coloured corset; Eddie Quinn Family Butcher.

('Eddie Quinn Family Butcher,' Ruth's father would read from the painted shop front. 'Now that's an unfortunate turn of events!')

Ruth would put her key in the door of the bungalow where her mother, measuring out her days with hospital visits and pyjama-washing, was still treating death with excessive politeness, as if it was an exhaustingly powerful guest. Ruth, stuffing her week's worth of washing into the drum of the machine, had wished her mother would tell death to get out of their kitchen and take its curdling yogurt pots and elasticized bed socks with it.

'Where is the fucking rage?' she would ask herself, blowing smoke out of her bedroom window, hiding her fags inside a fleecy hot-water-bottle cover when she'd finished.

'I'm off to see Daddy,' her mother would call from the hall. 'Will you come with me?' And Ruth would come out on to the landing shaking her head.

'I'll go up later.'

From the top of the stairs, Ruth would watch her mother, neat as a pin, pop two pots of yogurt and a pair of freshly ironed pyjamas into her basket before placing it on the front seat of her pine-scented car and reversing out of the gate. Alone, Ruth would go downstairs and lie in a shaft of sunlight on the kitchen floor, thinking about death and sex while one or other of her mother's cranky little dogs sniffed at her crotch.

On the night that Ruth's father died she had resolved that when he went, finally sinking into his bog-man body, she would leave this place. She would go to London, a city big enough to mourn in.

'I'm going to London.'

'Good for you.'

'Dan?'

'What?'

'Do you bless yourself in the dark?'

'Yes.'

'I don't bless myself in the dark.'

'In that case, you should definitely move to London.'

On the night that Ruth's father died, Ruth's mother had walked through the door of the Patriot as the JBFAs' cars zoomed away into the plentiful night.

'Get in the car with me, Ruth. Your daddy has gone.'

'I can't,' Ruth had said, and her mother had stood at the door looking around the empty pub which was already returning to its usual inglorious state.

'Please, Ruth,' she had asked quietly.

'I can't. I can't be with you right now. I can't.'

And her mother had momentarily held on to a chair to steady herself, then turned her back and left.

Dan had held her hand as they walked uphill to the county hospital, dipping under the hedge to the car park where her mother's car was parked under the watchful eye of a plaster Virgin.

'Your daddy slipped away,' the nurse had said, as Ruth stared at the blue eyeliner rimming the nurse's watery eyes.

'Amen,' Dan had solemnly responded, his hair curtaining his face as he bowed his head.

'Slipped away,' the nurse had said, as if her father had been biding his time until her back was turned. 'Slipped away,' she'd said, and Ruth had imagined a man drowning, dipping finally below the water, a man who could no longer hold on to his upturned craft.

Ruth and Dan had walked up the curving staircase to the room where Ruth's father lay. A little nun, moonlighting from the convent to tend to the dying, had opened the window next to his bed to let his soul escape. She had strung rosary beads through his fingers, which he clung to like a budgerigar gripping a swing. Looking at the open window, Ruth had imagined her father's soul swooping over the town, over the dark bars and curtained houses, over the crumpled flesh of sleeping spouses, under the doors of firm young girls to brush against them like a draught.

The little nun had placed a pillow under Ruth's father's jaw.

'Why is the pillow under his chin?' Ruth had whispered.

'Rigor mortis,' Dan had replied. 'If his jaw hangs open, it will stay like that.'

And Ruth had visualized her father lying in a pit in the ground, all the clay in the county being shovelled into his open mouth.

'Ruth? Ruth?'

Ruth replaced the photograph on top of the television and went into the bedroom, where her mother lay, clothed, under her quilt.

'I don't remember how I got here.'

'I made you scrambled eggs, but you just wanted to go to bed.'

'Could I have some water?'

Ruth brought water to her mother and then made tea and toast. She sat on a chair in her mother's bedroom, watching her eat.

'Do you remember my friend Dan?'

'Of course I do. He's on the town council. He organized a twelve-foot Christmas tree for the square last year. Twelve foot, Ruth.'

'His aunt, who owned the bar, whatever happened to her?'

'Bewildered somewhere. Mad as a brush. You could ask him yourself if you came home every now and again, Ruth.'

Ruth looked around the neat room, at the twitching dog spread out on the end of the bed, at the plastic Virgin on the bedside table, brimful of holy water, standing over a glossy magazine offering a step-by-step guide to a world-class orgasm.

'You can stay as long as you like, you know, Ruth. The dog won't object.'

'Actually, I'm going to go to London.'

'When?'

'Soon.'

'Oh.'

There was a silence while her mother brushed invisible crumbs from the sheet, her small hands veined and papery.

'Will you be here when I wake up?'

'Yes. I won't go straight away.'

'Good. We'll go shopping. You can buy yourself something that doesn't make you look like your own shadow.'

Ruth picked up the tray from her mother's bed.

'I wanted to thank you for something.'

'Oh?'

'When I came home pregnant with Sid.'

'Yes?'

'You were kind. Very kind. I'd underestimated you.'

'He was such a lovely baby, Ruth. Not a bit like you. Your father sent him to make up for leaving us.'

Ruth stood, the tray heavy in her hands. 'Go to sleep. You must be drunk.'

'I beg your pardon? I have never been drunk in my life.'

'Perish the thought.'

Ruth left the room, brought the tray into the kitchen and returned to the bedroom to turn off the light.

'Ruth?'

'Yes?'

'Will you be here when I wake up?'

'Yes. You asked me already. Remember?'

'Did I?'

The dog turned its head to watch her depart, its eyes glinting in the dark.

The following morning Ruth took the Pomeranian for a walk while her mother slept off the hangover she insisted she didn't have. The little dog endured a brisk stroll into town but dug its feathery heels in when Ruth tried to drag it any further. They were turning back towards home when Ruth spotted Dan going into the Patriot. He was heavier, prosperous looking, but Ruth would have recognized him anywhere.

'Ruth,' he said, taking her in his arms. 'Drink?'

'Coffee.'

She sat at the bar while Dan cranked up the machine, the nervy little dog eyeing up the optics like they were dangerous birds. Dan had bought the Patriot from his aunt years before. Recently, he'd bought Eddie Quinn Family Butcher and planned to turn the shop into a sushi bar. He was looking at other properties around town, he told her.

'You can't keep this town in tempura fucking prawns, Ruth.'

She smiled.

'I hear Robin is misbehaving.'

'Word travels fast.'

'You all right?'

'Dunno. Tired, mainly. My mother is appalled by me. She wants to bring me to Desirée's for a makeover.'

'You're lovely, Ruth. You never lost it.'

Ruth pulled her sleeves down over her fingers and picked up the hot cup.

'And Sid is in Berlin?'

'You're well informed.'

'Your mother tells me about him every time we meet. He wants to be a DJ?'

'That's the current plan.'

'She's very proud of him.'

They drank their coffee in silence, looking at one another, noting the changes that the years had made. The signs of their ageing were like a web, Ruth thought, easily brushed aside by memory.

'And you, Dan? Is life good?'

'Wonderful. Artem and I are getting married this summer.'

'Of course! I should have realized!'

'Beauty and the beast. I know.'

'That's not what I meant.'

'It's taken me a long time to be who I am. Longer than it should have.'

Ruth put down her coffee, reached across the bar for Dan's hand and held it.

'I'm so glad. So glad for you both.'

'You'll come to the wedding? Apparently it's a three-day event – if my knees hold up. Bring your mother and Sid. Bring that lanky German husband of yours if you've forgiven him.'

Ruth finished her coffee.

'Do you believe in forgiveness, Dan?'

'Oh god, yes. It's a different world to the one we grew up in, Ruth. I've forgiven everybody. Haven't you?'

Dan made Ruth take a snifter of brandy home for her mother, a hair of the dog. The actual dog, meanwhile, was whimpering to get back to its kingdom.

'How is your aunt, by the way?' Ruth asked.

'Good days, bad days. On the good days she thinks I've come to take her to Clive, the married boyfriend; on bad days she thinks I've come to rob her.'

'I'm sorry.'

'All her illicit joy. She couldn't give two hoots what anybody thought about her. She was a good friend to me.'

Ruth hugged Dan goodbye.

'I hope things work out for you two, Ruth.'

'Do you?'

'I'll never forget Robin coming here to find you. I was behind the bar when he walked in. "I'm looking for a girl called Ruth

Lennon," he said. And honestly, Ruth, you'd think he'd been looking for you all his life.'

Ruth phoned Sid from Dublin Airport.

'Where are you?' he said immediately. 'Robin's looking for you.'

'Is he?'

'He's in Popes Cove. Something to do with Ushi, he said I was to tell you if we spoke.'

'He say what's wrong?'

'She's not well. How come you don't know?'

'I was down home for a few days. Phone coverage.'

'Phone coverage? Yeah? What's going on behind you? You in an airport?'

'I'm going to London for a day or two.'

There was a silence.

'Sid? Can you hear me?'

'What are you going to do?'

'I don't know yet.'

Silence.

'Sid?'

'You and Robin had a row?'

'Yeah.'

'Because of me?'

'No. No, Sid, not because of you.'

'I didn't ask you to go to London.'

'I know you didn't.'

'Robin sounds freaked. You need to call him.'

'I'll call.'

'When will you be back?'

'Soon.'

Ruth had wandered into Duty-Free while she was talking; she found herself now trapped behind a display of plastic leprechauns.

'Sid . . .'

'What?'

'It'll be all right.'

'I didn't ask you to do this.'

'I know you didn't. I love you. I'll call Robin.'

They rang off. 'Kiss me, I'm Irish' was written on the leprechauns' made-in-China hats. More shit to clog up the universe, Ruth thought, turning off her phone and making her way to the gate.

SIX

London, October 1995

Ruth left Joseph's flat late on Sunday morning and returned to Streatham to pick up her rucksack and duffel coat and to tell the nurses that she wouldn't be coming back. Emerging from Brixton Station, the elation that had sustained her on the piss-scented Tube from King's Cross evaporated. The red buses pulling up outside the station seemed monolithic, immense, the ceaseless movement of people entering and exiting the Underground overwhelming. In the din and clatter of the traffic, the patter of jittery men hawking mirror-shine shades and the sonorous calls of the prophets standing on plastic crates, warning of callous ways and bitter deaths, she felt deaf, submerged. Hurrying to get on to the Streatham bus when it swung in towards the pavement, the sensation of being adrift intensified. Ruth felt separated from the husk of herself, released without warning to hover above herself and look down on a worn girl searching in her pockets for change. Relieved to find an empty seat upstairs, she sat down and closed her eyes.

Joseph. This morning she had stood in front of his bathroom mirror and looked at her swollen mouth, her stubble-grazed cheeks, the pupils of her eyes black and wide as a lake, and she had barely recognized herself. 'We've never really met before,' she'd whispered to her reflection, and then, feeling self-conscious and embarrassed by her strangeness, she'd stood in the dirty kitchen and cooked eggs. She'd brought the food to his bed and they'd sat under his quilt, and when she'd lifted her hand to her mouth her fingers smelt of him, and she'd felt as if she'd known him for ever, as if his soul had always been inside her, waiting to be made flesh.

'Don't leave me,' he'd said, putting their empty plates on the floor. 'I really can't be left again so soon.'

Later, she'd kissed his sleeping face and slipped out of the basement flat.

The nurses were not amused, Pauline insisting that Ruth relinquish her deposit, while Mairead, leaning her whippet-thin body against the cold fridge, waiting for a migraine to wilt, reminded Ruth that decisions made in haste were to be regretted at leisure.

'We'll all have plenty of time for regret,' Pauline snapped, returning the cake stand she had washed and dried to the kitchen cabinet.

'How was the birthday party?' Ruth asked, watching Mairead stalk out of the kitchen and remembering that there had been a celebration planned for Pauline's girlfriend, Dana, the night before.

'You were missed,' Pauline said.

'I didn't realize I was expected.'

'I didn't say you were expected. I said you were missed.'

'Who missed me?'

'Dana missed you,' Pauline said, smiling through her poker-straight hair, her raised eyebrows plucked to a string-thin arch. 'She left you a line; it's by your bed.'

'Why did she do that?'

'Who knows?' Pauline replied, leaving the kitchen.

Her rucksack packed, the clingfilm-wrapped generous line of cocaine from Dana tucked into the pocket of her coat, Ruth stood by the bathroom door watching Pauline pluck at her invisible eyebrows with the tweezers that no one was allowed to borrow and which usually sat in a sparkling dish on the bathroom shelf next to Helen's well-scrubbed rubber IUD and Mairead's many and varied oral-hygiene products.

'I'm sorry to let you down about the room.'

'Dana always said you wouldn't stay.'

'When did she say that?'

'First time she saw you. She calls you "the orphan". "The orphan won't stay," she said. She was right. You don't much like us, Ruth, do you?'

'Of course I like you.'

'Dana says we're too parochial for you.'

'Hardly.'

'I wouldn't mind the opportunity, Ruth.'

'To be what? Parochial?'

'To belong.'

Ruth watched Pauline's reflection, watched her replace the tweezers and examine the puffed arch of her brow in the bathroom mirror, her expression hardening, congealing. And Ruth saw them both reflected and reflected again, back and back and back, as if they were rippling out into the universe, Pauline in her nylon dressing gown and Ruth, pale and scuffed, leaning against the frame, an outsider.

'I'll take a month's rent for the inconvenience, and you forfeit your deposit.'

That was all the money Ruth had, everything she'd been saving in the pocket of the duffel coat she never usually wore. Ruth felt in the pocket for the stashed cash and handed Pauline the amount she'd demanded.

'Pauline!' Dana's voice called from the kitchen.

'Dana wants her breakfast. You might as well have something to eat before you abandon us,' Pauline said, in that characteristic way she had of giving and taking in the same shallow breath.

Pauline swept past, her silky pocket swollen with Ruth's cash. Ruth picked up her bag and followed her downstairs. Dana was sitting at the kitchen table, smoking.

'You're leaving, are you?'

'Yes.'

'What star sign are you?' Dana asked, while Pauline banged down a saucer in front of her for her forbidden cigarette ash and then stepped over her outstretched legs to fill the teapot.

'Gemini. Why?' Ruth asked, sitting down at the table and realizing that she was starving.

'And what star sign is your man?'

'I don't know.'

'You don't know? You're moving in with him, you haven't known him for a wet weekend and you don't know what sign he is?'

'I never thought to ask.'

Dana leant across the table. Ruth could smell her breath; tobacco and something sweeter.

'You'd have had to get his cock out of your mouth first. Am I right? Hey?'

Dana laughed, loud and sharp, looking to Pauline's rigid back for a response. Heavyset and beautiful, hard and raw, Dana didn't frighten Ruth half as much as she thought she did.

'Happy belated birthday, by the way.'

'We missed you last night.'

'So I believe.'

'Pauline made me a birthday cake.'

'Lemon drizzle,' Pauline said flatly, putting the teapot on the table.

'It was a thing of beauty,' Dana said to Ruth.

'You were too pissed to notice,' Pauline snapped, turning back to the cooker.

'I'm Libra, Pauline's Aquarius. We're a match made in heaven, Ruth. Geminis, though, are fickle; you can't help it. Find out what your man is before it all ends in disaster.'

'Right.'

Ruth drank her tea while Pauline banged pans around on the hob. Helen's arrival home from her shift at the Maudsley was a relief. Helen's random, strangely exciting eating habits were safe territory in which Pauline could vent her rage.

'We're about to have breakfast,' Pauline snapped as Helen placed a rotisserie chicken and six cans of Canadian beer on the table.

'Have what you like. We had a suicide last night. I'm having a drink.'

'What happened?' Ruth asked.

'Female, fifties,' Helen replied curtly. 'Hanged herself by her dressing-gown belt in the toilet during visiting hours.'

'Jesus.'

'She was supposed to be in a locked ward. There's fucking war.'

'Where were you?' Pauline asked.

'Upstairs with the alkies. Thank Christ.'

'What was wrong with her?' asked Ruth.

'Fuck knows,' Helen replied, cracking open a can. 'Life.'

Dana shook her head, wiped her hands on the legs of her jeans. 'Lord rest her.'

'What's all this in aid of?' Helen asked, nodding towards the table and the good milk jug that Pauline had placed in front of Ruth on the now crowded kitchen table.

'Ruth is leaving,' Pauline replied. 'She's moving in with a man.'

'Robin?'

'No,' Ruth answered.

'Not Robin?'

'No, not Robin. Robin's friend Joseph.'

'Robin's friend?'

'Yes.'

'Some friend. The boyo. Does Robin know yet?'

'It's got nothing to do with Robin.'

'Nice.'

Ruth drank her tea in silence.

They ate rashers and eggs and chicken and bread, Mairead wandering back in to join them, her face occluded beneath an oatmeal-and-egg-white face mask. Unable to allow herself to eat for fear of being revealed as human, she sat, legs akimbo, on the draining board, sucking a pint of lemon water through a straw.

'What's his name anyway, this bloke?' Helen asked.

'Joseph. Joseph Kazargazof.'

'Russian?' Mairead asked from her hungry perch, looking with fury at the glistening chicken. The culinary feast she'd plastered around her mouth having hardened, however, her mangled speech took some deciphering. 'Husschin?! Never trust a Husschin. They're all after something. You wouldn't catch me going near a Husschin,' she spat, the words cracking open her mask to reveal glimpses of her tight little mouth.

'Stick to the saliva suctioning, Mairead,' Helen replied. 'I don't think they're quite ready for you in the diplomatic corps.'

'I don't know if he's Russian. His mother is English, and she's dead.'

'Dead?' Helen repeated. 'How?'

Ruth thought about the woman hanging by her belt in the Maudsley, about the people who would come to claim her, about the endless geography of loss that would consume and obliterate them.

'I don't know how his mother died,' Ruth lied.

'Does he have family?' Helen was wiping up the grease from the bird's foil nest with a clutch of sliced pan.

'No, I don't think so.'

'You don't think so?'

Helen's curiosity was too much, her mouth chewing, relishing, interrogating. Ruth wanted to leave; she didn't need their approval. Pauline was right – Ruth didn't like them very much. They reminded her of home, of her convent school, of all those girls weeping and hissing and comforting and mocking.

'What does this lad do?'

'He's an artist,' Ruth replied defiantly.

'What does he paint?' – this from the draining board. 'Hot does he haint?'

'Portraits of his mother. They're beautiful. There's one of her sleeping with a dog by her feet.'

'What kind of dog?'

'A big dog, Mairead. A big yellow dog. All right? I need to go.'

'I don't think attraction has anything to do with astrology,' Pauline said, standing to clear Dana's plate. 'I think we find people who need us, because it makes us feel like we deserve to be alive. Mind you,' she added, turning to plunge her hands into the sink of dirty water, 'hating someone makes you feel alive too.'

After breakfast, Dana drove Ruth and her belongings to the Tube.

'Thanks for the line. You didn't need to do that.'

'Here,' Dana said, leaning across the passenger seat and shoving two fifty-pound notes at Ruth, who was reaching for her rucksack on the back seat. 'Your deposit.'

'Pauline said—'

'Don't worry about Pauline. I'll take care of Pauline.'

'Thank you.'

'You know where we are if you need us.'

On the Tube back to King's Cross, Ruth thought about what she might have told them but never would: how, after the rain and the drink, after she'd taken the cheese from the knife and after she'd shivered on his rug and lain awake while he slept, after she'd almost left, had almost lost him, after he'd pushed back the bedclothes and held her gaze, after she'd crawled across his broken bed and was naked, lying on the worn sheets, he'd looked at her in a way that made her feel as if she'd never been seen before. He'd looked at her pale breasts, at the line of her pubic hair, at her thighs and legs, at her feet, at her arms, at her hands, which he'd lifted, spreading her fingers out towards the light. He'd looked and looked, and when he'd finally seen what he wanted to see, when he'd imprinted her and she lay craving him on his mangled sheets, he'd opened her up and fucked her, and Ruth had felt herself shatter like glass.

At King's Cross, her rucksack on her back, Ruth retraced her footsteps to Midhope House, pushed open the broken gate and walked into the courtyard. Here, hidden between London's mephitic sheets, tenants in flimsy sweaters with fags in their mouths and paperbacks in their back pockets slipped in and out of battered doors. Here, children planted spring flowers in window boxes while ageing men, who'd planned on being something else entirely, carried their dirty washing in plastic bags to the laundrette on the corner. If London rang to the pitch of moneyed boys in leather loafers and crisply suited women with their high heels in their handbags, and if art was currency and music was currency and clubs were currency and drugs were currency, and a thin princess hurling herself down the palace stairs was currency, and if the traffic on Euston Road, streaming faster and faster until the metal blurred, was a sign of those loaded times, then these shabby flats on these forgotten streets had a different kind of value, or so it seemed to Ruth.

'I'm home,' Ruth whispered into Joseph's ear, slipping back into bed and rolling up one of her reimbursed banknotes so that they could snort two thin trails of cocaine from the cover of a sketchpad.

'Do I know you?' he asked, opening his eyes, and for a moment Ruth wasn't entirely sure he was joking.

Later, stepping out into the courtyard together, Ruth looked up at the washing lines strung overhead, hung with tea towels and withered socks, the nylon ropes tethered to balconies where bicycles leant against rusting ironwork. The shallow rectangle of sky above the flats looked as if it had been coloured bright blue by a single crayon. Underfoot, withered leaves from the pygmy trees lay palm-up on the ground, offering their lifelines to her as if she was a mystic who could read the future in their venation.

They walked to Camden Lock and sat on the canal bank under a cold sun, drinking cans of cheap cider, watching money being spent on the balconies of the lock-side bars. Ruth, indifferent to all that swagger, quenched by the day and the drink and the sheer beauty of Joseph, stretched out now on the bare grass, lay down beside him.

'I've been waiting for you for so long, Ruth,' he said.

Ruth spent the days cocooned in sex and sleep and the cavernous bath. Waking in the mornings in a nest of sheets, the broken bed herding them together limb to limb, she would drag herself up to go to work, resisting Joseph's suggestion that she spend the day with him so that he could draw her by the two-bar fire. As winter deepened and ice formed inside the frames and sparked around the wooden board covering the bathroom window, she'd wash at the sink, her breath frosting on the air, returning to his bed for a few last minutes of warmth. She'd dress under the duvet, batting his hands away as they lazily obstructed the clothes she was pulling on.

Leaving him, she'd walk fast up Gray's Inn Road, ducking into the schoolyard as the bell rang out. Hanging up her coat and scarf, she'd slip out on to the corridor to find her class, hoping that Veronica wouldn't be there checking her watch, hoping not to run into Robin, who smiled at her now without smiling, the memory of their shared lunches by the boiler room echoing in their polite exchanges.

'Joseph is well?'

'Good, yes, he's going to come in and paint the mural soon.'

'I look forward to it.'

'And you?'

'I'm absolutely fine, Ruth.'

'Great. Good. That's good. We should all go for a drink maybe.'

'Maybe.'

Joseph painted at night in the studio next to the bedroom. He was working from a series of photographs he'd taken of his mother in her Brighton flat before she died. The World Service on the radio, Joseph way beyond her reach, Ruth would fall asleep on his narrow studio couch while he worked, the disembodied talk from the airwaves weaving into her dreams. She dreamt of war and sometimes of summer gardens, and often she dreamt of her father. She dreamt that she found him alone in a derelict house, sitting naked on a chair, his mouth cracked and dry. 'I'm waiting for clearance,' he said, his voice utterly returned to her, but when she reached for him he disappeared. She would wake to hear Joseph telling her to go to bed, and after she'd done so he'd return to his work until five or six in the morning.

Usually when she let herself into the flat after school, she found him sleeping. Sometimes he was reading, sometimes drawing, the damp air warmed by cigarette smoke and the electric fire. Taking off her coat and boots, she'd heat soup for them on the hob and join him. Her legs across his lap, her head on the pillow, she'd close her eyes while he read to her, history or politics or art, always surprised by her ignorance.

'Didn't they teach you anything at school?'

'Hymns,' she'd answer, to amuse him.

Some winter nights he would decide to cook, surgically slicing onion and mushrooms with a Stanley knife, frying them in the pan with a cigarette in his mouth. He'd run over to Nish then for bread or bacon when his careful efforts shrank in the heat.

They'd eat in the kitchen that Ruth had scrubbed, and when the stray cats drew together on the ledge, as they had begun to do, Ruth fed them dregs from the frying pan.

Sometimes at night they walked to a bar he liked near Coram Fields, or when money was almost entirely absent, they just walked. Winding through the frosted parks of Bloomsbury, they might walk all the way to the river and back. Coming home marbled with cold, they would lie in the bath until there was no more warmth in the water, stepping out on to the ox-blood floor, leaving behind them a ring to rival Saturn's. On one of those frost-walk nights, as they lay head to toe in the deep bath, eking out the hot water from the tap, he told her that when, almost a year before, he had found his mother's body in her Brighton flat, there had been a bar of lavender soap by the sink in her room, and on the floor by her bed a single long-stemmed crystal glass, unlikely relics that must have been acquired from somewhere else, survivors of her wreckage.

He'd brought them both home, replacing the soap whenever he had any money.

'Tell me about her,' Ruth asked, scooping up warm water in her hands and watching it splay over her skin. 'Tell me whatever you want to tell me.'

He'd gone to Brighton to see her, he said, because it was almost Christmas and he wanted to get her outside of her flat, which she had become reluctant to leave, and photograph her on the wintry beach. They had talked on the phone the night before and agreed to meet in a cafe near the station, a cafe with a rubber shark in the window that she liked.

She'd been living in Brighton with a man called Dave. Dave had a dog, Victor, and when Dave had left, as Joseph knew he would, Victor had stayed. She'd loved that dog. She'd wanted Joseph to include Victor in the photographs on the beach. 'Victor likes mint ice cream,' she'd said. 'I'll bring him to the cafe with the rubber shark in the window and he can sit under the table with a bowl of ice cream while we talk.'

Joseph leant forward to turn on the tap. The water was lukewarm; soon it would run out.

His mother wasn't in the shark cafe when he arrived. He'd waited a long time. He'd phoned her, but the call rang out. She had a council flat near Hove, a bus ride away. It was on the ground floor, on account of her difficulties.

When she didn't answer her door, Joseph thought she might be sleeping. He'd broken in through her bedroom window. Victor had growled, or at least made an effort to growl.

Joseph had taken his mother's hand. There were laminated pictures of cats on her bedroom wall; there was an arc of blood decorating one of their mewling snouts. Cans and medication were scattered around. She'd asphyxiated on her own vomit. It looked like she'd been dead for a while. Victor had shat on the floor.

Ruth waited for Joseph to continue, but instead, closing his eyes, he leant back and submerged. The grey water covered his face, his black hair floating like a wreath.

Later that night, as she lay on his bed, barricaded from the marauding, unpredictable outside world, the two-bar electric heater perched for her comfort on the bedside table, Joseph began to draw her. 'I don't want you to move,' he told her, and she didn't. Lying back on the pillow, one knee raised, her hands folded across her stomach, she watched the yellow pencil move across the page.

As Christmas lit up the streets around King's Cross, Ruth walked home from work along Chapel Market, hoping to catch the traders before they packed up for the day. Sometimes she bought flat mushrooms, running her fingers over the frost-bruised gills, looking along the stands for something she could afford that would make him happy – dried apricots or walnuts maybe. Walking through the courtyard, her paper bag of shopping softening in the rain, she nodded to the muffled residents of the flats, who darted in and out of their front doors, keeping their eyes averted from the drunks sheltering under the stairwells lest some seasonal goodwill seep inside them like the raw cold and they ended up making promises they wouldn't keep.

'I'm home,' Ruth called into the silence. 'Joseph?'

Around the corner from the flats a glowing plastic Santa Claus hung over the door of the Duke of Wellington, and on Fridays, after Joseph had picked up his dole, Ruth would find him there, leaning back against a torn banquette, a pint of bitter on the table in front of him. Settling next to him in the conviviality of the dark afternoon, she'd watch him draw in the small sketchbook he kept in his pocket, watch the matronly women, who'd come in from the street to warm their hands around glasses of hot sugary port, materialize on the rough page.

On Saturdays Ruth could sleep, deep and dreamlessly, and Joseph would work, and when she woke up he'd run, head bowed against the cold, to Nish's corner shop for cigarettes and chocolate, before coming back to bed, his blue shoes on the floor, speckled from rain.

Later, her tights hanging on a loose plastic line above his bath, long wet dancers over their two wet bodies, they'd listen to a transistor radio balanced on the lip of the sink. The radio was tuned to a cricket match being played on the other side of the world. Leaning back against Joseph, Ruth could feel him hold his breath and then exhale with disappointment as the commentator spoke a language she would never understand.

'Are England all out?' she'd ask him. 'Did they put their legs before their wickets?'

She'd hand him a cup and he would wash her hair.

Ruth was naked but for a broken wristwatch Joseph had asked her to wear. It had belonged to his mother, or so his mother had said. It might be gold, he wasn't sure; he'd never thought to find out. The medics had removed it from her wrist and given it to him while they wrapped her body. Later that night, when Robin had driven to Brighton to bring him home, Joseph had taken away the watch, along with the crystal glass and the soap. Shielding them from the stained mattress, the ravenous dog, her pungent corpse, he'd brought the souvenirs back to London to spare their feelings.

'What happened to Victor?' Ruth asked.

'The medics called some service. He was taken away. I assume he was euthanized.'

'Euthanized? Didn't you want him?'

Joseph hesitated; he was preparing his materials to draw her, sharpening his pencils with a scalpel.

'Given the option, I would have chosen my ravaged mother over an incontinent dog, Ruth.'

Joseph didn't know where his mother had found the watch, or who might have given it to her. She'd been wearing it the last time he saw her alive, when he'd gone to Brighton to photograph her for his work. He'd wanted to photograph her on the beach then too, but she was too cold to leave the flat. He'd asked her to remove her jeans and sit on the side of her bathtub. She'd complied, the sinews in her emaciated legs stark against the white enamel. While he worked, she kept consulting the watch.

'Am I detaining you?' Joseph had asked.

'Yes. I'm expecting a caller.'

She'd kept her arms covered under layers of baggy jumpers.

Who gave it to you anyway?' he'd asked. 'What other woman might have awoken to find it gone, do you think?'

And his mother had pulled the watch from her wrist and thrown it at him, the catch glancing off his eye and scratching his cornea as he turned away.

He'd left her flat and walked as far as he could along the shore towards the railway station. He'd walked, watching the waves domesticate themselves as they reached land, masquerading as wavelets, doing a seriously fucking convincing job of pretending to be powerless. He'd bought himself an eyepatch in the pharmacy on the platform, the woman behind the counter handing him a mirror to show him his bloating cornea, and when he'd caught sight of himself wearing the eyepatch in the window of the train, he looked, he thought, like a cartoon, like an imposter. He'd photographed his imposter reflection in the window.

For weeks afterwards he couldn't see out of his right eye, and if you look now, he said to Ruth, putting down his pencil, if you really look, you can see a scar, watery and pale. And Ruth lifted herself to look into his eyes, and saw only her own anxious reflection. And Joseph lay her down again so that he wouldn't lose his line.

As Joseph continued to draw and Ruth struggled to stay awake in the tight heat of the two-bar fire, Joseph went on with his story. The buttery light of the Anglepoise reflecting off his page, he told Ruth that days after his trip to Brighton, when his eye was strong enough and he was sorting through the photographs of his mother that he had taken in her bathroom, he realized he had snapped her snatching the watch from her wrist. In the photograph her mouth was open, her bared teeth too big now for her shrunken face. It was what he'd been looking for, he said, and he'd finished the painting quickly in layers of white and grey and yellow; the bathtub, her withered legs, her teeth.

He'd taken a risk and grudgingly phoned an art dealer he knew, who had kept in touch with him since his degree show. She wasn't much of a dealer. If she was, Joseph told Ruth, he'd never have called her. She had come to the flat to see what he was doing the day before Joseph had first met Ruth. She'd looked at the work and asked to take that and two other portraits of his mother away with her from a series he had made of Stevie sleeping and Stevie smoking.

When the dealer had left, Joseph had sat in the studio and remembered something that had happened when he was maybe fourteen or fifteen, when his mother had spun around in the kitchen because of something he'd said to her and thrown a wine glass at him, which shattered and broke on the wall behind, the shards raining like ice. The doctor had picked out a tiny sliver of glass from Joseph's eye with a needle while Stevie covered her face with her hands and looked at her son through fingers anchored by heavy silver jewellery. And it was at that moment, Joseph told Ruth, that Stevie became his subject. It was at that moment the tables had turned.

Wrapping a bandage around Joseph's head, the doctor had asked Stevie what had happened, and while his mother hesitated, Joseph told the doctor that he had fallen. 'Fallen?' the doctor sighed, and sent them home with eyedrops.

They had gone back to their flat and Joseph had lain on his mother's bed and slept, and the next morning when he woke up there were paper and chalk and doughnuts beside the bed. Stevie had sat beside him all day while he tried to draw a still life, moving the withered fruit around and around on the kitchen table so that he could best observe the decay with his one good eye. Later Stevie had sat for him for the first time. When she complained of the cold he had refused to allow her to move.

Ruth lifted her hand to stroke his temple and, with the edge of the pencil, Joseph gently guided her hand back to where it had been. And Ruth was still, then, as a softening pear, while he worked on in silence.

The art dealer had been leaving messages on Joseph's very loud answering machine, which reminded Ruth of a Dalek. 'You. Haaave. One. Message.'

'Talk to me, please. I think I might have something. Joe, talk to me.'

'Why don't you talk to her?' Ruth asked.

'I'm not ready. Not yet.'

As the days darkened, Ruth sometimes woke at four or five in the morning to find all the lights on and Joseph in the studio drawing on butcher paper, lines and lines and lines, thin and gnarled, like tangled hair, the drawings getting darker and darker until Ruth thought they were just absence, they were just Stevie gone. And sometimes on these dark winter mornings, when Ruth was leaving for work, Joseph would be sitting in the studio looking at an empty canvas, the butcher-paper drawings balled up in a corner.

'Maybe you are finished with Stevie, maybe it is time to let someone else see the work now?' Ruth would say, putting down her coat and going to him: easing away his doubt, as if he were a frightened child.

Sometimes, on those frostbite mornings, after Ruth had found him glazed and empty, and had held him and spoken to him, and he was warm and reassured, she'd get as far as the front door and then, plagued by the thought that something would happen to him if she left, she'd go back again to see if he was still all right. And sometimes she'd think that she must feed him before leaving, because he didn't really eat unless she reminded him, and so she'd push up the sleeves of her duffel coat and break eggs into the Moroccan bowl that she'd washed and dried so many times, mixing the albumen and yolk with a metal fork, beating the egg in time to a folk tune that was being played in the flat upstairs, where the pianist lived, a silent hunched man that Ruth would sometimes salute in the courtyard when he was carrying his plastic sack of washing back and forth from the laundrette on the corner. And Ruth would beat the eggs, beat beat beat in time to the plonking tune, and it would make her late for work. But she had to do it; she had to take care of Joseph until he was ready to part with his work. When Ruth had complained once about the endless staccato piano seeping through their ceiling from the flat upstairs, Joseph had been surprised.

'Our neighbour,' he had told her, 'is an artist.'

'And is that a better thing to be than something else?' Ruth had asked, and Joseph had put down his brush and looked at her.

'What else *is* there to be?' he'd asked.

'A person?'

'People, Ruth, are just skin and death.'

And this morning the piano was mocking and jaunty and relentless, and Ruth brought Joseph the eggs she'd cooked for him, and stood for a moment at the door and watched him eat, and his eyes were bruised with exhaustion, pummelled by an invisible pugilist who lived inside him and beat the shit out of him.

'Thank you, Ruth,' he said, and she left.

One morning when she woke in his empty bed she got up and found him sleeping on the studio couch, his brushes on the floor.

'Is it today?' she asked, coming back into the room and handing him a mug of hot tea. 'Is it a year to the day since you found her?'

Joseph nodded.

'I'll stay with you.'

'Just go,' he said. 'Please.'

'Let me stay.'

'Go, Ruth, I don't need a fucking nurse. Why do you treat me like I'm sick? I'm not sick. I'm not an invalid. Why do you treat me like I'm a fucking invalid?'

And he hurled the mug of tea across the room, and Ruth saw it disperse almost in slow motion, falling in a spectacular arc across the easel and the walls and the bunched-up drawings in the corner.

Ruth held a towel doused in cold water to her face and left for work.

On the walk to school, she felt sick. His words felt like stones that she was carrying inside her.

'How is Joseph?'

Robin was in the schoolyard, unloading books from a pannier, a bright blue cycling helmet hanging over the bars, and it occurred to Ruth that he'd been waiting for her to arrive, because the schoolyard was empty and classes had already begun. Ruth looked at the sky. Something was falling; it could be snow or ash.

'New bike helmet?' she asked. 'It's very shiny.'

'Early Christmas present from Vicky. She fears for my safety.'

'That's nice of her. You're late for class.'

'So are you. How is he? How's Joseph?'

'Working. Some art dealer he knows thinks she has a gallery who might take the paintings and she wants him to put his drawings in for an art fair in an abattoir.'

'An abattoir? Can't ask for more than that.'

'She thinks he might sell.'

Ruth's heart felt strange; it was beating too fast.

'And has he agreed to all that?'

'Not yet.'

'Are you all right, Ruth?'

'Maybe you'd come over and see him? You and Vicky, I mean.'

'We're going to her parents' for Christmas.'

'Right. Christmas. I'm late.'

Ruth looked towards the side door of the school, wondering if she might make it to the domestic science kitchen to jettison her coat without being seen. The silence of the schoolyard was oppressive. Her stomach was churning. Her face felt tender where the drops of hot tea had scalded her.

'It's a year today since he found Stevie's body.'

'I know. I know it is.'

Ruth felt exhausted. The domestic science kitchen might as well have been on the moon. She was late, so late; she should've been with Ardu, herding numbers on to a page, he'd be anxious now, missing her. She was finding it hard to breathe. Above her, the sky looked loose, like it might come undone. Her heart felt fluid. Her mouth tasted of metal.

'Ruth?' Robin was staring at her. 'Are you sure you're all right?'

'I'd like a word with you.' Veronica was standing on the staffroom steps. There was a cardboard reindeer under her arm. 'As soon as you've finished speaking to Mr Wolfe. In my office.'

'Ms Lennon is ill,' Robin snapped, before informing Veronica, in a tone that brooked no argument, that Ms Lennon also needed to go home.

Ruth waited in the staffroom among the ugly jumpers. One of the Hazels had given her a cup of tea, staring with irritated curiosity at the side of Ruth's face.

'You need to put something on that burn,' she said, and walked away. Veronica called a taxi, her mouth so tight it looked like it might crack. Robin had given Ruth money for the fare before he'd gone to teach his class, money which she'd tried to refuse.

In the courtyard in King's Cross she could hear, from the flat above Joseph's, the dull thud of a polka. Ruth put her key in the door. Inside, she put down her satchel, inhaled the damp.

She didn't find him standing in his unmatched socks in front of the easel. She didn't find him sleeping next to the burnt-out butts in the ashtray. He was not lying in the cavernous bath.

She called his name and was startled by the fear in her voice. She pictured his clothes piled neatly on shale. She'd never been to Brighton, though she'd seen postcards of the esplanade, the boardwalk, the beach. She picked up the mug from the studio floor, remarkably intact given its unexpected flight. He was gone.

From the floor above the polka persisted. She wanted to run upstairs and smash the piano lid down on her neighbour's fingers, and then she thought that maybe he was a teacher; that would explain the notes, the same notes, over and over again – she could've sung them. Yes, the man upstairs was a piano teacher. He was teaching a child; functional fingers, persistence without promise. She'd have liked to sit in the man's warm room. (Was it warm, she wondered, was it lit pale and yellow?) She'd have liked to look at the back of the practising child's bent head. Anything, anything, but this emptiness.

Where was Joseph? She was losing the thread of herself. She waited. She slept. She woke to darkness and silence.

She went into his studio, turned on the light. She looked at the portrait of Stevie perched on the side of an unmade bed, and

Stevie looked right back at her with utter indifference. 'Fool,' Stevie whispered from her painted mouth. 'You are a fool.'

It was close to midnight; Ruth pulled on her boots and coat and left the flat. The cold had taken on a whole new personality. The cold was extravagant, the cold was the father of the bride, wanting everyone to witness his generosity, to envy his capacity for largesse.

Ruth crossed Euston Road and walked as fast as she could past the dank arches by the side of the station. The rain was starting again. Moss-green water gathered in mulch-blocked gutters. The city was saturated. The tower above St Pancras seemed to weep.

Ruth kept her head bowed and cut through the blocks of flats in Somers Town. She ran past Mornington Crescent and on to Camden High Street. She was elated; she knew now that she was going to find Joseph in the Man in the Moon, the same pub where they had gone on that first night with Robin and where only last week Joseph had bartered one of his sketches for two half-pints of bitter. The sketch was pinned up behind the bar; it was of one of the waitresses who worked there. The girl had stroked the nape of Joseph's neck as he drew, bent over his notebook, the girl's fingers gently lifting his hair.

Ruth would find him there, she knew she would, and he would tell her that he was sorry and that it was all too much. The loss. All the loss. Ruth's certainty carried her all the way to the pub's locked doors.

Ruth crossed the road and sat in the doorway of a barber's shop and watched all the people being rained on, on their way home to their beds. She saw two people leave the Man in the

Moon by the locked side door, a woman and a man, and although the twosome were huddled together against the rain and walking away from her, she thought that the man looked familiar – but he wasn't Joseph.

Her boots were soaked, the loose crêpe soles licking up the rainwater like thirsty dogs. She walked home slowly, retracing her route. She didn't have any money; she would have liked to have got on the night bus. She thought she saw Robin by the archways near King's Cross and, surprised and grateful, she called out to him, but when he turned around it was just a dead-eyed boy in a dirty beige coat, with a dog on a chain. And the dog snapped at the rain, and Ruth apologized and backed away.

Exhausted, she let herself back into the dark flat and lay still until morning, Joseph's scent on the pillow. And when it was light again she got up and phoned Robin. Hunkered down on the floor, she could keep the nausea at bay if she wrapped her arm tight around her stomach. Robin's phone rang out; he was not home.

Ruth dressed and ate bread, which seemed to quell the sickness. It was too early to go to school. Outside, under the rectangle of sky above Midhope, only the leaves moved. Ruth put on her duffel coat and walked into the studio, where she sat on the edge of the couch, waiting.

'Where is he?' she asked Stevie, and Stevie smirked.

Ruth stood and walked to the table under the window where Joseph kept his paints and brushes, the rags, turpentine and chalks. There was a drawer in the table, which she opened. Envelopes and bills and charcoals and pencils and an elastic band and a sprig of dried lavender and two papery banknotes from somewhere that she had never been. And underneath the loose haul, another, thicker, envelope and, inside it, photographs, Polaroids of Stevie, the photographs that Joseph had taken of her to make the paintings.

Ruth dealt the photographs out on the tabletop, one after another. When she had finished looking, she replaced the Polaroids in their envelope, placed the envelope at the bottom of the drawer and closed it. She picked up her satchel and left the basement flat as, upstairs, the piano began again.

Me Me Me Fah Me Fah So Me Doh So La So Fah Me . . .

Ruth arrived at school before the staffroom was even unlocked, and waited by the forbidden door.

'The dead arose and appeared to many,' Veronica sang, sweeping past Ruth and unlocking the room to which she was denied access.

'I'm waiting for Robin.'

'If I see Mr Wolfe, I'll be sure to tell him you're looking for him. Do you have a doctor's note to cover your absence yesterday?'

'I didn't go to the doctor.'

'You hardly needed to, I suppose.'

'What do you mean?'

'Ruth?'

One of the legs of Robin's jeans was tucked into his socks. He looked like he hadn't slept. His eyes were pink; he looked like a very thin rabbit. Ruth saw, and didn't want to see, the detail of him.

'Joseph didn't come home last night.'

Robin gently pulled the staffroom door closed on Veronica's loitering back, so that they were standing alone in the corridor.

He looked at Ruth with something she suspected might be pity. Ruth watched his hand tentatively lift towards her cheek and fall again without touching her, and she knew that the small blisters that had formed there looked like teardrops. She remembered that she hadn't washed properly; her hair was dirty, her duffel coat obscured her crumpled clothes.

'What do you want from me, Ruth?' Robin said, and she was surprised by how utterly defeated he sounded.

'Can you help me find him?'

'Ruth.'

Robin paused.

'What?'

'I looked after him for a long time, Ruth. I'm sorry.'

'But what if something has happened to him?'

'Joseph will survive, Ruth. You need to, too. I'm going to be late for class.'

Ruth waited with Ardu at home time. The day had been interminable, but, unable to face being alone again, she had stayed, dragging herself through class after class until it was time to go. Standing side by side in the empty Friday-afternoon schoolyard, Ruth and the child watched the snow begin to fall, watched the tarmac on Judd Street soften and float.

'When will the artist paint the trees?' Ardu asked.

'Soon.'

'To climb?'

'Lean against maybe. I don't think we could climb painted trees.'

'It can snow on painted trees.'

'I suppose it can.'

Ardu knelt on the frosted ground and opened his school bag.

'It's for you,' he said, handing her a card he had drawn.

Ruth looked at the picture. It was of the two of them in a blue basket, swinging through space. 'Are we in a spaceship?'

'We are inside the world.'

'Thank you, Ardu,' she said. 'It's beautiful.'

'I am an artist.'

'Yes, yes you are.'

Ruth didn't hear the staffroom door closing or Robin walking towards them. She had placed the card in her satchel and was holding the child's hand and looking into the thickening snow, searching for Ardu's mother, for her slow, familiar trudge up Judd Street.

'You know the way they say that no two snowflakes are alike?'

Robin was kneeling next to the boy, his jacket collar turned up against the weather, his sock still grasping the leg of his jeans.

'Yes,' Ardu replied, wary of this interruption.

'Well, a long time ago an American scientist found two identical snow crystals during a big storm in a place called Wisconsin.'

'Twins?' Ardu asked. 'Twin snowflakes?'

'Soulmates,' Robin replied.

When Ardu's mother appeared, she was alone, free of the buggy that she normally pushed ahead of her. Ruth watched Ardu run to her, watched the woman wrap her arms around her son and cradle him in her scarf as they disappeared together down the snow-blind road.

'Here,' Robin said, handing Ruth a tissue from the pocket of his skinny denim jacket. 'There might be chutney on that tissue, but it's all I've got.'

'Where's your coat?'

'Don't ask. Come on. You look like death.'

They pushed his bike along the familiar route, walking down Judd Street and winding their way through the slushy streets, their conversation silenced by the traffic and the falling snow, then turning into Woburn Walk, where the window of the Sorrento Cafe glowed pale and yellow in the dusk.

SEVEN

Ireland, May 2018

In Bantry town, roadworks on Chapel Street obliged Robin to sit behind the wheel and watch while, on the far side of the road, a minibus-load of Japanese walkers alighted on to the pavement, each earnest sightseer stepping out of the bus with a rucksack and a redundant sun hat to form an orderly queue outside a bar with a shillelagh in the window. Alone on the empty road, Robin became so focused on their diligence, on their conscientious participation in their distilled Irish experience, that he missed the temporary traffic lights changing from red to green and back to red. Pulled out of his reverie by an impatient car pulling up behind him, he was obliged to wait for the sequence all over again.

There was something urgent that he had forgotten, he thought, waiting for the light to change, something so vast it almost obliterated itself. What was it? As the green light flashed for the second time, the startling realization that he was going to visit his dying mother flipped over his half-empty stomach and sent perspiration racing down his neck. His mouth awash with saliva, he opened his window and coughed up a mouthful of undigested sardines. Silver-flecked fish skin adhering to the outside of his driver's door, the cars behind him sounding their impatience and incredulity, Robin saw the Japanese tourists, temporarily diverted from their schedule, look over at him brightly, as if he too might be an exotic cultural highlight. Vomiting man in cloudy country town – another Irish curiosity to tick off the list.

Robin drove, his head spinning, his mouth rancid, and parked outside the hospital's stippled yellow walls. Inside, he breathed in the already familiar soupy metallic smell and went to the public toilet, where he washed his face, rinsed his mouth and then took the stairs to St Canice's Ward on the second floor. Buzzed in from the nurses' station to the locked geriatric unit, Robin passed down the linoleum-covered corridor, trying not to look right or left. To either side of him, the wards held their own particular versions of hell: ancient men, their jaws trembling in an effort to speak, and old women, dry as sun-yellowed newspaper, corpse-still under cotton blankets.

Outside his mother's closed door, a marionette sat slumped in a wheelchair. On closer inspection Robin saw that the form was human, an old woman, a terrifying, toothless miniature, clutching a doll.

'Dada!' the ancient puppet shouted as he passed.

Robin sat by his mother's bed, looking at her swollen hands and sunken cheeks, and tried to convince himself that this moment was real. If he could only rouse himself from this endless fucking sitting, he might find his way back to a time and place where his mother was doing what she should be doing on a Sunday afternoon: cutting back the wild hydrangea, feeding an abandoned dog or wiping her glasses on her filthy overalls to read a thermostat or find her scissors.

'Ushi?' he asked, calling her name. 'Ushi? Can you hear me?' But his question hung in the stale air unanswered.

'What is the worst that can happen?' his mother used to ask him when he was prevaricating, when he was beached, unable to make the next step. 'Tell me, Robin, what is the worst that can happen?'

Beyond the sealed-up window in her room, Robin could hear singing, a choked, discordant song. On the lawn the peacocks were dancing, their magnificent trains spread out, their ornamental eye spots clear and sinister. As he watched them caw and sway, the rain started.

'Look at that,' Robin said to his sleeping mother. 'The peacocks called the rain.'

There was a knock on the door. It was Joy, with her tea urn and sympathy biscuits. A momentary Joy, Robin thought, returning to his mother's bedside with a cup and saucer in his hand to continue his vigil.

The older he got, the more Robin thought about his father, and now, witnessing his mother's final hours (if that was what was happening here, if that absurdity was indeed fact), his memory of the old man was as concrete as if his father had slipped into the room and taken a seat at the bedside, as if the meddlesome peacocks had called his father's ghost down with the rain.

His mother had taken Robin to meet the man just once – at his father's request, Robin assumed.

They had left Gilbert the knicker-eating goat with a reluctant Suzi and taken the bus to Dublin, where they boarded a flight to Germany. Robin was thirteen; he'd never been on an aeroplane before. When the air hostess bent down in front of him to pick up her safety demonstration equipment, he'd blushed from his throat to his hairline.

It was midsummer, the same wet, capricious summer that he'd first met Joe, and in his mind the two encounters – with Joe and with his father – remained connected.

Some weeks before Robin left to visit his unknown father, Joe had washed up, wild and careless and full of plans. And because he was on holiday in Ireland with his strange and alarming mother, who kept disappearing, Ushi had asked the boy to stay with them, and he had done so, for almost the whole summer. And then, *then*, just as Robin was beginning to get used to the English boy sleeping on his floor, and was cautiously interested to see what the unpredictable boy would make him do next (they'd already robbed and lied and smoked and spied on Suzi next door getting ready for a bath), Ushi had made an announcement.

Robin's mother had been making bread, her fists bashing into the dough, when she told him that they were going to visit his father in Germany. They were to go immediately. The English boy would have to go back to London with his mother, who had recently turned up giddy and apologetic and with a sprinkling of presents: vodka for Ushi, chocolate for Robin and Joe, and a motorcycle helmet for Joe, even though he didn't have a motorbike.

'What if Joe doesn't want to go home? What if I don't want to go to Germany?' Robin had asked his mother, looking at the pummelled dough and knowing how it felt.

On their last night together of that long first summer, Joe, lying in a sleeping bag on Robin's bedroom floor, his berth softened by Ushi's handmade quilt, had told Robin that Una McClafferty had voluntarily put her breasts in his mouth, one at a time, behind the broken wall on the Red Strand. Robin was stunned, and grudgingly impressed. Robin was in love with Una McClafferty, had been in love with her since the days of his mother's tattooed bananas in National School. Just last spring, in their final term of primary school, they'd done an astronomy project together and Una had gone red when she'd had to say 'Uranus' out loud. What was she doing with her breasts in this English boy's mouth? What was happening to Robin's world?

Robin had lain in his boyhood bed, trying to get the image of Joe and Una McClafferty (with her funny teeth and those unseen breasts that roamed under her school jumper like jellyfish) out of his head.

'You're a liar,' Robin had whispered to Joe, who was already asleep, cocooned in Robin's sleeping bag, the motorcycle helmet by his side. 'You're a liar,' Robin had whispered again, but with less conviction this time, listening to his friend exhale, slowly and deeply, his breath ebbing and flowing like waves.

That night Robin hadn't slept; there had been too much to think about. He understood that he was supposed to want a father and understood also, perfectly clearly, that he didn't. The fathers he saw around him were unpredictable. They drove their mud-splattered cars too fast and nearly knocked him off his bicycle. They shouted by the sides of pitches when things weren't going to plan, and they smelt like wet dogs. And anyway, he already had a mother and a goat and now a new best friend, almost a brother, and it was too much, it was overload. It was reckless, Robin thought, to acquire so many new people without warning; anything could happen.

Robin and his mother had landed in Cologne and taken the bus to Bonn, where she counted out her change and bought fruit salad and pastries in the bus-station cafe. Robin hated Bonn, everything from the cowed woman who swept under their feet as they ate to the pristine streets they walked along on their way to his father's riverside apartment. He felt defenceless and uneasy. He hated his mother most of all for exposing them to the scrutiny of this cultivated city; he hated her girth and her clogs and her swollen socks; he hated her smiling face.

They had stood outside a formal apartment building while she checked the address, Robin sick with embarrassment when she stopped a passer-by to check the name of the street from the note in her hand. He'd heard her speak to the man in her mother tongue and wanted to rip her tongue from her head. Why was she drawing attention to them? His mother, big and shiny and hot under a magnolia tree, had pointed up at the windows across the street, smiling and chatting and lapping at a line of perspiration over her lip, while Robin stood minding their rucksacks, too tall for his stupid corduroy trousers and with absolutely no-where to hide.

When his mother handed the stranger her camera, and gestured for Robin to join her under the magnolia tree, Robin had thought he was actually going to pass out. That she would choose to capture his moment of consternation under this prissy little tree was beyond Robin's comprehension.

'Am I OK?' his mother had asked him in English, while the stranger examined the ancient camera. Robin hadn't answered.

'Am I all right, Robin?' she'd asked again, showing him her teeth, white and strong, in case the remnants of her lunch had gathered there. Robin had seen kiwi seeds on her gums. He'd remained silent.

'What's the worst that can happen, Robin?' she'd asked after the stranger had gone on his way and they were crossing the road to his father's apartment building.

What's the worst that can happen? The worst was already happening! His world was being ripped apart, his certainties shattered.

His mother had rung a bell on a brass plate by the front door and they were clicked inside. On the second floor they'd walked down a tiled corridor and a door ahead of them opened before they'd even knocked. Inside, a gnarled woman had guided them down another short corridor, padding the carpeted ground like a tightrope walker, toe to hunched toe, as if she might fall into a gaping abyss.

She'd opened another door. There was a bed in the deep, silent room. There was a man on the bed and two hairless cats. Sphinxes.

The man was old and he was yellow. Robin had seen enough life to recognize death. His mother, in one movement, appeared to dart over to the bed and snatch the old man up from his sheets. The gnarled woman had watched from the bedroom door as Robin's mother held the old man on her knee. Robin's father's shrunken head had rested on Ushi's breasts, on her dress bought second-hand at the Friday market in Clonakilty, red and purple and studded with mirrored shards, heavy and thick with knotty embroidery. Robin saw the creased-up wadding of Indian cotton under her armpits. Her living-human smell, which had been lurking in the folds of her dress, drifted into the muffled room.

Robin thought he'd seen the woman at the door fight back a spit of repulsion at the sight of them. His father had been wearing some kind of floaty nappy; he'd looked like Jesus draped across his mother's knee. She had rocked the old man gently, as if they were alone, as if there was no one else there to witness his wrinkled nakedness, to see him smile and close his old monkey eyes.

The bald cats had raised their non-existent eyebrows and deserted the bed, dropping on to the floor in silence and arching around the woman at the door, and Robin had felt something rise in his throat. Shame. A kind of shame that he hadn't known until they arrived in this city.

'*Ich muss die Toilette benutzen,*' Robin had blurted out, and the woman had pointed to another door.

Robin had sat on an aubergine-coloured toilet bowl in the sour-smelling en suite and looked at the bottles and bandages, the swabs and powders stacked underneath his father's smoky mirror – the intimate accoutrements of illness.

Who *was* his father? What had happened? And why had he never wondered before? What was his mother to this man? A mistress? (Robin had heard the word; he understood the concept. But surely a mistress should be someone more like the air hostess, someone with smaller feet and less of an appetite, someone who wasn't so uncomplicatedly forgiving?)

When he'd come out of the bathroom, the gnarled woman had been saying something in German that he couldn't understand.

'Robin,' his mother had said gently, and Robin went to the bedside. His father had looked into his face. The old man's eyes were stained yellow like piano keys. Ushi had nodded, and Robin moved away, back to the safety of the wall.

Soon after, the woman had ushered them out and the three of them drank thin soup at a polished table while Robin's father slept. The woman spoke in German, looking at Robin from time to time to see if he understood. (He didn't.) She'd asked him a question, then repeated it in English: 'Do you have any talents?'

'None,' Robin had replied evenly, just like Joe would have done.

Across the table, his mother had smiled and wiped her eyes on the sleeve of her dress.

'Do you want to see him again?' the woman had asked Robin when all the soup was swallowed. He shook his head. They left soon afterwards.

On the flight home, Ushi had been quiet. Coming in to land over Dublin Airport, she had taken Robin's hand in hers.

'Your father loves you.'

'How could he love me? He doesn't know me.' Robin was furious, with her touch and her words.

'But why should love be diminished by absence, Robin? Why does it always have to be so ordinary?'

When they returned to the estuary, Robin had understood something he hadn't understood before, something fundamental. He understood that his mother was lonely. She was a foreigner everywhere; she belonged nowhere. No matter how long she lived in their little house, throwing and glazing her heavy pots, baking her sodden bread, feeding the feral cats, making tea out of nettles and friends out of strangers, she would always be a foreigner. 'Am I a foreigner?' he had asked himself, back in Popes Cove among the paraphernalia of his life, his schoolbooks and bicycle, his second-hand wetsuit and his fish hooks. Alone again in his bedroom, where Joe's berth had been unmade, the sleeping bag and quilt put back in the hot press, Robin had searched for his one and only Valentine's card, which had arrived in the post months before.

'With love from Anonymous,' the card read.

Looking at the writing now, in the light of his new discoveries, Robin had realized that he knew the sender, had always known the sender. He recognized her writing from all those banana skins he'd so hurriedly discarded.

Anonymous. Is that what being a foreigner meant to her?

USHI'S BREATHING SEEMED to have changed, the laboured, rattling breaths of earlier in the day cooling and lengthening into a slower rhythm. She was leaving slowly, stealthily slipping into a dark lake, knee-deep now in the still, brown water.

'How are we tonight?'

A nurse called Angel entered the room with swabs of wet cotton on wooden sticks and told Robin that the night shift had begun and that she would be looking after his mother for the next twelve hours.

Robin leant forward and gently applied the moist stick to his mother's parched lips.

Robin's father had been Ushi's teacher, a professor of arts, already in his sixties when he taught her. She had known, she told Robin in later years, that her infatuation was entirely one-sided. 'What can I do to help you?' he'd asked her when she'd told him she was pregnant. A pragmatist, she'd told him she'd need money to support the child. 'My wife is the one with money,' he'd said. 'We will arrange a meeting.' In the professor's office later, the wife had been courteous and savage. 'We won't see you again, but we trust that you will survive,' she'd said, taking out her chequebook.

Throughout Robin's childhood his mother would tell anyone who asked that her home found her, not she it. Ushi had come to Ireland in search of sea and air, and when she reached West Cork she found a fresh start. At the end of her first week in Clonakilty she had cycled out from the guesthouse in the town and along the estuary to meet a local auctioneer, her lover's wife's money in a canvas bag on her back. 'Cash is king,' the auctioneer had said, smiling. A small man with hard brown skin and black eyes, he'd left her in the low-ceilinged kitchen with six line-caught mackerel, wrapped in bloodied newspaper, which he had taken from the boot of his car, and a bottle of Irish whiskey, minus the two glasses they had shared to seal the deal.

'I'll throw the furnishings in with the house,' he had told her, and she'd thanked him, running her hands over the grain of the table, already imagining her own life denting its worn surface.

Robin put the moist cotton swab down in a dish on the bedside cabinet. 'Thank you,' he said to his lingering, drifting mother. 'Thank you.'

Pulled from a shredded sleep, Robin woke hours later in the hospital chair.

'Mr Wolfe?'

Disorientated, Robin scrambled for clarity.

'We need to look after your mother now,' Angel said. 'Maybe you'd like to go outside for a couple of minutes. We won't be long.'

'Yes. Yes, of course. Sorry, I must have fallen asleep.'

The hospital grounds were pale and damp, lit only by a half-moon and the bleed of fluorescence from the wards above. Robin walked, stretching out his arms and back. As his eyes adjusted to the light, he looked at the wet trees, and tried and failed to identify them. His mother would have known their names, had always known these ordinary things, hazel, ash, willow, maple, sycamore, lime, sweet chestnut, those solid, rooted words that she'd learnt first in German and then in English, words that she'd taught him, words that had leeched out of him over the years. To be replaced with what, he wondered – a vocabulary of regret? 'Why now, Robin, after all these years, are you behaving like someone who has been betrayed?'

The peacock screech above his head startled him: a command, an order, a warning not to take one step further. Robin had gone as far as he could go; he was not permitted to travel beyond this point. Peacocks roost in trees, his mother could have told him, while the hens, plain and practical, crouch under the bush. Robin looked up to where the call had come from – the bird, nesting in high branches, fanned out his tail, swift as a switchblade.

'You win,' Robin said, standing for a moment to watch the display of machismo before turning back towards the hospital. 'You win.'

The hospital cafe was closed. There was a porter herding wheelchairs under a stairwell. 'Of course it's closed,' he confirmed. 'It's nearly midnight.'

There was a late-night garage, he said, not far from the main gates, which might have a few sandwiches left, something anyway to see him through until morning.

'I'll be back,' Robin told him. 'My mother is upstairs.'

The porter nodded, whatever curiosity death's vigil might once have aroused in him long since spent. At the late-night garage, Robin considered the lone tuna-fish sandwich swimming around the empty fridge. His recent experience with the sardines won out, however, and he bought himself a bar of chocolate instead and an instant coffee that tasted remarkably like tea.

Walking back along the corridor of the darkened ward, Robin could see that his mother's door was ajar. Angel must still be in there with her. Robin went into the room. Ushi's bedclothes were pulled up tightly under her chin and a single yellow rose lay on top of the turned-down sheet.

'How is she?' Robin asked, trying to understand the theatre of the room he had so recently vacated.

'I'm so sorry, Robin,' Angel replied. 'We tried to find you. We couldn't.'

By the time Robin reached Popes Cove the sun was coming up over the water and the sky was mockingly beautiful. Robin stood outside his mother's gate, watching layers of pink and yellow and a sandy band of green gradually evaporate until finally the sky settled on a wishy-washy grey.

He turned his back on the horizon to go inside. Suzi's gnomes appeared to be sleeping underneath their cement hats.

'She's gone,' he called quietly over the garden wall to the biggest and ugliest of the pack. 'She's gone.'

He opened the cottage door, bracing himself to meet her shadows. Suzi had been in; there was a note on the kitchen table: 'Soup in the fridge. Your mother's recipe. Not as good. Fingers crossed. S.'

Fingers crossed for what? Robin wondered. Resurrection? A little less salt?

He tried Ruth's phone again.

'Leave a message.'

'Ruth, I'm in Popes Cove. I've called, often. I don't know where you are. Call me.'

In Ushi's bedroom he opened the book his mother had been reading on the page he'd marked the night he arrived. He began to read. He would sit in the kitchen and finish her book for her, and drink Suzi's hopeful soup, and wait for the gnomes to wake and for his wife to telephone to tell him if she was coming home. And then he would begin. Again.

'The sky the day we shot the boy was clear and blue . . .'

Robin closed the book and his eyes. The sadness was everywhere: in the inky text, in the last words, in the lost dawn, in Ushi's fleece slumped over a chair back, in the used tissue in the pocket, in the withered mandarin in the lopsided bowl, in the scrubbed table, in the innocence of a new morning, and in the lonely day ahead. Soon Robin would have to knock on Suzi's door and tell her that her friend had departed. Soon he'd have to face the outside world.

He stood and began to make himself a coffee, repeating the actions he'd watched his mother perform so many hundreds of times. As the years gradually accumulated Robin finally understood her enjoyment of the ritual: the hand grinder, the scalded pot, the deep perfume. Robin steadied himself, picked up the telephone from its cradle and lowered himself, with his mug of coffee, into the armchair where his mother used to sit on Friday evenings to ring him. As a young man in London these calls had driven him mad, a monstrous invasion, a reminder of what he was trying to escape. But later, in Dublin, as time went on and Sid got older, and he and Ruth settled into their courteous, twitchy marriage, he looked forward to the calls. Stirring a pot, pouring a glass, he was happy to settle down to an hour of meandering, uncomplicated conversation.

'How is Ruth?'

'Fine. Busy.'

'And you?'

'You know. Keeping my head down.'

In the last few months their conversations had been sporadic. Sometimes Ushi would forget what day it was, and when Robin telephoned her she would sound distracted, confused.

'I can't find my drill, Robin.'

'What are you drilling?'

'I'm not drilling anything.'

'Why do you need it, then?'

'Need what?'

'The drill.'

'I don't know why we're talking about this, Robin. How is Ruth?'

'Fine. Busy.'

'And you?'

'You know. Keeping my head down.'

Why hadn't he read the signs? Why hadn't he known? She hadn't been herself for the best part of a year. She'd been forgetful, irritable, strangely detached and then bubbling over with her mad, magical thinking.

He'd brought Celestine with him one weekend, partly because he knew that Ushi would not entirely remember that he had. They'd crawled along the lacy motorway out of Dublin, which was being dug up and re-stitched again, Celestine in the passenger seat eating Maltesers and singing along to some crap on the radio until Robin snapped it off.

'Can I smoke?'

'No.'

'What *can* I do?' Celestine had asked, throwing a chocolate ball into the air and catching it in her open mouth. Several options sprang to mind.

They'd stopped at a garage just beyond Cashel because Celestine needed to use the bathroom. While Robin was waiting for her in the forecourt, he'd called Suzi. He'd listened as Suzi agitatedly told him that that morning she'd found Ushi sitting on the beach in a nightdress. When Suzi had asked what she was doing there, Ushi told her she was waiting for the seal.

Robin had looked up, Celestine was walking back to the car. She'd bought a 99. He'd watched her pull the chocolate flake from the soft ice cream and, smiling at him through the dusty glass, snap it in half with her teeth.

Celestine's careful negotiation of his mother's kitchen had almost made Robin laugh. She'd picked her way over the flagstone floor in her high-heeled boots looking like one of Suzi's china figurines, shiny and stiff and breakable. His mother, dressed now in her overalls, and seemingly recovered, had put an abandoned kitten that she was struggling to nurse back in its cardboard box by the stove and stood to greet them.

'Ushi, this is a friend of mine, Celestine. Celestine, this is my mother, Ushi, and my mother's friend and neighbour, Suzi.'

'Hi, Ushi, thank you for having me in your home.'

Ushi had held on to the hand that Celestine offered and looked at her before she spoke.

'You look like a doll I owned when I was a child,' his mother had said, surprising Robin, who had been thinking almost exactly the same thing.

'Her name was Bathsheba and she had very black hair and a little mechanism in her back to lengthen and shorten it, and when you rocked her she cried. A haunting cry like a lost animal. I didn't know how to comfort her, so one day I cut off all her hair.'

'Tea, anyone?' Suzi asked.

All the usual props had been in place in the warm kitchen. His mother, generous and dishevelled and unable to find the tea cosy, had fussed around, trying to remember Celestine's name. The orphan kitten mewled in its box, while Suzi, her curiosity having gotten the better of her, decided to stay for tea and was laying the table with Ushi's better pottery. But Ushi had been different, altered. And Celestine was different. Celestine was not his wife.

'How old do you think it is?' Celestine had asked, kneeling to stroke the kitten in the box.

'Too young to be alone,' Ushi had replied, handing Celestine a saucer of milk and a rag and showing her how to dip the cloth into the milk and squeeze the drops into the cat's open mouth.

'I'm glad that Robin has a friend, I worry that since Joe went away he's been awfully lonely.'

'Joe?' Celestine had enquired.

'It's not important,' Robin had replied, retrieving the tea cosy from the coat-hook on the back of the door.

They'd been parked in the back of the IKEA car park when Robin told Celestine that he had to go and visit his mother. They were on the back seat, Celestine still straddling his lap.

'I have to go and see my mother.'

'This minute?'

'Hardly.'

Her fearlessness terrified him. The first time they'd fucked in the furniture-store car park, he'd thought he was going to have a heart attack, if not from the sheer joy of simply fucking without conversation or negotiation or history, he was also convinced they were going to be discovered.

'Believe me,' Celestine had said. 'You and I are far less fascinating to them than their flatpacks.'

'Ruth is going to Berlin to see Sid. I suspect there's something up with him, but she's not saying what,' Robin had said, lifting Celestine's hips and slightly adjusting her position.

'Am I hurting you?'

'I think my hip is crumbling.'

'You say the sweetest things. Dylan's marching to save the planet on Saturday and my father's flying to Tenerife to do his cha cha chas; come to the flat, we can do this lying down.'

'I'd like to, but I need to see my mother. She's not well.'

Celestine was buttoning her shirt. 'What's wrong with her?'

'She's not eating, wandering around the place at weird hours. Her neighbour is worried,' Robin had said, unbuttoning Celestine's shirt again and tracing his fingers over her scarred breast.

'I'll come with you,' she'd said, lightly batting away his hand.

Robin had watched the kitten mewl and squirm in Celestine's painted fingers, watched it blink its blind eyes in confusion until finally it accepted the milk squeezed from the rag.

He would walk away, should walk away, any day now. Walk away from what though? They had made no plans, no declarations, no promises.

Their friendship (relationship? Robin baulked at using the word) was strangely uncomplicated. They had sex when and where they could. They went to awful films together, which she chose, and sometimes they'd stop off on the way home and eat in an Italian cafe she knew, near the hospital where she had had her treatment and where the staff all greeted her by name.

It was comforting to live within their reduced routines, Robin thought, comforting to hold her hand in the dark while, on the screen, people ran through Manhattan looking for love or dresses.

The second time they'd met they'd gone for the walk that Celestine had suggested. Robin had driven to Howth, a pretty fishing village on the northern reaches of the city, and parked at the summit of the hill. They'd walked through bracken for a while, emerging on to the cliff path, where he'd tried to interest her in the habits of the black-legged kittiwakes reeling above them in the wet sky.

'They're monogamous, certainly during the breeding season.'

'Yeah?'

'Apparently.'

'The breeding season doesn't last for ever though, Robin, does it?'

Afterwards they'd gone for an awkwardly polite drink in a bar full of elderly American tourists who were gingerly sipping glasses of Guinness and hoping to engage in conversation. Celestine's feet were soaked, her canvas runners stained yellow from the dry paths they'd walked. She was tired and wanted to get back to

Dylan. He'd taken her home, watched her disappear into the canister of the stairwell of her flats, and he hadn't heard from her for a week. Just as he'd become convinced that their interlude was over before it had begun, she'd rung and offered to take him to a film. He'd sat next to her in the dark wondering what he was doing there while on the screen warring lovers united over a slobbering canine. Afterwards she'd taken him to a cocktail bar and asked him to order her a Porn Star.

'I think you're lonely, Robin,' she'd said, sipping her drink while he knocked back a beer.

'You think I'm lonely?'

'Yes, I do.'

'I'm not lonely.'

'I think you'll find that you are.'

She'd laughed. He'd ordered her another Porn Star.

'I had breast cancer. I was sick. And now I'm not sick any more.'

'I'm sorry.'

'The things that mattered before are different to the things that matter now.'

'What matters now?'

'Dylan. Being the best I can be for him.'

'What else?'

'Other people know what they want. Money. Love. I just want the next day and the next.'

Robin had watched her. He remembered when they'd first met across his desk at the parent–teacher meeting and he'd mistaken her warmth, her openness, for some kind of provocation.

'When my hair grew back after the chemo, it was entirely grey. Look!'

She'd bent her head to show him the grey roots he'd noticed on that first encounter.

'Why do you dye it?'

'I don't want to be grey, not yet. I'm not like you, Robin, I don't want to go quietly.'

'So what do you want?'

'At the moment, you.'

Across the room a couple sat at a low table. The woman was complaining to the waitress; under the sinuous bar music, Robin couldn't tell what about. Her husband, or lover, or whoever he was, was sitting back in his chair, smiling frankly at the indifferent waitress, who was possibly the most beautiful young woman Robin had ever seen. He'd looked back to Celestine; she'd held his gaze.

'Where?' Robin had asked.

They had fucked in the ladies' bathroom, inside a blue tiled cubicle that smelt like almonds. The silence was sublime. He held her hands above her head, gripped at the wrist. When she came he felt her breath, hot against his neck.

Celestine had put the sleeping kitten back in the box by the stove. After politely asking where the bathroom was, she'd excused herself from the kitchen, catching Robin's eye as she left.

'You're brilliant,' he'd mouthed to her, and she smiled.

'Your friend is awfully good with animals,' Suzi had remarked, rinsing out the stoneware, while Ushi went in search of clean sheets for Robin's bed.

'She's got a lot of experience with reptiles, and frozen mice.'

'She might need it,' Suzi had said, snapping out the tea towel before heading back to her own chaste cottage.

Robin had taken the sheets from his mother and made up a bed for himself and Celestine in his old room. He'd decided to drive back into town to buy something special that he could cook for dinner.

'You go,' Celestine had said. 'I'll stay with Ushi.'

Driving back, the shopping on the front seat, he'd seen them both walk slowly up from the shore, Celestine's high-heeled boots sinking into the grey sand, his mother turning back to look at the water, as if there was something there that she had left behind.

Robin had briefly closed his eyes, and when he looked again he could have sworn he saw his father leaning back against the gable wall, languidly, waiting for the two women to return. And Robin had experienced a moment of intense relief, a moment when he didn't feel alone, and then his father was gone, and there was just rationality and a tint of shame and the shadowy space where the old man had or hadn't stood.

Later, after the mussels Robin had bought in town were scrubbed and simmered, and the fish seared, and Suzi had joined them with bottles of bitter home-made wine that quickly blew their heads off, Robin had excused himself from the table and gone outside to breathe in the night air. All evening Celestine had been by his side; she'd been funny and warm. She'd told the two old women, both thirsty for her story, about her father's passion for ballroom dancing, a passion he'd developed when Celestine was a child and he'd been trying to find a pastime he could share with his young daughter after her mother died of breast cancer.

'We danced together on the kitchen lino,' Celestine had said. 'I would stand on his feet and he would twirl me around the room.'

'And do you dance now?' Suzi had asked.

'I've two left feet,' Celestine replied, and Ushi, who had barely picked at her food all evening, had looked under the table in confusion.

Robin had stood looking at the sea, at a moon so round and white it looked like painted scenery. He didn't hear the back door open.

'I've seen your father out here twice,' his mother had said, startling him. 'He's been here in the evening, when I have come out to feed the mother cat. I think he's been sent for me.'

'What happened to you this morning?' Robin had asked her, unwilling, unable, to hear what she'd said. 'Why were you on the beach in your nightdress? You'll make yourself ill. Suzi is worried about you.'

Ushi was looking at the moon, illuminating the living and the dead with equal dispassion.

'Your father also presents himself to me as a seal,' she said. 'I don't think he'll be able to stay much longer. I imagine there's only so much time that they're allowed before they have to go back.'

'I take it you're not actually trying to kill yourself, are you? Or maybe you are? Any other old ghosts you're planning on floating around with in the brine, besides my father?'

'Why are you talking to me like this, Robin?'

'You need to see a different doctor. Wandering down to the beach in your nightdress and talking to seals – you'll get pneumonia. You're not eating. You're not working, not driving. You're thin, Ushi! You're thin because you won't eat. I don't understand why you won't see a different doctor. I've asked you and asked you.'

Robin had felt untethered: Suzi's wine, Celestine's closeness. His mother's strange absence, her preoccupation.

Ushi hadn't replied immediately.

'I don't need to see any more doctors, Robin,' she'd said eventually. 'I have a diagnosis. I have a tumour on my brain. It cannot be treated. It doesn't hurt, it just alters what I see, it alters what I understand. Sometimes with spectacular grace. Sometimes not.'

The mother cat had sauntered out of the woodshed, turning back to look at Robin with cold amusement. Tit for tat. Mother for cat.

'When were you going to tell me?'

'I like your friend. I will give her the kitten.'

'When were you going to tell me, Ushi?'

'As soon as you were able to hear.'

He'd watched his mother walk back to the kitchen. He stood in the garden, alone, he assumed, underneath the curious moon.

That night he lay with Celestine in his boyhood bed and lost himself in her beautiful, injured body.

ROBIN COULDN'T ALLOW himself to start thinking about Celestine now. Not now. Sitting in Ushi's kitchen, his coffee cold, he had calls to make. He'd be reckless, because caution got you fucking nowhere.

'Ruth, I assume you don't want to speak. Ushi is dead. I'm in Popes Cove. I've called you and called you. It's morning now. I don't know where you are. I'm beginning not to give a shit.'

The hospital was efficient when he called, the undertaker silky. Sid's number rang out, so Robin tried it again.

'What time is it?'

'I woke you, Sid. I'm sorry.'

'You all right?'

'I'm still in Popes Cove.'

'Ushi?'

'She died late last night.'

Robin felt like an imposter, he felt as if the words belonged in another mouth. He looked around his mother's kitchen as he spoke to his son, wondering if the pots and pans had heard the news, wondering if the mother cat on the windowsill, ragged and thin, would chase the information down the lane. He wondered if the wind would scatter the news over the townland like dandelion seed.

'I'll come home, Robin.'

'You're working.'

'I can change things.'

'Give me a couple of days to sort things out, Sid, then come. Yeah?'

'You sure?'

'I'm sure.'

'I'm sorry for your loss, Robbie,' Colm commiserated, and Robin could visualize him, tense and embarrassed and wishing that Helen had been there to take the call.

The school secretary was punctilious. 'I'll get the details from the funeral website as soon as they're available and disseminate them among your colleagues.'

When Robin put the phone down her words seemed to hang in the empty air.

Nine thirty in the morning; Suzi must have seen Robin's car by now. One more call to make, then he'd brave the stuffed dogs and china shepherdesses.

'Hello?' Celestine sounded wary.

'Were you asleep?'

'Robin, is that you?'

'Yes.'

'It's early. I was working last night.'

'Focus group?'

'Yeah.'

'What for?'

'Sausage-flavoured gin. Why are you asking?'

'How's Dylan?'

'He's asleep. Where are you?'

'My mother's house.'

'Is she all right?'

'Actually, Celestine, she's gone. Last night.'

'I don't understand.'

'She died, last night.'

'Oh, Robin. I'm so sorry.'

(What's the worst that can happen, Robin, what's the very worst that can happen?)

'I need to see you.'

Robin heard the rustle of Celestine's bedcovers, heard the rescued cat's indignant cry.

'Celestine?'

'We agreed to stop, Robin. I'm not the person you should be talking to.'

'Celestine?'

'What?'

'I miss you.'

Robin showered and put back on the clothes he'd driven down from Dublin in, which he'd washed and hung over the old wooden horse in Ushi's empty studio. Sun-dried and stiffened under the corrugated-plastic roof, the clothes felt like a suit of armour, just the protection he needed to face the day.

Leaving the studio, Robin saw a photograph pinned to the wall above Ushi's glazing table, muddied and faded. Robin unpinned it and looked at it more closely. It was a recent picture of Sid, tall and thin and dark, a cigarette between his fingers, his arm around Ushi. The two of them were leaning against the cottage door, smiling. Beautiful boy, Robin thought as if seeing him for the first time. Beautiful boy. The best thing that had happened.

Robin was leaving the cottage when the phone in the kitchen rang. Assuming it was the undertaker with questions that he didn't want to answer, he was tempted to ignore it.

'Fuck it,' he said and, deciding to face whatever it was that needed to be faced, he went back to the kitchen and lifted the receiver.

'Robin.'

'I thought you were the undertaker.'

'Robin, I'm so sorry. Are you OK?'

Her voice seemed to belong to a different time and place, a time and place where Ushi was still alive and where he was still blithely scribbling over his life, unaware of how close he was to this moment of utter loss.

'Robin? Robin, are you there?'

'Where are you?'

'London.'

'I see.'

'I'm coming home.'

'There are things to do. Arrangements.'

'I'm coming home, Robin.'

'Ruth.'

'What?'

'Give me some time.'

'Time?'

So much of him wanted to retreat, to plead with her to come straight away. He held his ground.

'Don't you need me, Robin?'

'I don't know, Ruth. I don't know.'

'TAUT AS A drum, you two,' Colm had said to Robin.

It was a summer evening in Dublin in the fading years of the old millennium, shortly after Robin and Ruth had begun to see each other. They were in Colm and Helen's back garden, looking at the ornamental pond, Colm showing Robin the one remaining bloated fish that had consumed all the smaller ones. The two men stood watching it dart around the pond, lonely and confused, looking for a friend to eat.

'I thought it was a Shubunkin,' Colm said.

'What is a Shubunkin?'

'I don't know, but whatever it is, it's not that.'

Inside the house Helen was resting between bouts of feeding baby Kelly, who she described as a milk machine, and Ruth was at the kitchen table drawing with Sid and with Erin, the elder of Colm and Helen's two young daughters. Colm, a beer in his hand, looked away from the pond and down the length of the garden. Beyond his daughters' trampoline and curtained Wendy house, beyond the bird feeders and parasol, the gazebo and boxed hedging, an identical garden backed on to theirs.

'See that house there?'

'Yes,' Robin answered.

'Just sold again. Prices round here have nearly doubled in fourteen months. Doubled!'

'Right.'

'They'll gut it. Sunken kitchen, the works.'

'Right.'

'You might be looking for a sunken kitchen yourself?'

'Why would that be?'

'Taut as a drum, you two. Eh?'

Robin, still enjoying looking at the remorseful fish, had yet to grasp his meaning.

'You and Ruth. Life and that. The way it turns out.'

'Apparently we're taut as a drum,' he'd said to Ruth that night, vaguely drunk, watching her undress. She'd slipped her grey dress over her head, over her small, efficient breasts, and stepped out of her underwear and into his bed.

'I don't think Sid is fully asleep,' she'd said, her hand stilling his.

Robin had lain back, her presence in his bed, in his home, where Ruth and Sid had begun spending the weekends, was enough.

'Do you hate it?' he'd whispered.

'Hate what?'

'The domesticity. Colm and Helen, the fishpond, the gazebo.'

'I could live without the ornamental pagoda.'

They lay in silence.

'Thank you.'

'For what, Robin?'

'For being here. You and Sid.'

'I didn't think you'd want us in your life.'

'I never stopped wanting you in my life,' Robin had said. 'Ever.' And astonishingly, and for the first time in twenty years, more, he had felt tears on his face, and in the stillness he had turned away before Ruth could see him cry.

'Stay,' Robin had said to her the following morning. Ruth was sitting on the kitchen floor, with Sid, in his Teletubbies pyjamas, facing her across her lap.

'Don't go back down to your mother's. Stay.'

Sid was opening Ruth's mouth, posting Lego inside and closing it again.

'Stay?' she'd asked, gently spitting a yellow brick into her cupped hand.

'Live with me. Marry me. Whatever you like. Just stay.'

Later that afternoon, eye to eye with a young falcon loosely chained to a perch, Ruth had turned to Robin and, looking levelly at him, had mouthed the word 'yes', and Robin knew that had they been alone in this cold outhouse they would have made love against the mildewed walls.

'Thank you,' Robin had mouthed back, and Ruth had looked away to where the falcon handler was pointing at a baby chick in his hand, its neck lolling like a drunk.

At dinner the night before, Helen had presented Robin and Ruth with a gift voucher to visit the raptor sanctuary. She'd won it, she said, in a raffle in aid of the tennis club.

'Aid? For the tennis club? In the name of Jaysus,' Colm had said, sighing through a mouthful of creamy chicken curry.

'That's not the point,' Helen had replied. 'I don't like birds, and neither does Erin. Take it, Robin, I insist.'

Robin had held Sid as the handler whistled for the falcon to leave its perch. He'd felt the child struggle to get down from his arms, heard his rapid, open-mouthed breathing, felt his heart accelerate as the bird landed on the trainer's other gloved hand and swiped at the chick with its beak.

'The chicks are gassed,' the handler, a pragmatic Dutchman, had told them in loud tones of honky-tonk practicality. 'Three hundred at a time. It's more humane that way.'

'Not if you're a chick,' Robin had said quietly, lowering Sid to the ground.

Politely turning down the opportunity to examine the larder of chick corpses and grateful that the feeding demonstration was over, they had thanked the Dutchman and left, strapping Sid into the car seat in the back of Robin's car, the seat that Helen had given Robin on the first weekend that Ruth had come to stay with the toddler in tow. ('I insist. I never use it. It's a spare. Take it, Robin, I insist.')

Driving home through long lines of motorway traffic, Ruth and Robin had talked quietly, while Sid slept, about the practicalities of the move.

'It's all possible,' Robin had assured her. 'What's the worst that can happen?'

Nearing home, they'd stopped to get diesel, Ruth going into the service-station shop to buy something for dinner while Robin filled the tank. We're like normal people, Robin thought, looking through the window at Sid's sweet sleeping face and at Ruth wandering the shop's scant aisles.

'We mustn't forget to thank Helen for the voucher to that awful place,' Ruth had said, getting back in the car with a plastic-wrapped chicken.

'Shit,' she said, looking down at the headless bird in her lap. 'I should have got the frozen fish.'

'I don't want to eat the birdie,' Sid had said from the back seat. 'It's too sad.'

There was happiness, Robin considered, in the early years making their life together, in their routines, pushing their bikes out on to the long road in the mornings, Robin cycling to the city-centre school where he taught, Ruth dropping Sid to his playgroup and then going on to the framer's where she'd found a place to continue her apprenticeship. Every day spent with Sid erased Robin's fears that somehow he wouldn't be a good enough father. Father? What did the word even mean? He had no template, no map. 'So what?' Ruth said. 'Love him like you were loved.' And so he did.

Sid was four, almost five, when Ruth miscarried. It was high summer. They'd been on the beach, Robin swimming, Sid burying Ruth in the sand.

'Help me,' she'd said, smiling, when Robin came out of the water. He'd thought she wanted him to pull her from the sand. 'Help me,' she had said again, and as his long shadow fell over her mummified form, he'd seen that she wasn't smiling at all.

That night, when he'd been putting Sid to bed, the boy had reached across the sheets for Robin, who was sitting up in the bed with his back to the wall. Robin had put down the book he'd been reading and held the child close to his chest.

'Where is she gone?' Sid had asked.

'She's in the hospital. Remember?'

'Why?'

'Because she had a pain that she needed the doctor to mend. And tomorrow, when she's feeling better, we can pick her up and drive her home.'

'Is the other little boy in the hospital too?'

Robin had hesitated.

'What other little boy, Sid?'

'The little boy inside her.'

'I didn't know that you knew about that.'

'You said I'd be five when the other boy would be born.'

Robin thought back to a conversation they'd had in the car when they thought Sid was sleeping. They'd just discovered that Ruth was carrying a boy, and they'd begun to imagine their life with the two little boys, and Robin had felt exhilarated and terrified and full of gratitude for this new dispensation.

Sid's pyjamaed leg cupped the duvet. Robin had stroked the boy's small back, his silky hair. 'I'm sorry, Sid, that baby wasn't well enough to be born. But he's asleep now and he's peaceful and he's OK.'

'Where is he asleep?'

Robin hadn't trusted himself to speak, and even if he could, he didn't know how to answer. Sid had broken the silence.

'Joachim in my class has three mothers. That's too many mothers to have.'

'Joachim has three mothers?'

'When Joachim was born the doctor had to cut one of his mothers in half to take him out.'

'That's pretty unusual, Sid.'

'The two halves grew legs and arms and a head, and turned into two mothers.'

'I've met Joachim's mothers, Sid. They seemed fine.'

'Well, if you cut a worm in half you get two worms.'

'Worms aren't people, Sid.'

'They might think they're people.'

Robin had kissed Sid's head. They lay together in silence until Robin thought Sid was finally asleep. Moving slowly so as not to wake him, Robin stood.

'I think the other boy is in heaven,' Sid had whispered. 'Granny Lennon said my granddad is there fixing God's lawnmowers.'

'Did she?'

'There's a lot of grass in heaven, Robin. An awful, awful lot. When the little boy is bigger he can play football on it.'

'I love you, Sid.'

Robin turned off the child's bedside lamp. It was late, beyond the curtains the night had barely thought of darkening.

EIGHT

London, December 1995

December: a month of relentless cold and almost permanent dark, and orange street light washing over wet pavements. Nobody wanted to look at the thin boys sitting under the arches, dog chains gripped in tattooed fists. Nobody wanted to be burdened with sympathy at rush hour on a freezing December Thursday. Walking towards Camden Town, Robin glanced down at a bed of corrugated-cardboard wadding where one of the homeless boys sat. He smelt dog and piss and, hating himself for the pointless grandiosity of the gesture, put his hands in the pockets of his jeans, found a couple of quid and bent down to give the coins to the boy. The dog bared its teeth, maybe in thanks. The boy said nothing, just looked at the hard, cold money. Robin was straightening up when the boy asked for his coat. You want my coat, Robin thought, walking away, my almost brand-new wool gaberdine coat? My almost brand-new wool gaberdine coat that keeps me warm and dry, that my girlfriend, Vicky, who loves me, gave me? My almost brand-new wool gaberdine coat that I detest? You must be fucking joking.

Like a mechanical thing, like a man made of nuts and bolts, Robin turned and retraced his steps. He felt the warmth leave his body, he could almost see its spectre evaporate as the coat transferred to its new owner and hung itself around the boy's thin shoulders. Robin didn't look back. The rain soaking his grey sweater, plastering his jeans to his legs, he looked up at the saturated London sky and it was as if the street lights were tall, beneficent beings, illuminating the city with their tiny sparks.

Vicky was waiting for Robin in the sushi bar, her briefcase on the floor beside her chair.

'Where's your coat?' she asked as soon as Robin approached the table.

Robin saw that she looked tired. He thought of all the legal work packed into her case, the stern words she had written and rewritten to protect other people's money, each crafted paragraph a credit to her professionalism.

'Your coat, Robin, where's your coat?'

Sitting down, he thought of the thoroughly excellent education she had ploughed through in order to be trusted with all that money in the first place. He thought of her diligence and ambition, her unflinching belief in the market, in the solid assumptions that furnished her world – the absolute necessity of insulating oneself from the rain apparently being one of them.

'Your coat, Robin? Did you walk here without your coat?'

He remembered the rosettes glued around the mirror in her girlhood bedroom in Berkshire – Thatcham gymkhana runner-up, three years running. He remembered her grown-up face in the glass, he remembered her fear and pleasure as they fucked in front of it, her hand, when she reached back to him, knocking over a porcelain piggybank while, downstairs in the warm kitchen, her mother tested the temperature of the beef.

'You're completely soaked, Robin. Where's your coat?'

'Vicky . . .'

He thought about her very specific generosity to him: barbells and a bicycle helmet. Once he had bought her a hand-turned wooden box, cylindrical, with a lid. 'What's it for?' she'd asked. He thought hard about his wool gaberdine coat, the coat she liked so much, with the tortoiseshell buttons and the silky lining. 'Now!' she'd said when she buttoned him into it. 'Now you look like someone!' And when he still couldn't manage to give a fuck about giving it away, he decided to lie.

'I lost it.'

'That coat cost three hundred pounds! What do you mean, you lost it?'

'I didn't lose it. I left it somewhere.'

'Well, which? Did you lose it or didn't you?'

'No.'

'No what?'

'No, I didn't lose it.'

'You're all wet, Robin!'

'It's raining.'

Robin and Vicky met in the same Japanese restaurant every Thursday evening. Vicky didn't have time for lunch on Thursday, any day really, and she looked forward to their Thursday-evening early bird all week. (The phrase 'early bird' made Robin feel queasy, though he was never sure why.) Vicky liked to make plans for their future on their shared Thursday evenings, and for some months now she had been urging Robin to give up his flat and move into hers in Kentish Town so that they could save for a place of their own.

'We're throwing good money after bad,' Vicky declared now, finally reassured that the coat would be gracing Robin's back forthwith. 'Dead money,' she added, her tongue flicking out to retrieve a globule of wasabi paste on the end of her chopstick.

Robin put down his own chopsticks and lifted up the roll of raw fish and wet rice with his fingers. He could only eat sushi if he didn't have to think about it too much, and the longer he arsed around with chopsticks the less likely he was to go through with the whole mastication bit. He'd suggested to Vicky, after their second visit to the sushi bar, that they might try the Thai restaurant next door, where the menu was firmly orientated towards cooked things in batter, but Vicky had an allergy to monosodium glutamate, an invisible ingredient that she could spot at a hundred paces.

'Robin?'

'What?'

'I said we're throwing good money after bad.'

'I like my flat,' Robin replied, surprised at how easy it was, having lied about the coat, to tell the truth about his living arrangements. Vicky, about to dip a bright pink shrimp into a puddle of soy sauce, moved with terrifying rapidity towards outrage.

'Why are you trying to upset me, Robin? What's liking your flat got to do with our future?'

Her tone was in danger of alerting the attention of the establishment's other perspicacious diners, who'd all be home in time for the news safe in the knowledge that they'd bagged a fucking bargain.

He hadn't meant to upset her; anything but. Navigating the swampland of Vicky's tears was a highly developed skill, and he was especially cautious in restaurants where her potentiality for weeping seemed to peak.

Watching Vicky's mouth open and close, and aware that her words were in danger of flooding the table, Robin wondered if maybe he should retract. Recant. Just take her up on her offer. Whatever the financial benefit of a shared rent, there were, after all, other pluses to consider too, not least her indisputably generous posterior, her work ethic and her experimental quiches. And, more importantly right now, if he could just bring himself to say 'yes, thank you, I'll move in tomorrow', they could finish their meal without drama and leave quietly.

'Do you love me, Robin?'

'Do I love you?'

Robin felt oddly disconnected, his thoughts hitting each other without a buffer. He felt around blindly for his usual protections – circumspection and deliberation – but his mind felt raw, stripped back. He didn't know why he'd given away his coat.

'Robin?'

He needed to get a grip. Normally he wouldn't have allowed even a modicum of uncomfortable truth to seep out into the cathedral quiet of the early-evening sushi bar, especially when Vicky still had a dish of wilting seaweed to negotiate.

'How is your shrimp, Vicky?'

'I'm getting very tired of your ambivalence, Robin.'

Ambivalence! There it was again. They were back on safer ground. Vicky presided over a personal library of popular psychology. Robin had spent many Saturday mornings lying in her plump bed staring down the long row of pastel-coloured self-help paperbacks that sat spine to spine along her window-sill, the collection disarmingly bookended by plaster effigies of Eeyore and Pooh. 'Ambivalence' was the word Vicky had settled on to describe Robin's generally less than adequate responses to most of her suggestions (skiing with her college mates, Christmas with her parents and their two flatulent Labradors, parenthood).

Ambivalence. Funny, every time he tried to remember the word he forgot it again. Presumably Vicky would say he was ambivalent about ambivalence.

'Robin?'

Was it only this morning that Ruth had stood in front of him and looked up at the sleet falling in the schoolyard? It felt like a lifetime ago. She'd looked exhausted; exhausted and shaken. And Robin had brought her into the staffroom and insisted that Veronica phone a taxi to take Ruth back to Joseph's flat. She'd looked ill, papery and ill. He'd struggled to concentrate on his classes all day. When, during last period, Lai, a student he admired, had interrupted their reading of Emily Dickinson to ask where everyone in the class wanted their ashes scattered, he'd been grateful to sit back and let the discussion she'd initiated wind down the clock.

'Robin? Are you listening to me?'

Mainly he tried not to think about Ruth at all; sometimes he succeeded. Mainly he told himself that she was just another of Joseph's girlfriends. Ruth did not haunt his sleep. That did not happen.

'We talked about cremation in class today. Lai asked everyone where they wanted their ashes scattered.'

'Robin, I'm asking you a question.'

'I told the class that I wanted my ashes scattered on the Long Strand. I lost my virginity on that beach. Did I ever tell you? It was a significant moment in my life.'

'And am I significant in your life, Robin?'

There was half a tomato on his dish, carved into the shape of a swan. He wondered if someone actually came into work to sit at a stainless-steel table and carve tomato swans. Maybe they bought them in from some kind of vegetable-origami-swan provider.

'Robin?'

'Yes, Vicky?'

'I said why not have your ashes buried in our beautiful garden, Robin.'

Vicky was whispering, her chin dimpling with grief. Robin knew the signs; he should backtrack, fast.

'We don't have a beautiful garden, Vicky.'

That was close to provocation. That *was* provocation.

'And if you don't want to move in with me and save up for a home together, we never will.'

Blinking back her tears, she looked around for the waiter. She was going to ask for a doggy bag for his damp sushi.

'No.'

'Sorry?'

'You asked me if I love you, and in some ways I do.'

Robin's heart was pounding. He could see the proprietor approach their table. Robin put his hand up to stop him moving any closer.

'I'm sorry that you thought I was someone I'm not. But the truth is that I don't love you, Vicky. Not the way you should be loved.'

He couldn't be entirely sure whether he was saying the words aloud or just thinking them. When she went completely white, he knew he had articulated a truth he had carried for far too long.

'I'm sorry, truly sorry.'

She didn't move, didn't speak, didn't cry.

Robin decapitated the blood-red swan with one of his unused chopsticks. The proprietor, having been hovering mid-stride, finally came to the table, and Robin asked for the bill. Someone seemed to have turned down the sound on the world. Robin felt as if he were swimming underwater.

They sat in silence until the bill came. Returning his card to his wallet, he stood and helped Vicky into her coat, then he picked up her bag and guided her towards the exit, the proprietor smiling encouragingly at them as they left.

'Next week, yes? Merry Christmas!'

Outside, the rain was returning to sleet. Robin noticed that the bookshop across the road was still open. He was freezing. If he hadn't just fucked over his own life he could have walked up the road to Vicky's warm flat and made hot chocolate while she slipped into her teddy-bear pyjamas.

He took her hand in his and they crossed the icy street together. She still hadn't spoken. On the other side, he turned her towards him; her face was a plate of tears, round and wet and pale.

'I'm sorry. I'm so sorry.'

He held her, smelt her hair, damp and lemony. He traced his thumbs over the pillowy line of her cheeks and jaw. He kissed her mouth, her tender, competent mouth. Vicky remained entirely still.

'Goodbye, Robin,' she said, so quietly that he almost couldn't hear her words.

He watched her walk away, grateful for her restraint. He watched until she turned off the main road, the big bag in her raw hand, to walk back to her empty flat.

In the hip little bookshop a few minutes later, a woman approached Robin and told him that she was a writer. Robin was grateful for the distraction, pleased to have a reason to return the novel he'd been holding in his freezing hands, and was unable to focus on or read a word of, to the shelf.

'Wonderful book,' the writer said.

'Yeah?'

Robin looked at the cover. 'Two soulmates who have met too late,' the blurb helpfully explained.

'It's a love story, simultaneously uplifting and soul-destroying.'

'Brilliant.'

Robin, embarrassed now to put the book back on the shelf, weighed it in his hand as if it was a bag of rice, as if he could tell to the gram the quality of the fiction.

'Brilliant,' he said again.

The writer was about to give a reading from a poetry collection she'd written about growing up on a farm. 'Come and hear my story,' she said, and although he realized that she was simply drumming up an audience for her event, he was flattered. Fuck it, he was elated. The writer, Robin observed, had a lazy eye, the pupil slinking towards the corner of her nose in a way that suggested intimacy. Intimacy? He should go home. He was feeling worryingly rash.

The writer was telling him her name; it evaporated on the air before he had time to catch it.

'That sounds . . . brilliant,' Robin lied. He couldn't think of a less alluring subject for a poetry collection, or any other kind of collection, than farming life, which was hard and relentless and which he had known was not for him since he was knee-high to a Holstein Friesian. But Laura? Leah? had made her way across the shop specifically to ask him to attend her reading.

'Well?'

She looked at him with her disconcerting gaze. He wasn't about to say no.

'Absolutely.'

'And your name is?'

'Robin,' Robin replied, as smoothly as the name allowed.

'Well, Robin, there's a free glass of just about drinkable wine after, if you'd like to hang around.'

'And your book is about farming?' Robin asked brightly. Too brightly.

'Growing up on a farm,' the writer corrected him, her fallen eye twitching slightly.

Climbing the bookshop stairs to hear Lilly?/Lana? read, Robin decided that from now on he would, at the very least, tell himself the truth. There were choices to be made. He was free. He was a free man. He thought about Vicky's sorrow and hated himself, hated his cowardice. He should have had the courage to leave long before. He stood at the back of a narrow upstairs room with a handful of apparently enthusiastic listeners while the declamatory writer read an extremely long poem about the death of an ancient ewe called Mother, a metaphor, Robin presumed, for something he had entirely failed to grasp. When the writer (Libby?) stopped reading, Robin clapped along with everyone else, grateful to have something to do after all the stillness. And when the bookshop owner offered Robin a plastic glass of wine and said something meaningful about the cunning bitterness of the breast, Robin nodded solemnly and swallowed fast.

He made his way to a small table at the front of the room where the writer was signing copies of her oeuvre. He picked one up; her name was on the cover. Alison. Brilliant – he was deaf as well as selfish and reckless.

'So?' Alison asked him as she autographed his purchase.

'So that was, that was . . . moving, really moving,' Robin replied.

'Stay,' the writer commanded, her gaze unfaltering.

When the wine and the people were all gone, he and Alison left the shop and walked across the intersection to the Man in the

Moon. Robin went to the bar to order wine. To his disappointment, a gloomy performance poet called Edwin, whom he hadn't noticed at the reading, had turned up at their table by the time he returned with the two glasses. Shortly afterwards, the gentle bookshop owner also turned up and the night seemed to accelerate. Later, already drunk, Robin asked them all where they wanted their ashes scattered, and the writer told him that she wanted to be turned into some kind of tree pod, which Robin thought was asking quite a lot of whoever survived her, and the performance poet said he wanted to be embalmed and propped up in the British Library, and the bookshop owner said he would simply be buried according to Muslim tradition. Then they all talked about the bestselling novel Robin had been looking at in the bookshop, the love story that everyone except Robin had read, about an architect and a woman temporarily released from domesticity, the two soulmates who met too late. The performance poet said it was nothing more than pinafore porn and the bookshop owner said it was about our need to return to a state of grace. The writer said that the lovers were so much more than fuckable parts; they are lost souls, she asserted. Robin said he didn't know what a soul was, and the writer held his hand under the table and said she would enlighten him.

Having a slash in the gents, propping himself up with one hand against the stained tiles above the urinal, Robin was momentarily sure that when he went outside he would find an empty picnic table under withered baskets and his coat, still holding Ruth's warmth, abandoned on the table's frosted surface.

Robin and the writer were the last to leave the pub, the floor staff letting them out through a side door as the place was already locked up. Hunched against the rain, Robin coatless, they walked through the closed-up city. They walked past tall, shabby houses that looked down on them like disappointed parents. Leaning against some noble pillar, unable to walk much further, Robin told the writer that he wasn't worth following home, and she laughed and told him that she wasn't following him home, he was following her home.

They had sex in her bathroom, cramped up in a mildewed shower.

'Why are you so unhappy?' she asked him, wrapping her strong thigh around him.

He was sitting in the base of the shower, his back against the cold tiles, watching her dry herself with a red towel when he finally answered. 'I miss someone I never had.'

He woke up on a couch, dawn bleeding through the windows. He used the bathroom, saw the red towel on the floor, remembered his half-hearted attempts to make Alison come, his numb fingers, his indifference. He decided to find her, to offer to make amends. In the hallway, he heard chanting and opened what he assumed to be her bedroom door. The glum performance poet was sitting, legs crossed on a rattan mat, next to a low bed where the writer slept, her long, dark hair occluding her half-remembered face.

'Namaste,' Edwin murmured. 'Now you really should fuck off.'

When Robin finally got back to his flat, he was ravenous. The fridge was empty. He considered the two bananas dying on his windowsill, but there was something alien about their slimy purpling skin.

He closed the fridge and was assaulted by the single fridge magnet stuck to the door. It was a gift that Vicky had bought for him to hold up her typed and laminated list of allergies. 'Today is the Beginning of the Rest of Your Life!' the magnet read.

Robin thought about delaying that particular inevitability by going to bed. It was only Friday; he had to be in school in an hour.

From behind the staffroom window Robin watched the children gather up the melting snow and crush it into each other's hair and faces as they swarmed out of the gates. Only Ruth and Ardu remained in the empty schoolyard. As Robin gathered his books together he watched the boy give Ruth something from his bag, saw her kneel to put it in her satchel.

'Are you joining us for a drink later in The Lamb? Season of good cheer and all that?'

One of the Hazels was speaking to him. Chemistry Hazel or Geography Hazel, he could never remember which was which.

'Right, drinks, sorry, thanks but I've got, eh, plans.'

Chemistry/Geography Hazel looked out the window.

'Well, don't let us detain you.'

Robin hunkered down next to Ardu, the snow falling on his denim jacket, which, in his rush to leave the flat that morning, already late for work, was the only thing he could find. The boy was watchful, mistrustful; he listened to Robin tell him about the identical Wisconsin snowflakes with his hand firmly holding Ruth's.

'Twin snowflakes?' the child asked.

'Soulmates,' Robin replied.

After the child and his mother had departed he and Ruth walked slowly down Judd Street together.

'Where's your coat?'

'Don't ask.'

They sat at the table in the window of the Sorrento Cafe. Outside, the streets were softening under the snow, the wrought-iron railings opposite outlined in feathery whiteness.

Warming her hands around her cup, Ruth told Robin that she and Joseph had had some kind of row. Joseph had thrown a mug across the room and she'd gone to work, and when she went home he was gone. He hadn't been back since.

'Did he throw the mug at you?'

'I don't think he'd do that.'

'How long has he been gone?'

'Just a night.'

Joseph, Robin speculated, was in some bar somewhere, nursing old wounds, sketching people's faces in his little black book in return for pints of bitter.

Ruth had searched the studio when he hadn't come home, she told Robin, and she'd found photographs that she didn't think she was supposed to see.

'What photographs?'

They were photographs of Stevie, Ruth said, Polaroid photographs that Joseph must have taken, studies to make his paintings of her.

Robin finished his coffee and put the cup back on the table. He felt so fucking tired. When was the last time he'd slept, he asked himself, and then remembered the writer's cramped couch and waking up under her thin Aztec-inspired blanket.

The photos of Stevie had freaked Ruth out. In the first photograph Stevie was naked, and so slight and insubstantial she seemed to float on the surface of Joseph's deep bath. In the next, she was reflected in his damp-speckled mirror, looking at her own spent body, Joseph behind her, holding the camera. In the last, Stevie was dancing on Joseph's mangled bed. Wild. Pagan.

Ruth looked out of the window, the pastry Robin had bought her untouched on her plate. She looked like a child, Robin thought, young and earnest and afraid of something she thought she saw in the shadows. He wanted to tell her that it didn't matter, it didn't matter what she saw in Joe's cold and inhospitable studio. None of it mattered, not as far as Ruth should be concerned. Joe was only ever going to crave one woman, and that woman was dead. Stevie, for all her spitting and raging, for all her remorse, for all her empty promises and burnt vows, was gone. Stevie was dead.

Robin left her at the table and went to pay the bill. He watched her from the counter, wrapping the uneaten pastry in a napkin and putting it in her pocket.

Refusing Robin's offer to walk with her back to King's Cross to see if Joseph had returned, they stood outside the cafe while Robin unlocked his bike from the railings. Unsure as to how she might react, Robin tentatively suggested that Ruth might like to come back with him to his flat in Chalk Farm.

'I don't know about you but I'm starving,' he said. 'I could cook for us.'

He was surprised when she gratefully agreed. They trailed through the slushy streets, talking about nothing much, about Veronica's horror at having Ruth sully the staffroom the day before, let alone Ruth's effrontery at having Veronica call her a taxi to take her home. They talked about Ardu's growing confidence, about the pictures he made for her, each one more and more elaborate and fantastical.

'I've been giving Ardu things, presents. Don't tell Veronica, I don't think I'm allowed to do that.'

'What have you been giving him?'

'Paints and brushes, the ones that Joseph doesn't use.'

'Sounds all right to me.'

They walked on in companionable silence, Robin and Ruth, the gleaming bicycle helmet slung over the handlebars, and it was almost, Robin thought, as if the intervening months had somehow never happened.

'Helen made me that cake, by the way.'

'What cake?'

'The cake she threatened to make for me after the night we drank all her Absolut. Remember?'

'Kind of.'

'Colm works in a bathroom suppliers near my flat, ran in to him once or twice, next thing Helen was on the doorstep with a Christmas pudding.'

'I think she has a soft spot for you.'

'I was going to give it to Vicky's mother when we went down there for Christmas.' Robin hesitated before continuing. 'Anyway.'

'How is she?'

'Helen? Pissed off. They're going back to Ireland early in the New Year. Colm's starting up on his own.'

'I thought Helen liked London?'

'Colm doesn't think it's a good place to bring up kids.'

'What's that got to do with anything?'

'Helen's pregnant.'

They had reached the supermarket where Robin planned to pick up some food.

'Ruth, are you all right?'

'I'm fine.'

They had stopped walking, Ruth put her hands on the bike to steady herself.

'Are you ill?'

'No, no. I'm just starving.'

Lashing through the fluorescent supermarket while Ruth stayed outside minding the bicycle, Robin threw two fat cellophane-wrapped steaks that looked like a pair of bloodied fists into the basket. Then, on impulse, he fired in a scented candle, and next to the bread and fruit and chocolate and cheese that he collected, he threw in a jar of jam-like stuff that wasn't jam and was meant to be spread on crackers.

Ruth's embarrassed admission that she hadn't any money to contribute to the bill only spurred on his desire to get her anything and everything she might possibly want. He threw in ice cream and wine and a small yellow melon and a net of mandarin oranges and just stopped short of buying a bright red poinsettia in a plastic pot. You can't eat houseplants, he told himself.

He wondered if he should buy her a dozen eggs.

Ruth was gobsmacked by the size of the haul. They had to hang the shopping bags over the handlebars to get it all back to Robin's flat.

The small amount of cash she'd been saving, Ruth had told him outside the shop, had disappeared along with Joseph.

You fucker, Joe, Robin thought, pushing the bike up the hill. You selfish fucker.

Inside Robin's shipshape second-floor flat, he told Ruth to make herself at home and then, feeling like a maiden aunt, he went to put the kettle on and fiddled around with the heat switches to warm the place up. In his neat galley kitchen he made her another cup of coffee and then started on dinner while she wandered around, cupping the warm mug in her hands, putting it down every now and again to examine pieces of Ushi's heavy pottery.

'What's this?' she asked, picking up an awkward piece of ceramic that must have weighed more than a small lamb.

'A pipe-holder,' Robin answered from the kitchen.

'A pipe-holder?' Ruth repeated, carefully putting it back down on the windowsill. 'It's . . . substantial.'

'Yep, and extremely useful if you were a pipe-smoker, I imagine.'

She looked through his CD collection, stacked neatly on Perspex shelves. She chose a Sex Pistols album to listen to, turning it off after a few minutes and replacing it with Annie Lennox.

'You don't like the Sex Pistols?'

'Joseph plays it all the time. Can I look in the other room?'

'Sure.'

After a few minutes he went to find her, standing there in his sparse bedroom. He was suddenly acutely self-conscious and embarrassed by his neatness, by his artily framed photographs of raging seas. He rarely had a visitor here, occasionally Joe, and sometimes Vicky, who had preferred to sleep with him in the prettified softness of her own place.

The last time Joe had been here was a year ago, on the night Stevie died. They'd driven up from Brighton together and had drunk Irish whiskey in front of Robin's muted television, watching a pouting girl band stomp around in glittery hot pants. Joe had stayed on the couch for a week and stayed drunk for a week, finally getting back into Robin's car to drive to Brighton and make the funeral arrangements for Stevie, whose body had just been released. Cause of death asphyxia, the coroner concluded. The toxicology report remained unopened.

Ruth was flicking through the book of poetry that Robin had thrown on the bed that morning.

'I didn't know you liked poetry.'

'I'm not sure if I do.'

'What are the poems about?'

'Farming.'

'Farming?'

'Growing up on a farm.'

'Are they any good?'

'Possibly not. I think they're about mothers. Maybe. Or maybe sheep.'

'That's pretty comprehensive.'

'Dinner is more or less ready, by the way.'

'Are you sure this is OK, Robin?' Ruth asked, putting the book down on his empty bed.

'That you're here?'

'Yes.'

'Well, it's OK with me if it's OK with you, and I don't see anyone else here that might have an opinion.'

'Thank you.'

She hugged him. He could feel her bones through her thin dress. Her hair smelt oily.

'Eat, then sleep.'

Seeing how ravenously she devoured her steak, he gave her half of his as well, claiming sudden-onset vegetarianism. After she'd finished most of the fruit and, finally, when they'd eaten the cheese and crackers (abandoning the savoury jam, which tasted like incense), she pushed her plate away and looked at him across the table.

'Are you pregnant, Ruth?'

'I think maybe I am,' she whispered, covering her face and looking at him through her fingers.

Ruth lay sleeping on his bed, her body segmented by the low pink light of the winter morning seeping through the slatted blinds. Robin, having spent the night on his couch, had been going to ask her if she wanted breakfast, but she looked so peaceful that he retreated from his bedroom again without waking her. He was gently closing the bedroom door when he heard her call.

'Robin?'

'Sorry, I didn't mean to wake you.'

'Stay.'

He lay next to her, conscious of her strangely altered state.

'Big seas,' she said, looking at the photographs on the wall. 'Do you ever think about drowning?'

'I have thought about drowning, yes.'

'My baby is in a big sea now. I am a big sea.'

Robin waited until her breathing slowed and deepened. He brushed a web of hair from her cheek and went back to his berth on the couch. Unable to sleep there either, he made himself a mug of coffee and picked up the poetry book from the floor. He read a couple of lines about the stifling embrace of the mountain and the dry kiss of the berry and then he put the book down again and stood and looked out of his windows at the parked cars below and the neat row of communal bins that served his block. It was less interesting to read verses written by someone you'd had sex with in a mildewed shower than it should have been, the words blurring into images of the greenish paste between the shower tiles and of the poet's lovely brown back and the way the water suddenly ran stone-cold.

Ruth was pregnant. She was lost to him.

The next poem concerned rage and flax, and Robin was struggling. The truth was actually so ordinary, Robin considered, that it hardly bore thinking about. He was in love with a woman who was in love with someone else. He was in love with a woman carrying a child who was not his. Joe's lover. Joe's child.

Robin wanted Ruth to wake up. He wanted her to read the poems and tell him what he was failing to understand. He wanted to ask Ruth if there was any possibility of ignoring the ordinary truth and making it less than ordinary. Couldn't she just stay here, in his bed, in his home? He wanted to tell Ruth that he would relinquish it all, all of the unknown future, to take care of her here in his second-floor Chalk Farm maisonette.

Robin dressed and left the flat, returning twenty minutes later with a chicken to roast. Ruth was still sleeping. He put the food in the fridge and lay down again on the couch. He must have finally drifted off because when he awoke the lush morning sky had been entirely absorbed by ordinary day. Ruth was up and washed and dressed and wearing his old blue sweater over her flimsy dress, and Robin thought that she had never looked so beautiful. She had lit the scented candle and was sitting on the floor, looking at the small leather photograph album Vicky had bought him last Christmas.

'Which one are you looking at?' Robin asked.

She handed Robin the album. The photograph was of Joe and Robin on the Long Strand. It had been taken, probably by Stevie, during that summer they first met, when Robin was thirteen and Joe almost a year older. In the photograph, Robin, sunburnt and lanky and holding a colourful bodyboard, was standing next to Joe, who was small and dark and dressed in a droopy sweater and baggy jeans. Joe was looking at the camera with contempt, while Robin almost managed a nervy smile.

'The day we met,' Robin said, handing the album back to Ruth.

'Tell me,' she asked, following Robin into the kitchen and sitting up on the counter while he took the bird out of the fridge and prepared to roast it, packing butter under its pink-veined skin.

'Tell me,' she asked again, leaning back against the smooth tiled surface.

When Robin had first encountered Joe, lying flat out under a watery sun on an almost empty beach, lying, to be precise, on a strip of pink cotton, a scarf or towel or something that Robin couldn't quite make out, Joe hadn't been alone. And if Robin was to be entirely honest about it, if he was to be entirely accurate about it, it wasn't Joe he first noticed at all; it was Joe's mother, Stevie.

Belting along on his bicycle on the marram-grass track over Long Strand, it had been a glimpse of her through the dunes that halted him. A shot of pink and the shape of her, the images not making sense, had made him brake hard to see if what he thought he'd seen was real.

She *was* real. Bleached hair knotted at her neck, legs akimbo on the pink fabric, she'd been sitting up, her back to the sea. She must have been reading; she was bending over, blonde head bowed, breasts bare, small and brown and hanging down in front of her like ice-cream cones.

Robin had imagined his mouth on those melting breasts, and the thought bloomed large and vivid, obliterating the familiar horizon, and he'd flung himself and his bicycle off the track and into the dunes, pushing his crotch into the sand and closing his eyes.

When he'd opened them again, he'd seen the woman stand up and turn to look at the water. A piece of greenish-white cloth around her waist floated and lifted in the breeze. Her hips were thin, shank-like; she reminded Robin of a foal. One hand blocking the sun, she'd lifted the other and waved to a swimming man, who plunged towards the shore and walked out of the water. Robin had watched the man put his arms around the woman, even though she squirmed away, and Robin could hear her yelps and laughter when the water, streaming from the man's body, bit into hers.

As Robin looked on through the dry grasses, the man had picked the woman up and carried her back to the scarf and put her down again, then stood over her, his lanky shadow falling across her. That was when Robin noticed the boy, a black-haired boy, wrapped up in layers of clothes despite it being the only almost hot day so far in a squally, wet summer. The boy was wearing a jumper and jeans, and he was barefoot. Robin saw his pale feet pushing in and out of the sand, pedalling to nowhere.

Robin had watched as the boy stood up and walked towards the sea, and kept watching as he wandered along the beach and then turned back towards the dunes, keeping a distance between himself and the woman on the pink rug and the wet man who had lain down beside her. Robin had stopped watching the boy then, and watched the woman instead. The woman was lying alongside the man, propped up on her elbow, her breasts disappearing right into his side. She was so close to him you couldn't tell skin from skin, and she was leaning into him, picking something out of his hair, which was drying now to grey.

'Do you want to fuck my mother?'

Robin had turned. The boy was beside him, brushing dry sand off the bottom of his jeans. The boy's words were startling, astounding even, but he had spoken softly and with quite a bit of disinterest for such an incendiary enquiry.

'What mother?'

'My mother,' the boy had replied. 'The one you're staring at.'

Robin had not for one split second considered the possibility that the woman with the brown breasts could be anyone's mother, let alone the mother of the boy now standing next to him.

'Is that your mother?' Robin had asked.

The mothers Robin knew (and all his friends seemed to have one) were entirely unlike the one on this beach. His friends' mothers had mother faces, mouths that opened and closed in butcher's shops and eyes that squinted on the sidelines.

'Well, do you?'

'What?'

'Want to do it to her?'

'No. I don't.'

'Everyone else does,' the boy had said, and they'd both looked down on to the beach, where the woman who was the boy's mother was pecking at the man's sandy mouth like a gannet.

'Is he your dad?' Robin had asked.

'You must be joking.'

The boy had looked down at the couple on the beach and then turned back to Robin and held out his hand.

'My name is Joey Kazargazof,' the boy had said. 'I'm half Russian. You can call me Joe.'

It was the first time Robin remembered shaking hands with anyone.

Robin had a bodyboard tied to his bicycle. It wasn't a proper bodyboard; it was short and had a picture of a mermaid on it. His mother had bought it for two pounds at the Friday market.

'It's a girl's board,' Robin had said when she brought it home.

'There's no such thing,' his mother had replied. 'Is there a boy's sea and a girl's sea? Is there a boy's moon and a girl's sun? No. It's a board. Use it, or give it to someone who will.'

'Yeah, give it to some girl,' Robin had muttered, attaching it to the back of his bike with a manly bungee cord.

Robin and the boy had taken the board down to the water, Joe pushing Robin's bicycle all the way along the beach, almost to the tide mark, even though Robin had told him it was safe to leave it in the dunes.

Joe hadn't gone into the water. Instead, he'd kept watch for sharks from the shore. Robin had paddled out, lying face down on the board, and looked at the horizon. But the waves weren't really waves that day, and there was a quietness in the bay that was disappointing, as if the sea was preoccupied with something else, so Robin had just messed around a bit, and every now and again, when the boy shouted 'Waaatch ouuuuut!' in an accent that didn't sound one bit Russian, Robin pretended to drown, one leg sticking up in the water like a flagpole, while an imaginary shark pulled chunks of him down to the depths.

'You want to come in?' Robin had shouted towards the shore, gesturing at the board. But the boy shook his head and hunched into his jumper, so Robin got out, and when his goosepimples had faded he'd seen that, despite the clouds, the sun had burnt through the chalky sunblock his mother always insisted on slathering over him. His arms were red, his throat was dry and his stomach was empty.

'I'm going home,' Robin had told the boy, and the boy just shrugged, so they walked the bicycle and board back along the beach. But before they reached the path to the dunes, Robin saw the woman walking towards them. She was wearing a floaty top over her breasts and blue beads around her neck, and she was holding a tiny cigarette and smiling as if the sight of the two of them was the best thing she could ever have hoped to see.

'Joey!' she'd called. 'Introduce me to your friend.'

'What's your name?' Joe had asked.

'Robin.'

'That's shit.'

'I know.'

'He's Robin.'

'Hi, Robin. I'm Stevie.'

She'd held out her hand, and her fingers were sandy and had silver rings on them that were wider than her knuckles. And for the second time in his life, and all in a matter of hours, Robin shook someone's hand. He reckoned it must be an English thing, because no Irish person had ever shaken his hand, and he knew three separate Dutch people who had never shaken his hand, and his mother had a friend from Wales who visited every Christmas and had never shaken his hand, and there was a boy in his class who was born in Tunisia and had never shaken his hand.

'Guess what, Joey,' Stevie had said. 'Adrian is bringing us back to his castle for supper under the stars.'

'That's because Adrian's castle doesn't have a roof,' Joe had replied.

'Bring your friend. It'll stop you moping around all night being miserable.'

Hours and hours and hours of inky night came and went, and Adrian's supper under the stars still hadn't materialized. The two boys had wandered all around the ruins of Castlefreke, a place Robin knew well from blackberrying with his mother in autumn among the crumbling walls. The boys had amused themselves by terrifying each other with sightings of giant rats and headless ghosts and old women with babies' limbs hanging from their teeth. They'd read the dull graffiti on the half-burnt walls, all the scrawled names loving and hating each other in equal measure, and finally, crouched in a urine-scented corner of the old keep, they'd told each other about the weirdest things they'd ever seen in their entire lives.

'A dead shark,' Robin had said, 'washed up on Inchydoney beach, its belly all bloated and crawling with maggots. What's the weirdest thing *you've* ever seen?'

Joe had thought about the question for so long that Robin wondered if he'd forgotten it.

'I have to go home now anyway,' Robin had said eventually.

'A boy,' Joe had declared, 'sitting on the window ledge of a high-up window and all the people inside; a boy sitting way up over the street while, inside, there was a party.'

They'd wandered back to the campfire, to Adrian and Stevie huddling around the dying flames.

'There you are, darlings! Have you been having the most fantastic fun?'

Stevie's mouth had worked hard to make the words stand up straight. Adrian raised his bottle in salute.

'Two fine young men,' he'd spat, pushing back his long grey hair and appraising the two boys standing loosely in front of them. 'Two young gentlemen with your whole lives ahead of you. Am I right?'

Scuffing their runners in the damp and the ash, the boys hadn't answered. Adrian's voice dropped; he sounded more English than Stevie, even though his family owned this Irish castle.

'When I was your age I understood pain,' he'd said. 'If you don't understand pain, you understand nothing.'

'Is this really your castle?' Robin had asked, because he wanted to know.

Adrian threw back his head and laughed. Robin could see where his teeth were missing.

'It fucking well should be.'

Robin was starving. Ushi had said he had to be home by ten o'clock, no later. And it was later now, much much later.

'What do you see when you look at me? Tell me.' Adrian was talking to Robin. 'Look at me, you, blond boy, look at me and tell me what you see.'

Robin hadn't answered. He'd only wanted to know about the castle.

'He sees a pisshead,' Joe had replied calmly. 'What else do you think he'd see?'

Robin and Joe had walked back to Popes Cove along the marram track, silver and blue under the moonlight.

'Did the boy you saw sitting outside the high-up window fall?'

'Nah. He didn't fall. He was never going to fall. He was just pulled back inside and given an ice cream.'

Ushi had been waiting by the cottage door with a cigarette in her hand.

'Do you smoke?' Robin had asked her.

'Again and now,' Ushi had answered, and Robin saw that she was relieved and that her relief was bigger than her anger with him for being late.

'I'm sorry I'm late. This is Joe.'

'I'm very glad to see you both,' Ushi had replied, stubbing out her cigarette in a tub of rosemary. They went inside and ate and ate.

'Can Joe stay?' Robin had asked, while Ushi made chamomile tea. 'Adrian's castle doesn't have a roof.'

RUTH WAS DOZING on the couch, Robin reading, the chicken roasting in the oven, when the phone rang. It was dark outside, the living room infused with the scent of the burning candle.

'Is it Joseph?' Ruth asked, waking immediately, and the hope in her voice hit Robin like a blow.

Robin stood to answer. 'It might be Ushi, I missed her call last night.'

'She's here,' he said, after a moment. 'She's with me.'

He handed Ruth the receiver and went into the kitchen to find a beer, turning on all the lights as he went.

'Joseph,' he heard her whisper. 'Joseph.'

Robin drove her back to King's Cross, the wheels of the car spinning over the ice as he pulled out of the car park.

'Thank you,' she said, as he finally managed to reverse over the impacted snow. 'I was so frightened.'

The traffic was light, London deadened by snow. They drove in silence.

'I'm not going to tell him,' Ruth said.

Robin didn't want to know what she was talking about.

'The baby. I'm not going to tell him yet.'

Robin wished she would just sit there and not speak.

'I think it might be too much for him to handle.'

'Fuck him! Fuck him.'

Robin was shouting. He didn't mean to shout, he didn't know why he was shouting. He never shouted.

'Fuck him. He's a self-obsessed cunt. He always has been and he always will be. Fuck him, Ruth, just fuck him!'

'He's not well!' Ruth was shouting too.

'That's right, he's not well. And you can't fucking cure him.'

'I can take care of him.'

'You don't matter to him, Ruth. I don't matter to him. No one matters to him. There is only his work and the memory of his fucked-up mother. There is only the glorification of his own fucking past. He doesn't want to be well, Ruth. "Well" is too ordinary for Joey Kazargazof. You think you're going to change him, Ruth? You're pissing into the wind.'

'Stop the car, Robin. Let me out. Stop the car. I want to walk!'

Robin dropped the gears and swerved into the pavement, the car skidding on the ice and lurching to a stop inches from a parked van. He was shaking. He could have killed her. Maybe he wanted to kill her. Maybe he wanted to kill her rather than relinquish her.

She was in tears, gripping the seatbelt that was digging into her neck.

'I don't want to see you any more, Robin,' she said quietly. 'I don't want to see you again.'

'Ruth.'

'Don't touch me!'

'Ruth.'

'No!'

'Listen, Ruth.'

'No, you listen. You're angry with me and you're angry with Joseph, and I feel sorry for you, Robin, really I do, because I know what it is to be lonely. I know what that's like. I love him, Robin. Nothing you can say is going to change that.'

She picked up her satchel and opened the door.

'Maybe it's better if we're not part of each other's lives any more. Robin? Robin?'

'I heard you.'

'Goodbye, Robin.'

It was the second time he'd been told goodbye in two days. He'd told the truth and finally alienated everyone. Robin watched her walk away, watched as she broke into a run towards the lights on Euston Road, watched until she was obliterated by the falling snow.

Robin turfed the burnt chicken into the bin and sat hunched over the photograph album he so rarely looked at, stopping at a photograph of himself and Joe taken the summer after he'd finished school. They had been guests at a local wedding, or at least, Robin was a guest at a local wedding and Joe had tagged along.

That summer, Joe, dark and delicate, with his beryl-blue eyes, had been at the height of his iridescent boyish beauty, while Robin, endlessly pale, endlessly self-conscious, was still searching his body for a place to settle.

Robin had done all right in his exams. When the letter arrived, offering him a place at university in the city, Ushi had made a celebratory banana bread and given him twenty quid. Robin, angrily weary with her lack of worldliness, defeated by her insouciance, had sat opposite her staring at the moist bread, the letter of acceptance from the university lying between them on the scoured table.

'You're not happy,' Ushi had said, watching him push the banana bread around his plate. Her eyes were round and sad, her strong teeth bit her bottom lip. She sometimes reminded Robin of a cartoon. Happy Ushi. Sad Ushi. His mother's face, like his mother's art, held no ambiguity. What you saw was what you got. Big, strong pot; big, sad mother.

He'd wanted to ask her if she really thought he was going to survive life outside the cottage with a hand-knitted tank top and a Tupperware box full of home-made granola bars, dense enough to hold up a crumbling coliseum. Night after night he'd lain in his single bed wondering when his life would begin, and now that there was a chink of light, a possibility of escape, he realized that his mother's childlike trust that the universe would provide was going to scupper his chances of independence.

'I have good news,' Ushi had said brightly.

'Yeah?'

'Yes, indeed. Joe telephoned while you were sleeping. He has been given a scholarship to go to art school. He's coming to stay. He'll be on the evening bus, we can celebrate his good news!'

Robin had pushed his chair back from the table with as much force as he could and gone outside, banging the door behind him. The tinkling outrage of his mother's startled wind chimes followed him all the way down to the beach.

Robin and Joe had applauded the best man and danced with the bridesmaids and eaten chicken and chips in a basket and swallowed as much free drink as the barman was prepared to give them, and then they had left the wedding party and gone to smoke a joint on the wet sand of the Long Strand, with two bottles of vodka that Joe had pilfered from the stores.

On the beach, Robin had reached into his jacket pocket for a cigarette and skins and found instead a piece of wedding cake, wrapped in a paper napkin embossed with the names of the bride and groom.

'That is a halogen moon,' Joe had said, unscrewing one of the bottle tops and lying on his back on the sand. It was a statement that Robin distrusted.

'I've no skins,' Robin had said.

'Buy some.'

'I've no money.'

Robin had broken the cake in half and handed some to Joe. Behind them, in the new hotel that had sprung out of the soft-gummed earth above the shore, the wedding they had so recently departed continued. If Robin and Joe had been sober or interested enough to stand up and watch, they might have seen the bride and groom and the lilac-gowned bridesmaids and all the happy couple's upholstered aunts and uncles and first and second cousins do the chain-dance around the hotel's glass-panelled ballroom.

'If you'd put that wedding cake under your pillow instead of eating it, you'd have dreamt of the person you're going to marry.'

'Who told you that?'

'Can't remember. Someone's aunt at the wedding. I think her name was Bendy Mary. We did the chicken dance together. Unfortunately.'

'I'm not going to marry anyone.'

'Of course you will, Robin, you're reliable and reasonable and you know how to add, subtract, multiply and divide and you can spell. People who can spell always marry someone.'

Una McClafferty was sitting on the low stone wall that separated the beach from the road. Robin could have sworn she hadn't been there a second ago.

'Hello, Una. Where did you come from?'

'Hello, Una,' Joe repeated. 'You don't have any skins, do you?'

'I don't smoke, Joey. It's bad for my health.'

'Una, ask Robin to spell something.'

'Spell "marijuana", Robin.'

'No.'

Una had come and sat between them, her lilac bridesmaid dress darkening in the damp sand. She had a fat joint and a lighter tucked into her shot-silk bodice. She lit up, and Robin passed along the bottle.

'Do you ever think about me, Joey, when you're back in London?' Una had asked, the vodka bottle hovering around her glossy mouth.

'I think about you often, Una,' Joe had said, exhaling and passing the joint on to Robin.

'I think you're a liar, Joey Kazargazof,' Una had said, and drank by the neck.

Summer after summer since they were thirteen, Una had darted around Joe like a jack snipe while Robin watched from the sidelines.

'Robin thinks about you night and day, Una.'

'Do ya, Robin?'

'No I don't. Fuck off, Joe.'

'Robin is a virgin,' Joe had said, and Robin felt himself disintegrate.

'You're not, Robin, are you?'

'Course I'm not.'

'He wanted to fuck my mother when he was twelve and he still hasn't managed to do anything.'

'Is that right, Robin?'

'No, it fucking isn't.'

'It's a cruel world out there, I used to want to crawl back inside my mother too.'

'You're fucked up,' Robin had spluttered, the raw vodka burning his throat.

'What kind of thing is that to say, Joey, about your own mam?'

'I wanted to live inside her, so that I'd never lose her. I wanted to get back into her womb and read the graffiti of her unborn children by the light of a halogen moon.'

'Where is she anyway?' Robin had asked, hoping to change the subject of his virginity.

'Stevie? Following a donkey's arse around India, apparently.'

Una had taken off her satin shoes. Her feet were white under the moonlight.

'Are you really a virgin, Robin?' she'd asked, reaching over and laying her hand on his belt.

'I don't want you feeling sorry for me,' he'd said, his face flushing.

Her lilac breasts swung in his direction.

'Do you fancy me, Robin?'

'He's fancied you since he was ten.'

'Has he now? Well, I tell you something, Robin, you're looking gorgeous tonight in that jacket and the hair and everything.'

Robin had wanted to go back up to the hotel. He'd been enjoying the party; it hadn't been his idea to leave. There were going to be sandwiches. As soon as he could feel his legs again he was going to stand up and go back to the hotel. He'd friends up there, hadn't he? Boys he'd known all his life, crowding around flat pints and talking about big futures. He'd go back there as soon as he could stand up.

Una was looking at Robin, her hand still on his belt, looking at him like she either hated him or wanted to conquer him, but maybe, Robin thought, that's the same thing.

'Isn't it mad the way we never want what's put in front of us?' she'd said. 'The sun is always brighter on the other side, Robin, isn't that what they say?'

'Is it? Don't you mean the grass is always greener?'

'What I mean is maybe they're wrong about that, do you think?'

Joe was sitting on the low wall, placing his feet in his new shoes, carefully tying the leather laces in even bows.

'We're in our prime,' Una had said. 'Some day I'll be hauling some hairy-arsed husband up and down these boreens and Joey there will be in London, starving in his garret, and you, Robin, what will you be doing?'

Her fingers had found his fly.

'I dunno.'

'You'll be married, I'd say, and teaching German up in the Tech.'

'I'm not marrying anyone.' He was finding it hard to speak.

'We'll look back on tonight and it will feel like the time of our lives,' Una had said, kneeling up and straddling him on the wet beach. She leant down and kissed him. Her tongue tasted of ketchup and vodka. Robin lay back on the sand, engulfed in layers of damp silk.

Joe stood up on the low wall, brushing sand off his soles. For a boy with absolutely no money whatsoever, he was oddly neurotic about his shoes. Robin had watched the gleaming two-tone loafers turn away and walk towards the ballroom lights.

Robin's brain was crumbling; he chased particles of himself down starlit alleyways. What the fuck was happening? He felt Una slip down on to him. Gripping her waist, he pushed his fingers into her heliotrope folds. He was aware of the August moon, of its singular buttery, all-encompassing light.

Afterwards, Una had rolled off him and pulled down her skirts. Kneeling on the wet sand, she'd regarded him with a kind of blank surprise. It was as if the drink and the night had fallen away and there was just the ordinary fact of what had transpired, which was, her look seemed to say, hardly worth remembering. She had gone back up to the hotel in search of the other bridesmaids and a round of triangular ham sandwiches. And surely, Robin thought, to whisper in their ears about his floundering, his snivelling, his juvenile gratitude. Robin had lain there, regarding the smirking stars.

He'd stood up and taken off his clothes. He had walked towards the moonlight until he was waist-deep in the night water. Plunging into the inky sea, he swam, the tide pulling him sideways, away from the shore, towards Owenahincha. He swam with his head down, arms trundling through the water, each stroke an effort to escape the mocking faces that crowded his mind; Joe, Una, the bride and groom, the lilac bridesmaids, the lads from school, the whole room whispering about his innocence, his desperation, his shameful suddenness, his pathetic relief. He saw his monkey-eyed father dying in his mother's mephitic embrace. 'Do you have any talents?' the gnarled-up old woman had asked him all those years before, and no, ma'am, he didn't, ne'er a one, as they say in this neck of the woods, ne'er a one.

Robin had stopped swimming, the exertion punctured somehow by ordinary sadness. He felt the cold suck the strength from his arms. He floated in the corrugated moonlight. He felt tired, so fucking tired. He felt himself become still, and in that stillness the cold had left him and he dipped quietly under the water. He heard his name being called and, relinquishing sleep, he obeyed his instinct, took a huge breath and struck for the shore. He had kicked on and kicked on and kicked on until the calling became louder and then he felt himself being lifted from the water and dragged towards the tideline. He could barely breathe. His chest heaving, he retched up vodka and sea water.

His head bent over the black sand, he saw Joe's saturated shoes, saw Joe too, heaving and spitting on to the sand. Together they made for the low wall and Robin's deserted clothes. They sat next to each other for a moment until their breathing stilled.

'Fuck it, Robin,' Joe had said. 'I can't even swim, man.'

'I'm sorry.'

'Killing yourself isn't as easy as it looks, eh?'

The following morning, while Joseph lay passed out on Robin's bedroom floor in a pile of quilts and cushions, Robin, unable to sleep, had got up and gone into the kitchen. Ushi was already in the studio: Robin could hear her radio playing and the low, spasmodic buzz of her potter's wheel.

There was a banana on the tabletop with an arrow drawn on it. The arrow was pointing towards a small blue book. He picked it up. His post-office deposit book – he had opened the account when he was about thirteen, in a fit of determination to save enough money to buy himself a decent bodyboard. He had, until this moment, forgotten about it entirely. He turned the pages, witnessed Ushi's carefully recorded, modest monthly lodgements. Month after month, year after diligent year, she had saved for this moment when she could quietly gift him a new beginning.

NINE

Dublin, May 2018

'OK, Helen! Hop up there on the scales and we'll see how you got on this week.'

Helen got back into the Passat at half past twelve and opened all the windows before she put on her seatbelt. May, and the weather was warm, too warm, unseasonably warm. If she'd wanted her thighs to chafe in May, she'd have moved to Magaluf. She put the car in gear and rolled out of the community-centre car park, narrowly avoiding a bunch of zippy little women trotting up to the hall for their yogalates class. Half past twelve and, despite the wall-to-wall egg-white omelettes, she was three pounds heavier than last week. And now, having endured the ritual humiliation of the Wednesday weigh-in, she had barely enough time to get to the supermarket and pick up a tub of low-fat cottage cheese and a pineapple before she was due back at her mother's to make sure she'd eaten the lunch that the carer would have left for her. Cottage cheese, a pineapple – and cat food, she mustn't forget cat food, cat food that the cat would turn her little pink nose up at anyway. Oh-so-meaty it may well be, Helen thought as she slowed for the lights, but that wouldn't cut it with the querulous animal.

The cat had cancer. Or at least the cat had had cancer – of the ear. The vet had snipped off half of the cat's left ear last Thursday, and hey presto, it didn't have cancer any more. It was lopsided now, and had stitches, and looked at Helen as if it was all her fault.

It had been Helen, naturally, who'd taken the damn thing to the vet, Helen who'd waited outside the surgery door for a quarter of an hour studying a poster for ringworm, Helen who'd handed the vet one hundred and seventy-three euro, which included an analgesic, a spray-on antiseptic and a post-operative care plan but failed to explain how lopping a bit of ear off a shrieking feline could cost more than an air fare to the Algarve. It was Helen who'd put the dazed and spitting animal back in its travel carrier and driven it home, and it was Helen who'd chased it out from under the beds to zap its seeping wound.

The vet (no little ray of sunshine himself), had peered at Helen through his bifocals and told her that global warming was responsible for the cat's ear cancer, which Helen thought was going it a bit. And even if it was global warming, what was Helen supposed to do about it? Knit a bed-hat for the hole in the ozone?

Ruth, of course, being Ruth, concurred with the depressed vet on the global threat to cats' ears. Ruth had arrived late for a long-planned get-together at Helen's house last Saturday night. She had been ridiculously late, if truth be told, tapping on the patio doors just as Helen was standing up from the table to take dessert out of the fridge. She had a habit of popping up out of nowhere, but even so Helen nearly had a heart attack when she saw Ruth's pale little face shimmering outside the window.

Apologizing for her lateness, Ruth had picked the lopsided cat up out of its basket, stroked its haughty chin and launched into a monologue about how ear cancer in felines was first noticed in Australia by a bunch of sentimental Irish émigrés who had brought their cats with them to live in Sydney or Perth or wherever. The Antipodean sun beating down on those translucent little Celtic cats, Ruth had explained, shrugging off her jacket, caused skin cancer.

'Why do you know that, Ruth?' Helen had asked, looking at her in her jeans and T-shirt and those awful clodhoppers she wore, and thinking that she might have made a bit of an effort for the evening.

'I must have read it somewhere,' Ruth had answered, putting the intoxicated cat back in its bed. 'It's one of the advantages of being an insomniac – there are hours and hours of the dark night to fill with useless pieces of information.'

Robin had stood up from the table as soon as Ruth sat down, and had gone to open another bottle.

'It's an interesting theory, Ruth, but we're in Castleknock, not Canberra,' Colm had said, emptying the end of the warm white wine into an unused glass and handing it to her. 'There's more chance of the cat catching venereal disease from the postbox.'

'Why, what's so alluring about Castleknock postboxes?' Robin had asked.

Ruth had lifted the lid on the remains of Helen's creamy chicken chasseur, which was congealing in its oven-to-tableware pot.

'Looks lovely, Helen. I'm sorry for being so late, but we'd just managed to suspend the globe when one of the stays snapped.'

'I got your texts. We decided to start without you,' Helen had said, bringing the dish back to the hob to heat it up.

'We've all eaten,' Robin had confirmed. He was leaning against the kitchen island, pulling the cork out of the bottle.

'I've apologized,' Ruth had replied evenly.

'Your oven-to-tableware pot is fucking surpassing itself, Helen,' Robin had said quietly, refilling his glass before he brought the bottle to the table. It occurred to Helen that he was already pissed.

Twelve forty: supermarket first, then she would nip over to her mother's house and then back to her own house to make lunch – a bacon sandwich for Colm and a cottage cheese and pineapple salad for herself – and then she'd grab a minute to try to fix the baggy Velux in Erin's room.

Supermarket. Cottage cheese. Mother. Velux. Then she'd quickly catch up with a bit of invoicing for Colm and then she'd drop Erin to her 'group', which her daughter had sworn blind to Helen that she would definitely go to this week.

Supermarket. Cottage cheese. Mother. Velux. Invoicing. Group. Then she'd scoot back over to her mother's, make sure the evening home help had got her into her nightdress and that she was ready for bed and not poking around the cold old kitchen in her dressing gown, and then she'd whiz back to pick Erin up from group. Helen knew the ropes; she'd wait outside in the car and when Erin emerged from the clinic she'd plaster a smile on her face and remember not to ask any probing questions on the drive home.

Supermarket. Cottage cheese. Mother. Velux. Invoicing. Group. Mother. Group. Smile. And then she'd think about dinner. What in the name of god was she supposed to make for dinner? She couldn't look at another chickpea.

'Fail to prepare, Helen, prepare to fail!' her leader had said at the weigh-in when the digital scales pinged.

'I haven't a minute,' Helen told her leader. 'Not a minute.'

'Hectic is not active!' the leader replied, crossing the fake-tanned bits of sinew that passed for her arms and trapping Helen between her sanctimonious little leader's face and the pulsing digits.

Helen was going to be sensible. She was going to have a golden week, she decided, freeing one of the trolleys from its chain gang. She would aim to shift a pound, maybe two. Helen knew she had been too ambitious in the past, too willing to please, eating nothing and then, ravenous, eating everything. Pushing the trolley down the yeasty bread aisle, Helen remembered something cheering: she was allowed to eat the supermarket's own-brand fat-free bagels.

'In moderation, Helen,' the leader had warned, as Helen swung off the scales.

The supermarket didn't have any own-brand fat-free bagels, so Helen bought ordinary bagels instead, and some little glazed pastries that the girls might like, and then she popped an almond ring in the trolley, which she'd take over to her mother, and then she got the cottage cheese and the pineapple and a big bottle of fizzy grapefruit something, which was on special offer, and at the checkout she threw in a packet of seaweed crisps, which she opened as soon as she got back to the car. They tasted like the inside of a cistern.

'I don't like almonds,' Helen's mother sniffed when Helen presented her with three buttered slices on a side plate.

'Fine,' Helen replied briskly. 'Did you eat the lunch Madeleine left out for you?'

'She doesn't speak. I told her to wash the bathroom floor. She ignored me.'

'She has a name and she does speak. Her English is terrific actually.'

'If you're so fond of her, let her go to your house and drag you out of bed in the morning.'

'She's not a skivvy. Sit up until I change your bed jacket.'

'Once they sent a Chinese man. I sent him packing.'

'"Once" being the operative word.'

'What did you say?'

'Nothing. You can lean back now.'

Helen carried the dishes downstairs and washed up her mother's lunch things and rinsed out the tea towel and steeped last night's bed jacket in Vanish to get the tomato soup out of the fabric. Picking up her car keys, she noticed that she'd somehow managed to eat the three almond slices.

'For god's sake, Helen, lose some weight,' her mother had said the day before when Helen, having knelt down to plug the nebulizer into the socket behind the bed, struggled to get back up again.

'I might,' Helen had answered, 'if I had five minutes to myself.'

When Helen got home from her mother's, the cat was mewling on the doorstep. There was a note from Colm on the kitchen island to say he had to meet a possible client and wouldn't be back until later that evening and, beside it, a note from Erin to say she'd gone out and would make her own way to group today.

The cat was arching around Helen's ankles. The cat food! She knew she'd forgotten something.

Helen opened the fridge to put away the warm cottage cheese that had spent the last hour fermenting on the back seat of the car. Standing in front of the refrigerator's cavernous interior, she steeled herself to enumerate Erin's overnight casualties: the entire family pack of ham, all the yogurts, every last jalapeno pepper and half a packet of breadcrumbs. Breadcrumbs, for god's sake.

Helen found an out-of-date packet of salami in the salad drawer that had survived the slaughter, and threw the cat a slice. Out-of-date salami, Helen observed, popping a slice into her own mouth, tasted exactly the same as in-date salami. She closed the fridge and looked at her elder daughter's note again. Erin had no intention of going to her group today, of course she didn't.

Helen walked over to the patio doors and looked out into the garden, at the mildewed trampoline, at the rotting Wendy house, at the fishpond silted over with emerald fronds. She took in her misty reflection, her heavy breasts and arms, her thighs languid in the summer skirt she had finally allowed herself to wear on this ordinary morning.

'What do you think of my new skirt?' she'd asked Colm on Saturday night before Ruth and Robin were due to arrive. Helen had everything ready: the chicken was simmering, the tiramisu was in the fridge, there were night lights and nibbles multiplying on every surface.

The receipt was in a bag on the bed. Helen had bought the skirt in a sale at a shop called Ms Fecundity. 'That's a dangerous yellow!' the assistant had smirked, pulling back the dressing-room curtain.

It wasn't too late to take it back; her hands had barely touched the fabric.

The skirt was soft, the colour of buttercups. Stepping into it, it had occurred to Helen that she would like to be fucked by someone, sublimely.

'Colm, look at me. Do you like my skirt?'

'I do, yeah,' Colm had answered, before glancing up from his laptop.

Helen had taken off the skirt and put it back in the bag and dug out her navy trousers. There was a Werther's Original in the pocket.

'You really are the least of my worries,' she said now to the billowing yellow skirt, reflected in the patio window, as her phone started to ring. It would be Colm, again. Since the downturn, when the business had almost been destroyed, he'd lost confidence in his decision-making, turning to Helen for advice on everything from slip-mats to shower heads.

'What is it, Colm?'

'Helen? It's Robin. Look, I was wondering if you had an hour to kill. I need to talk to you.'

Erin had been home on Saturday evening when Robin and then, finally, Ruth had come over for dinner. Helen had invited her daughter to sit down and join them. Erin had reluctantly agreed, but in the end she hadn't sat with them to eat the chicken chasseur and the creamy mash, instead drifting away in that untethered way she had, and navigating the kitchen in her layers of baggy jumpers. Picking at bits of breadstick and pretzel, she had politely answered Robin's questions about her plans for the future. No, she didn't think she would defer college again for another year. Yes, she was going to try to go back in the autumn and carry on with her degree. Yes, this time she would definitely try to participate more. Maybe, she offered, she might even sign up with a running club. Running club? Helen could have screamed.

Robin had listened attentively enough, although you could see that he was edgy, looking at his watch, crossing and uncrossing his legs, wondering, Helen supposed, when Ruth would get there. It was only when Ruth had finally turned up and was sitting down with a wine glass in her paint-splattered hand that Erin, too, had floated towards the table as if her string had been cut.

While Ruth spoke about her work with the refugee children and the drama of the semi-suspended globe she'd left behind to be worked on again on Sunday, Helen had brought the reheated casserole dish back to the table. She'd served Ruth, who was ravenous, and then surreptitiously filled another plate with nicely arranged chicken pieces and a whisper of mashed potatoes, and slipped it in front of her daughter.

Ruth was telling Erin that she and the other volunteers had helped the children to make the enormous papier-mâché globe that they had then decorated with their memories of home and their hopes for the future. Ruth had used every contact she'd made in the art business to have the globe temporarily hung in the foyer of a gallery hosting an exhibition of contemporary art. Visitors to the exhibition, Ruth explained, wouldn't be able to avoid the globe on their way upstairs to float past prints of Damien Hirst's butterflies.

While Ruth spoke, Helen had watched Erin shred up the chicken she had put in front of her and slip it to the cat, who was out of its sick box and stretching up its open claw towards her plate.

'Stop it, Erin,' Helen said sharply, too sharply, and Ruth had stopped speaking and everyone had looked at Helen, and Erin had blushed and pushed the plate away.

'Stop what, Helen?' Colm had echoed softly. 'Sure, what harm?'

What harm? Plenty of harm. Harm all around them, harm seeping under the doors, whether Colm could see it or not. What harm? The cat vomiting on the carpet, their daughter's footsteps slithering down the stairs at three o'clock in the morning to stand barefoot in front of the American fridge-freezer, to eat and eat, to fill herself up until there was no space left. What harm?

'Sorry,' Helen said, as lightly as she could manage, and Ruth had resumed eating and Erin had begun to trace her fingers along the table's edge as if she wasn't entirely convinced by its existence.

Helen, in need of a drink, had reached for her glass, and Robin had momentarily covered her hand with his own and she was grateful.

'How much would that kind of a thing be worth anyway?' Colm had asked, refilling Ruth's glass.

'The globe?'

'Your man Hirst. How much would one of his prints be worth?'

'It depends on your interpretation of worth,' Ruth replied, smiling, and Colm, who had no patience for Ruth's tricks, had sighed and raised his eyes and asked Helen if it was true that the tiramisu had been forcibly repatriated to Italy, and Ruth, having finished her food, had pushed back in her chair and had already started to look restless.

'Do you think it makes any difference?' Erin had asked Ruth.

'Difference?'

'The voluntary stuff with the children and the art. What difference can it make?'

'I don't know,' Ruth had replied simply. 'But doing something has to be better than doing nothing. Doesn't it?'

'I don't know if that's true. I think we're destroying everything just by being. Even our breathing hurts the earth. Maybe it would be better if we all did absolutely nothing.'

'So,' Colm had interrupted loudly, 'I was thinking about clearing out the fishpond and buying myself a Shubunkin!'

'You bought a Shubunkin a long time ago and it ate its mother. It ate its mother and then it ate everyone else's mother.'

'That wasn't a Shubunkin, Robin. That was a shark in Shubunkin's clothing.'

Helen, standing to finally get the tiramisu out of the fridge, had watched Ruth examine her daughter's face as Erin, too, stood to leave the table.

'Why don't you come along to the gallery and see what we're doing, Erin. It would be good to have your input.'

'Maybe,' Erin had replied softly, slipping out of the room.

The four of them had already finished dessert when Colm remembered that one of his clients had given him a dessert wine, quite possibly in lieu of payment. He went off and crawled around under the stairs and found the wine, as well as three-quarters of a bottle of Irish whiskey and a forgotten bottle of Tia Maria. When he came back into the kitchen, Ruth had moved on to minty tea, but she was certainly the only one.

'Where's Kelly tonight?' Ruth had enquired about Helen and Colm's youngest daughter when they were all back at the table.

'She's at a play with her new friend who isn't her boyfriend. I asked. I said, "Is Dylan your boyfriend?" She said I was being reductive. She's sixteen, I'm forty-six. I don't actually know what reductive means.'

'It's all bullshit.' Colm was refilling the glasses again and Helen knew that he was now moving through his familiar idiosyncratic dance of drunkenness. There'd be mild belligerence around his lack of parental prowess and his failure to have smashed bathroom retailing, followed by a dose of sentimentality around how

Helen had stuck with him through thick and thin. (I'm like durable grouting, Helen thought.) And finally he'd insist on the accumulated personnel around the table joining him in a trip down memory lane.

'I live in a house full of women,' Colm was saying, interrupting his monologue to leave the table on his way to having a slash. 'My daughters tell me I know nothing. My wife tells me I notice nothing. I'm obsolete. I'm blind. I am an old fucking man.'

'Robin?' Ruth had said quietly, leaning across the table and putting her hand on Robin's arm, and Helen had realized that she wanted to go home already. She'd hardly arrived. It wasn't much beyond midnight.

'What is it, Ruth?'

'We might think about calling it a night?'

'I have runny cheese with walnuts in it,' Helen said, deciding to ignore Ruth's obvious exhaustion, and that seemed to settle that.

When Colm came back to the table, he was already in the mood to reminisce, about nights spent with Helen in the flat in Streatham, and the nurses and the drink, and Pauline and her air fresheners and her neat little lines of cocaine, and Dana, who could get her hands on all kinds of everything, and Mairead, the dental nurse, scaring the shite out of him wandering around the flat underneath her egg-white face mask. And the nights he and Helen had spent in the back of his Transit van on holidays in the New Forest, with *The Joy of Sex* in the glove compartment.

'Those were the days, Helen, eh?'

'I wouldn't like to be crawling around that van now,' Helen had said, to dampen his ardour.

'My first and last.'

Colm had raised his glass to her, and Helen, embarrassed by his uxoriousness, and even more by his lack of worldliness, had asked Robin who his first love had been. Robin had looked up at the ceiling and laughed.

'You must remember,' Helen had persisted, and finally Robin recalled losing his virginity, on a wet beach, to a girl called Una, who had voluminous breasts and a purple dress.

'Did you love each other?' Helen asked, bringing the runny cheese to the table.

'God no,' Robin replied, emptying his glass. 'She was just being charitable.'

'What about Vicky?' Ruth had asked, declining the cheese and producing a tobacco pouch and papers that she'd found in Sid's room after he'd gone to Berlin, which she hadn't quite been able to part with.

'What about her?' Robin had asked, taking the pouch from Ruth and methodically beginning to roll a cigarette.

'Vicky loved you.'

Ruth took the pouch back and rolled her own, with decidedly more panache.

'Vicky?' Colm had asked.

'Vicky was a solicitor.'

'A lawyer actually.'

'Sorry. Vicky was a lawyer who Robin went out with in London.'

'She make any money?'

'She made lots of money, Colm,' Robin answered. 'Then moved back to Berkshire and married someone else with lots of money.'

'Who?'

'Fuck knows. Someone with dogs and a horse box.'

Ruth stood to go outside and smoke.

'There's no need to ask you who your first love was, Ruth, eh?'

Ruth had hesitated. 'Why's that, Robin?'

'Nothing.'

Helen had watched Ruth hold her ground.

'Why do you say that?'

'Forget it. I shouldn't have spoken.'

'The first time I fell in love was with a total stranger, just an ordinary stranger walking through St Stephen's Green.' Helen had heard herself speak, heard herself break the silence that hung between Robin and Ruth with the weight of their petulant history, and was grateful that she had found her voice. 'I was twelve,' she'd continued. 'I mustn't have seen him for more than minutes and I swear to god if he walked into this kitchen now I would know him. Every inch of him.'

'Jesus, Helen.'

'I can see him, in my mind's eye. He was a king.'

'A king? What do you mean, a king?'

'Do you want to join me?' Ruth had asked Robin.

'You're on your own,' Robin had replied.

Helen had watched Ruth go outside and light up her cigarette beyond the patio doors. As Colm muttered about kings and fiddled around with the CD player, Helen asked Robin about Ushi, who had been back in hospital for more tests.

'We'll know more in a day or two. There's no point in worrying unnecessarily.'

Helen had kept her counsel. It wasn't the night to interrogate the truth of that particular statement either.

Helen had wanted to hold on to the tender lull of drunkenness before sobriety returned, and, with it, the realities of her life: her lonely mother, her fragile daughter, her frightened spouse, her unrecognizable reflection in the glass. She wanted to feel like she used to in the black-forest nights in Colm's accommodating van.

'Roll us one of those, Robin. I haven't had one for years.'

'Have mine.'

Robin handed her his solidly constructed cigarette, his fingers momentarily touching hers.

Helen had found Ruth wandering around the silted-up fishpond, her cigarette almost spent. They'd sat on the steps of the Wendy house, the cold of the late-spring night seeping out of the wooden slats and through Helen's clumsy trousers.

Helen took a few laborious puffs and, when the rollie died, gave it to Ruth and told her to keep it. Ruth relit it, and in the sudden illumination Helen could see, in the bleached contour of her face, how she had aged.

The two women had sat in silence for a while. There were no stars to look at, no constellations to name, no lights burning over a distant city. Through the glass doors leading into the kitchen, they watched the two men. Colm had found the track he was looking for and was animatedly pointing out chord sequences to Robin, who, looking bemused and speculative, was pouring himself another glass of wine.

'Do you ever miss London?' Ruth had asked.

'I miss being young. I don't miss the city any more. Do you?'

'I think about it.'

'London?'

'I think about the past.'

They were silent. Strains of Oasis drifted towards them from the kitchen.

'Do you ever hear from the girls in Streatham?' Ruth had asked.

'Christmas cards from Pauline. Herself and Dana moved to Hastings, bought a place of their own.'

'Good for them.'

'Pauline isn't always well.'

'No?'

'Up and down. She was always very hard on herself. Dana's been good to her.'

'I liked Dana. She was kind, generous, she saved my life.'

'She could be generous, when she wanted to be. Apparently she's given up the drugs trade and gone into seaweed manufacturing.'

'What drugs trade? I thought Dana worked in the car industry? Didn't she? She always had wads of cash and shiny new cars.'

'You know, Ruth, for all your arty ways, your flaky tobacco and your dreadful shoes, you can be very naive sometimes. Very gullible.'

'I suppose. How's Mairead?'

'Living in St Albans with her dentist. According to Pauline, Mairead has a maid and a full set of molars to eat her with.'

Ruth ground out the cigarette in the dewy grass.

'Erin seems fragile.'

'I wish you were more economical with the truth, Ruth.'

'Sorry.'

'Colm won't see it, can't see it. I don't know what's going to happen to her.'

There was a pause. Helen regretted her haste in giving away the cigarette.

'I think Robin is having an affair.'

'What are you talking about, Ruth?'

'It's not you, is it?'

'What's not me?'

'I don't blame him. Not really. He thinks he's failed. And I don't dispute it, at least not enough. I'm of the opinion that we all fail. In the end. I don't think there's another option.'

'Jesus, Ruth.'

'Sorry. I'll shut up. I'm a lousy dinner guest. Your chicken chasseur was brilliant. No failure there.'

Helen had stretched her legs out on the un-mown lawn. She was wearing her favourite sandals, the ones with the kitten heels. Funnily enough, she thought to herself, she'd always had nice neat feet.

'I'm flattered.'

'By?'

'You thinking that your husband would have an affair with me.'

'Why wouldn't he? You're lovely.'

'Fat.'

'Fuck's sake, Helen. Give yourself a break.'

Ruth stood, stretched, her T-shirt lifting from the waistband of her jeans. She wasn't perfect, Helen thought. She was ordinary. Ordinary and real. Actual.

'What do you think about when you think about the past?'

Ruth had taken the cigarette pouch from her back pocket, sat back down and begun to roll another cigarette.

'I think how stupid I was to keep it alive in my mind for so long.'

'Joseph?'

'Yes, Joseph.'

'He was brought in, you know, not long after you left London. I was in my last weeks at the Maudsley. Kazargazof, not a name you'd forget. He'd been splashing around in the traffic on Euston Road. Funny the things you remember.'

Helen had watched Ruth's fingers roll her cigarette; she was shaky, unlike her earlier competitive display at the kitchen table.

'In the beginning, after Robin and I got together, he'd phone Ushi, threatening to come and find Sid. I told Robin to keep him away. I don't know what Robin said to him, but he stopped calling, disappeared. I started to believe he was dead.'

Ruth tried to light up, the Bic scratching out blue sparks before it ignited.

'Then a few months ago, out of the blue, a drawing arrived at the framers. It was addressed to me. A beautiful drawing of a boy on a beach, barefoot, skirting the water's edge. The boy was so like Sid, it was almost as if he knew him.'

'Did you tell Robin?'

'No.'

'Why?'

'I don't know. It was addressed to me. It felt personal, like an apology.'

Helen could smell Ruth's smoky breath.

'What about Sid? He has a right to know that his father is alive.'

'When Sid went to Berlin he started looking for him. I knew he would eventually. He doesn't want Robin to know. He loves him, doesn't want him to feel betrayed.'

'Has he found him?'

'There was a return address on the package. As soon as Sid told me what he was doing I gave it to him.'

'Has he seen him?'

'Not yet.'

'Where is he?'

'Midhope. He's back in the old flat.'

'You have to tell Robin.'

'I know I do. I will. Tomorrow. I would have told him, but he's so silent recently. Absent.'

In the kitchen Colm was waving them in, brandishing the Tia Maria around like it was a prize worth fighting for.

'Why do you think Robin's having an affair?'

Ruth had closed her eyes before she spoke. Helen could see Ruth's weariness, and something else. Defeat?

'He's stopped being kind. People underestimate kindness. I never did.'

Robin was in the downstairs bathroom when Kelly had bounced into the kitchen with her definitely-not-boyfriend. They'd caught the last bus home and had stopped for spice bags in the village. At sixteen, Kelly had none of her sister Erin's terse anxiety; a friendly and passionate child with a warm, open face, she had introduced Ruth and her parents to her not-boyfriend with verve.

'This is Dylan,' she'd said. 'Dylan's going to be the most amazing writer you've ever known.'

'Thank god for that,' Colm had responded.

'I'm delighted to hear it,' Ruth replied, extending her hand to the delicate boy. 'What do you write about?'

'He writes about reptiles breaking out of their cages and recalibrating the world. It's a metaphor,' Kelly had replied.

'In the name of Jaysus.'

'Colm, why don't you make Kelly and Dylan a cup of tea?'

'What would they want tea for? They've reptiles to recalibrate.'

'I'm looking forward to reading your work, Dylan,' Ruth said. 'My husband is an English teacher. I'm sure he'd love to talk to you.'

'Mr Wolfe,' Dylan said. 'Kelly told me he might be here.'

'Mr Wolfe, yes. Robin. Do you . . . ?'

'He's my English teacher.'

'Goodness. Robin is your teacher? Does he know that you write?'

'My mother wanted me to give him one of my stories but . . .' The child had trailed off.

'Oh, but you must give him your work, he'd be delighted.' Hearing Robin come back into the kitchen Ruth had turned towards him.

'Robin, Dylan is here, isn't it a small world!'

Robin had looked, it later occurred to Helen, like one of Colm's mother-eating Shubunkins, opening and closing his mouth in a dumbshow of confusion.

'Dylan,' he'd finally said.

'Mr Wolfe. Sir.'

After Kelly had told Robin that Dylan was a talent to be reckoned with, there had been a smattering of conversation about coincidences and then Robin had become decisive in that instant way that drinkers often do. It was suddenly too late for another glass, too late to sit in Colm and Helen's wet spring garden, blowing smoke rings at the moonless sky. It was suddenly and unarguably time for Ruth and Robin to put on their jackets and begin their familiar walk home.

'HELEN? IT'S ROBIN. Look, I was wondering if you had an hour to kill. I need to talk to you.'

When Helen had finished speaking to Robin on the phone, she'd gone upstairs and brushed her teeth and put on tinted moisturizer and lipstick and brushed her hair, first to one side and then the other. She was tempted to change out of the dangerous skirt, to slip into something more invisible, but, looking at herself in the long mirror on the landing, she decided to stay as she was.

Her phone rang again the minute she got back into the car to first sort out her mother.

'How was your weigh-in anyway?' Colm asked.

'Difficult to tell. I had my shoes on. Are you eating something?'

'Tofu burger. I'm waiting for a guy called Oisín who wants to fit out his eco hostel with solar shower heads. I'm not going to be sitting here with a quarter-pounder when he shows up.'

'Tofu? Why didn't you have chicken?'

'I dunno. I've started to feel sorry for chickens recently. Did Erin go to her group?'

'No, I don't think so. We'll talk later, Colm, will we? I'm going to be a while at my mother's. I mightn't be back before you.'

'Mind yourself. There's very little compassion for matricide.'

'Thanks. Don't choke on your bean curd.'

Not once, Helen considered, turning into her mother's driveway, ignoring the overgrown hedges and flattened grass, had anyone ever asked her if she wanted the two couples, Robin and Ruth and Colm and Helen, to become friends. Not once had she been asked if she wanted to sit across the table from Ruth, year after year, dinner after dinner, watching her pick at her marriage and her food, choosing the bits she'd swallow and the bits she'd discard. And yet somehow Ruth had grown on her, she was solid, Helen thought. She didn't promise more than she could give.

It had been two decades, two whole decades, since Robin had first brought Ruth to the house in Dublin, twenty years since he'd arrived on the doorstep with her, without explaining things properly, without clearly setting out the territory, without giving Helen the full picture. So much so that while Helen had been preparing dinner for them on that evening of their reunion, when she had been making the white sauce for the chicken pillows and filling up the filo pastries with the plump white breast, she had felt full of indignation on Robin's behalf.

Robin had left London not long after Colm and Helen. He'd let his flat go and had sold his car and come back to Ireland. Helen had run into him on Grafton Street when they'd all been home for at least a year. They'd stood together in the drizzle outside the Oriental Cafe, talking about Dublin and how the city had changed in their absence. And wasn't it mad how the gloom had lifted, they said, and wasn't it mad the way everyone was running around the place, getting jobs in information technology and drinking beers by the neck and eating chilli jam on their overpriced sandwiches? And wasn't it madder again to think that they, Helen and Colm, and Robin and all the rest, had had to emigrate to London only a handful of years before because there wasn't a damn job to be had in this country?

But being home could be a bit lonely too, sometimes, couldn't it, Robin had said, and then he'd looked embarrassed and said he had to go, but Helen had delayed him a bit longer, asking him how he'd been since his return. He'd been temping, he said, in a couple of schools, and now he had an interview for a permanent position with one of them, a fairly prestigious boys' school in the city. Helen had straight away invited him to dinner on the following Friday, to meet Colm again. Colm was doing well, she'd said, more than well; he couldn't keep up with the demand for power showers and art deco soap-pumps, or so it seemed. And

Robin had said that he'd love to come to their new home. And was there anything Robin was allergic to, Helen had asked, and he'd said: 'Too much of my own company, I think, Helen.' And maybe it was at that moment that Helen had fallen in love with him, a private kind of love, a pebble-sized love that you could turn over in your pocket without anyone at all being aware of its weight in your hand.

They'd been saying goodbye, keying each other's numbers into their Nokias, when Helen asked after Ruth. Robin had laughed like a bad actor and told her that he hadn't seen or heard from Ruth since she'd so hurriedly left London.

'She has a child now, you know. A son.'

'Yes, I'd heard that all right, he'd be almost the same age as Erin,' Helen had replied, looking at him and stretching out her gloved hand to brush at the drizzle on his shoulders.

'Of course, I'm so sorry, I forgot. So you and Colm had a daughter, congratulations.'

'She's with her dad at a tiling exhibition. I came into town to have my hair dyed. What do you think of me as a redhead?'

'I think you look great, Helen, as always.'

Before Helen left her mother, she popped the old lady into her bed with the panic medallion around her neck and the two remote controls well within her reach.

'You're in a bit of a hurry to get me off your hands, aren't you?'

'I've got to meet someone in town in an hour. Do you want your nebulizer?'

'No,' her mother replied as Helen was preparing to dive under the bed again and wrestle with the plug. 'I don't want my nebulizer, I want to die.'

'Yes, so you've said, more than once. How about a cup of tea instead?'

'You can bring me a hot port, with lemon and cloves.'

'Fabulous,' Helen muttered to herself, descending the stairs again and putting on the kettle. There hadn't been a drop of alcohol in the house when she was growing up. It was an orchestra of teaspoons I listened to, she thought, filling her mother's glass with port and studding the lemon slice with the pungent cloves. As soon as Helen, the youngest, had left home to do nursing in London, her parents, it seemed, had anchored their old age to ruby port and the occasional trip to Medjugorje.

Her father had had a heart attack, just after Helen and Colm had moved into the new house. He'd died just as Helen had feared, leaving her to take care of his truculent wife.

One eye on the bedside clock, Helen watched her mother drink. Each day the woman seemed to sink deeper and deeper into her own sinews.

'Are you proud of me?' Helen asked suddenly, surprised at the initiative her mouth had taken with so little warning.

'Am I proud of you?'

'Are you?'

'Is that a new skirt?'

'Do you hate it?'

'You look like a field of daffodils.'

'I'll take that as a compliment.'

'And so you should. It suits you.'

'Do you need me to do anything else before I go?'

'I'm all right. You should head on.'

'Right, I'll see you in the morning.'

'I'm grateful to you, Helen.'

Her mother's voice halted her before she closed the bedroom door.

'I don't see your brothers from one end of the month till the next. You're a good girl, Helen. You always have been.'

Helen left her car at the park-and-ride, took the bus into town and walked down Grafton Street. They were to meet in Bewley's, where Helen and her mother used to go sometimes on a Saturday afternoon when her father was on duty. Helen remembered the waitresses in white pinafores carrying triple-layered cake stands to the marble-topped tables; she remembered the eclairs, their chocolate tongues jewelled with moisture.

'You may choose one cake, Helen,' her mother would say, and the waitress would wink at her across the table.

The refurbished cafe didn't feel the same. The magnificent stained-glass windows were still there, but the cavernous room was crowded and noisy. Tourists were efficiently shepherded towards three-bean salads and vegan tarts; there wasn't an iced fancy in sight. Helen stood in a queue to be seated until a brisk woman with a bouncing high ponytail led her to a red velvet banquette, where she sat and waited for Robin to arrive.

'I'd like a cappuccino and an eclair,' she told the young man who was sweeping the floor underneath her feet and, despite the odds against her success (he could have been a janitor for all she knew), he actually came back minutes later with a latte and an eclair that was sweeter and more manufactured than her mouth remembered, but entirely palatable nonetheless.

On the night that Robin had first brought Ruth to dinner in their house in Castleknock, Helen had spent the afternoon in the kitchen confidently stuffing the chicken pillows. She was quite looking forward to seeing Ruth again. She was looking forward to showing her the house, looking forward to showing her how much a part of their lives Robin had become. Looking forward, maybe, to showing Ruth what she had missed.

Since they'd bumped into each other outside the Oriental Cafe that day and Helen had first invited him over, Robin had got the permanent job and found a home of his own in Dublin. He'd been a guest in Colm and Helen's house dozens of times now. 'Guest' was hardly the right word; Robin was like family, Robin belonged. And Ruth – Ruth, who had somehow been resurrected – could, if she was interested, easily see what good friends Helen and Colm had been to Robin during the years of her absence, and how Robin had come to rely on Helen herself, Helen in her fine house, with her two little daughters now and the mewling kitten, and with Colm, of course, Colm who'd entirely missed the point about Ruth re-entering Robin's life.

'Ruth?' he'd hollered when Robin had phoned to say that he was thinking of bringing her over.

'Bring her over! Of course bring her over. God almighty. Ruth! Haven't seen her for years!'

While Erin played in the garden and Kelly slept in her pram on the sunlit patio, Helen had put the chicken pillows in the fridge, to glaze later with beaten egg. The rest of the menu sat on the refrigerated shelves: creamy dauphinoise, Eton mess and a slab of blue cheese that she'd need to bring back to room temperature. Helen had closed the fridge and stood back to look at what they'd achieved, at what Ruth might see when she arrived: the American fridge-freezer that made its own ice; the home gym where Colm kept his portable stock; the showstopper stairway; the family room with the gun-metal-grey couch that fitted together like a jigsaw (not entirely successfully, it had to be said); the kidney-shaped bath in Helen and Colm's en suite, with the temperamental jacuzzi that had given up the ghost altogether on the night Colm had been named runner-up in the excellence in the retail plumbing category, and she and he had gone at it like lunatics, the bubbles haloing her hanging breasts.

Usually Helen worried all day when Robin was coming to dinner, worried about the food and the house and her stomach and her thighs and even her fingers, which sometimes felt tight. She worried about Colm laughing with potato in his mouth. She worried that Colm bored Robin with his endless messing around with gadgets and buttons and remote controls. She worried that Robin secretly dreaded Helen's weekly 'just checking in' calls.

Sometimes when Robin came over for his dinner, you could tell by his restlessness that he was preoccupied. Sometimes though, the three of them, Helen and Colm and Robin, would watch a film together in the home cinema (which was really just an enormous television in the den) while Erin and Kelly slept upstairs. Helen liked those nights, the three of them on the big sofa, Colm shouting about the surround sound while Robin tried to focus on the plot. Helen liked to look from one to the other in the flicker of the Hollywood light.

Once, Robin had turned up for a home-cinema night with a girl called Ita, who had fantastic legs and one of those chins that give up on themselves like a good idea long forgotten. Halfway through the film, Ita had thrown up in the downstairs toilet. Helen had knocked on the door after Ita had been in there for over twenty minutes and had found her sitting on the floor. Ita had turned the same colour as the new auto-flush toilet, bluey-green and slightly shiny. Colm might have been a bit unrestrained with the Tia Maria, but no one had been pouring it down her neck.

Colm had gotten great mileage out of Ita. He'd even put the card Ita sent them on the fridge door, stuck it up with a magnet so that Robin could see the picture of the coy little kitten with the speech bubble that read: 'Can You Forgive Me-ow?'

'Where's Ita?' Colm had joked when Robin turned up the following Friday, unaccompanied bar a bottle of Rioja. Robin had shrugged his shoulders and smiled, and they hadn't bothered with a film after dinner that night, the three of them instead sitting out on the patio until it got too cold and Robin said: 'We're not all as lucky as you, Colm.' And he'd smiled at Helen over his glass, and Helen had felt . . . complete.

Later that night, after Robin had left to walk back along the side of the park, practically all the way down to the river, to the little two-up-two-down they'd advised him to buy just in time, Colm had rolled over in their king-size bed (which could sit itself up at the touch of a button and lie itself down at the touch of another one) and said: 'He's right. I am one lucky man.'

She'd lost three pounds that week. A golden week.

Helen sipped her latte and kept an eye on the entrance to see Robin when he came in. She watched a parade of couples enter the cafe: older couples, younger couples, men and women, women and men, men and men, women and women, persons and persons, they and theys, as Kelly would insist. I wonder, she thought, if they all feel as alone as I do.

When Robin had moved into his house, Helen had driven him to the supermarket to stock up on 'store-cupboard essentials'. She'd even written out a list. Robin had piloted the trolley around the aisles and Helen had filled it up for him, and afterwards, even though it was only four in the afternoon, Robin had suggested a drink.

He'd bought her a gin and slimline tonic in the ugly hotel next to the supermarket car park. They'd talked about his job teaching English in the boys' school in the city. He'd rather have worked in a mixed school, he said, or a school with more diversity, but it was a start, and in a year or two he'd look for something more to his liking. Robin hadn't wanted another drink; Helen had offered, twice. Walking back to her car she'd let herself imagine, just for a second, a stale hotel bedroom and her sandals kicked against a scuffed skirting board.

She'd dropped Robin and his bags off outside his house. He'd kissed her cheek, hopped himself and the bags out, and was saluting her from his new front door before she'd even turned the engine off. She'd slipped the brand-new Passat into drive and proceeded carefully down the narrow road for fear that a child, growing up on these labyrinthine streets without the benefit of a garden, would dart out in front of her.

Colm thought that the night Robin first brought Ruth to their home had been a great night. He'd swished the curtains open and closed for Ruth's entertainment and, after the chicken pillows and meringue and cheese had been eaten and they were standing out on the patio to get a bit of air, he had turned the pond lights on and off and off and on, and the lights had flashed red and green and orange. And Helen had realized, for the first time, that the pond looked like a traffic junction, and as she turned to tell Colm to stop it, she saw Ruth look at Robin with something wild in her eyes, some kind of want. And Robin had touched the arch of Ruth's back, his fingers grazing the line of her skin between the waistband of her jeans and her floppy jacket and Helen could almost feel the touch on her own back, a back momentarily constructed of pale skin and narrow bone.

After they'd left, Helen had finished the Eton mess, leaning against the fridge-freezer, while Colm disarmed the pond lights and triple-locked the outside doors. In bed, in their vast bed that could incline, recline and decline, she'd lain down and waited for sleep.

'Peas in a pod, those two,' Colm had said to the dark.

Helen hadn't slept. She alone had heard the deluge, heard the rain beat down on the darkened fishpond.

The following Saturday, a week after that first dinner, Helen had been warming up to run, walk or crawl five kilometres around the park, in a tutu and cerise-pink wig, with a bunch of similarly attired parents from the play-school group, in aid of a new kidney for someone, when Robin had phoned. Helen had propped herself up against the obelisk and taken his call. He was phoning from the supermarket to say that he and Ruth were going west. Ruth's mother was minding Sid for a few days.

They planned to visit Popes Cove, he'd said, then move farther along the coast and rent a cottage for a couple of days. They were leaving straight away, stocking up first on red wine and pasta and things in jars that you couldn't buy in the middle of nowhere. They were going to walk and talk and catch up on lost years. And gaze and fuck, Helen thought, and fuck and gaze, and let their morning coffees go cold.

They would be in touch on their return, Robin had said. 'We'll cook for you next time.'

'Enjoy,' Helen sang. 'Don't do anything I wouldn't do!'

Everything. They would do everything she had never done. She didn't mean the sex, although you could let your imagination run away with you. But to be lost and then found. To be sought. To be made flesh.

Helen had looked down the long misty avenue; the other runners were like a distant mirage of living dolls.

Helen watched Robin walk towards her table in the Oriental Cafe. He looked tougher somehow, more closed off than he used to, his hair shorter, his shoulders tensed. He looked, she thought, less breakable.

He ordered a cup of coffee and smiled at her, and Helen saw straight away that the smile was perfunctory and that there was business to attend to.

'The boy Dylan, Kelly's friend, my student, whom I met in your house on Saturday?'

'Kelly's not-boyfriend boyfriend, yes, what about him?'

'She hasn't said anything to you, no?'

Robin thanked the waiter for the coffee.

'Said what?'

'Did he know I was going to be there on Saturday night, with Ruth?'

'Robin, it's a small city. Surely it's not that unusual to bump into one of the boys from your school?'

'Maybe not.'

Robin looked around the cafe. Helen saw the manageress with the officious ponytail glance in their direction. That was the odd thing about some men, Helen thought, men like Colm seemed to blur into a watery, genderless puddle as they got older, while other men, men like Robin, aged like leather or oak; they became more than what they might once have been.

'I've been sleeping with Dylan's mother.'

Helen thought she was hearing things. She could have sworn that Robin just said that he was sleeping with the mother of Kelly's friend.

'Neither of us want Dylan to know. Neither of us wanted anyone to know.'

Us. Who was this 'us'? What was he talking about?

'Helen, I'm not asking you to do anything for me, I'm not asking for your understanding. I just need to know if the boy knows.'

The boy. What had this to do with the boy? Ruth! They should be talking about Ruth.

'Ruth knew you were seeing someone. She guessed.'

'How?'

'She asked if it was me.'

'You?'

'You sound amazed. Why not me? Why shouldn't it be me?'

'I don't know what we're talking about, Helen.'

Helen didn't know why she felt so angry. She was tempted to smash a cream slice down her throat to quell the rage.

'As long as I've known you, Robin, you've thought about no one else, only Ruth. You just wouldn't leave it, would you? You had to prove your point. You had to win. Well, you got her. You got what you wanted.'

'Helen . . .'

'When did you stop wanting her, Robin? When she started wanting you, was it?'

'Ruth knows. I told her after Dylan showed up at your house.'

Helen waved the waiter over to their table. She'd eat what she damn well liked.

'How is she?'

'She's gone.'

'Where?'

'I don't know.'

He put his head in his hands. Helen could see where his blond hair was thinning, his scalp showing through. We're revealed, she thought, as we age; we are revealed, the gloss falls away, we are exposed. She thought of her mother propped up in bed with her remote controls, sinking into the bog of herself, into the folds of her powdery skin.

'You're getting old,' Helen said to him. 'I can see your scalp.'

He smiled.

'Why?'

'Why? Why does anyone end up with someone else? I don't know. Because you feel excluded from your own life? Immaterial? I don't know. Fuck it, Helen. I didn't plan this.'

'Oh well, that's all right then. As long as you didn't plan it.'

'I'm not looking for your support.'

'Thank goodness for that.' She gestured to the waiter again.

'There was no reason,' he said. Sid going. Ruth's work, the children she was teaching, her belief. He used to give a fuck once too. It had all felt distant, as if he was living someone else's life, and she was living her own. 'You wake up, Helen, and it's all too late for plans.'

The waiter came to the table. Robin didn't want anything.

'Tell me about Ushi,' Helen said, while she waited for her Swiss roll to skim its way towards her through the Edelweiss.

'She's in Bantry Hospital. More tests. I'm due to go down Friday. Maybe they'll let me bring her back to Popes Cove for the weekend.'

'That would be nice.'

Helen's cake arrived, haloed in a sprinkling of sugar. It was a thing of beauty.

Robin looked at her. 'You haven't asked me anything about her.'

'No, I haven't.'

'Her name is Celestine. She was sick. She's recovered. It's a cliché. I know it's a cliché. She knows it's a cliché. But she's been given a second chance.'

'You want me to sing hallelujah?' Helen asked, sinking her fork into the snow.

Helen walked back to her bus through St Stephen's Green. It was a beautiful evening, the sun dipping behind the trees in the park, the water smooth and brown. The ducks looked ornamental, too precisely marked, too perfectly symmetrical to be real.

'I'm not allowed to feed you any more,' Helen said to a curious duck who watched her sit down on an empty bench next to the pond. 'You're not allowed carbs either. It's a damn swizz. You and me on the algae, eh?'

The duck ignored her, turning its decorative face away to follow the arc of a tired fly.

If Robin or Ruth or Colm had asked her that night in her house to tell them about the first time she fell in love – if they'd had the patience or the interest or the curiosity, if Colm had wanted to hear her rather than imagine that she was entirely known to him, entirely domesticated, entirely understood – if any of them had asked, she would have told them that the first time she fell in love was with a beautiful man who was black and who walked past her in St Stephen's Green without noticing her. It was late spring: brown daffodils and loose tulips wilted in circular beds; young men lay under weeping willows, pretending the dappled light was a flurry of kisses; purposeful people rushed along, ignoring the ducks.

The man had walked slowly. He wore a magnificent coat. He was his own procession. Helen had seen the man and the coat, and thought of kings. Helen had seen the man and the coat, and wanted to run her hands up and down both of them.

Helen and her mother were scurrying right towards him, her mother whipping along in her cold mackintosh, Helen in her wake.

The man's coat hung over his shoulders, unbuttoned, afloat. Close up, the coat was squirrel-grey. And Helen, in that tiniest of moments, the kind of moment that hides itself in the toe of a sock, imagined spreading herself all over him like butter.

Helen's mother had tugged her daughter onwards and through a wrought-iron gate back on to the solid street. And Helen had turned and the beautiful man was gone.

Helen's mother had brought her into town that afternoon for a medical appointment, a consultation. They'd come in on the bus.

'Can I hold the ticket?' Helen had asked after the conductor had returned to slouch in the open stairwell.

'You're too old to be holding tickets,' her mother had replied, looking out of the dirty window.

'I'm twelve,' Helen had whispered.

'You don't need to remind me,' her mother had said to her sullied reflection.

The word 'consultation' had rolled around Helen's tongue on the long journey into town, getting mixed up with other words that had yet to reveal their true meaning to her: delicatessen, delirious, abandon, rotisserie.

When the slow bus had finally reached its destination, Helen had had to run behind her mother all the way up from Abbey Street across the bridge over the River Liffey, past women sitting on the ground, hands raised for money, faces burnt red from rain, babies snuffling inside their blankets.

'Mammy?' Helen had said, but her mother didn't stop.

They had run past the Protestant university, Helen's ankle socks catching under her heel in her good patent-leather shoes. They had burrowed fast up Grafton Street, darting through powdery women who sauntered past Switzer's windows, women who slowed to view cashmere cardigans and the strings of grey pearls that hung around the mannequins' necks like old ladies' teeth.

'Would we not have got a taxi?' Helen had panted at the mouth of the green, and her mother slowed for a split second and it occurred to Helen that she might get a slap.

Helen had been in a taxi once before, slotted in between her narrow mother and her wide father, whose two legs took up half the back seat. Her father was dressed in his uniform, the silver medal in his hands. Her mother smelt of Tweed talcum powder. No one sat beside the driver.

'Is this a taxi?' Helen had whispered.

'It is,' her father had whispered back. 'Make a wish.'

Helen had wished for peanut butter, which she knew existed.

The things you saw out of taxi windows that you might never see again: a statue with a brass penis; a barking dog with a studded collar; a woman crying in a swinging skirt.

'I'd prefer the medal to some nice Waterford glass anyhow,' Helen's mother had said, breaking her silence, and Helen knew that that was a lie. Even that pink-eyed poodle with the studded collar, craning its frilly leg against the plinth, knew she was telling a lie.

'She's an elephant,' Helen's mother had said to the doctor as soon as they were admitted into his consulting rooms in the big Georgian building opposite the back gates of the green. The consultant, who was, much to her mother's relief, so entirely white and chalky that you could have spat on him and rubbed him out, had raised a transparent eyebrow and asked Helen to sit down and stick her tongue out. He shone a torch into each of Helen's ears and finally he handed her mother a bill, the amount of which would easily have done the electricity for the winter.

'Is that it?' her mother had asked incredulously. 'Are you even going to weigh her?'

'Come back to me when she begins to menstruate,' said the doctor, opening a drawer in his big brown desk and looking inside in case there was something to interest him in its caliginous interior. And Helen's mother had reddened and snatched up her handbag, and Helen had looked from one to the other and rolled the word 'menstruate' around in her mouth to get a good grip of it before her mother could run her all the way back down to the bus and shake it clean out of her.

Not even that word though, not even the whispered crumbs of explanation from her mother on the rattling bus back home, suggesting the leaking of blood and juice from the sugary cavity inside of her, could blur the image of the beautiful black man in the park. And when Helen closed her eyes that night, it was his image that flickered over all the knotted-up unopened parts of her.

TEN

London, May 2018

Exiting the terminal, Ruth took the escalator down to the ground floor and followed the signs for the Underground. Briefly finding herself outdoors between arrivals and departures, she was aware of a grainy sky and a familiar but forgotten metallic scent in the air. Around her, mobile phones were bleating. She should really turn hers on; she'd promised Sid that she'd phone Robin.

In the Underground the platform walls were plastered with images of a British bulldog advertising bamboo razors. Inside the train, advertisements for pain relief, financial relief and haemorrhoid relief sat alongside images of happy families gasping in awe at shit-stained lions on Trafalgar Square. Ruth had never much cared for London's visitor attractions; for her, the city's allure lay in its anonymity. Here, occupying a seat on the crowded train among all the other silent travellers, she was invisible.

Hounslow West, Hounslow Central, Hounslow East.

Monogamy, Ruth considered, is fatally flawed. You can choose to be present, to sign off on every shared breath, you can walk, talk, fuck, eat, laugh, wash, row, sleep, weep, care, worry, hope. You can love. You can make an identity and name it – Robin and Ruth, Ruth and Robin – but you cannot forget the past. You cannot monogamize memory.

Northfields. South Ealing. Acton Town.

That first time that Robin had brought both Ruth and Sid home to meet Ushi, his mother had stood in her warm kitchen kneading bread. Blowing a strand of hair off her forehead, she had turned to put the kettle on the hob, and Ruth had recognized a wariness under Ushi's hospitality, an acknowledgement that Ruth and now Sid's presence in her home heralded an end to how things had been before. Robin had become part of another entity.

While Sid ran around the cottage, Ushi, refusing all help, had measured stock and chopped vegetables and aired sheets, finally agreeing to walk on the beach with them while dinner cooked in the range. And even as Ushi took Sid's hand in hers and began to tell him the names of the headlands they could see – Seven Heads, Toe Head, Galley Head – that sense Ruth had of being an outsider, an intruder, refused to lift.

The following morning Ruth had lain awake next to Robin in his boyhood bedroom while he slept, wondering if she should have allowed herself to be persuaded there. Tracing the pattern of the hand-sewn quilt that covered their makeshift arrangement of mattresses on the floor, she'd listened to Sid talking to Ushi in the room next door, in that breathless, unpunctuated way he had. His questions, each patiently answered by Ushi, had gathered more and more momentum, until finally Ruth heard him running down the short passageway towards their room. He was looking for his rubber boots so that he could go walking with the lady, he said, to find cats and rabbits and a black-and-white 'kuh'.

'A kuh has four stomachs,' the child had told Ruth, while she sat on the floor with him to help him put socks over his socks so that his boots would fit.

'Yes, I think I knew about that,' she'd whispered.

'They use one stomach for their breakfast and one for their dinner and one for making pee and poo and one for making baby kuhs.'

'Wow. That's efficient.'

'I told the lady that you peed sitting down, and she said that was fine and not to worry about it.'

'That's good to hear, Sid, thanks. Do you know who the lady is?'

'No.'

'The lady is Robin's mother, and soon she will be your granny.'

'I have a granny already.'

'Ushi will be another granny.'

'A spare granny?'

'Kind of.'

'Will she be sad when we go home?'

'Do you think she'll be sad when we go home?'

'Yeah. She probably will be crying.'

Ruth had tried to kiss Sid goodbye before he tore back out of the room. Hearing the back door close, she slid back into bed beside Robin, putting her cold hands on his stomach.

'We've got twenty minutes,' he'd said to the pillow.

'I thought you were asleep.'

'I never knew you peed sitting down,' he said, turning to her and slipping his hand between her legs.

'I'm an anatomical fucking miracle,' she replied.

Later, still inside her, he rolled her back on to the mattress.

'Tell me,' he'd said. 'Tell me that there is no one else, Ruth. Tell me.'

'There is no one else.'

'Tell me, Ruth. Tell me.'

'There is no one else.'

When he came, he had cried out, his face on her shoulder, his blond hair touching her breast.

By the time Sid had arrived home with a dead starfish, Ruth was sitting naked on the edge of the bath in Ushi's tiny bathroom. She'd listened to Sid outside the door, telling Robin that starfishes had no blood and no brains.

'Sid thought he would like to have a starfish as a pet,' she heard Ushi gently interrupt. 'I explained that starfishes cannot exist outside of their element.'

'They simply die,' Sid concurred. 'They just simply die, Robin.'

Ruth had put the tips of her fingers into the scalding water, to obliterate the image of Joseph's face, his black hair splayed out in a tenebrous, tangled halo.

That afternoon, while Sid and Ushi mixed clay in the pug bucket, Ruth and Robin had driven into town. They picked up what was needed for dinner and then sat by the fire in an empty afternoon pub, the walls decorated with a lifetime of paraphernalia, memories crowding memories.

Robin had wanted Ruth to know that his past relationships felt insignificant, that everything had been leading to this moment, to Ruth.

Ruth had looked around the old bar, suffused with random ephemera, with other people's histories, and told Robin that she'd never thought sex and love had much in common anyway. When she was younger, she told him, finding herself in some boy's bed had never been unpleasant but it was always just an attempt to feel actual, to feel present – until Joseph, she had almost said out loud, but hadn't.

She and Joseph had never spoken about her past, she might have added, Joseph probably always assuming that he was greater than the sum of its parts. And Ruth had never felt threatened by some girl from Joseph's past that they might encounter on their walks around Camden Town or when they were drinking in a King's Cross pub. It had seemed to Ruth that there were always going to be smoky-eyed girls in slivers of tartan asking him for a light for their hand-rolled cigarettes. She was never sure what Joseph saw in her though. Something about her that could carry his weight maybe. And she was from a brooding country, of course, where girls were well versed in knowing their place.

Robin had taken their empty glasses back to the bar and they had left and walked down to the river, stopping by a memorial bench dedicated to a local child.

'Who was she?' Ruth had asked, leaning forward to read the plaque.

'I don't remember her. She was before my time,' Robin answered. 'Just some drowned girl.'

The following day, before the drive back to Dublin, Robin had taken Sid down to the beach to bury the dead starfish, which had spent the night in his sand-bucket by the back door, while Ruth stayed behind to gather together the clothes and toys she had brought for their visit.

'Thank you for everything. It's been lovely,' Ruth had said, carrying their bedding into the kitchen, where Ushi was filling a box with bottles and jars.

'Sid is a sweet little boy.'

'You've been so kind to him. He's loved it here.'

'His father loved it here too.'

Ruth felt her throat constrict.

'Joseph.'

'Joseph? That is what you call him? Joseph? It suits him. Joseph. Maybe you think he needs gravitas, Ruth, maybe you need to weight him down? I understand that. I tried to hold on to him too, to make a home for him here. But he was always a stray.'

Ushi had stopped packing the box and looked directly at Ruth.

'He was a beautiful young boy, clever, disguised his fear.'

Ruth stood still, the bundled washing in her arms.

'Everyone wanted to take care of him,' Ushi had continued. 'To heal him, to please him. All Robin's little girlfriends, flitting by the cottage to see if Joey was back yet for the summer. Tell Joey this, tell Joey that. When will Joey be here? Is Joey on the evening bus? A boy destined to break hearts. Poor Robin – he was feeling, I think, always second best.'

'Would you like me to put this washing in the machine?'

'Did he break your heart, Ruth?'

'I should really put these sheets somewhere, get on with packing.'

'It is not impossible to be second best, I know this, but it is not easy, Ruth. You should understand that. It is not an easy role to inhabit.'

Ruth had heard Sid's tumbling words as he and Robin approached the kitchen door.

'There's been a reprieve,' Robin had said, opening the door and coming into the kitchen with Sid, the dead starfish displayed on Sid's yellow plastic spade. 'Sid reckoned this guy deserved a second chance. Apparently your mother's been filling him in on the miracle of resurrection, Ruth.'

Robin had driven them back to Dublin, jams and chutneys and pickled things in jars in a box in the boot, Sid's noisome starfish on the back seat. When Sid had fallen asleep, Robin had taken his hand off the wheel and found hers.

'What's up?'

'Nothing.'

'Ruth?'

'I've been thinking about my father actually. I wish he could have known Sid. And you. I think he'd have liked you.'

'You could take me to meet your mother.'

'I could. We certainly won't be returning from there with a bootful of jams and chutney.'

'No?'

'More like a bellyful of her regret.'

'What does she regret most?'

'Me probably.'

'Fuck it, Ruth, there's only so much chutney you can eat anyway.'

But that hadn't been what Ruth was thinking about, or not entirely what she had been thinking about. She had been thinking about Ushi's words and she had been thinking about London, about that place she had inhabited between griefs, before the true weight of loss had seeped inside her.

THE TUBE TRAIN was at Leicester Square now, passengers being warned to mind the gap. That treacherous single step, Ruth thought, closing her eyes, as more and more anonymous people alighted and departed.

In a cafe on the concourse outside King's Cross Station, Ruth bought herself a chicken wrap and a mind-bogglingly expensive coffee. After handing her sterling to a young man with a tongue stud, she went and stood at a table with her lunch and read a flyer propped against a jug. According to the text, the coffee beans had been hand-picked and roasted by a bunch of ecstatic Costa Ricans whose one and only thought was Ruth's pure drinking pleasure. Nice to know someone's in your corner, she thought, scrunching up her paper napkin and firing it into the correct bin on her way out the door.

The glistening granite concourse outside the station, criss-crossed by purposeful people tugging pretty toddlers and silent wheelie-bags, almost made her laugh. She felt a moment of nostalgia for the old King's Cross, for broken pavements and urinating drunks and mad old men and sad young women and rotting wooden escalators descending to quotidian rush-hour hell.

On the other side of the boulevard the familiar burger bars and kebab shops were still trading, Ruth noticed, still peddling plates of fuck-knows-what to a clientele long past caring. Crossing Euston Road, Ruth saw that the boarding houses and cheap hotels around Argyle Street seemed unchanged. Some had 'Vacant' signs in the windows. She randomly chose the nearest one.

The room was a pleasant surprise. The bed was clean, there was a table and a chair. The toilet seat was covered by a paper necklace, the shower stall small but spotless. It was a room that demanded nothing. It reminded her of a hospital cubicle – she might have been there for a day procedure, some kind of test invasive enough to require recovery. (Which, she thought, was pretty accurate actually.)

After the early-morning flight and long Tube journey, Ruth wanted to sleep, but she knew she had to face turning on her phone first. She had made a promise to Sid. The phone chimed to life; there were missed calls from Robin, seven of them. She listened to his last message.

'Ruth, I assume you don't want to speak. Ushi is dead. I'm in Popes Cove. I've called you and called you. It's morning now. I don't know where you are. I'm beginning not to give a shit.'

She telephoned Popes Cove. Robin answered.

'Robin.'

'I thought you were the undertaker.'

'Robin, I'm so sorry. Are you OK?'

He didn't respond.

'Robin? Robin, are you there?'

'Where are you?'

'London.'

'I see.'

'I'm coming home.'

'There are things to do. Arrangements.'

'I'm coming home, Robin.'

'Ruth.'

'What?'

'Give me some time.'

'Time?'

Outside the hotel window, the clouds parted. It was going to be a beautiful day.

'Don't you need me, Robin?'

'I don't know, Ruth, I don't know.'

Ruth stood in front of Nish's corner shop, which was no longer Nish's corner shop. In its place stood a sleek establishment selling handmade leather bags. The shop was closed, a couple of potted bay trees standing sentry next to an elegant but locked concertinaed gate. Ruth would've liked to have gone inside and enquired after Nish, although whether anyone would remember a sleepless man in a knitted cardigan twenty years later was debatable.

Across the road from not-Nish's the flats were looking confident, the brickwork steam-cleaned, the window frames restored, the flaking paint and mottled glass replaced. Ruth pushed the gate leading into the courtyard, but the broken mechanism was no longer broken and the gate remained closed. She walked up the street, turning right towards the laundrette where they used to sit together in the muggy warmth watching their clothes chase each other around the half-empty drum. The laundrette was still the same, as was the dingy food shop next to it. Ruth used to be scared to go into that shop alone, where everything had smelt like yesterday and the rice spilt out of split sacks that lay belly-up on the floor. 'Come with me,' she'd say to Joseph, and he would, and the men behind the counter would stop talking to watch as the two of them stood together considering the blackening fruit.

There was a new cafe on the corner, opposite the old Episcopalian church, a prosperous-looking place that took Ruth by surprise. Light and glassy inside, there were tables outside on the pavement and people eating and drinking in the May sunshine. Ruth sat down at a table littered with the previous occupants' dirty crockery and asked the boy who came to clear it if she could have a coffee and some water.

It had somehow become easier over the years to absent herself from much of Robin's life, Ruth thought. The occasional social events around his job held no allure for her, for either of them really. She didn't get on with Harry, his colleague whom he occasionally went off with on a Friday-night skite. And his relationship with Ushi was so particular, so ingrained, and Ruth's own sense of being an intruder on their history so persistent, that she had found ways to slip the net there too. She didn't need to be there for every visit to Popes Cove, did she? Finally she persuaded herself that she didn't need to be there for most of them. When Ushi came to visit them in Dublin, albeit rarely, Ruth would go out of her way to be welcoming, but Ushi would quickly become restless.

'Give me something to do with my hands, Ruth!'

Sid's clothes shelves had overflowed with sweaters in ribbons of primary colour that Ushi had knitted, sitting in the red chair in their kitchen, while Sid rolled racing cars over her feet. Once Sid had discovered football, however, he'd refused to wear Ushi's efforts any longer.

'Granny was asking Robin if you liked the new jumper she knitted you. She was saying that she hasn't seen you wearing it.'

'What did Robin say?'

'He said that we all really liked the jumper. He said you had lots of jumpers now.'

'I don't like it.'

'No?'

'Joachim said I look like a girl.'

'Did he?'

'I don't want to look like a girl. I want to look like a footballer.'

'Right. Footballers probably wear jumpers at home, you know, when they're just hanging about doing, you know, whatever footballers do.'

'Footballers don't hang about.'

'No?'

'They train.'

'Right.'

'And they get scouted.'

'Oh, OK.'

'And they don't wear jumpers.'

They'd been walking down the long road of two-up-two-downs to the local shop, Sid's small body decked in the livery of his favourite football club, Everton, his chest obliterated by crests and insignia.

'Wayne Rooney was scouted when he was six. And I'm already nearly eight.'

'Six? That's immoral.'

'What is a moral?'

'Im-moral. No little boy should have to decide what they want to be at six.'

Sid had stopped by the graffitied wall next to the post office and looked up at her. Ruth remembered wanting to kneel down, to be level with his lovely face, but he hated her treating him like a baby, so they had stood, hip to eye, to continue their conversation.

'It's not about deciding; there is no deciding. If you are Rooney, you are Rooney. You're a striker. And I am who I am. I'm a striker too.'

'Did Rooney have to leave his mum when he was six?'

'No, I think she was allowed to keep him 'til he was twelve.'

A mean little flurry had blown around their ankles. Ruth had taken Sid's hand, even though he didn't want her to, and they had sought the warmth of the newsagent's.

'I know that some day I will have to lose him,' she had whispered to Robin that night. She hadn't been able to sleep, her dreams full of rotting rooms and sinister places rank with neglect.

'You won't lose him,' Robin had said, his arm around her, a grey dawn falling across their muffled bodies. 'But some day you will have to let him go.'

'Will I lose you?'

She had lifted her hand, traced the lines of his face, stubbled, pillow-wrinkled, dry-lipped.

'No, Ruth, you won't lose me, you won't have to let me go.'

'Beautiful day,' the cafe proprietor said, coming to her table with her coffee.

'Isn't it?'

Ruth smiled, watching prosperous young Londoners at nearby tables lift their faces to the sun.

As she stood to go inside to pay the bill, a woman of about her own age, in a green dress, her long hair loose and grey, asked if the table was free.

'Of course,' Ruth replied. 'Be my guest.'

'Thank you,' the woman answered, sitting down at Ruth's vacated place.

Ruth walked around the block again. The courtyard gate was being propped open by a young mother with a bicycle, a small child strapped into the bucket seat on its back-carrier. Ruth went up to them and held the gate open as mother and child manoeuvred their way out.

'Tell me if you need to pee-pee, Lucy,' the mother said, giving Ruth a smile of thanks.

'No I won't,' Lucy replied.

Neither the recalcitrant Lucy nor her apprehensive mother looked twice at her as Ruth walked on into the courtyard.

Inside, the atmosphere was botanical, splendid, exhilarating. The once dwarfed trees were now dense and luscious. The newly fashioned balconies above Ruth's head were bulbous and weighted down with triumphant plants. Ruth heard wind chimes and birdsong. Late daffodils bloomed in window boxes outside the ground-floor flats. The washing lines that were once strung from balcony to balcony across the rectangle of open sky, and hung with shirts and socks like notes on a stave, were gone; dispelled, Ruth assumed, by the vigilant new aesthetic.

She walked to the far end of the courtyard and sat down opposite Joseph's old flat, on a bench that used not to be there. The kitchen window was dark. Behind the frosted bathroom glass, Ruth could see the blurred imprint of bottles on the sill.

'I'M NOT GOING to tell him.'

'Fuck him, Ruth, just fuck him!'

'He's not well!'

'He doesn't want to be well, Ruth. "Well" is too ordinary for Joey Kazargazof.'

'Stop the car.'

'Ruth.'

'Don't touch me!'

'Ruth.'

Ruth had run from Robin's car, through the slush and across Euston Road. She'd pushed open the courtyard gate; inside, the snow was deep and unadulterated, obliterating the stunted trees, muffling the windowsills, balancing like a high-wire act across the handlebars of abandoned bicycles. Shaking, she'd put her key in the door. The hallway was dark, the kitchen as she'd left it, her cup and plate in the sink, the turquoise bowl on the table empty except for her note to him. She'd gone into the studio and turned on the overhead light. At first it wasn't entirely clear what she was seeing. The walls were bare, the canvases and drawings gone. Under the naked bulb there was just the shadow of their absence, fine straight lines of dust drawn on the emptiness. Ruth had called his name.

The bedroom door was ajar; she'd pushed it open. The woman was sitting on the unmade bed. Ruth saw her cigarette tip illuminate her features in the darkened room before she assembled the face into a recognizable whole. Stevie was fragile and wrinkled, sinewy and blonde; the fingers holding her cigarette were weighted with silver rings. She looked up at Ruth and her eyes were the colour of trapped things, of subterranean things, of things that are lost. Ruth had felt the blood drain from her body. She'd reached for the switch. The room flooded with harsh light. The bed was empty.

Ruth had heard his key in the door and there he was, alive, breathing. She'd held on to him, her face pressed into the shoulder of the ratty black jacket he wore as if in mourning.

'She's in there.'

'Who's in there?'

'Stevie. Stevie is in there. She was there. I saw her.'

'My mother is dead.'

'I saw her.'

He was moving away from her, he was in the bedroom, sitting on the side of the bed where Stevie had sat. He was rolling a cigarette. He was asking her if she was hungry. She'd realized, watching him fumble with the tobacco and the skins, that he was drunk.

'Are you fucking Robin, by the way?'

'What are you talking about?'

'Are you?'

'Am I what?'

'Hungry.'

'No.'

'No what? No, you're not hungry, or no, you're not fucking Robin?'

'Robin has nothing to do with us, not any more.'

'Robin is my friend,' Joseph had said.

'Where are the paintings, Joseph? Where have they gone?'

'They're sold.'

And then they were walking fast towards Gray's Inn Road, to where there was an Indian restaurant on the corner that they'd never had enough money to go into before. And inside everything was womb-like and spicy, and Ruth felt ill, shaken, assaulted by the image of Stevie looking up at her with such depth of contempt.

Joseph ate and drank and piled up money on the table, hundreds of pounds. Food and money and words littering the pale pink tablecloth, he'd told her that after the row, after he'd hurled his mug across the room and watched Ruth leave, he'd gone to the art dealer Zaggy's place in Dalston. He finally wanted to sell the paintings, he'd told her, all of them, as many as she could get shot of, he didn't care to whom or for how much. Zaggy said that she knew a woman, ambitious, based in Brighton, who was setting up a gallery there and trying to create some buzz around it. Zaggy knew the kind of work this woman might be on the lookout for, she said, and told Joseph that if he waited a while, she'd set up a meeting.

'What's she called?' Joseph had asked.

Joseph had been in a hurry. He'd gone back to the flat and selected a painting to bring with him as a calling card. He'd chosen a knowingly kitschy, yet still slightly disturbing, portrait of Stevie with the bright yellow dog at her feet. He'd searched until he found Ruth's money and then he'd taken the train to Brighton. He'd gone to the shark cafe near the station where, a year ago, he'd waited for his mother to materialize. He found the number of the gallery woman in the phone book.

Her answering-machine message gave the address and phone number of the gallery space where she could now usually be found. Joseph decided not to call again but to go there straight away.

An elegantly dressed woman with lousy teeth was locking up the huge, opulent-looking new space as he arrived. He'd introduced himself and handed her the painting.

Later, in a bar with sawdust on the floor, the gallery woman, Esther, had told him she was intrigued.

'Intrigued,' Joseph repeated.

She'd bought him another drink and, later still, brought him back to her flat on a Regency square set back from the seafront.

There was an ironwork lift in the lobby, shaped like a birdcage. ('It was a beautiful thing, Ruth,' he said, 'to be incarcerated in such fine craftsmanship.')

Esther's flat was full of art, paintings, pieces of sculpture. There was a winged bird-man with outstretched hands, against which she propped Joseph's painting. They drank, slowly now. At Esther's suggestion, Joseph lay on her deep couch and, at her prompting, he'd talked about Stevie.

He'd told her about finding Stevie dead in her council flat, not far from where they were. He'd told her that the yellow dog had shat on the floor. He'd told her about the laminated pictures of kittens on Stevie's walls, speckled with her blood.

They'd drunk some more, looking out of the long windows at the pleasure pier, while Esther lay on the other end of the broad couch and stretched out her leg and placed her bare, gnarled foot against his crotch.

'Tell me about your father,' she'd said.

And Joseph had told her that he'd never met his father but that he'd seen him. He'd looked at him. When he was a child of maybe ten or eleven, Stevie had brought him to a party, he'd told Esther, glancing with disinterest at her grey foot in his lap. The party was in a rambling, shabby house in West London. He remembered a room, high and cold and hung with vast canvases. The paintings – life-sized portraits of a young man, an anxious, watchful man, whose arms hung down by his sides – looked gargantuan to Joseph. He had gone from picture to picture, following the man around the room, the defeated man resigned to standing naked in his marbled skin, to wait and serve the watcher.

In the last painting, if it was the last and not the first, the man was hunkered down, his eyes raw as if he'd needed sleep.

There were no more paintings of the frightened man, so Joseph had left that room and began searching for his mother among the faces at the party, face after talking, drinking, smirking, laughing, kissing, howling face.

Joseph had searched for Stevie and, unable to find her and thinking that she'd left without him, had tried to find a way out of that bilious house. There was an open window, and he remembered climbing on to the sill, searching for his mother on the street below. He remembered looking down at parked cars and overflowing bins and at a dog or maybe a fox mooching from scent to scent on the empty road. He remembered a woman trying to coax him back inside with ice cream, which he didn't want. He remembered her hand clasping his wrist and bringing him to Stevie, who was sitting at a table heavy with drink and chicken bones. And she'd looked up at him and waved. He remembered crawling underneath the table and lying across his mother's feet and knowing that were he to fall asleep, she could not leave without him.

'The portraits were of my father,' he'd told Esther. 'They turn up now and again at auction. Even if I could afford him, I don't want him any more.'

Joseph had woken on the couch the following morning to the light on the sea.

'I think I knew your father,' Esther had said, driving Joseph back to London later that day. 'He was on the edges of things for a couple of years. A scene painter – Polish, I think, wasn't he?'

Joseph had invited Esther into his flat and laid Stevie out end to end on the studio floor, the portraits and the other looser, darker drawings he had recently made.

'It was a clean transaction,' he told Ruth. Esther had appraised Stevie's potential to make her a buck, handed Joseph a down payment of two thousand quid, with the promise of significantly more to follow and, tootie-sweetie, he'd packed his mother into her boot.

'Sold her by the yard, Ruth. I was tired of living with her ghost.'

'She wasn't tired of living with you,' Ruth had murmured.

'Art,' Joseph had said, signalling for the bill, 'can't resurrect the dead, but it can buy a chicken korma.'

Esther was staying at her London club. Joseph was to join her there, to celebrate their deal. The club was in Chelsea.

'I wasn't invited,' Ruth had said.

'I'm inviting you.'

'Come home, Joseph.'

'I don't want to go home, Ruth. I'm finally free of the place.'

In the taxi, Ruth had looked out of the window at the sleeting snow, at the beams from the street lights raining down their illuminations, fire sparks in the night.

The taxi had stopped at a crescent of elegant white houses; pillars and porticoes, and gracious windows, illuminated by Christmas lights.

'Where are we?'

'Another universe,' Joseph had replied, getting out of the car.

They'd walked a little way down the road, rung the bell of a low door in a long white wall. In the hallway of the club there was wood panelling and a coat stand and a man in yellow trousers putting on his overcoat, who blew them a kiss as he departed. In the spacious old bar there was a Christmas tree, tasteful and traditional, fixed with white lights. The walls were lined with paintings, the bar with long-stemmed glasses and people lapping at them. The talk, as far as Ruth could tell, was of art and death, and of how tiresome it was having to die before one was discovered.

Ruth had turned to smile at Joseph, to share the strangeness of this new place, but he was shouldering his way through to the bar. His pockets saturated with cash, he ordered a bottle of champagne.

Ruth stood back and watched Joseph introduce himself, watched him high-dive into the members' mutable attention until they tired of him and turned back to one another, to talk again about all their marvellous friends, dead as doornails but immortalized by abstract oils of olive groves or charcoal drawings of flowering cunts.

'There you are!' Esther with the lousy teeth had said to Joseph when she swooped into the bar. 'Ah, you decided to bring a friend?'

'This is Ruth.'

'Of course. Come out to the yurt, Ruth, and we can all get to know each other better.'

They'd followed Esther into the garden, where people were drinking and smoking inside a stupendous tent. There was more champagne, and then wine and then whiskies, and later, when Joseph's eyes had lost focus and there was no light of recognition burning in them, just a smouldering cigarette in his slack mouth,

Esther had leant across him, her hand resting high on his thigh, and, speaking directly to Ruth for the first time all night, asked her if she was Irish.

'Yes,' Ruth had replied.

'Catholic?'

'Once.'

'My mother was Catholic. I'm afraid I was a tremendous irritation to her. Always peeking between my fingers at the moment of transubstantiation, desperate to see the naked Christ. Are you a painter?'

'No.'

'Thank goodness for that! Irish girls are such a find; so loyal, enduring. You were clever to find her,' Esther had said, turning back to Joseph, cutting off Ruth's chance to reply. 'So very very clever,' she repeated, her hand squeezing his thigh.

'Go fuck yourself,' Ruth had said.

She'd stood and left the yurt, making her way back to the bar, circumnavigating a billiard table where a couple of old grotesques were chasing balls across the baize. She found the ladies' toilet and, locking herself in a cubicle, leant her head against the door.

In the bar, a fat man was warbling a tune; peace and love and goodwill to men.

When Ruth had returned, the table in the yurt was empty.

Joseph wasn't in the garden. He wasn't in the bar. Ruth went back to the hallway where they had come in. A narrow staircase led to the upper floors, a velvet rope across it hung with a sign reading 'Members Only'. Ruth had unclipped the brass hook and walked up the stairs, past khaki-toned watercolours, their frames garlanded with tinsel. At the top of the stairs a corridor ran to her left and to her right. Ahead, a thin staircase led to more rooms above.

She'd turned right: a door ajar, an empty bathroom, an algae-stained claw-foot bath. She'd walked to the end of the corridor; the rooms were locked. The corridor to the left was silent. She'd ascended the narrower staircase.

She could hear Joseph's slow, spittle-drooped voice from behind a door. She turned the handle; the door opened. Joseph was leaning against the wall. Esther was on her knees, Joseph's cock in her withered mouth.

Ruth had found her way back down the stairs. Holding on to the side of the stained bath, she ran the cold tap over her wrists. She needed to slow down her breathing, calm the rolling nausea in her gut. The door opened. Esther leant against the frame, her hair, long and pinkish, loose around her face.

'There are rules, you know. "Members Only" means "Members Only".'

Ruth had stood and walked past her, back up the narrow staircase and into the bedroom, where Joseph now lay on a crumpled bed.

'Ruth. What are you doing here?'

'Leave. Come with me now.'

'You should go.'

'This doesn't matter, none of this matters.'

'Go, Ruth.'

'Come home.'

'No.'

'Joseph, come with me.'

'What do you fucking want from me, Ruth?'

She had lunged at him. He'd caught her wrists. Spittle had gathered at the corners of his mouth.

'Come home!'

He'd dropped her wrists, lain back on the bed. There were cigarettes on the bedside table. He lit one up, blew smoke at the ceiling. When he spoke, his words were slow, considered.

'I want to be free, of the past. Do you understand me?'

'I'm not your past.'

'It's only the beginning for me, Ruth. This is only the beginning.'

'You said you'd been waiting for me for your whole life.'

'Did I?'

'I'm pregnant.'

Joseph had stood up, ground the cigarette out on a saucer next to the bed. He'd walked across the room to where there was a table and chair, Esther's clothes – silky, willowy – draped over them. There was a water jug and a glass. He filled the glass and drank, filled the glass and drank again. He filled the glass a third time and handed it to Ruth. She took it and drank.

'Whose is it?'

'What do you mean?'

'Mine or Robin's?'

'How can you ask me that?'

'I'm asking.'

'Yours. Yours yours yours.' She didn't want to cry; she wanted to spit, to maim.

'I don't want it, Ruth. I don't need someone else to fuck up. I'm not finished fucking up myself.'

There was a gentle knock on the door, then a man's voice, apologetic, insistent. 'Members and their guests only, I'm afraid. I'm sorry, but could you kindly ask the young lady to leave?'

Ruth watched herself hurl the water glass at the door.

IT WAS GETTING cold, the rectangle of sky above the courtyard of Midhope House clouding over. Ruth opened her backpack, unrolled her jacket and put it on. Her phone was in the pocket. She replayed Robin's message: 'Ruth, I assume you don't want to speak. Ushi is dead. I'm in Popes Cove. I've called you and called you. It's morning now. I don't know where you are. I'm beginning not to give a shit.'

'Give me some time,' Robin had said. He hadn't said how much.

Ahead of her, an elderly man descended the staircase from the flat above. She recognized her former neighbour straight away. Carrying out his bag of washing in his gloved hands, he seemed to have been overlooked by the block's modernization. He walked past. Ruth would have liked to tell him that if she tried hard to remember, she could still hear his bullying polkas, still hear the mocking folk tunes he played, over and over, seeping through the ceiling. She would like to have asked him if he had any recollection of her, if she had made any impression at all on this hidden place.

She watched him leave, watched as his path crossed that of a couple entering the courtyard through the gate.

Ruth found herself becoming entirely still as the woman in the green dress, the same woman who had earlier asked her if the cafe table was vacant, walked towards her, Joseph beside her, his fingers loosely around her wrist. The couple walked slowly, enjoying their conversation.

Joseph wore a shabby black jacket; he was thin, head bent down, smiling, as if he was listening. The woman in the green dress wore pretty sandals. Humorous, animated, a little worn, she was speaking to him, smiling. She looked the kind of woman Ruth would like to have had as a friend, in another city, in another life. But they weren't friends; they were just ordinary strangers on a cloudy London afternoon, and this wasn't Ruth's city and this wasn't Ruth's life.

Neither Joseph nor his lover looked over at Ruth sitting on the bench. She was invisible to them. She watched them turn into the entranceway of his flat. She waited, unmoving, until she saw the light go on behind the kitchen window, illuminating that low room which had never caught the afternoon sun.

At the cafe on the corner, the proprietor stepped out from behind the service area to see what he could do for her.

'I was in here a short time ago.'

'Of course. I remember.'

'I'm looking for an old friend: Kazargazof, Joseph Kazargazof. He's a painter. I think I may have just missed him.'

'Are you the taxman?' The proprietor smiled, and Ruth shook her head.

'We were friends. A long time ago. I just thought . . . It doesn't matter. I'm sorry to bother you.'

'Yes, I know Joey. He's a regular.'

'My name is Ruth Lennon. I'll be in London for a day or two. I was wondering, if you saw him, could you give him my number? I'll write it down.'

Ruth walked with no particular destination in mind, the area's changes becoming less confusing to her as familiar landmarks reappeared: Cosmo Place, Russell Square, Woburn Walk. The Sorrento Cafe was closed; through the glass she saw her own reflection imprinted on the empty chairs.

She walked on, retracing her steps until she found herself outside the Clerkenwell comprehensive where she and Robin had first met and where Joseph had come on that wet autumn afternoon to see about painting a mural on the schoolyard wall. The school was unchanged, a little more dilapidated maybe. Unlike the flats, it must not have been deemed worthy of regeneration.

Ruth stood outside the locked gates. There was a mural on the schoolyard wall, its whole expanse covered in a fading, flaking forest. Through the iron railing, Ruth could clearly see the muralist's signature: 'ARDU 2002'.

Ruth looked for a long time at Ardu's evanescent trees, then walked back to Cosmo Place and bought herself a plate of pasta in the Italian cafe there. Unable to finish her meal, she left, walking back through the dusk to her room on Argyle Street.

'You want to pay now?' the woman behind the reception desk asked, looking not at Ruth but at her own decorated fingernails, so long they were beginning to curl inwards towards her palm.

'I'd like another night.'

'Suit yourself.'

Back in her medicinal room, Ruth phoned Sid. His mobile went straight to voicemail.

'I spoke to Robin,' Ruth said. 'I'm in London. There's no other news. I'll see you soon in Popes Cove. I love you.'

Hanging up, she realized that her tears were falling without bothering to wait for her consent.

WALKING FAST THROUGH Chelsea, her head bent against the rain, Ruth hadn't known where she was. The elegant white houses with their ebony doors were inscrutable. She had begun to run down a side street and found herself cut off by a set of electronic gates, beyond which was an enclave of red-brick houses, each one uniformly aglow with a textbook Christmas. She'd doubled back on herself, walking and running until she came to an intersection, a shopping street, bars and restaurants, women laughing, ankles turning, money murmuring. The shops were closed. In their windows were ski jackets and silk dressing gowns and featureless mannequins with Perspex faces. She should've stuffed her pockets with Joseph's money earlier in the night when it was loose on the restaurant table. She had nothing.

At South Kensington Tube, she'd slipped through the barrier behind a party of drunk boys in grown-up suits and tasselled loafers and dissolved on to the crowded platform. Changing trains at Victoria, she'd travelled to the end of the line. At Brixton, the elderly inspector had allowed her through the barrier without a ticket. His kindness almost undid her. She began to walk.

When Ruth was a little girl, she and her father used to walk together on the beach beyond their town. Holding her hand inside his jacket pocket, he would tell her important things she needed to know: the best breed of dog to catch a rat, how to read a compass or gut a fish. Sometimes he wouldn't talk at all. Sometimes he'd talk too much, telling her how the Christian Brothers in his boyhood school would crack their leathers over the boys' small hands, how he'd once seen a Brother hold a child by the ankles out of the school's high windows – and worse, he'd mutter, worse, worse. He mightn't talk after that, not for the whole length of the beach and for the whole drive back to the bungalow beside the co-operative store.

Sometimes, though, on those beach walks, they would stop to look at the big grey sea and he would talk about all the places he'd never seen but wished he had: Africa, India, the Far East. He'd love to see Uluru, he'd say, he'd love to get a look at that great burnt rock. Uluru, he'd say, as if it was a spell, an incantation, as if just singing that word could make it real.

Ruth had walked up Brixton Hill, imagining that she was walking to Uluru. She'd passed council blocks and closed-up supermarkets and a petrol garage where a fistful of young men milled around on the forecourt. Still on her way to Uluru, she saw kebab shops and darkened bars and a woman running from a raging man, and heard voices call, but not to her. On familiar ground now, she passed the mini-cab office and betting shop and slumbering nail salon.

The nurses' flat was above a solicitor's office. She'd rung the bell, leant against the doorframe, and waited. She rang the bell again, for longer this time and with more force. She waited, and thought about praying.

'I don't blame God,' her father used to say on their cold beach walks. 'I blame men for having the arrogance to think they're doing God's work.'

Ruth could hear someone coming down the stairs. Dana had opened the door. Her hair tied back in a bobbin, she looked like a child.

'What the fuck, Ruth? It's three o'clock in the morning.'

Dana had made Ruth tea and a bed on the couch and told her that Pauline hadn't been feeling well and had taken something to help her sleep. Helen was on nights, Dana said, and Mairead was at an implant conference in Coventry.

'We put the new tumble dryer in your old bedroom. There isn't room for a bed.'

'I'm fine on the couch. I'm sorry.'

Dana had filled Ruth a hot-water bottle and took Mairead's duvet off her bed and put it over Ruth, along with the rugs and blankets that she had already gathered.

'Mairead will go mad.'

'Mairead will never know.'

'Did you ever find out your man's star sign?' Dana had whispered when Ruth finally felt warm enough to sleep.

'Scorpio.'

'Fuck's sake!' Dana exploded. 'What did you expect?'

'Dana?'

'What?'

'Have you ever been to Uluru?'

The next morning Pauline had sat at the kitchen table in her nylon dressing gown while Dana, an unlit fag in her mouth, beat six eggs into a metal bowl.

'You're both eating,' Dana had said, pouring the eggs into a saucepan. 'I'm not taking any messing.'

Pauline's eyes looked loose in her head. 'Dana told me what happened,' she said.

'Did she?'

'You'll be all right.'

'Will I?'

'It ebbs and flows.'

'What does?'

'Love? Call it what you like.'

'Eat,' Dana said, firing scrambled egg on to their plates.

Helen, back from night duty, her uniform crumpled, her white tights bagging at the knee, had joined them, with a box of barbecued chicken wings.

'We're having breakfast, Helen,' Pauline sighed.

'Long night.'

'Suicide?'

'Two attempts. Boys. They took them from the canal. Brothers.'

'I'm sorry,' Ruth said.

'God, lads, I'm tired,' Helen had said, snapping a wing in two. 'I'm so shagging tired.'

Dana had driven Ruth down Brixton Hill with the roof down, the December wind whipping around their faces.

'What do you think of her, Ruth?'

'Scirocco, isn't it?'

'Wouldn't have taken you for an aficionado.'

'I know a woman who drives hers barefoot, knocking spots off the Limerick road.'

'Fair play to her. I bought mine off a bloke who's going back to Ireland. Fuckin' buzzing over there, he said. The country's hopping, he said. He's going back to be a restaurateur! He's a fuckin' salad chef. You wouldn't catch me dead back in that country, I told him. They might have a few bob in their pockets, but they're still a crowd of sanctimonious pricks.'

Crossing Waterloo Bridge, Ruth had looked along the river at the luxurious city opening up on either side.

'I'm going to go home myself for a while.'

'Are you?'

'I left without saying goodbye. I need to go home to say goodbye.'

They'd stopped on Cromer Street in front of the old Episcopalian church.

'How are you going to get home, Ruth?'

'I'll manage.'

Dana pulled out a wad of notes and handed Ruth two fifties.

'I can't, Dana, not again. It's too much. I can't pay you back.'

'Pauline was charging you far too much for that old room. It's only a hole.'

'I kind of liked it.'

'You did, did you? More fool you.'

Ruth had put her arms around Dana, felt her solidity, her strength, smelt her sweet floral perfume. 'I hope Pauline will be OK.'

'I'll take care of her.'

Turning down Whidborne Street to Midhope House, Ruth heard the Scirocco blast away.

RUTH LAY AWAKE in the neat bed in the plain guesthouse room and listened to London sleep: occasional muffled shouts, laughter, a burst of something mocking from a passing car. She listened as the subterranean rumble of the trains became more frequent, and sometime after dawn she fell asleep.

She dreamt that she had been ordered to guard a corpse, to keep it utterly still. But the corpse was unruly, lifting itself up from its hospital bed, pulling at the wadding that forced its jaw closed. The corpse wore a wedding band. The ring was tight, the corpse's yellow skin bubbling around its line. Ruth lifted the washed-out hospital pillow from under its head and thought to smother it. But the corpse opened its mouth, and instead she bent her head to hear it warn that a worm had invaded an egg. And then the corpse vanished, and now Dan was sitting behind the bar in the Patriot, and he was painting his nails and he was speaking: 'I've forgiven everyone, Ruth. Haven't you? Ruth?'

And then Dan disappeared and then there was sex, sudden, wild, joyous. And someone was inside her, and it was stupefying, astonishing, and she knew those limbs. Long, pale, it was Robin's body, and his fingers were touching her, and it wasn't Robin, it was someone else, behind her now, black hair falling over her neck, and she could hear herself cry out and she looked down between her legs and saw blood, blood streaming down her thighs, pooling on the tangled sheet. And she was alone, entirely alone.

'My baby,' she said, to no one. 'Look, my baby is gone.'

'Do you want a tissue?' a nurse was asking her.

'Yes, please.'

'Well, you can't have one. You were asked to do one thing, Ruth! One thing! And now your daddy has slipped away and we can't find him anywhere!'

She woke, shaken. It was late. Beyond the window, the sun was high in the sky.

She stood in the shower. Head back, she opened her mouth in the vain hope that the water might obliterate the broken night.

Ruth looked at herself in the mirror above the sink, her hair wet, her eyes dull, the line of her jaw smudged, baggy.

There was a missed call on her mobile, which she found wrapped in the damp sheets. 'One neeeew message,' said the phone's alien voice.

The cafe on the corner of Cromer Street was quiet, the lunchtime crowd long departed. When Ruth arrived, the tables on the street were empty, the sky overcast. She went inside and took a table by the window.

'I saw Joey this morning,' the proprietor said, coming to her table. 'I gave him your message.'

'Thank you, yes. He got in touch. We're meeting shortly.'

'I think he was happy to get your note. He tells me you were the one who . . . what is that expression? The one that ran away?'

'The one that got away?'

'That's it.'

'I'm sure he didn't mean that,' Ruth said gently. 'I doubt he'll even recognize me.'

Drinking her coffee, Ruth watched out of the window as an elderly, dishevelled woman made a slow pilgrimage across the road from the church opposite, then came into the cafe freighted with bags and sat heavily at a table nearby. Laboriously removing her wallet from one of her shopping bags, the old woman brought it to the counter and showed a card to the proprietor, who was busy refilling the coffee machine.

Ruth watched him shake his head and refuse her card.

'No,' he said. 'That card won't do.'

The woman made her dilatory way back out of the cafe again, stopping by the door to adjust her bags and stick, hovering for a while on the pavement before she walked across the road again. Ruth watched her disappear beyond the church. She felt ashamed of herself. Why hadn't she intervened? Why hadn't she offered to buy the old woman whatever she had come in here for? Why had she sat, her head averted, pretending not to notice?

As Ruth watched through the window, the old woman reappeared from behind the church and, repeating her actions, crossed the road, opened the cafe door and once more sat heavily at the table nearby. She laboriously found her purse in her bag and brought it to the counter and, as before, the proprietor, the same man who had shown Ruth kindness, declined her card.

Ruth was on her feet. 'Please, let me pay for whatever it is that the lady wants.'

'No no,' he murmured, while the old woman moved past Ruth as if she wasn't there, once again picking up her bags and stick, and leaving.

'It's her habit to come in three times. On the third time I will serve her. If I serve her on the first visit or the second, she walks out anyway. It is the pattern of her mind. It is her peculiar wish. But we understand her.'

As Ruth turned to go back to her table, the door opened and Joseph walked into the cafe. She stood still.

'Ruth.'

'Joseph.'

For a moment neither of them moved, just stood, looking into each other's unfamiliar faces. He walked towards her, lifting his hand and then resting it on her shoulder. He lightly kissed her cheek. She could smell cigarettes and soap.

'Can I get you a . . . ?'

'I have one, thanks.'

They sat at her table by the window. Neither spoke. She found herself staring at his face, figuring out the puzzle of its altered configuration, weighing up skin and bone, categorizing shape and shadow, measuring, proportioning. He had aged more than Ruth might have imagined: his hair was streaked with grey, his skin coarse, his teeth when he smiled were thin, delph-like. His eyes, though, were unmistakable: vigilant, pale, unworldly.

He was speaking to her, asking if she was staying nearby.

'Argyle Street.'

He laughed, taking a leathery notebook from his inside pocket as the proprietor, without needing to be asked, brought him a coffee.

'*Come stai?*'

'All right? Alfie, this is Ruth. Ruth, Alfie.'

'But we are friends already, Ruth and I, are we not?' Alfie said as the cafe door opened and the old woman returned for her third visit to her table and searched in her bags for her card.

'Our neighbour – she has complicated habits,' Joseph said as Alfie returned to the counter to take her order.

'So I believe.'

'You're not going to draw me, are you?' Ruth asked, nodding towards the small sketchbook that lay now on the table between them.

'No, I was going to give you this. It's something I found.'

He picked up the book and handed it to her.

'They're all of you, pretty much. One or two of the old boys in the Kurdistani cafe, some of the clients in the Duke of Wellington, but most of the drawings are you.'

'Me?'

Ruth took the book from his hand and began to look through the dry pages. The words 'Midhope '95' were written on the inside cover. The drawings were simple, some of them just one continuous line: Ruth cooking, Ruth sleeping, Ruth beating eggs, Ruth reading, Ruth feeding cats on the windowsill, Ruth in her duffel coat standing by the bedroom door, Ruth in the deep bath, her tights strung overhead like long, thin dancers.

'Can I keep this?' she asked, grateful that her words sounded solid enough to have been spoken.

'Of course.'

Ruth placed the sketchbook on the table. She held her hands in her lap, unwilling for the moment to pick up her cup. They were silent. Ruth watched Joseph stir sugar into his coffee, his movements tentative, slow.

'How is Robin?'

'Ushi is gone. She died on Saturday. She'd hardly been ill. It's a shock. I think everyone is shocked.'

Joseph sat back in his chair, looked out of the window.

'I'm sorry,' Ruth said. 'Robin just told me yesterday.'

Ruth watched Alfie bring the old woman a tall glass of orange juice with a paper straw.

Joseph cleared his throat. 'I'd like to write to him. Is he in Popes Cove?'

'Yes. Yes, he is. I'm sure he'd appreciate that.'

Ruth looked across the table. After the initial elation of seeing him, there was just this formality. Had she just used the word 'elation'? Maybe she meant mania, maybe she meant idiocy. He was speaking to her, talking about Sid, leaning towards her, apologizing. The wrinkles around his eyes were deep, the pores on his cheeks wide, his skin yellow.

'I'm sorry, Ruth. I'm sorry I wasn't up to the task.'

Memory, she thought, is just layers and layers of colour and tricks of the light.

'Sid is fine. He never needed you.'

Joseph fell silent.

Ruth looked out of the window. She could see the old lady reflected in the glass, the straw in her mouth, her two hands flat on the table.

'I have very little to offer him, Ruth. I haven't made much of a success of my life.'

'I'm not asking you for anything. I'm giving you a chance.'

Joseph had stopped trying to speak. He was listening.

'Sid has been looking for you. He didn't tell me for a long time. And then your drawing came in the post . . .'

She broke off. She had wanted to sound practical, concise, authoritative, but she didn't know where to begin, where to end.

'He doesn't want to hurt Robin. He loves him. He's trying to figure himself out. He left art college, left home, went to Berlin. He's struggling. He's stopped drawing, makes a bit of music. I've listened to the lyrics; it wasn't hard to read between the lines, to know that he thinks about you.'

'And I him.'

'Why did you send me the fucking drawing, Joseph? Why? Twenty years of silence and then you send me a drawing? How did you even know where I worked? What right had you to reappear? What? Tell me! What right had you to track me down?'

Ruth didn't know where her own anger was coming from. Behind the counter, Alfie was looking in their direction.

'I was trying to make amends,' Joseph answered quietly.

The old woman, temporarily put off her stride by Ruth's outburst, resumed her ingurgitation.

'Amends? Are you in recovery?'

'Yes. I suppose.'

'From what?'

'Everything, really.'

'Is this some kind of twelve-step thing? Are you looking for forgiveness? Because if you are, you can look elsewhere.'

'No.'

'What, then?'

'Peace. I want to make peace with the past.'

'Are you dying?'

'Currently, no more than any of us.'

'Currently?'

'No, I'm not dying.'

There was a pause. The old lady was now sucking her biscotti like a lollipop.

'Tell me about Sid.'

'Why should I?'

'I don't want to hurt anyone,' Sid had said.

They'd been sitting outside in the yard, the night before he left for Berlin. He was rolling a cigarette, and Ruth had wanted to snap it out of his hand.

'I don't want to hurt Robin, I don't want to hurt either of you, but I need to know him. I need to know who I am.'

'What do you want to know about him?'

'Anything.'

Beyond the restaurant window, the sun was filtering through the cloud bank. She shouldn't have come here. Why did she come here?

'He used to say . . .' Ruth hesitated. 'When Sid was a little boy, he used to say that the word "hello" tasted like popcorn.'

Ruth took the paper napkin out from under her cup and blew her nose. She was fucked if she was going to cry.

'Thank you,' Joseph said.

'He's going to contact you. I've told him where you are.'

Ruth leant in towards Joseph. Aware now of their audience, she lowered her voice.

'He's going to come looking for you and I swear, Joseph, that if you hurt him or betray his affection, or reject him, or shit on him in any way, I will come after you and I will tear your fucking heart out.'

'My life wasn't simple.'

'Nobody's life is simple, Joseph.'

Ruth watched the old lady reflected in the glass. Sated now, she was applying lipstick without the help of a mirror. Her precision was remarkable.

'Robin has been a good father to him?'

'Of course Robin's been a good father to him,' Ruth snapped. 'He's a good man.'

Alfie came back to the table to see if they wanted anything else. Ruth asked for the bill. But there was no bill, not if you were a friend of Joey's.

They walked in the late-afternoon sunshine to Russell Square and sat together on a bench, the earth dry and dusty beneath their feet. Office workers freed from their desks hurried past, young women in pencil skirts and clunky runners, loud boys on their phones, gym bags slung over their shoulders.

'It's not as lovely as I remember,' Ruth said.

'The park?'

'The park is not as lovely as I remember.'

They stood. Retracing their steps, they began to walk back towards King's Cross.

'Are you ill?' Ruth asked, keeping step beside him, her arms folded against her body.

She had a strange sensation of control. She felt immune, free to ask what she wanted to ask, to behave as she wanted to behave.

'I *was* ill. Hepatitis. There were complications. The liver is a forgiving organ, if you give it a chance, which I didn't always. I look after myself now, Ruth. I lead a quiet life.'

'Drink?'

'Drink, yeah. Lot of drink. I was using for a bit. Briefly. I got lucky. A woman I met, a sculptor, brought me to India and then to Spain. We lived together for a time in the High Alpujarras. Us and a bunch of goats. I was pretending to be a painter.'

'What happened?'

'To the goats?'

'To your girlfriend.'

'She got sense, Ruth, threw me out.'

They walked on a little.

'Robin had a goat once.'

'I know. Gilbert. Decent chap. I met him.'

The pub at the end of Argyle Street smelt of old beer and disinfectant. Ruth's wine tasted like tin.

'After Spain I came back to London. I'd sublet Midhope, the only intelligent thing I managed to do in about a decade. I'd somewhere to come back to. I moved back in, tried to work. I was drinking. Skint. Nish used to save me the unsold bread. I had one tab with him and another in the Duke. Paid up in the Duke whenever I sold a bit of work.'

'And did you sell?'

'Illustrations. Couple of cookery magazines used to use me. I was a dab hand at knocking out a pomegranate or a sheaf of wheat.'

'And now? Do you work? Can you survive?'

'I get some teaching. Bit of illustration still. It's enough. I live simply.'

Joseph was drinking water, his hand shaking a little when he raised his glass.

'I sublet again, before I became ill, and went to Poland. I was looking for my father.'

'Did you find him?'

'Found a brother in Łódź who drank me into a coma. An actual coma. Our father remained at large.'

'Is your brother an artist?'

'He's a policeman.'

Joseph needed to eat. When Ruth suggested that she leave him and return to her guesthouse, he invited her back to the flat to eat with him. There was a Tesco Metro near the station, he said, he could pick something up. He bought bread and cheese and tomatoes, refusing Ruth's offer to pay. Joseph asked her if she wanted wine, but she demurred. At the till, he bought cigarettes. She changed her mind, bought herself a bottle of red.

'I have my own code to open the gate,' Joseph said as they reached the flats. 'Tell Sid. He'll need it if he wants to visit. He'll remember it.'

'Why?'

'It's 1996, the year of his birth.'

Ruth waited in the hallway for Joseph to turn on a light. He gestured her ahead towards the kitchen, however, explaining that he needed to get a new bulb.

'The kitchen light works,' he told her, but she knew that already.

The kitchen was clean. On his table was the lovely turquoise bowl that she'd forgotten she remembered.

His studio was warm; there was a rug on the floor, a record player, his punk albums stacked next to it in a wooden box. In the bathroom, a dry towel hung on a rail. On the floor under the sink there was a basket that held bits and pieces of jewellery, a square of cotton, cleansing oil in a blue bottle, a toothbrush in a plastic box.

Back in the studio, where Joseph had directed her, Ruth sat on the narrow bed that served as a couch. On the walls there were paintings and drawings, some of the woman she had seen him with yesterday, some of a child, a girl. A wide piece dominated the wall opposite the bed: a dark forest, a still lake. Poland, she thought.

Framed over Joseph's desk, Robin stood waist-deep in green water. He had been trapped in that lake for decades, Ruth thought, standing to look at it, becoming more luminous with age.

'I'm tempted to ask,' Joseph said, coming in from the kitchen with her wine, 'if Robin knows you're here?'

'No,' Ruth answered. 'He doesn't.'

There were drawings of the woman in the green dress on the desk. Ruth liked the way Joseph had depicted his lover's body, the weight of her breasts, the ordinary generosity of her stomach and thighs.

'Someone you love?' Ruth asked.

'Maria? Yes. She won't live with me. I've asked. She tells me I'm better in small doses.'

'She looks kind.'

'She's a teacher, like Robin. Music. She teaches in a comprehensive in Coventry. We see each other at weekends.'

Ruth sat down again. A silence descended between them.

'Tell me, how did you and Robin . . . ?' He paused.

'Begin?'

'Resume.'

Ruth sipped her wine.

'Sid was about two; we were living with my mother. I wrote to Robin at Popes Cove. I knew his mother's name; the address wasn't hard to find. I'd thought about him. I wanted to apologize for how I'd left things in London. He'd been trying to protect me and I'd been ungracious, cruel. Part of me wanted to know if Robin knew where you were, how you were. I waited a long time before I posted the letter. Waited until I was sure that I wanted to know about him more than about you.'

'He wrote back?'

'He got in his car and came to find us. Walked into a bar and asked for me. My friend Dan was behind the counter. The way he tells it, Robin rode into our town, guns blazing. I think it was more tentative than that.'

Ruth looked around the low room. There was an austerity to it that she hadn't immediately spotted. The evening had grown cold, the residual warmth from the day long spent.

'There's something I'd like to show you,' Joseph said, standing to leave the room.

He returned moments later with a framed drawing in his hands. 'I don't know if you remember.'

The lines were faded, but Ruth knew herself in the same way you know your own child, in the intrinsic way you can pick their small body out in a crowd. In Joseph's drawing, Ruth lay on his unmade bed, barricaded from the marauding, unpredictable outside world, the two-bar electric heater perched for her comfort on the bedside table. 'I don't want you to move,' he'd told her, and she hadn't. Lying back on the pillow, one knee raised, her hands folded across her stomach, she'd watched his yellow pencil move across the page.

They ate the bread and cheese sitting on the studio floor. There were certain drawings that he couldn't let go, he told Ruth. The drawing of Robin in the lake, of Ruth by the two-bar fire, some of Maria sleeping, one or two of Stevie that he had managed to retrieve after the Brighton show. He'd had a couple of promising years after that exhibition, before he'd definitively blown that candle out by being too fucked to produce any work.

'It could come around again maybe?'

'No, Ruth, not now. I'm too old, too staid.'

'Do you think about Stevie?'

They were smoking, sitting in the courtyard on the bench where only yesterday Ruth had sat and watched Joseph go into the flat with Maria. They were flicking their ash into a broken plant pot. Ruth's wine glass was empty.

'I do, but differently. I'm older now than she ever managed to become. I have out-aged her, and now I'd like to know her better and she's gone.'

'Is she?'

'I feel her presence here. Sometimes, when I come in from being out somewhere, I get the feeling that she's just left. I can smell her cigarette smoke, almost see it. Depressing to think we maintain our addictions beyond the grave, eh, Ruth?' he asked, stubbing out his cigarette in the pot.

They sat on the floor in the studio, sipping tea and listening to the Buzzcocks. When the album was over, Joseph stood, put Siouxsie and the Banshees on the turntable and went into the kitchen to make another pot.

'Well?'

'Nope. Sorry.'

'How can you still not appreciate punk?'

'Sid says the same thing to me.'

'Tell him I saw the Banshees on stage. In the early days. And the Buzzcocks. At the Vortex in '77.'

'You were a child!'

'Twelve, thirteen maybe. I don't know how Stevie got me past the door, but she did. Fucking mind-blowing. I loved her for that. Tell Sid that I still have Stevie's original membership card for the Roxy. He'll like that.'

'Maybe you can tell him yourself.'

'Maybe.' There was a pause. 'Ruth?'

'Yeah?'

'I thought . . . No, it doesn't matter.'

'What?'

'I wondered if you named Sid after Sid Vicious.'

'Why?' She laughed. 'Why would I name him after Sid Vicious? Sydney Lennon! I named him after my father!'

Beyond the basement window, Ruth watched a pair of boots walk down the silvery pavement towards St Pancras.

'I need to go, Joseph. It's late.'

She stood, gathered up her backpack and checked inside to make sure she had the leather-bound sketchbook Joseph had given her in the cafe and the key to Argyle Street, which she transferred into her jacket pocket.

Joseph sat on the floor and watched her.

'I have a daughter.'

Ruth slung her bag over her shoulder, leant against the doorframe.

'Stephanie. She's almost fifteen. I haven't lived with her since she was five.'

'Where is she?'

'Spain. She lives with her mother.'

Sid had a sister. The news had come too fast. Ruth felt herself slip, become uncontained.

'She's Sid's sister.'

'Half-sister,' Ruth countered.

'Where is the little boy now?' Sid used to ask her over and over again in the days and weeks after the miscarriage. 'What is the little boy doing? Who gives him his dinner? Is he allowed to watch the television? What does he watch on the television? Does he watch football?'

Ruth had been unable to answer him, leaving it to Robin to tackle the hokum of heaven, and instead going off on her own for a desultory walk up and down their long, long, unbroken street.

'She used to cry when I left the finca, used to try to stay awake until I came back.'

'The finca?'

'The farm in Spain where her mother and I lived, where she was born. There were rows. I'd leave, drink, lose days.'

'I'm sure it was all very difficult,' Ruth replied briskly, running her fingers over the key in her pocket, picturing the sanctuary of her single bed.

'I'd go back, apologize, tell them that it was never going to happen again. Stephanie was just a little thing. Wouldn't let me hold her, wouldn't look at me. I was being punished. And then she'd call out to me in the night and I'd pick her up and bring her into our bed. I loved those nights, Ruth. Her asleep between us. Just breathing.'

'Love.'

'Love doesn't cover it.'

There was silence. Beyond the window, Ruth could see rain.

'Last summer she came to England to visit her grandmother. She stayed with me for a night. Maria and I took her to the Notting Hill Carnival.'

'She like it?'

'Bit freaked out by the crowds. I think she missed her mother.'

'What about this summer?'

'Don't think so. She hasn't said. That's her there.' Joseph indicated a watercolour that Ruth had noticed earlier, of a delicate young woman, fair, with ice-blue eyes gazing cautiously at the painter. Ruth had thought the painting was of Stevie, before the unravelling had begun.

'I have to come to terms with my own failures, Ruth. I can't afford to look away.'

Ruth put her bag down and knelt opposite him. She took his hand.

'I never let you be a part of Sid's life. Or Robin's. We all fail. We just have to learn to forgive ourselves.'

He rested his forehead on her hand. She stroked his greying Indian hair.

'Stay, Ruth. Stay.'

Ruth lay on her side and watched Joseph sleep, saw from the spill of the street light his chest rise and fall, the hollow sockets of his eyes. Earlier, when he'd sat on the bed to take off his shoes and socks and shirt, she'd seen the white scar that ran from his right side to halfway across his abdomen, cutting into his musculature like a badly sewn seam. He'd asked if it disgusted her.

'Disgust?' she'd repeated. 'Why would it disgust me?'

'I'm not asking you for anything, Ruth,' he'd said.

She'd leant back against the doorframe, wondering what she had to give him anyway.

He'd stood to unbutton his jeans. Between them was his bed, a grey cotton throw smoothed over its surface. He'd walked over to her, his body compact, heavier, squared off. He was darker than she remembered, his skin compressed, toughened. She'd wondered how she would set him if he were to stand entirely still, become an image of himself, a life drawing – barefoot man, injured man, man in loose black jeans reaching for someone beyond the frame.

'Ruth?'

He'd kissed her neck. She'd felt him lift the hem of her shirt.

Complying, she'd reached her arms over her head, then unhooked her bra and let it fall, her back cold against the bedroom door.

'You're beautiful, Ruth. You never understood that.'

'You don't know me,' she'd said quietly.

She'd looked beyond him. Already she felt a weariness with this place, with his shoes arranged side by side at the foot of the bed, with the dampish underground smell, with the drawings tacked to the wall, the paint-spattered lamp on the card table, the stacked paperbacks, the empty mug.

'Aren't you cold, Ruth?' he'd asked her, decades ago, on that first night. She'd been standing on his rug, on a small blue oval of frozen tundra, and he'd reached for her and she'd gone to him, every infinitesimal part of her anticipating the next moment and the next.

'Ruth? Are you cold?'

'Yes.'

They'd finished undressing. He'd lifted the bedcover and she'd lain on his sheets. Beside her, he'd looked along the length of her body. She'd dismissed the dull thoughts crowding her head, of how she'd changed, how she'd aged. He was looking at her intently. His interest felt almost – she searched for a word – botanical? Scientific? It was, she thought, as if she were a cask that held something invisible inside, something alchemical, that could reconnect them both to a past they hadn't lived.

They'd fucked slowly, not unpleasantly. In deference to how she thought she should be feeling or behaving, she'd opened up to him, held him, run her fingers over his back, still beautiful, over his shoulders, robust and staunch.

'I loved you,' Ruth said.

'And I you.'

'I don't think so.'

She'd tried to find herself in the mirror of his pupils, but all she saw there was the low gleam of the bedside light. He'd closed his eyes, stopped. He hadn't come.

'I'm sorry,' he'd said. 'Sometimes it happens that way.'

She'd told him to sleep, told him that nothing mattered, that this moment was for them and them alone.

He'd lain back, reached for her hand.

When Sid was a tiny baby, Ruth had watched him sleeping, afraid that if she took her eyes off him he would disappear. Her mother would come into the bedroom and take the infant away with her so that Ruth could rest. She'd sleep then, as if at the bottom of a well, weighted down by exhaustion, waking in a flash of consciousness, her body already ahead of her, her breasts leaking, seeking the child she was almost sure she'd lost.

Years later, not long after Ruth and Sid had begun living with Robin, when Sid was no more than four, Ruth had returned from the toilet in a Spanish airport to find Robin where she'd left him with Sid, on a plastic bank of seats, their luggage spread out around them. Robin was reading, one long leg crossed over the other. 'Where's Sid?' she'd asked and Robin had paled.

Ruth remembered running and calling, the only sound in her ears the drumming of her useless blood. She wanted to annihilate everyone on the concourse, every foul living, breathing piece of shit obscuring her view, blocking her way. She ran to the ladies' room, sure that he had followed her there. She slammed open cubicle doors, banged her fists on others, calling his name. She ran to Duty-Free, where earlier Sid had asked for the lollipop that she'd bought and put in her bag for landing. She couldn't see him anywhere. Just people, other people: seething, lurching, insouciant people. She'd searched the cafes, the sweet shop with its troughs of lurid candy. He'd been gone for ten minutes – more, maybe twenty. She heard his name announced over the intercom – Robin had gone to Security. She felt a numbness around her mouth, felt her stomach drop further. He was nowhere. She'd tried to get a breath. She'd looked up. Robin was walking towards her, holding Sid in his arms. Her son had wandered off to play with a child he'd seen waiting at a nearby departure gate, who was rolling a ball across the airport's smoothly tiled floor. The child's mother, who was Danish, had heard the announcements and brought him to Security.

The three of them had boarded their flight to Dublin, Ruth holding Sid's hand so tightly he stared up at her in frightened trepidation. She couldn't look at Robin, couldn't speak to him.

That night, back in their own kitchen, Sid safely in his bed, Robin had sat with his head in his hands.

'I'm sorry, Ruth,' he'd said.

'He's *my* son,' she'd hissed. 'Mine.'

'Mine,' she said aloud now in the silent bedroom. But the word was empty.

Dawn. She slipped out from under Joseph's sheets. He didn't stir. Picking up her jeans and shirt from the floor, she stood for a moment in the doorway and looked around her. She wanted to go home. Whatever home was, wherever she had left it. She turned her back on his subterranean world. From the small oval of blue rug, she watched herself depart.

RUTH LISTENED TO the roar of the engine, felt the aircraft climb, shaky as a rickety step, felt it level out, felt a barely perceptible knot of tension unravel from passenger to passenger.

Held in place by her seatbelt and the greasy chair back, she felt something inside of herself detach and, like the surprise of finding your own tooth lying in the well of your mouth, it occurred to her that something rooted had come undone.

EPILOGUE

Dublin, July 2018

'Robin!' Kelly said, sitting up in her sun lounger to apply more lotion to her well-oiled arms.

Robin's eyes were closed; he had drifted off, his legs stretched out in front of him, in one of the old wicker chairs that Colm had unearthed from the Wendy house when it became clear that Dublin's much-anticipated heatwave had actually materialized.

'Robin! Are you awake?'

'Um-hum?'

The warmth from the late-afternoon sun was perfect. He didn't want to open his eyes.

'You promised you'd tell me what you thought of Dylan's book.'

'Did I?'

'You said you'd read it and tell me exactly what you thought.'

'When did I say that?'

'I want the truth, Robin. Don't teacher me. I don't want to be patronized.'

'I wouldn't dare.'

Helen's lunch had been, as Helen's lunches always were, excessively generous. This time they'd finished with a vegan almond cake that Erin had made.

'I think it might need cream,' Helen had said, her fork hovering.

'It does not need cream,' Erin had replied.

'Robin! Tell me!'

Robin opened his eyes and looked across the garden to where Ruth and Colm were kneeling next to the fishpond, seemingly trying to enumerate Colm's new shoal of darting Shubunkins.

'How many do you count, Ruth?'

'I'm not sure. They keep hiding in the underwater castle.'

'Nice, eh?'

'As plastic castles go, it's a winner.'

Ruth had rolled her jeans up. Her legs were getting freckled.

'It may not be up to your standards, Ruth, but the bloke in the pet shop said the fish needed stimulation.'

'He saw you coming,' Helen muttered from the paddling pool, where she was sitting in her polka-dot swimsuit, her arms and legs dangling over the sides.

'So! Tell me. Were you blown away by Dylan's talent? Robin?'

'I'm only counting thirteen.'

'Robin?'

'There's supposed to be seventeen. I bought seventeen Shubunkins.'

'Robin, I'm asking you a question.'

Ruth looked up from her fish-counting, held Robin's gaze across the hot garden.

'It's a very long book, Kelly.'

'Long?'

'Long. One thousand, one hundred and fifty-eight pages is a long book.'

'You finished it, then?'

'Yes, I did.'

'It's actually three books. A triptych.'

'That fact didn't escape me, Kelly.'

'And?'

'And I'm full of admiration for Dylan. It's quite a feat.'

If Colm knelt any further into the fishpond, Robin thought, he'd drown.

'Eleven, twelve, thirteen. You're right. Thirteen. There's a killer on the loose in there. That pet-shop owner sold me another cannibal.'

'I'm starting to feel patronized, Robin.'

Robin glanced over at Helen and Colm's youngest daughter, parked alongside him on her sun lounger, a pair of enormous star-shaped sunglasses covering her eyes. Kelly was looking dangerous; well oiled and dangerous.

'Maybe,' Robin suggested, 'Dylan might think about condensing the book a little.'

'The Reptile Wars, you mean?'

'Maybe the Reptile Wars, yes. Yes, actually. Definitely the Reptile Wars.'

'They're intrinsic to the plot.'

'All seven of them?'

'God, I can't take much more of this heat. Colm!'

'What, Helen? We're trying to count the fish.'

'I think the paddling pool is deflating.'

'Well, I'm not going back down to the petrol station to pump it up again.'

'I'm so hot. I'm too hot to get out of this thing and I'm too hot to stay in it. I need to find the cat. Where's the cat? Ruth says I've to put sunblock on its ears.'

'Yep. Thirteen. No more than that,' Ruth announced, standing up from the fishpond.

'Definitely?'

'Definitely thirteen.'

'Jaysus. Now we're in trouble.'

'Did you like the bit where he transmogrified into the frozen snake, so that he could pass through the narrow portal into the other world?' Kelly asked Robin.

'I remember that bit.'

'And the quest to save the queen?'

'Yep.'

'The queen's flesh-eating disease is a metaphor.'

'I suspected as much.'

Ruth had wandered over to join them, sitting on the arm of Robin's wicker chair. Robin closed his eyes again; the light beat orange against his lids. Gently, he laid his hand on the small of her back. Her skin under her T-shirt was damp.

'What are you guys talking about?'

'Dylan's book,' Kelly replied.

Robin felt Ruth's back stiffen. He had a sudden, unprovoked memory of fucking her up against a wardrobe door, in a guest-house in Achill, of holding her up, her legs wrapped around his waist. The next morning they'd lain on the empty beach with their hoods up and kissed.

'So,' Kelly explained to Ruth, 'the Reptile Wars are fought to free the queen, who is actually dying of flesh-eating loneliness on this distant planet where she's being held by this, like, despot.'

'Despot?'

'Half dragon, half despot, but the thing is, the queen is based on Dylan's actual mother, Celestine, who was actually, actually dying when he was writing the middle section of the trilogy.'

'Dying? I hadn't realized.'

'Breast cancer. She's fine now. They're all in Tenerife. Dylan's granddad is in the finals of a ballroom-dancing competition.'

'Glad to hear it.'

'Robin,' Helen called. 'You don't want to help me up, do you?'

Helen was sitting in a puddle on the yellow grass, the deflating pool listing around her, the water sinking into the dry earth. Robin got up and helped her to stand. His arm around her waist, they joined Colm at the pond to examine the diminishing stock of inhabitants. The three of them looked into the greenish shallows, trying to find Judas among the frightened Apostles.

'I think it's him,' Colm said, pointing at one of the darting fish.

'How can you tell?' Helen asked. 'They all look like the one odd shoe.'

'Maybe it's something else, a predator. Maybe you should cover the pond with a net,' Robin suggested.

'If you do, I'll take it off again,' Erin said, leaving the shaded steps of the Wendy house to join them. 'The fish are being taken by the heron. She swoops down at sunset and catches them in her beak. She's magnificent.'

'What heron? I've never seen a heron.' Colm sounded indignant.

'You've never looked,' Erin said.

Standing on one long, skinny leg, yawning, Erin, it occurred to Robin, didn't look unlike a heron herself.

'She's going to get a sharp twist of the neck if I catch her.'

'She'll haunt you,' Erin said lightly. 'Your life will be blighted by your own ignorance.'

'Helen, our daughter is frightening me.'

'Erin's right. Let the heron have the fish, and when she's eaten these ones we'll go back to the pet shop and get her some more.'

'Terrific. I'm the one who cleaned this pond out, wading around pulling dollies' prams out of it! I'm the one who drove to the pet shop and lugged home a bucket of Shubunkins, and now you're telling me that I have no control over who eats what in my own fishpond! Is that it, Helen? Is it?'

'That's correct. You have no control over the fate of your fish-pond, Colm. It's life. Live with it.'

Robin found Ruth in the kitchen stacking used dishes on the draining board.

'Let me help.'

'Up to you.'

Robin looked at her. The earlier calm in the sunlit garden had dissipated. She looked tense. It was cold in the kitchen; she'd put a cardigan on over her T-shirt.

'I didn't realize that your friend had been so ill.'

'She's fine now,' Robin said, picking up a bowl of half-eaten potato salad from the kitchen table.

'So I hear.'

'Should I put this in the fridge?'

'You'll need to cover it first.'

Robin chose an empty plate and rinsed it under the tap. He watched as, beyond the kitchen window, Kelly and her mother leapt around the garden, shrieking, while Erin sprayed them with the garden hose. Colm continued to glare earnestly at the condemned fish.

'Are you still seeing her? Celestine?'

Robin found a tea cloth hanging over the cooker rail and began to dry the plate.

'Occasionally.'

There was silence as they moved around Helen's chaotic kitchen.

'Have you been OK? Ruth?'

'I'm fine.'

'Busy?'

'Project with the kids is finished for summer. Work's quiet.'

'Yeah? Why don't you come down to Popes Cove for a couple of days?'

'Does Celestine go to Popes Cove?'

Robin didn't want to answer the question.

'Does she?'

'Sometimes.'

'Does she bring her son?'

'No.'

He covered the dish of potato salad with the plate, tried to find a place for it in Helen's crowded fridge. 'Do you think we should load the dishwasher?'

'No,' Ruth replied dully. 'Just stack.'

They scraped and stacked the dinner plates and dessert plates. Robin began to gather the glasses.

'Did she go to Popes Cove when Ushi was alive?'

'Once.'

'Did Ushi like her?'

'I think so. It wasn't easy to tell.'

'More than she liked me, I'm sure.'

'Ushi loved you.'

'No she didn't.'

'Ruth . . .'

'She thought I treated you like you were second best. She never believed in me.'

'Ruth?' He reached out for her.

'It doesn't matter any more,' she said. 'None of it matters any more.'

When Robin turned back to the sink, he saw that Erin was standing by the open kitchen door.

'Mum says you're to come outside and enjoy the last of the sun. She said to leave the dishes.'

'Helen, thank you for lunch,' Robin said.

'You shouldn't be wasting the sunshine. The dishes can wait until later.'

'I need to make a move anyway.'

He watched Ruth follow Erin to the Wendy house step, where they both sat down.

'So soon?'

'If I get on the road now, I'll be in Popes Cove before the light goes.'

'See ya, Robin.'

'Cheers, Kelly. Tell Dylan not to give up.'

'Oh, he won't. He says giving up is the only failure.'

Robin said goodbye to Colm, commiserating on the fate of the fish. He looked again across the pond to Ruth. She smiled from the shadows and raised her hand.

He thought about blowing her a kiss, but then thought that would be ridiculous. He thought about walking across the garden and shaking her. He did neither. After raising his hand to echo her salute, he turned and walked towards the house.

Helen followed Robin through the shadowy kitchen, tying some kind of dressing-gown thing around her and offering him a varied assortment of supplies for his journey, all of which he declined.

'Ham sandwich? Coleslaw? I have tons of cottage cheese and pineapple.'

'It's a three-hour drive, Helen. I think I'll survive.'

In the hallway, Robin bent to kiss Helen goodbye. She looked up at him.

'We're worried about Ruth.'

'We?'

'Colm and I.'

'Has she said something?'

'She's not saying anything, that's the point. It's like she's stopped. It's like she's waiting for something, only we don't know what it is. Why don't you invite her back to Popes Cove with you?'

'I did. She declined.'

'Are you still seeing that woman?'

'I've already been through this, Helen. Occasionally. It's not what you think.'

'What do you mean, it's not what I think? You sleep with her! You eat with her! Presumably you think about her! It's perfectly clear what it is.'

'We don't make demands on one another. We're friends.'

'Lovely. I wish my friends were so accommodating.'

She looked away then, aware maybe of her wet footprints on the carpet underfoot.

'She's sad. That's what I have to tell you. All that I have to tell you. In my opinion, in our opinion, Ruth is sad. Anyway, there you are. She knows where we are if she needs us. The same thing applies to you.'

'Thank you, Helen.'

'Don't hug me. I'm soaking. I'll ruin your shirt.'

'Hey.'

Robin turned from the open boot, where he'd been searching in the pockets of his jacket for his glasses.

'Hi.'

'New glasses?' Ruth asked.

'Just for driving.'

'Nice.'

'Yeah? You don't think they're a bit . . . ?'

'What?'

'Hip?'

'There are worse looks.'

'Suppose.'

'I just thought I'd say goodbye.'

'Thank you. It felt strange to be leaving without.'

They moved together. Robin held her, her head on his shoulder. Her stillness always reminded him of a small animal. She was all caution, all vigilance.

'I meant to tell you that I heard from Sid yesterday,' Robin said, resting his chin on her head.

'Me too. Joe is bringing him for long, long walks around London. Camden, Bloomsbury, Soho, Covent Garden. The river, the whole length of the river, Sid said.'

They stood together in silence, the distant conversation from the back garden drifting towards them in the stillness. Beyond them the Dublin Mountains shimmered blue and mauve in the heat.

'You called him Joe.'

'Did I?'

'You said Joe. You used to only ever call him Joseph.'

Joseph, Robin thought, as if his name held water she didn't want to spill.

'Sid calls him Joe. That's his name.'

'Joe sent me a card and a drawing to Popes Cove.'

'Yeah?'

'He must have drawn it thirty years ago. It's me standing waist-deep in a lake. Half of me solid, the other half obscured. I don't remember the occasion, don't remember any lake. He wrote kind words about Ushi. Her soups.'

'Ushi's soups! You could tap dance on them, as my mother would say.'

'Like Helen, Ushi thought the world could be fed into submission.'

Their bodies parted. Robin tried to read Ruth's expression, but she was looking away and the light was undependable in the smoky summer haze.

'Anyway, I don't want to delay you.'

'Are you sad, Ruth?'

'Aren't you?'

'A lot of the time. You kind of get used to it.'

He opened the driver's door, threw his jacket on the front seat. Leant back against the roof of the car, he looked at her. She smiled, scuffed her flip-flop on the ground.

'I don't know who we are any more,' she said, 'Ruth and Robin. Robin and Ruth. Those people don't exist. They belonged to some other time.'

'Maybe we've outlived those versions of ourselves. Maybe they no longer serve us.'

'Maybe.'

Ruth looked around the suburban garden, at Helen's wilting hydrangeas, at a pot of dwarf roses steadily climbing the stippled wall.

'The stupid thing is, Robin, that I love you and it would probably be more convenient if I didn't. And I wanted to say something. I wanted to say sorry.'

'For what?'

'For taking so long to know that.'

The sun slid behind a cloud. Momentarily the garden became monochrome and Ruth, so slight, seemed almost to evaporate.

'Maybe it's best if I go, Ruth.'

'Safe trip,' she whispered, and turned to go.

'It said on the news that the cows are thirsty.'

'Sorry?'

She turned back to face him at the door of Colm and Helen's fine, hospitable, exhausting house.

'Cows, all over the country, are thirsty. It's a phenomenon.'

'Is it?'

'Maybe not a phenomenon. But when I go out to the yard to feed Ushi's cats, they're there, the cows in the top field, croaking at me.'

'Ask the farmer to give them water.'

'I would, but unfortunately he married Una McClafferty and I don't think he likes me.'

'Una McClafferty?'

'Una's the very generous girl who relieved me of my virginity on a wet beach when I was seventeen and came over to the house in her Subaru to drop me in a meatloaf when Ushi died.'

'A Subaru, eh?'

'Una married Pat. Big bloke, Pat. Big Pat.'

'Big Pat? I don't remember Ushi talking about anyone called Big Pat.'

'No?'

'You're afraid of Big Pat because you lost your virginity to his wife who baked you a meatloaf?'

'That's it. In a nutshell.'

'You've a complicated life, Robin.'

'Tell me about it.'

He stepped towards her, reached for her, touched the familiar contour of her face, her neck, the freckled skin on her shoulders.

'It can't be the same between us.'

'No, Ruth, it can't. But we can choose to be together for today, to not worry about what comes next.'

He looked beyond her at the parched street, once so familiar, now dry and foreign-looking in the long evening light.

'You could go inside and say goodbye to them, Ruth, or you can say goodbye to me here and turn away. All that matters is that it's what you want. All that matters is what you choose.'

Erin waited for sunset, sitting still on the mossy steps. She waited until she saw the heron approach. She watched her glide through the pink night, neck retracted, wings stretched. She watched her dipping her beak into the suburban pond and take what she wanted from the ink.

Acknowledgements

Warmest thanks to everyone at Penguin Random House in both Ireland and the UK, especially Patsy Irwin, Kate Samano, Josh Benn, Fíodhna Ni Ghríofa, and all in the sales team. I'm also deeply grateful to my copy editor, Katherine Ailes, and to Marianne Issa El-Khoury for the jacket design which so eloquently expresses the mood of the book. And, of course, much appreciation is due to my two editors, Fiona Murphy and Alice Youell, both of whom have been simply wonderful to work with.

Much gratitude and affection also to Sharon Bowers, Michèle Forbes and Maureen White for their invaluable advice and support. And a special thank-you to Professor Deirdre Madden, an inspirational writer and teacher, at Trinity College Dublin.

Hilary Fannin is a playwright and newspaper columnist. Her plays have been performed in Ireland, London, Europe and Canada. She was writer in association at the Abbey Theatre, Dublin, in its centenary year, 2004. Her plays are published by Methuen.

Having written for *The Irish Times* for almost two decades, she now contributes a weekly personal column to the paper. Her memoir *Hopscotch* was published by Doubleday in 2015. *The Weight of Love* is her first novel.

Hilary lives in Dublin and has two sons, Peter and Jake.

Hopscotch
A memoir
Hilary Fannin

For four-year-old Hilary, the world is a bewildering place. Her unconventional home life in 1960s suburban Dublin doesn't fit well with her rule-bound convent education.

Seen through the eyes of her childhood self, Hilary Fannin's stunning memoir gradually leads us from a confusing mosaic of half-understood conversations, bizarre rituals and surreal religious symbolism, to a growing awareness of the eccentricities of the adult world around her, where money is tight, ideas are unorthodox and where living life to the full is the goal. Soon the cracks begin to appear: siblings are expelled from school; final demands litter the hallway; and Hilary discovers the truth about the always-present but never-to-be-mentioned golden-haired lady.

Hopscotch is a funny, poignant and beautifully written memoir, a spellbinding meditation on innocence, love and memory itself.

'Wonderfully funny and moving' Dermot Bolger, *Sunday Independent*

'Lucid, crystalline and intoxicating' Carlo Gébler, *Irish Times*

'Destined to become a classic of the form' Donal Ryan

'Quite brilliant; beautifully, cleverly observed; funny, heart-breaking' Roddy Doyle